THE STRATEGIST

By

William H. Cunningham

Creative Content Corporation
Darien, Connecticut

To the best of the author's knowledge, *The Strategist* is a work of fiction. References to real people, organizations, establishments, companies and events, as well as any imaginary characters, names, organizations, firms and events, are only included to provide an authentic context for this creative, fictional story.

The Strategist. Copyright © 2012 by William H. Cunningham. All rights reserved.

No part of this publication may be reproduced, distributed, transmitted, or used in any form or by any means without the express written permission of the publisher, except in the case of brief quotations embodied in critical review and certain other noncommercial uses permitted by copyright law.

ISBN-13: 978-0-9897695-2-5
ISBN: 0989769534

Cover design: www.ebooklaunch.com and Robert Cunningham

For Dylan and Evan . . . always pursue your dreams.

Acknowledgements

This work, whatever it's worth, if anything, to anyone else, is a dream I would never have pursued or realized without the support, urging, and help of two people—my wife, Patty, and my brother, Bob. Thank you, forever.

CHAPTER 1
Wednesday, May 2, 2012

483,000!

She knew the number would explode onto everyone's computer screens, smart phones, and televisions Friday morning, shocking financial markets around the world. Billions would be made and lost because of it. But that was the price that had to be paid to expose everything. It was the only way. She was certain.

The number had to be too big to believe, so that people couldn't accept it, no matter how desperate they were for it to be real.

Still, one month's data might be dismissed, or worse—believed. That's why she was there, to revise February and March as well, to make sure it was all too good to be true. With the revisions and 483,000 for April, everyone would realize something was wrong. Then she'd tell the media what she knew.

The Commissioner, the FBI, the SEC—they'd all ask why she hadn't gone to them first. She'd lose her job, maybe worse. But it was the only way to guarantee the truth came out, she told herself again. No one could be trusted. It was too explosive—too destructive.

She pulled her car into one of the many vacant spaces on the first level of the underground parking garage. Her office would be empty, like the past two nights—like all government office buildings after five o'clock. She hated coming there this late. It felt like a mausoleum. But it would be over after tonight, except for the fallout.

She stepped out of her car, locked it and hurried to the garage elevator.

"Again?" she muttered anxiously, seeing the sign that the elevator to the lobby was out of service. She'd have to take the stairs. She shuddered. *Stay calm. You're almost done.*

She blew out slowly through pursed lips as her eyes darted from one shadow to the next in the vacant cement garage, finally settling on the dark corner to her left where an exit sign glowed above the stairwell door. It should still only take fifteen minutes to get to her office, run the program and change the data. Then it would be all set—no going back.

As she started to run towards the stairwell, she saw a shadow move across the dull yellow light oozing from the thin vertical window in the door. She stopped. Was someone waiting for her? No, she'd been careful. No one knew what she was doing.

Then she remembered the woman who was attacked last week in the building garage down the street but managed to get away. *Mugged while I'm committing a crime. That would be ironic.*

She heard the faint sound of shoes clicking down steps and realized the person was in the stairwell. She stepped closer and squinted—a man in a suit coming down the stairs from the building lobby. She breathed out in relief . . . *someone working late.*

She walked over and reached for the stairwell door. It flew open—

"Whoa!" she exclaimed, pulling her hand back as the door slammed into the cement wall, the spring to restrain it clearly broken.

"Sorry," the man said, barely looking at her.

She detected an accent of some sort and glanced at him. He was wearing a gray blazer, not a suit, and black slacks, with a light blue dress shirt but no tie. His head was closely shaven, and he was stocky, muscular. He held the door open for her.

"Thank you," she said, smiling nervously and stepping quickly by him.

"Nice ass," he muttered.

She walked towards the stairs, then looked back as the comment registered.

Warm breath touched her cheek, and the smell of cigarette smoke closed in on her. A strong hand suddenly reached around her right arm, grabbed her across the stomach, and pulled her back near the door. She screamed, her voice echoing in the empty, cinder block stairwell.

Another powerful hand came around quickly over her left shoulder and covered her mouth. It yanked her head back towards his shoulder, his rough, unshaven chin grinding into the side of her neck. She tried to scream again, but only muffled gasps escaped. She dropped her wallet and cell phone to pull frantically on his arm with her left hand. She gripped her keys tightly in her right hand, planning to stab him if she could free her arm that was trapped under his overpowering embrace. She looked up, searching desperately . . . *No cameras!*

He lifted her up and whipped her around, slamming her up against the wall, her forehead banging hard against the cement. Her head tingled and the wall blurred, then everything went dark for a moment. She dropped her keys.

Feeling her resistance lessen, he pressed his pelvis against her buttocks, the pungent smell of tobacco choking her nostrils like smelling salts. He whispered, his accent more pronounced, "I like to fuck you like this, but no time . . . too bad."

He pulled his right arm away, pushing harder on her back and pinning her against the cold, cement wall. The pressure was suffocating. She gasped for small breaths, then sensed him reach for something in his blazer pocket.

"Click . . ."

The sound reverberated in her ears and everything rushed back into focus. *A knife!* He wasn't going to rape her—he was going to kill her!

She relaxed all her muscles instantly, as if she had fainted, and started to slide slowly down the cement wall. Either he would loosen his hold or she would die now.

He mumbled something in a language she didn't recognize and planted his knee between her legs to prop her up. Then he took his left hand from her mouth and grabbed around her stomach to stop her from falling, his right hand still holding the knife.

If she hesitated, she would die . . .

Now! She quickly planted her hands and right foot against the wall and pushed back as hard as she could, snapping her head to butt him in the face as she did. She heard something crack and felt a painful throb on the back of her head. He groaned as they propelled backwards.

Her body tensed, anticipating hitting the floor, but the falling sensation continued. She realized they were plunging down the stairs to the level below, his arm still wrapped around her waist, pulling her down with him.

They continued to drop. She reached out with her right hand and clawed against the cinder block wall, the dull stairwell light above moving away, as if in slow motion. She felt a metal railing and clasped it frantically, her hand sliding down until it hit a fastener holding the railing to the wall. Her right arm and shoulder snapped taut, and her left arm and leg swung around wildly, crashing onto the cement stairs. She stopped abruptly, straddled diagonally across the stairs, her right arm stretched painfully above her, still gripping the metal railing.

A loud thud and grunt echoed as the man slammed onto the steps, flipped over and slid to the landing below. She gasped as she looked at him lying face down at the bottom of the stairs. He moaned and stirred.

RUN! She let go of the railing, lifted herself up and leapt two steps at a time to the top of the stairs. She saw her keys and wallet on the floor and grabbed them, then shoved the door open and ran out to the garage. The door flew against the wall, ricocheting back and slamming against her shoulder, sending her sprawling onto the hard cement garage floor.

GET UP! She scrambled to her feet and sprinted to her car. She climbed in and fumbled to get the key in the ignition. The engine roared and the doors locked. She shifted to reverse and stomped on the accelerator. The car jumped backwards. She spun the steering wheel, slammed on the brakes and shifted to drive. The tires screeched as she sped towards the exit.

The stairwell entrance grew smaller as she stared in her rearview mirror, expecting him to come running out—he never did. She turned her eyes forward and gasped, skidding to a stop just before ramming the gate. She waved her pass at the sensor, and the gate lifted. She accelerated, turning a sharp right out of the garage and driving away.

Horns blared as she drove through a red light, half hoping the police would pull her over—they never did. She stopped at the next red light and checked to see if he was following her—no one there. She took a deep breath, her lower lip quivering. She let go and sobbed. The light turned green, but she continued to cry, not moving, hoping someone would stop to help her—no one did. Instead, the taxi driver behind her sat on his horn for several seconds before pulling around her and flashing his middle finger as he raced through the light, now red.

The light switched back to green. She wiped away her tears and drove slowly down the street. She felt a stinging pain, like a bad paper cut, on her right forearm. She looked at it—blood. She grabbed her sweatshirt from the passenger seat and dabbed the blood away. A six inch slice stretched up her arm from her wrist. Blood seeped out, but she sensed it wasn't deep.

It was from his knife, she realized, and began to tremble. He was going to kill her and try to make it look like a rape, or robbery. She knew who he worked for.

"Where are you, Brad?" she cried softly.

But she couldn't call him. Her cell phone was back in the stairwell. She had to find a way to reach him. She could go to her apartment and call him from there.

The thought of speaking to Brad calmed her. After she talked to him, she'd report the attack to the police. But she'd need an excuse for why she was at her office so late. She didn't want to reveal anything until Friday, after the number was released.

She pulled her car into an empty space on the street in front of her apartment building and sat there thinking, the engine still running. *Is this smart?*

Maybe she should go straight to the police. No, she had to talk to Brad first. He could help. He had experience with these situations. And the man probably assumed she had gone straight to the police anyway. She looked around from inside her car—no one there. She'd be safe once she was inside her building.

She turned off the engine, stepped half way out of her car and looked around again. It was quiet and dark, the sound of not too distant traffic floating across the cool air. She reached back in her car and grabbed her wallet, then stepped all the way out and closed the door.

The sudden roar of a powerful engine startled her. She turned quickly and looked down the street—nothing. She whipped around and saw a silver and black grill racing towards her . . .

RUN—

483,000 . . . Everyone will think it's real . . . I have to tell Brad I forgive him . . .

The asphalt felt cold and rough on her cheek. She pushed herself up to a sitting position and leaned against her car. She couldn't feel her right leg. It looked strange, misshapen. She coughed—blood . . . *Blood!*

"Get up!" she shouted, spitting blood.

She grabbed the handle of her car door and pulled herself up, balancing on her left leg, trembling. The slice on her wrist was bleeding again. She dragged her limp right foot underneath her, then looked down. Her new, white sneakers were stained red. Something thick and moist seeped down her neck. The darkness swirled around her, the pain dull and distant.

Get in the car . . . get to Florida Avenue . . . someone will help . . . where are my keys . . .

She heard the engine roar again. It grew louder. She looked . . .

Red lights coming—

No more pain . . . can't lift my head . . . the number . . .
"Brad . . ."

Detective Garcia stepped out of his car and walked over to the police officer standing in the middle of Beekman Place, a narrow side street in the Adams Morgan neighborhood of Washington, D.C. Garcia looked at his cell phone—8:31 a.m., Thursday, May 3, 2012. He noticed a scratched and dented black Ford Focus sedan parked on the street behind the officer. A yellow plastic sheet covered a figure at his feet. Garcia handed the officer his styrofoam coffee cup to hold and then bent down.

"Jesus Christ," he muttered as he lifted the plastic sheet and looked at the mutilated woman's body. "How many cars ran her over?"

"Who knows? It was probably so dark no one even saw her," the officer replied. He shook his head slowly. "What goes through your head while you're dying like that?"

CHAPTER 2
Thursday, May 3, 2012

DYLAN REGAN tasted the red wine. He didn't know what it was, but it was good—smooth and full, what he expected from Del Frisco's, a glitzy, overpriced steak house in midtown Manhattan.

He turned and looked at the older man sitting on his left, forty-something, balding and smug. The man was a fixed income portfolio manager for a small investment management firm. Dylan nodded his approval of the wine.

The man nodded back, acknowledging with false humility his own unique ability to order the second most expensive wine on the list, as the client. He said, "So Dylan, what are you expecting for the employment number tomorrow?"

Dylan was a strategist, an evolved form of an economist to most institutional investors like the portfolio manager. He worked for Financial Trust Securities, or FTS, a small Wall Street firm. FTS hired him three years ago after he was fired by Merrill Lynch following the collapse of Lehman Brothers and the start of the global financial crisis—*The Great Recession*. His job was to develop investment recommendations for clients—investment managers, pension plans, hedge funds—the "buyside" in Wall Street terms. He specialized in bond markets, the same ones that had imploded like a nuclear meltdown during the crisis. His Merrill Lynch experience made him a draw for an FTS salesman trying to convince a client to go to dinner.

Before Dylan could respond, the portfolio manager looked at the young man across the table and said loudly, "Hey, you should listen to Dylan. He's been on a roll with his strategy calls."

Dylan glanced at the young man, a recently hired bond trader who worked for the portfolio manager. He was a few years Dylan's junior, maybe thirty, and already slightly drunk from several beers he'd consumed at the bar before they had all sat down for dinner.

It was a round table, perfect for five. Bob Berkley, the FTS bond salesman who had arranged the dinner, sat between the two clients. Billy McDonald, the head of bond trading for FTS, sat between the young trader and Dylan.

"Forget the employment number," the young trader blurted out, smirked and looked at Dylan. "Bob here says you used to go out with Mary Gannon. I wanna hear about her!"

Dylan's eyes darted to Bob Berkley. Berkley looked back at him, smiled and shrugged.

"Mary Gannon?" the portfolio manager exclaimed, forgetting his question about the employment number. "That sexy internet news reporter? My teenage daughter idolizes her. You dated her?" Then he grinned, leaned towards Dylan and asked in a low voice so only their table could hear, "You fucked her, right? Was she as good as she looks?"

Everyone except Dylan broke out in loud laughter, turning heads at a number of other tables. He feigned a smile, trying to appear humble, as if he didn't want to boast. He'd been asked the same question by other clients enough times to be good at pretending it didn't bother him. It did.

"That was a long time ago, and I never kiss and tell," he replied. "That's her job."

"She's the real strategist," Billy McDonald interjected. "She dumped him as soon as Merrill Lynch dumped him." The table erupted in another round of laughter.

Dylan stared coldly at McDonald, who flashed a sardonic grin in return.

Billy McDonald was thirty-eight, five-feet seven inches tall, and at least two-hundred fifteen pounds. With his thinning white hair, he looked closer to fifty. He was an asshole, Dylan thought, like most Wall Street bond traders.

"Anyway, as far as the April employment number tomorrow," Dylan said, "I'm looking for a loss of about fifty thousand jobs and for the unemployment rate to tick up a tenth. The economy's momentum from earlier in the year is starting to fade. There's a real risk we could turn down hard, maybe back into recession, especially if Europe continues to drag confidence down and China stalls, never mind the tax hikes and budget battle waiting at the end of the year."

"It's the goddamn Presidential election," the portfolio manager said. "How can anyone have confidence to do anything in this shitty economy when the best we can come up with for candidates are Romney and Obama? Left and lefter. Bring back Ross Perot."

"Who the hell is that?" the young trader bellowed. "I say Mary Gannon for President!"

Bob Berkley was there to make money and didn't want to squander the opportunity. He cut off the young client and said, "Dylan, why don't you tell these guys about your two new trade ideas while I order some appetizers?"

"Okay. Sure—"

"Hold on," the young trader interrupted again, uninhibited after quickly downing two glasses of wine, "I gotta tell you I don't really see what value FTS brings to the table for us."

Berkley quickly responded, "A lot if you'll work with us. We have a very experienced sales force that covers all the big money managers, pension plans and hedge funds. We can find you bonds that big firms like JPMorgan and Goldman Sachs can't, but it helps if we can get a look at your portfolios."

"Come on, you just wanna see what we own so you can shop our bonds around," the young trader argued, slurring a few words. He then looked at Dylan and said, "And you were wrong big time on the jobs number last month. Aren't you the guy who recommended buying Lehman bonds right before they filed bankruptcy? Dude . . ."

The portfolio manager glared at his young, inebriated trader and snapped, "Hey, you're the new guy, remember? They're buying dinner. What do you know anyway? You weren't even trading back then. Everyone got Lehman wrong. You think you're going to do all your trades with Goldman? They do business with everyone. Our small trades don't mean shit to them."

After the dressing down, the young trader behaved for the rest of the dinner. The conversation was light and mostly sports related, with a particular focus on golf. Dylan played basketball and didn't consider golf a real sport, yet. He wasn't sure he ever would.

As Dylan returned from the men's room after dinner, he noticed the rest of them leaning over the table whispering to each other. They quickly stopped, sat back and smiled.

No one was interested in dessert. Bob Berkley signed the credit card receipt for dinner, then turned to Dylan and said, "I know you wanted to make it an early night so you can be fresh for the employment report in the morning. We're going to grab a beer at the bar. I'll see you tomorrow, okay. This was great. Thanks buddy."

Dylan understood he wasn't invited to join them, but he wasn't sure why. While he tried to flag down a taxi on Sixth Avenue, he glanced in the large window by the bar. Berkley and McDonald were introducing the portfolio manager and young trader to three suggestively dressed women. He had noticed the women when he was leaving and assumed they were working. He hadn't realized it was for FTS. If the young trader had any doubt, he would soon understand the value FTS brought to the table.

With one woman for each client, Berkley and McDonald would have to share the third. The recession was over, but times were still tough. Expense control, Dylan mused.

CHAPTER 3
Friday, May 4, 2012

483,000!

"I don't fucking believe it," Dylan exclaimed, staring in shock at the headline that had just flashed across the Bloomberg screen on his computer. It was Lehman Brothers all over again—the sinking feeling of realizing he'd been completely wrong, watching his credibility and career vanish before him.

He shook his head in denial as he sat at his desk on the small trading floor of FTS's midtown Manhattan office. Then he quickly typed in a command on his Bloomberg screen. A list of all the morning's economic headlines scrolled down. There it was: "8:31 May 4: U.S. April Employment – Statistical Summary".

At 8:30 a.m. on the first Friday of every month, the Bureau of Labor Statistics, the BLS, issued its report on the U.S. employment situation, announcing the most important piece of economic data in the world—U.S. job growth. Every month for the past four years, investors, business leaders and politicians across the globe had waited and hoped for a sign that the largest economy in the world was finally awakening from its financial crisis induced coma. With this morning's announcement that 483,000 new jobs had been created in April—the largest one month gain in fifteen years—the BLS had declared the U.S. economy alive.

Jobs were supposed to be lost, roughly 10,000 according to the Wall Street fortune tellers—economists and strategists like Dylan who made substantial livings predicting what had already happened. Today, their forecasts had all been wrong, more wrong than anyone in the profession could remember, and he had been one of the worst, for the second month in a row.

"It can't be real," he muttered and clicked to open the story, bringing up a table summarizing the report. The number "483", in thousands, appeared under "April 2012" next to "Change in Total Nonfarm Employment".

Maybe government jobs were artificially boosting the number somehow, he thought. He looked at the line labeled "Change in Private Employment", which excluded government workers. The number was "487", in thousands—the largest private job growth in almost thirty years. *That can't be right.*

He quickly scanned for revisions to the previous two months of jobs data since they were updated with each report. His prediction last month of a loss of 150,000 jobs for March had been way off too. The actual number was zero, but he had expected downward revisions in April's report would make that forecast look more accurate. He was wrong. The revisions were insignificant. But that made no sense. There were almost always major revisions to the previous data when such a surprisingly strong number printed.

What am I missing? There were no major strikes or temporary lay-offs or weather related distortions that could have produced a strong rebound in hiring, and the BLS hadn't reported any special factors affecting the data.

"Damn," he blurted between his gritted teeth. The number seemed real.

Dylan examined the rest of the employment report. It painted a much weaker picture of the U.S. economy, more in line with the other economic indicators he followed.

But he knew it didn't matter. Investors, business leaders and politicians would only focus on April's new jobs number. They'd celebrate it like a savior, leading them out of the depths of four years of economic despair, the likes of which they had not suffered since *The Great Depression*. Four years that were atonement for three decades of unbridled borrowing—from their futures and their children's futures. Borrowing that had enabled anyone and everyone to have it all, until it all crashed with the financial crisis. The number was absolution, finally. Everyone wanted it to be real and, therefore, would believe it was real.

"Crack!"

The loud, sharp sound of a plastic phone receiver smashing against a desk pulled Dylan out of his shock.

"Hey Regan! What the fuck's the story with your forecast?" Billy McDonald shouted from across the trading floor, standing with a broken phone receiver in his hand. "You said it would be down fifty thousand! I'm getting killed. This is bullshit!"

McDonald tossed the broken receiver onto his desk, then sat down to look at the four bond trading screens in front of him. Salespeople who had paused in their phone calls to see what was going on went back to trying to get panicked clients to trade their bonds. Dylan shook his head, knowing McDonald didn't have the balls to take any real trading risk betting on the jobs report.

Dylan turned back to look at his Bloomberg screens. Interest rates in every fixed income market around the world were shooting higher, sending bond prices tumbling, while stock markets soared. Billions were being made and lost because of the jobs number.

"Dylan, I need some color!" Andrew Cantor, the head of fixed income sales, yelled from several seats down as he squeezed the mute button on his receiver.

Cantor was tall, slim and in his mid-forties, with thinning sandy hair. He had toured on the professional golf circuit for a few years before realizing he could make more money talking about his game and selling bonds than actually playing.

"I've got Proctor Management on my line," Cantor shouted. "They sold corporate bonds yesterday and bought a hundred million Treasuries on the other side based on your forecast. The thirty-year yield is up fifty fucking basis points! They're pissed and being real pricks."

Cantor was talking about the interest rate on the thirty-year Treasury bond, Dylan knew. He did a quick calculation in his head—fifty basis points was half of one percent, times the bond's duration . . . the rise in rates had cut the value of Proctor's bonds by seven million dollars.

"Do you want me to jump on?" Dylan shouted back.

"Yeah, but tell them not to sell now. Billy won't buy anything until things settle down."

Dylan picked up the receiver and pressed the flashing red button on his phone turret. Cantor immediately dropped off the call. After fifteen minutes, Dylan convinced the two portfolio managers on the phone to hold off selling their Treasuries until the markets quieted down and bond prices rebounded. They hadn't been pricks, unless the definition of a prick was trying to understand why the bonds you bought yesterday were down seven million dollars today. By that standard, every client was a prick.

"*483K Is Wrong But Too Big To Ignore*" was the title of the email Dylan sent to clients to provide some analysis of the April employment report. He argued that the economy was too weak to produce that many new jobs and that the BLS might have made an estimation or data collection error. Despite his conviction, he recommended that clients cut their losses by reducing their holdings of Treasury bonds—losses that had likely resulted from listening to him. He was hedging his call, something he hated doing, but he had to salvage some credibility.

By noon, he had talked to a dozen anxious buyside clients and swallowed verbal assaults from several irate FTS salesmen. Fortunately, treasury bonds had recovered half of their earlier losses and stocks had pared their gains, although he figured it was only temporary.

Andrew Cantor rolled his chair down to him. "The Proctor guys took your advice and waited. They used this rebound to sell half the Treasuries they bought from us and gave Billy an order to sell the rest. They're feeling better. Good job . . . except that shitty forecast."

Dylan shot back, "If my shitty forecast got them to buy the bonds, why do you get the commission?"

"Because I sold the bonds," Cantor replied and slapped him on the shoulder. "We're called the sellside, not the research side. Remember?"

"I keep forgetting," Dylan quipped.

Cantor smiled, shook his head and rolled back to his desk.

Dylan decided he needed some lunch. He slipped out the back door of the trading floor, took the elevator down to the lobby and headed for Dunkin Donuts at 42nd Street and Madison Avenue. He bought a medium coffee, cream only, and a jelly donut, then went downstairs to the seating area he called the "coffee cave", his refuge when he needed to think. He sat at his usual table in the corner. The coffee was good, but the donut was stale. He closed his eyes.

It had been almost four years since he made his disastrous call to buy Lehman bonds just before it went bankrupt. He thought he had finally rebuilt his credibility. His successful investment recommendations over the past two years had started to attract attention again from clients, the media and recruiters. The chance to escape FTS and move back to a real Wall Street firm seemed within his reach. But today's jobs number threatened everything.

He opened his eyes and saw a middle-aged woman in a dirty, faded green sweat suit staring at him from another table, talking to herself. Homeless, he guessed, maybe a former strategist.

As he stared back at her, he felt the same hopeless inevitability of his fate as that night before Lehman Brothers went under, with one exception—he knew he was right this time. But to prove it, he had to figure out how the jobs data could be wrong. He needed to speak to Caroline. If something was wrong with the data, she would know.

"There you are," Breck, the young and happy receptionist, said as Dylan swung open the glass door to the FTS office. "I've been looking everywhere for you. Is your cell phone on?"

"I was having coffee with a client, so I turned it off," Dylan replied. It was an easy excuse that he had come to rely on to cover himself when he wanted to get away from the office. He didn't like telling white lies. He thought they added up over time, like pennies, but he seemed to be using them a lot of late.

"A Mary Gannon called twice. She insisted I track you down," Breck said.

He paused, surprised, and then took the message slips. "Thanks."

"Is that Marry Gannon, the reporter for ICIN?" Breck asked, a hint of awe in her voice.

"Probably," he said and walked away.

He turned the corner and walked onto the FTS trading floor. After three years, he still noticed how underwhelming it was. With its low, dingy ceiling panels and narrow, dirty windows looking out onto Madison Avenue, it didn't compare to Merrill Lynch. But the Merrill he knew didn't exist anymore. It had been absorbed during the financial crisis by Bank of America before it could collapse like Lehman Brothers, while FTS had survived, unchanged.

His desk was a space at the end of one of several long rows of generic desk tops with computers, a nearby window giving it a modicum of status. He sat down and looked at the two message slips from MG.

It had been a year and a half since they last spoke, and almost three years since they had broken off their engagement. After he was fired from Merrill, their relationship spiraled down. He blamed her, especially after the article she had written about him and other Wall Street analysts who had recommended buying Lehman before it filed bankruptcy. When he finally suggested they separate, she was eager to agree—too eager. He got angry, and they didn't talk again for six months until she called to have coffee one afternoon. They met, but all she wanted was to return the engagement ring. He snapped at her, and she left with tears in her eyes.

She probably wasn't calling to have coffee.

MG was a financial reporter at Reuters when they broke up. He knew she had jumped to ICIN—International Cable and Internet News—seven months ago. A relatively new venture in online and cable media, ICIN employed a provocative and sensationalist approach to the news that had become extremely popular with the under thirty population. The edgy applications it had developed for smart phones were attracting an even younger audience not usually enamored with real news. It was a big step up for her, and everyone seemed to want to tell him how well she was doing there.

He was curious and dialed the number on the slip. MG's voicemail answered. Her greeting sounded playful and happy. He didn't leave a message.

Turning back to his Bloomberg screens, he saw that the bond market was selling off again, and equities had resumed their torrid rally. He was expecting both, but anxiety over not knowing why he'd been so wrong still flooded his body. Or maybe it was the third cup of coffee. Either way, he had to talk to Caroline.

Caroline Brenner was a Senior Economist at the Bureau of Labor Statistics. She helped him whenever he had questions about an economic indicator. He had gotten to know her through his best friend, Brad Johnson, who worked for the Federal Reserve in Washington, D.C. Caroline and Brad had been dating seriously for a while, but she broke it off suddenly about a year ago. Dylan still didn't know why.

He dialed Caroline's office number. After several rings, it went into her voicemail.

"Damn," he muttered and waited for the beep. "Hi Caroline, it's Dylan. Can you call me when you get this? I think there's something wrong with the employment data. It doesn't make sense. It looks corrupted. Do you think you could help explain it to me? Thanks."

He hung up and tried her cell. He thought someone picked up and said, "Caroline, you there?" Then his call was disconnected. He called back, but her voicemail answered immediately. "Caroline, it's Dylan.

Sorry about that. I guess we were cut off. Anyway, I left a message on your office phone too. Can you call me as soon as possible? Bye."

He hung up and sent her a text message. Then he slid back in his chair and waited. His anxiety grew with the silence. After ten minutes, he shook his head in frustration, sat up and placed his fingers on his computer keyboard. He started downloading the April employment data to his economic spreadsheets. He had to figure out what was going on. The data would eventually tell him. It never lied—to him.

By five o'clock, his spreadsheets were all updated, and he was ready to begin some statistical analysis of the data. He paused and looked around. Most of the FTS trading floor was gone, probably over at Annie Moore's, a local Irish pub, having their usual Friday night drinks. An instant message from Tom Sygowski, a bond trader he used to work with at Merrill Lynch, flashed on his Bloomberg screen.

"Tom Sygowski . . . Jesus Christ," he muttered, then opened the message.

"You're famous!" it read, with a link to a video.

Dylan clicked on the link. The ICIN banner crossed the screen, and then MG appeared in front of the New York Stock Exchange. She was wearing a short, black leather skirt, a tight, red, sleeveless zippered blouse—barely zipped—black leather wrist bands and black high heels. Her brunette hair was longer now and waved lightly in the wind. She looked like a hooker doing the news—a beautiful, high-class hooker. Her familiar, playful voice tingled in his ears.

"Wake up new grads everywhere! I know you're sleeping in because you haven't been able to find a job to move out of your parent's house or pay off your $200,000 in school loans, but the work whistle blew for you this morning with the surprising announcement that 483,000 new American jobs were created in April. After four years of financial repression, employment depression, and Democratic and Republican impotency, the U.S. economy looks like it's finally coming out of its coma—on Viagra! But you would never have guessed by listening to those high paid Wall Street fortune tellers. One top strategist, Dylan Regan of Financial Trust Securities, actually predicted a loss of 50,000 jobs for April. He could probably use a little blue pill himself right now. So, is Dylan Regan just another overpaid, seldom right Wall Street weatherman, or is he the canary in the coal mine for the U.S. economy? Text us with *your* thoughts at ICIN.com. I'm Mary Gannon, body and news, for ICIN!"

Dylan sat back in his chair, clenched his teeth and breathed quickly through his nose, trying to control his anger. *That's why she called . . . to tell me I'm bleeding.*

CHAPTER 4
Saturday, May 5, 2012

DYLAN'S HEAD vibrated as he dozed off leaning against the window of the Metro-North train jouncing its way towards New Haven, Connecticut. His head suddenly bounced painfully off the glass as the train clicked over new joints leaving the Stamford station, jolting him awake.

He hadn't slept much last night, the number "483" flashing constantly in his anxious dreams, waking him every half hour it seemed. Five beers on an empty stomach after a late, long workout—his first in over a month—probably had something to do with it too.

He stretched his eyes and looked out the window. They were zipping through Darien, a small, wealthy town dominated by Wall Street types. He knew several traders who lived there. He took a sip of his coffee and contemplated calling his sister in Bridgeport, since that's where he was headed. But she'd suspect something was wrong, since he never called. Calling at nine o'clock on a Saturday morning would only confirm it.

He glanced at his Wall Street Journal. The weekend press was saturated with stories about the extraordinarily strong April jobs number and the dramatic stock market rally and bond market selloff it had ignited. President Obama had given a speech not so subtly taking credit for the job creation, while skeptical Republicans argued the jobs would have been created sooner if not for the Democrats. Well known economists and strategists debated whether it was really the start of the long hoped for economic revival. Yet, no one seemed to be aggressively questioning whether the number was real, except him, and no one was listening to him.

An hour and a half after leaving New York, the train pulled into Bridgeport. He got off and surveyed the downtown area from the station platform. Bridgeport was the largest city in Connecticut and the home of P.T. Barnum, but few knew or cared about either fact. To most people, it was the city on I-95 that you never wanted to break down in, the city that tried to file bankruptcy in 1991, the city with a two building skyline. It was also the city he had grown up in and managed to escape. Now, it was the city he looked to for grounding.

Despite Bridgeport's damaged history, he saw small signs of a city finding ways to adapt, the same hope he had found there three years ago when he was unemployed and depressed. It was the weekend right after he was fired by Merrill Lynch. He had come up to visit his mother and was approached by a young man begging for money with a sign that read: "Back From Iraq But No Jobs – Please Help". It made him think of his older brother Kyle who had died in the first Gulf war. He decided to stop feeling sorry for himself and do something.

Although he wasn't having any success at the time landing another half a million dollar a year Wall Street position for himself, he knew how to help other people find jobs. He was a strategist, a good one, despite Lehman Brothers, and he had a plan. He went to the Colonel Charles Young American Legion Post 140 and arranged to set up a table in their banquet hall one Saturday morning a month to provide free employment counseling to veterans—anything from helping with resumes, to strategies for identifying jobs, to career advice, to preparing for interviews, to simply listening.

He had initially expected to meet with mostly young veterans returning from Iraq and Afghanistan, but a large number of older men and woman had also shown up over the past three years. He didn't know how to measure the impact he'd had, other than it was more than nothing. Shortly after he started, he landed his job with FTS. At the time, he thought it was serendipity—something good that had happened because he was doing something good. He shook his head now at the irony.

He grabbed a large coffee and two dozen donuts from the Dunkin Donuts downtown, then walked along Stratford Avenue, over the bridge that crossed the inlet separating downtown from the East Side, over the bridge that connected to the East End, and finally to the rundown building that housed the American Legion Post 140. It was a long walk, and he usually took a taxi, but today he wanted to remember where he'd come from.

When he arrived, a long wooden folding table was already set up, with a chair for himself on one side and two on the other. He put the donuts on one end and opened up the top box. He sat down, pulled out his notebook and pen from his leather bag, and took the lid off his coffee. He took a sip. It was good. He grabbed a jelly donut. It was fresh.

After an hour, he had only talked to one young man, a veteran who had served in Iraq and wanted some help with his resume and suggestions on how to pursue a career in restaurant and hotel management. Dylan had a friend who owned a restaurant in Providence, Rhode Island. He promised to set up an informational phone call.

By the end of his second hour, he had still only spoken to one veteran. Most of the donuts were gone, eaten by people wandering in from the bar in the next room. He started to put away the folding chairs when a tall man walked in from the door to the outside, the bright sunlight wrapping around him and blinding Dylan's view. As the man approached, Dylan saw that he was wearing a heavy blue wool blazer, a red tie, and dark gray slacks. He looked in his early twenties, six foot three or more, lanky, with a dark complexion and straight brown hair.

"Mr. Regan? Hi, I'm Ron Pahlavi. Am I too late to meet with you?" the young man asked and caught his breath as if he'd been running. He extended his right hand to shake.

Dylan grabbed it firmly and noticed the young man was wearing a black glove. His hand felt hard and his fingers barely bent. It was a prosthetic hand, he realized, but the grip was surprisingly strong.

"No, I have a little time," Dylan replied. "Sit down. Want a donut? Last one."

"No, thank you," Pahlavi said. "I'm sorry I'm late. Traffic on 95 was brutal."

"That's okay. Where were you coming from?"

"UConn. I'm finishing up my bachelor's degree there."

"UConn's a great school. I'm guessing they have some good placement services. I'm not sure I can do any better, but go ahead and tell me what help you're looking for."

"Well, my mother knows your mother," Pahlavi started.

"She does?" Dylan replied, smiling. He remembered he was supposed to call her.

"Yeah, they work together at Bridgeport Hospital. She's a nurse too. I guess my mother was telling her about my frustrations with getting job interviews, and your mother suggested that I come by and talk to you. She told me about your brother Kyle. I'm sorry."

Dylan's shoulders tensed. He stared into Pahlavi's blue eyes and said, "It was a long time ago."

"I . . . I didn't mean to upset you," Pahlavi stammered and reached to scratch his right forearm where his prosthetic hand was attached.

Dylan caught the gesture in his peripheral vision. He relaxed his shoulders, nodded slightly towards Pahlavi's hand, and said, "Do you mind if I ask what happened?"

"Uh, no. I used to, but not anymore. If I don't feel sorry for myself, then there's no reason for anyone else to. Anyway, I joined the Army right out of Central here in Bridgeport. I heard you went to Harding. Big basketball player, right?"

"Yeah," Dylan replied and feigned a smile.

"I'm tall but no good at basketball," Pahlavi confessed. "Anyway, they sent me right over to Afghanistan after basic, probably because of my name and the way I look."

"What nationality is Pahlavi?" Dylan asked.

"Persian, not Iranian. My mother's German, first generation. My father was Persian. He was killed fifteen years ago when someone tried to rob his store in Queens. My mother moved me and my younger sister up here to get away. Some difference, but she didn't know. Sorry, I guess I'm talking your ear off. Anyway, I was doing mine duty. I don't mean the real stuff. Just lugging hardware that was supposedly defused. Next thing I know, there's a small explosion and most of my hand is gone. Real freak thing. I was active for all of three months, then a year of rehabilitation. That's when I decided I'm not going to spend the rest of my life like it's over. I got out and started at UConn."

"That's impressive," Dylan said and looked warmly at him.

"Only if it gets me a job . . . Um, do you mind if I ask what happened to your brother?"

Dylan tensed again but then took a deep breath and let it out slowly. "No, it's okay. Like I said, it was a long time ago. Kyle joined the Marines right out of high school, like you. I was eleven. He died in a helicopter crash in Kuwait at the end of the first Gulf War. Mechanical problem. He wasn't shot down."

"Doesn't matter," Pahlavi insisted. "He was there to fight for his country."

Dylan smiled slightly. "I know. Enough about me. What kind of career are you looking for when you graduate?"

Pahlavi smiled back and said, "I want your job . . ."

After their meeting, Ron Pahlavi gave Dylan a lift to the train station. Pahlavi wanted a job on Wall Street. Apparently, he hadn't seen enough of the dark side of people in Afghanistan. Dylan promised to set up a few informational interviews for him.

The ride back to New York seemed faster. After Dylan got off the train at Grand Central Station, he grabbed a cup of coffee and two cheeseburgers at the McDonalds on 42nd Street and headed to his office. He needed to finish analyzing the employment data to write up his weekly strategy note to clients. He was still hoping Caroline would call him back to explain why he'd been so wrong about the jobs number the past two months after being so right the past two years. But he couldn't wait. He had to try to figure it out.

The dark, empty FTS trading floor with streaks of light seeping through the thin, dirty windows felt strange—serene and safe, like the clearing in the middle of the woods he would go to in his mind growing up in Bridgeport after he'd been beaten up in a fight or, when he got older, after he'd done the beating up. Nothing to threaten him. Just the hum of computers and a dingy, utilitarian office . . . until Monday.

He took a big gulp of coffee and ate one of his cheeseburgers. Then he logged onto his computer and pulled up all of his spreadsheets. For the next five hours, he immersed himself in the jobs data going back to the 1940s, performing extensive statistical analysis to determine if something was going on with the economy that he didn't see or understand. But there was no precedent he could find for the April employment number in any of the ten post-World War II recessions preceding *The Great Recession*. The April jobs number was an intruder to the data history—an outlier that you would only believe if you were desperate to believe. And he knew that every unemployed voter in the country was desperate to believe.

Frustrated, Dylan slumped back in his chair and grabbed his coffee. It was cold and almost gone. He decided to try to reach Caroline again on her cell phone. Her voicemail picked up immediately. He left another message. Then he realized that Brad might know where she was. Brad had told him last week that they were close to getting back together.

Sophomore year at Brown University was when he first met Brad Johnson. They were on the same team during a pick-up basketball game playing against some varsity players. Dylan dominated from the point guard position, feeding Brad for short ten foot jumpers that won the game. It was a meaningless victory, but Brad was ecstatic since he had been cut from the Brown team earlier that year.

When Brad saw him later that night at a fraternity party, he walked up and said, "You're not bad for a small, white guy."

"I'm six feet, and you're not very good for a tall, black guy," Dylan shot back.

"If you're six feet, I'm white," Brad replied.

"Nice tan," Dylan quipped. Brad laughed. They were friends from then on.

After Brown, Dylan went to work for the Boston Federal Reserve, while Brad moved to Washington to work for the Bureau of Industry and Security, a branch of the Department of Commerce. Dylan headed to Georgetown two years later for his MBA, and Brad followed a year after that. From business school, Dylan joined Merrill Lynch in New York, and Brad went to the Federal Reserve in Washington. That's where Brad met and fell in love with Caroline Brenner.

Brad was devastated when Caroline suddenly broke up with him. He had tried to hide it, but Dylan knew. Things between her and Brad seemed to get better after she left the Federal Reserve last summer to take a position as a Senior Economist with the BLS. Dylan hoped they'd eventually get back together. They loved each other. It was obvious. He and MG were like that once, a long time ago.

Dylan called Brad's cell but got a greeting saying he was away at a conference until Monday. He left Brad a message, then texted him. There was nothing more he could do to get in touch with Caroline. He finished his cold coffee, sat up and started typing his strategy note.

It was dark outside and late when he finally placed his fingers lightly on the keyboard, paused and then typed the last lines of his strategy note:

The obvious beneficial political ramifications of April's surprisingly strong job creation make us wonder if the number was a convenient data error that will soon correct itself or if this economy has been transformed overnight into the vibrant job producing engine we all want it to be. Conspiracy theories anyone?

CHAPTER 5
Sunday, May 6, 2012

BRAD JOHNSON leaned down to pick up the folded white piece of notebook paper on the floor inside his apartment door.

"Not another leak," he muttered, remembering the obnoxious note he had received two months ago from the old couple who lived below him in the brownstone on Buchanan Street in the Fort Totten neighborhood of Washington, D.C. His shower had leaked through the grout around his bathtub and was dripping through their ceiling. They threatened to sue him. Now, they no longer acknowledged him. He was their mortal enemy, the scourge of the neighborhood at their senior center socials.

He closed his door, put down his duffle bag and brief case, and unfolded the note. It was handwritten from Caroline:

Brad, I thought I might catch you after work, but I guess not. Sorry for snapping last night. My fault. A lot going on. Need your help with a problem. It's important. Also, I broke up with Chris. Love! Caroline!

Brad smiled, relieved and excited. Her exclamation points were a message—her sign of affection. She had told him that when they first started dating. And she wasn't angry at him anymore for the other night. Although, he still didn't understood why she had snapped at him over dinner and then stormed off. Maybe it was the problem she needed his help with. Either way, it didn't matter anymore because she had broken up with that worm of a lawyer boyfriend. He knew it meant she wanted to get back together. *Finally!*

He took out his cell phone, pressed "2" and then "Send". It went straight into Caroline's voicemail. "Hey Caroline, it's me. It's about nine Sunday night. Just got home and saw your note. I don't know if you got the messages I left, but I've been at a conference since Wednesday. Never heard back from you. Hope everything's okay . . . I missed you. Call me."

He read the note again. She had obviously left it last Wednesday since they had gone out to dinner Tuesday night. But then why hadn't she returned his calls?

She probably lost her cell phone again, he told himself—the third time in two years. She had a Ph.D. in economics and was a computer genius, but she couldn't manage to hold onto a cell phone for more than six months.

Then he remembered that Dylan had left a message trying to track down Caroline to ask her about the April employment report. He had sounded a little frantic. Brad called his cell.

"Hey Brad," Dylan groaned. "You back?"

"Yeah. You sleeping?"

"Just went to bed. Didn't get much sleep over the weekend. What's up?"

"Sorry for waking you. Did you ever talk to Caroline?"

"Uh, no, she never called me back," Dylan answered.

"Did you call her office or cell?"

"Both. Why?"

"Um, it's nothing. She left me a note under my apartment door last week while I was at my conference. I called her a few times, but I never heard back. I thought you might have heard from her."

"She's probably just busy with that ridiculous jobs number the BLS put out Friday. The markets are going crazy over it. You saw it, right?"

"I did. That makes sense. You're probably right. Well, go back to sleep. I'll call you tomorrow to catch up."

"Hey, when you talk to Caroline, can you ask her to give me a call?" Dylan said. "Something's wrong with the jobs data. I'm sure of it."

"I will. Goodnight," Brad said and hung up.

He started to unpack, trying to keep his mind from imagining different things that might have happened to Caroline. Even though they had broken up over a year ago, he still worried about her every night.

He took a deep breath and blew out slowly. He realized the anticipation of possibly getting back together with Caroline was making him anxious, sending his mind to bad places. He shook his head. *Nothing's wrong. She just lost her phone. Nothing's wrong.*

CHAPTER 6
Monday, May 7, 2012

THE STREETS of Washington were quiet at 6:30 Monday morning. Brad stood outside the Metro station near his office and dialed Caroline's cell phone again, hoping to catch her still in bed. It went immediately to her voicemail. He left another message, then called her office voicemail. He texted her again too.

She definitely lost her phone.

A pile of pink message slips sat in the middle of his desk when he walked into his office on the fifth floor of the Federal Reserve's New York Avenue building. He hung his suit jacket on the back of the door, sat down and turned on his computer. He took a sip of the black coffee and bit off a piece of the plain cinnamon raisin bagel he had bought, the same breakfast he had every day. Then he flipped through his messages.

Shannon Dunn, one of Caroline's friends at the Bureau of Labor Statistics, had called Thursday afternoon. He had met her several times. The message asked him to call her back on her cell. It was still early, but he decided to call anyway.

"Hello?" a raspy woman's voice answered.

"Is this Shannon?"

"Yeah. Who's this?" she asked, clearing her throat.

"Shannon, it's Brad Johnson, Caroline's friend. I have a message you called."

He heard her voice tremble as she tried to clear her throat again.

"Oh, Brad. Then you haven't heard yet . . ."

"Heard what?"

"I'm . . . I'm sorry to be the one to tell you," she said and started to cry. "Caroline was hit by a car and killed Wednesday night. I'm so sorry. It's awful. I'm sorry to tell you this way."

The walls moved towards him, and the lights dimmed. Blood rushed from his head, and his chair seemed to spin. His fingers felt numb.

He shook his head, blinked his eyes and squeezed the receiver. The room brightened.

"What? What did you say?"

He heard Shannon sobbing.

"I'm so sorry Brad. I got a call Thursday from the police. They said she was killed by a hit-and-run driver in front of her apartment. I tried to call you. I didn't know how to get in touch other than your work. I don't know what to say."

"What do you mean, she's dead . . . She can't . . . What—"

"Caroline's dead, Brad . . ."

No, no, no . . . He breathed quickly, then deeply, squeezing his eyes closed and clenching his jaw. He couldn't talk. He gripped the phone tighter and made a fist with his right hand. He pressed down as hard as he could on his desk. If he said anything, he'd explode. Just silence— silent anger, silent pain. She was dead—he was dead.

"Brad, are you—"

"Where is she?"

"Uh, I don't know where—there's a Detective Garcia at the Third District police station. I think he's handling it."

"Did they catch the driver?"

"I don't know. They hadn't when he talked to me last, but that was Friday."

"Anything else?"

"No . . . just that I'm so sorry," she said, struggling to hold back from crying again.

He hung up.

No one was ahead of Brad when he walked up to the window at the visitor's desk of the Third District police station on V Street. An average sized, thirty-something male police officer was standing in the back talking to a young female officer by a desk. Brad waited a couple of seconds to be noticed, then tapped on the window. The male officer glanced over, turned and finished whatever he was saying. Then he walked slowly towards the window.

"I'm Brad Johnson. I just got a message that my girl friend, Caroline Brenner, was killed in a hit-and-run last week. I was told Detective Garcia is handling the investigation. Could I speak with him, please?" His voice broke slightly as he focused on the officer's blank eyes.

"Take a seat. Someone will be out to talk to you," the officer said and typed something into the computer.

Brad sat down in one of four plastic and metal seats in a corner against the wall. After ten minutes, a stocky, slightly bald and graying man in a white, buttoned down shirt, green tie, and gray slacks came out a side door carrying a notebook and looked towards him.

"Mr. Johnson? I'm Detective Garcia," the man said with a slight Hispanic accent. Before Brad could stand, the man sat down one seat away. "You say you were Ms. Brenner's boyfriend? My notes say that Chris Smith was her boyfriend. You're the old boyfriend, right?"

"He wasn't her boyfriend," Brad replied. "She broke up with him. We were getting back together."

"Okay, when did you see her last?"

Brad realized he was being interrogated. "Last Tuesday night. I left for a conference on Wednesday—"

"Where was the conference?" Garcia interrupted.

"The Virginia Conference Center, outside of Richmond. I left yesterday. You can check."

"We will."

Brad pressed his lips, then asked, "Wasn't Caroline killed by a hit-and-run driver?"

"That's what it looks like. We're waiting on the Medical Examiner's report."

"Then you haven't caught the driver yet?"

Garcia glanced up from his notes and stared at Brad without any emotion. "Assuming it was a hit-and-run, we still don't know who it was or the circumstances. Now, what about the last time you saw Ms. Brenner?"

Brad took a deep breath and released it slowly through his nose. "We had dinner last Tuesday night. She left a note under my apartment door, sometime Wednesday, I'm pretty sure. I picked it up when I got home last night. Then I had a message at my office this morning from one of her work colleagues. I called and found out she was . . . she was dead."

"Do you have the note with you?"

Brad took the folded note out of his pocket and handed it to Garcia. "I tried calling her several times from my conference and—"

"What were you fighting about?" Garcia interrupted, looking up from the note.

"We weren't fighting. She was upset about something and snapped at me, like the note—"

"What was she upset over?" Garcia interrupted again.

Brad glared at Garcia. "We never got that far. She left before I found out. But she was okay when she wrote the note."

"How do you know that?"

"The way she used exclamation points. It was her code for when she was happy. Have—"

"What do you think the problem was that she wanted your help with?" Garcia asked, cutting him off again.

Brad was silent for several seconds, breathing quickly through his nose, his jaw clenched. "If I knew, I'd tell you . . . There's a reason you're grilling me, Detective. What is it? Do you suspect foul play?"

Garcia turned his eyes down and wrote something in his notebook. Without looking up, he asked, "Why did Ms. Brenner write you a note instead of calling?"

"I don't know," Brad snapped. "She wrote me little notes all the time. She liked it. It's her hand writing. You can check."

"We will," Garcia said calmly.

"Or maybe she lost her cell phone, since she didn't return any of my calls," Brad said, clearly angry. "She did that a lot too. Did you find it?"

Garcia looked up from his notes and scrutinized Brad. "Did she always drive to work?"

"No, just when she planned to work late. She didn't like taking the Metro late at night. Was she coming from work when she was hit?"

"You said you two were getting back together. Why did you break up?" Garcia asked.

"What the—" Brad stopped and took a deep breath. "Are you married, Detective?"

"Divorced."

"It happens, right?"

"Hmm . . . Okay, you have a car, Mr. Johnson?" Garcia asked.

"Yes, a Chevy Impala. I park it in a lot by my apartment."

"I need you to write down all your personal information and the details of your conference. We'll need to take a look at your car, if you don't object."

"I don't, but can you please tell me what happened and where the investigation stands?"

Garcia closed his notebook and asked, "Is there anything else you can think of regarding Ms. Brenner that could help in our investigation? Anything at all?"

"No, Detective. You're the one with all the information. Can you share any with me?"

Garcia cleared his throat and said, "Okay, I can give you some information, but it's an ongoing investigation. These are the facts that have been released to the media so far. About four o'clock Thursday morning, two men and a woman walking by Ms. Brenner's apartment building found her lying in the street next to her car. They called 911, but she was ruled dead at the scene. By the impact, the driver was definitely speeding. Her car was scraped along the driver's side, likely from the car that hit her. It was late and that street's dark at night. Could have been a drunk driver, or someone who didn't see her. There are other possibilities too."

"You mean that it was intentional, right?" Brad replied. "You have to have a reason for thinking that. What is it, Detective?"

Garcia seemed to grumble, then said, "Ms. Brenner's parents asked me to share what I told them with you. It's unusual, but you'll just get it from them if I don't. So, I'll make it easy on everyone . . . Alright, it appears from the body that Ms. Brenner might have been run over more than once, maybe by another car that didn't see her because it was so dark. We don't know yet, but the trauma was very severe."

Brad looked down, the image of Caroline's body lying in the street flooding his mind. His eyes started to water. He wiped them and asked, "Were there any witnesses?"

Garcia paused, then answered, "That's all I can tell you."

Brad lifted his eyes and looked at Garcia. "Have you spoken to Chris Smith yet?"

"Mr. Johnson, we know how to do our job. We'll find whoever did this. I won't have any more information for you until the ME's report is issued, probably in a couple of weeks. Can I suggest you call and talk to her parents? That might help, and they seemed worried about you."

Brad knew he wouldn't get anything more out of Garcia. He left the station and walked for a while before sitting down on a bench outside a generic gray cement building. He closed his eyes and put his face in his hands. The image of Caroline lying on a metal table being cut open spread in his head.

"Nooo," he moaned quietly.

The sun warmed the late morning air as it always did in Washington this time of year. Caroline had been excited about the coming warm weather, he remembered. She was Southern, and Washington was always colder than she liked.

CHAPTER 7
Monday, May 7, 2012

JEFF SCHWINN walked quickly into the office and smiled. "Good morning, Senator. Early as always. After twenty years, I think you've earned the right to just be on time, at least Monday mornings. You make me look bad."

James Murphy, the Senate Majority Leader and Democrat from New York State, was sitting on the front edge of his desk in his office in the Hart Senate Building in Washington, D.C., reading a report. Slightly above average height, he sported a full head of white hair and a wide middle, accentuating his small shoulders and thin legs. He looked over his glasses at the shorter, thin and well dressed man with curly brown hair, in his mid-thirties.

"Hah, we both know you work harder than me, Jeff," Murphy said. "You just like to stay up late. I've been a morning person since basic training forty years ago."

"I see you're reading my write-up on the employment report. Is it what you wanted?"

"Yes, it's excellent," Murphy replied, "but I don't think my Chief of Staff should be putting this stuff together. We have junior people for that."

"Well, with that jobs number being such a surprise, I wanted to make sure you were prepared for today's session and any press opportunities."

"Thanks, Jeff . . . 483,000 new jobs is remarkable. And economists were predicting we'd lose jobs," Murphy said, shaking his head.

"That's why Harry Truman always wanted one-armed economists," Schwinn remarked, "so they could never say, 'But on the other hand'."

"That's one of my favorite quotes," Murphy said. "So, do the markets believe the number?"

"Uh, are you asking if investors and Wall Street expect the data to be revised away next month?" Schwinn replied.

"I mean do they think the data's real and the start of a stronger trend?" Murphy responded, his tone a little impatient.

"Well, based on Friday's stock market rally and bond market sell-off, everyone is clearly hoping it's real," Schwinn answered. "A few economists are saying it's unsustainable, but most pundits are waiting to see what next month's number is before they commit to a view. Only one insignificant strategist is arguing the number was an actual error. Republicans are grumbling, of course, because it hurts their Presidential hopes, but business leaders are ecstatic."

"I caught Mary's piece on the jobs report Friday," Murphy said. "Provocative, and not just her comments."

"Well, that's ICIN's style, not hers," Schwinn replied. "I don't like it either, but they're getting viewers, especially college aged kids who can vote."

"If young people are listening to her, then everyone else will soon be listening too, if they aren't already," Murphy said.

"I hope that's true," Schwinn replied. "That's good for her and good for us. She's been giving you good press recently."

"So you say, but that's only because you two are dating. You know I'm not a fan of ICIN. Still, I'm not going to complain about good press." Murphy paused, stood up from leaning against his desk and stared at Schwinn. "Jeff, if everyone's listening to her, then they know

46

about that insignificant strategist she highlighted in her segment on Friday, the same one you say in this here report thinks the jobs number is a mistake, maybe even a manipulation."

"Uh, that's right, I mentioned him in the report. Well, I doubt that anyone will pay much attention to him or his theory. Are you worried about something, Senator?"

Murphy looked back at the report and flipped a couple of pages. "Always . . . hmm, Dylan Regan . . . Wasn't Mary engaged to him before you two started dating?"

Schwinn raised his eyebrows and said, "Yes, she was."

"What if she continues to spotlight him?"

Schwinn smiled slightly. "Ah, I see your point. A conspiracy claim about the jobs data could hurt Democrats in November's elections if Mary and ICIN gave it credibility by hyping it. And she might be a bit too willing to go along with Regan given their history. I'll talk to her . . . point out that he's just using her to get attention for himself. I'll let her know it doesn't look professional to be promoting a fringe conspiracy theory by your former fiancé."

Murphy nodded and said, "Good, but don't be too rough on her. You two make a nice couple. And if you don't mind a little advice, she could be good for your political career too. She shows well. Besides, I don't want to lose that good press coverage before the elections."

"Don't worry. I'll make our point gently. On the topic of elections, has Governor Hayes told you yet if he's running for President?" Schwinn asked.

"Not yet," Murphy replied. "He's attending the Saint Thomas Moore CP fund raiser this weekend. We're going to spend some time together then. I'm sure he'll try to gauge my interest in the VP role, assuming he's going to declare as an independent. That has to stay confidential."

"I understand."

"Oh, and I need a call with Donald Granger before I meet with Hayes. I want to know if I can count on his financial support again if Hayes gives me the nod."

"I'll call him today. Anything else?"

"No, that's all. Just close the door on your way out."

Schwinn left, and Murphy walked around his desk to sit down. He picked up his IPhone and dialed a number.

"Patricia, it's Jim Murphy. . . . Fine, thank you. We need to meet. . . . Well, that jobs number wasn't protocol either. The rest of the group wants to know what happened too. . . . No, just me and Randy. . . . Yes, Mitch knows about it. It was his idea. . . . Next week? But this is important, Patricia. . . . Saturday? Alright, that'll have to do. . . . Early, say eight o'clock. Where? . . . There again? . . . I understand. I'll expect some answers by then. . . . My apologies. I didn't mean to strike that tone. We need to work together on—. . . But it affects national secur—. . . Very well, Patricia. Your way. I'll see you Saturday."

Murphy leaned back in his chair and tapped his IPhone on his lips. He sat up and dialed another number. "Hello, Mitch. It's Jim. We need to meet . . ."

CHAPTER 8
Monday, May 7, 2012

DYLAN WAS skeptical as he sat at his desk and read the message slip late Monday morning that Blair Armstrong had called. He knew he was good, but he didn't delude himself that top hedge fund managers wanted to talk to a strategist at a third-tier Wall Street firm.

Blair Armstrong was the Chief Investment Officer of Differential Capital Management, a large and aggressive hedge fund that focused on fixed income markets, Dylan's specialty. Differential traded billions of dollars worth of bonds and derivatives with Wall Street firms every month. Claiming Differential as a client could be the boost he needed to get back to a bulge bracket firm like JPMorgan or Goldman Sachs. At the least, Andrew Cantor would be thrilled since he'd been trying to break in with Differential for years. But it had to be a mistake.

Dylan dialed the number anyway. A receptionist answered and told him that Blair Armstrong wasn't available. He left a message that he was returning her call.

Clients were already emailing him in response to his provocative strategy note hinting at a politically motivated conspiracy to inflate the employment data. Compliance would normally have deleted anything controversial from his note, but there was a new, young woman in the group. He nicknamed her Duke, since she had graduated from there. He knew she would be the only one working this morning. It took just a little flirtation to get his note approved and sent out before anyone senior could review it. He never would have gotten away with that at Merrill.

Andrew Cantor rolled his chair up next to Dylan. "So, the government's manipulating the data to make the economy look better . . . That's why your past two forecasts have sucked? I'd tone down that conspiracy crap before Joe flies up here and fires your ass."

Joe Brooks was the head of all of fixed income and their boss. He worked out of the main FTS office in Charlotte, North Carolina.

Before Dylan could respond, Breck's voice came over the intercom on his phone turret. "Dylan, Rick Jones from Differential Capital is on the line. Do you want to take it?"

Rick Jones was the head portfolio manager at Differential and Blair Armstrong's right hand man. Dylan smiled wryly at Cantor, then picked up the receiver.

"This is Dylan . . ."

"Hi, Dylan, it's Rick Jones at Differential Capital. Blair Armstrong, our CIO, asked me to call and invite you in to make a strategy presentation. I know we've never done business with FTS before, but this would be a good introduction. Are you up for it?"

"Absolutely. When?"

"How about this Friday for lunch here in our office on Sixth Avenue?"

"Friday for lunch at your office. That works. I think Andrew Cantor covers you. Want me to have him follow-up?"

"No, but tell him he needs to have lunch brought in for the team. See you Friday."

Dylan hung up and turned to look at Cantor.

"I heard," Cantor snapped before he could say anything. "You blow your jobs forecast and blame it on a government conspiracy. Then they invite you for a meeting and tell me to be the fucking waiter . . . Unbelievable." He shook his head and rolled back to his desk.

Dylan laughed briefly, but he knew Cantor was right. No matter how good he'd been the past two years, his call on the April jobs number was dead wrong. Anyone who'd followed it was losing money. This sudden attention from a major hedge fund didn't make sense. Differential had an agenda. Hedge funds always did.

It didn't matter. He wasn't going to squander an opportunity that could help him escape FTS. But before he met with them, he had to get more insight into what was wrong with the jobs data. He started to call Brad to see if he had talked to Caroline yet when his Blackberry rang.

"It's Dylan . . ."

"Hi, it's Mary."

Dylan was silent for a moment. Then he said, "Why are you calling?"

"I'm fine and how are you? Anyway, you probably already saw that I mentioned you in my segment Friday. I thought you'd be happy with the publicity."

"Yeah, well, if being the poster child for the thousands of economists and strategists who got that number wrong is supposed to make me happy, I'm ecstatic."

"You're welcome . . . God, Dylan, the national exposure is good for you. Even if I poked fun, I was fair. You know the media game. I gave you great press, and that's all that counts, especially when you're at a small firm like FTS."

That stung, Dylan thought. "And it doesn't hurt you either. What do you want, MG?"

"It's Mary. No one's called me MG since we broke off our engagement. And yes, it doesn't hurt me either. That's why I called. I just read your new research note. I'd like to use it in a special series I'm planning. Would you talk to me about it?"

"*WE* didn't break off the engagement—you did, and how did you get a copy of my note?"

"I'm a reporter, remember? I have lots of contacts. Are you interested or not? It'll be good for you. I promise."

She was convincing, as always. He recognized the playful seduction of her coaxing tone from when they were engaged. "Are you asking to meet?"

"Yes, are you afraid?" she asked.

"Will I have to wear armor?"

"Kind of sensitive. What happened to that strategist confidence?"

"It filed bankruptcy, remember?"

"Okay, can we just move forward and not rehash things?"

"Fine. What's involved?" He was giving in to her, but he knew the visibility would help him, and he was curious to see her.

"I'm planning a series of reports on the November elections. I'd love your input on the likely impact on the economy. Can you grab a drink tomorrow night at Sofia to discuss it?"

"Um, sure," he replied, even though he didn't really want to meet at what used to be their favorite wine bar. Another subtle manipulation on her part, he knew.

"Great. Six o'clock work?"

"Yeah."

"Thank you. See you then." She hung up before he could respond.

He threw his Blackberry down on his desk. He was furious, but he wasn't sure why. His Blackberry rang again. It was Brad.

"Hey Brad, you talk to Caroline?"

Brad's breathing was raspy and hollow. "Caroline's dead."

CHAPTER 9
Tuesday, May 8, 2012

MARY GANNON knew what she wanted—to reach the pinnacle of professional journalism. She didn't need to win a Pulitzer. She had her own standards. But she dreamed of it.

Becoming a professional journalist was a goal she'd set for herself during high school in New Jersey. After being wait-listed at New York University, where she was determined to study journalism, she showed up at the Dean of Admission's brownstone co-op in Greenwich Village with a PowerPoint presentation on why she should be admitted, an article she'd written on the failings of elite college admissions, and flowers for his wife. Two weeks later, she received her letter of acceptance. Getting into the Columbia Graduate School of Journalism for her Masters was easier.

Mary knew what she wanted, and ICIN could help her get it, but she'd have to go through Gary Rothstein.

"Gannon!" a voice boomed through the wall of the reception area where Mary was waiting.

Mary walked confidently into the office of ICIN's Managing Producer and stopped. She eyed the short, paunchy and balding sixty-something man behind the large oak desk and smiled coyly. "Is there something wrong, boss? I've only been waiting an hour."

"Your humor isn't any better than your reporting," Gary Rothstein quipped and stood up from his desk. He shuffled over to the couch in front of his office window, sat down and put one foot up on his coffee table. He didn't apologize for keeping her waiting. He never did.

Mary walked over to a chair by the coffee table, sat down and opened her notebook. Rothstein looked at her as if she should have waited for his permission. She smiled again.

"You got a segment Thursday, right? What are you doing, and why don't I know about it already?" Rothstein grumbled.

"Because I just started working on an idea for a special series on how the economy will influence the upcoming elections. I want to start out focusing on the employment situation since it's likely to determine the next President. In response to that incredible April jobs report, I'm going to raise the possibility that there's a conspiracy to inflate the data to make the economy look like its improving leading up to the elections. What do you think?"

"I think you want to highlight your old boyfriend's bullshit ideas to create a sensationalist story to hype yourself."

Mary was expecting an obnoxious comment, but the reference to Dylan surprised her. She didn't say anything, knowing he liked to growl before giving a real response.

Rothstein took his foot off the table and sat up. "It's not great, but it'll work if it's done right. I don't want us looking like a bunch of amateur, paranoid hacks trying to invent news, like the Times. And don't come across like a Wall Street Journal reporter either. Our viewers will click to another website to jerk off. Give me a write-up by noon tomorrow. Tell Reyes I want to see it before it airs."

Jane Reyes was Rothstein's right hand woman. In six months of working with her, Mary had already learned more about the business than she had in her entire career before ICIN. She knew Reyes would be surprised that Rothstein wanted to review her segment since he seldom got involved with actual production anymore.

"Okay, thank you," she said, trying to contain her excitement.

"I'm done. Get out."

Mary stood up and walked to the door.

"Gannon!" Rothstein snapped. She turned and smiled. He barked, "Don't let your history with Regan affect your reporting on this. Got it?"

"Got it, boss. If he can't help the story, I won't let him hurt it."

She closed the door, walked a few steps and stopped to look at herself in a mirror. She'd be a little late for drinks with Dylan, but he'd wait. He wanted to see her, she knew.

CHAPTER 10
Tuesday, May 8, 2012

DYLAN WAS sitting at one end of the bar at Sofia reading messages on his Blackberry, an empty wine glass in front of him, when Mary strolled in. He saw her immediately as she took off her sun glasses to look for him, pausing to let her eyes adjust, or maybe posing. Several men stared at her as she walked purposefully across the floor towards him.

She wore a sleeveless, form fitting, purple dress that ended several inches above her knees, accentuating her long shapely legs. She appeared taller and thinner, he thought, but it might have been because he had shrunk and widened. Lightly tanned and in great shape, she exuded a playful confidence without being aloof, the way he remembered her.

He hadn't seen her in over a year. Although she seemed familiar as she approached, she was a stranger now. No longer his fiancée, he didn't even know if she was a friend. He could recall the last time they slept together, but he didn't want to. This was what he wanted to avoid in meeting her there—the memory of a previous life, unfinished and no longer his, with Mary seemingly better for it.

"Hi there," she said, then paused to allow the initial awkwardness to pass. "You look good. How have you been?"

Dylan stood up, forced a smile, but made no gesture to embrace her. He was uncomfortable and self-conscious. He knew he didn't look good, but she hadn't lost her ability to make him want to believe her.

"I'm fine. Want to grab a table?"

"Sure, maybe by the window? But I'm not hungry."

"Okay, neither am I. Something to drink?"

"Yes, my favorite, please, assuming you still remember."

She was playing with him, Dylan knew. He asked the young woman bartender to send over another glass of Chianti for him and a glass of Marco Martin Pinot Grigio for Mary. They sat down, and he glanced into Mary's eyes. She looked back, but her big brown eyes only revealed a woman who wanted to discuss business. It was a relief—no emotion to remind him of anything he had said or done before.

"How's Brad?" she asked. "I've been meaning to give him a call."

"Uh—"

"I think he could help with my series. How are he and Caroline doing?" She noticed Dylan's expression change and asked, "What is it?"

Dylan hesitated, wanting to yell at her for not knowing, but he just breathed out slowly. "Brad called me yesterday . . . Caroline was killed in a hit-and-run last week in Washington."

Mary sat back in her chair and raised her hand to block the gasp that came out of her month. Her eyes suddenly seemed disoriented, her tanned face now white. She looked visibly shocked.

He was skeptical but quickly felt guilty about it. "You alright?" he asked.

"No . . . Yes. What happened? How is Brad?"

"How do you think? He's devastated. You *do* know they broke up over a year ago?"

"Yes, I do," she replied defensively, "but I thought they'd get back together."

A waiter delivered their wine and asked with a warm smile directed at Mary, "Will you be having dinner tonight?"

"No," she snapped, sending him away, bruised. She took a deep breath, looked out the window and asked, "Can you please just tell me what happened?"

Dylan stared at her almost too perfect profile. He saw a tear seep out of her eye, pause as if undecided and then roll down her cheek. He took a gulp of wine and said, "Sure . . . Sorry."

Mary turned and looked at him, her brown eyes glistening. "I'm sorry too."

Dylan cleared his throat. "It happened late last Wednesday night in front of her apartment building. Some people found her lying in the street next to her car early Thursday morning. The police think it was probably a drunk driver. They said he must have been speeding given the force of the hit . . ."

Mary stared at him, leaned forward slightly and said, "There's something else, isn't there? I can tell."

"Well, her body was in pretty bad shape. The police think she might have been run over again by another car."

"What?" Mary exclaimed and turned away again.

"It's apparently a dark street," Dylan replied. "The police think the second guy may not have even realized he did it."

Mary looked back at him, streaks from tears marking her face. "It was a man?"

"No, they don't know who hit her or might have run her over again afterwards. No witnesses have come forward yet."

"When's the funeral?" she asked, drying her eyes.

"Tomorrow in Atlanta. I can't make it."

"Can you forward me her parents' address so I can send some flowers?"

"Yeah, I'll send it tonight," he replied, sat back in his chair and took another gulp of wine.

They were silent for a while. Then Mary took a sip of wine, swallowed slowly, and said, "It probably isn't the best time, but I might not get another chance before I need to move ahead. Can we talk about my series?"

Dylan had expected that she wouldn't be able to continue, but she was more driven than ever, he realized. He smiled briefly at his own naivety, then nodded to her to continue.

"Well, it's a multi-part special series on the economy and the upcoming elections," Mary started. "I'd like to use your research as a lot of the source material. You'll be spotlighted, and I'll want to interview you for one of the segments." She paused, then added, "It could be the best media attention you've ever had, and on the hottest news network in the country."

Dylan clenched his jaw as he struggled with his response. He was angry at her, but he wasn't sure it had anything to do with Caroline's death. He said, "I have to think about it."

"I'm doing the first segment on Thursday," Mary shot back, clearly annoyed. "I don't have time for you to think about it, Dylan. I want to start off highlighting your last strategy note. This is all good for you. What's your hesitation?" Her eyes were determined, no longer glistening.

"Besides the fact that Caroline's dead?" he quipped and took a gulp of wine. "Besides that, you're going to make me look like a crazy Wall Street strategist who can't admit he's wrong."

Mary sighed and said, "Dylan, not helping me won't bring Caroline back. Didn't she always help you? This will help you too, and you won't look bad. I want to spotlight your conspiracy theory. You'll get a lot of great publicity. Trust me. It might even help you move back to a top firm."

She was convincing, or maybe he just wanted to believe, like everyone who wanted to believe the jobs number. He gulped down some more wine. "You can use my strategy note, but I have to think about the rest of it."

Mary pressed her lips tightly, then said, "Don't make this about us. That's over, but if you can't work with me because of our history, just say so and stop pretending it's something else."

Her anger seemed more sexual than intimidating to Dylan. But she was right, he knew, on both counts. Whatever they had once was over for her a long time ago, and the media exposure on ICIN would be good for him, as long as he could trust her, which he couldn't but wanted to.

"Fine," he said, "but I need a couple of days to organize my thoughts."

Mary smiled warmly, knowing she had gotten what she wanted. She insisted on paying for the drinks. They walked out of Sofia, and he hailed her a taxi. She stepped in quickly, avoiding any awkward goodbye.

As Dylan watched her taxi speed away, his mind drifted back to Caroline. Who was going to help him figure out the jobs data now? Then he thought of Brad and felt guilty. Another glass of wine would help. Maybe the young woman bartender wanted to hear his conspiracy theory.

CHAPTER 11
Wednesday, May 9, 2012

SHE ISN'T here. She can't be.

With the late morning sun streaming through the stained glass windows, the Middletown Presbyterian Church looked different from the last time Brad had been there.

It was Christmas Eve, 2008. He had flown down to Atlanta to meet Caroline's family for the first time. He remembered sitting next to her in a pew while she argued quietly with her mother about her father not attending service with them. Her younger sister, Jackie, sat on the other side of him, talking his ear off about something.

Caroline's father was barely Jewish, her mother very Protestant. Dating a black man should not have been shocking, but Caroline was very sensitive that night, he remembered. Her parents had not said anything to her yet, and she was worried their silence meant they didn't approve.

When he left the day after Christmas, her father gave him a strong, warm handshake and said, "I heard you're African-American. Is that true?"

"I wish someone would have told me," Brad replied. "I heard a rumor you're Jewish."

"Well, it seems we're both the victims of idle gossip," he said and laughed.

Caroline was happy as she drove him to the airport that day. The sun danced on her long, blond hair. He remembered her turning and catching him staring at her. Her blue eyes sparkled as she smiled and said, "I love you." He was happy.

Brad scanned the crowded church and saw Lindsey Cho, Caroline's best friend from college, waving to him from the front. Then he saw it. The air suddenly felt dense, almost too heavy to breathe. The noise of people shuffling into pews grew deafening. He stared, helpless.

At the end of the long aisle, a few feet in front of the altar, sat a maple brown coffin adorned with various shades of lilacs. It rushed towards him . . . *Oh, God . . . she's dead . . .*

The service was emotional, but the graveside ceremony was more painful for Brad. He was leaving Caroline there in a box. He'd never see or talk to her again. As he drove back to her parents' house, he struggled to accept why he was there, how she could be dead. He had lost her once, when she broke up with him, but he had always clung to the hope that she would eventually forgive him. She finally had, he believed. But now, there was no hope.

Brad was nervous about how Caroline's family would receive him. They were supposedly very upset when they learned she had broken up with him, but she had never told them why. Still, Caroline had joked with him two weeks ago that if they ever got back together, they would have to elope quickly so her mother didn't have a heart attack worrying about whether they'd get married. That's when he knew Caroline had just about forgiven him.

"Thanks for coming, Brad. It means a lot to us," Caroline's father said, embracing him as he walked into the house. Her mother and sister Jackie both came over and gave him long, warm hugs as tears streamed down their faces. Even their little rat of a dog seemed to be happy to see him. Only Caroline was missing.

Brad was looking at Caroline's framed undergraduate degree from Dartmouth and pictures of her Ph.D. graduation at the University of Chicago when Lindsey Cho stopped to talk to him.

"Well, I just wanted to see how you're doing," she said.

"Hey Lindsey. I'm okay. Thanks for asking."

"The lilacs were beautiful. They were her favorite. She always said she was going to get married with a million lilacs around her." Lindsey choked up realizing the irony.

"I remember," Brad said and looked down.

"I still can't believe it," she said. "I just saw her the weekend before."

"Where was that?" Brad asked, turning his eyes back up to her.

"Well, she came up to New York City to visit me. We hung out, went shopping and had dinner. We talked about you and her. She told me she had broken up with Chris, the guy she was sort of seeing, because she thought you two were going to get back together. She was excited—you knew she broke up with him, didn't you?"

"I didn't . . . not until after she was killed," Brad replied.

"Well, you did want to get back together with her, right? She wasn't imagining that?"

"No, she wasn't imagining it."

"Well, why did you guys break up in the first place? Caroline was heartbroken. She said it was because of your job, but she never explained. Was it another woman?"

"Stop it, Lindsey!" Brad snapped.

Lindsey flinched. "I . . . I'm sorry, Brad. That was insensitive."

Brad took a deep breath, bowed his head and said, "No, I'm sorry . . . I hurt her, but not with anyone else. It doesn't matter now. She knew I loved her." He looked at Lindsey and said, "She left me a note the night she was killed saying she needed my help with a problem. Do you know what it was?"

"Well, she was kind of in a strange mood that weekend she visited."

"What do you mean?"

"You know, preoccupied, but she never shared with me why. I assumed it had to do with you two. Didn't you guys have dinner the night before she . . . that night before?"

"Yes, but she snapped at me right at the beginning and stormed off. I thought I did something wrong, but she apologized in her note and implied this problem was the reason she was upset. You sure she didn't mention anything, about work or anything else?"

"Well, no, she didn't. But you know she had been thinking of taking another job, right?"

"No, with whom?"

"Well, some money manager in New York," Lindsey said. "She didn't tell you? I think she turned it down. I assume because she didn't want to leave you."

"Did she tell you the name of the firm?"

"Well, um . . . I don't remember. It might have been a hedge fund or something like that, but I'm not sure. She probably told her mother or Jackie. But why are you so obsessed with this problem, whatever it was? Is something going on?"

"Sorry, it's just that it was the last thing she asked me for, but I never got a chance . . ." He paused, then said, "It's probably nothing."

"Well, stop punishing yourself," Lindsey said, gently touching his arm. "It's just a horrible tragedy. You couldn't have done anything. I'm going to see how Jackie's doing." She started to walk away, then turned and whispered, "That's Chris Smith over there talking to her. Maybe he gave Caroline a hard time about dumping him. That might have been the problem."

A bland looking, medium-sized man with stylishly cut blond hair and round rim glasses was talking to Jackie in the corner of the living room. Nothing about Chris Smith was special, Brad thought. Why would Caroline ever date him?

Lindsey leaned back and added, "But I think Caroline could have beaten him up herself." She caught Brad's pained look, smiled sympathetically and walked away.

Brad glared at Smith for a few seconds. He wanted to question him about Caroline, but now wasn't the time. He looked around the packed living room—memories of Caroline everywhere. Anxiety filled his body. He felt like he was drowning. He had to get out. He said a quick but painful goodbye to Caroline's parents and left.

Brad slept most of the plane ride back to Washington, jolted awake by a hard landing. His mind was still filled with images from a dream he had of Chris Smith speeding in a car towards Caroline, and his head was pounding from the five shots of Jack Daniel's he had downed.

He walked into his apartment, went immediately to his desk and took out a blank notebook. He sat down at his kitchen table and wrote on the first page: "DID CHRIS SMITH KILL CAROLINE?"

His cell phone rang, startling him. "Hello?"

"Mr. Johnson, this is Detective Garcia from the Third District—"

"Did you find the driver?" Brad interrupted.

"No, not yet," Garcia answered. "I just wanted to let you know that the ME's office will be releasing its autopsy report tomorrow. That's quick for them. I called Ms. Brenner's parents to let them know. They asked me to give you a call. Stop by if you want a copy."

"Have you seen the findings? Can you share them with me?"

"Mr. Johnson, this is just a courtesy call. You'll have to wait until tomorrow. Goodnight."

The next day, Brad went to the police station at eight o'clock and waited, sitting in the same plastic and metal chair as before. At ten o'clock, an officer came out and gave him a copy of the report. He read the standard language at the beginning and quickly found the cause of death—"Severe head trauma." Moisture filled his eyes. He read the rest of the summary. His eyes widened in disbelief as he read the last line: "Manner of Death: Pending."

CHAPTER 12
Thursday, May 10, 2012

THE FTS trading floor had long since been deserted Thursday night when Dylan finished his presentation for tomorrow's meeting with Differential Capital. He debated whether to work on his weekly strategy note or go for a run around the Central Park Reservoir. He was still sore from his long workout last night, but the pain felt good. He felt alive.

As he leaned back in his chair and stretched, he sensed someone next to him. He whipped around—the cleaning lady.

"Jesus, where'd she come from?" he muttered, turning back to his computer.

The cleaning lady turned around, thinking he was talking to her. He waved his hand dismissively. Probably an unemployed ninja settling for any job she can get in this economy, he mused. That made no sense, he realized. She was clearly Hispanic.

His Blackberry rang. "Hello?" he answered.

"Ah, Mr. Regan. Demitri Petropoulos here, returning your call. How is my Wall Street prodigy doing?"

Professor Petropoulos, or Petro as his students called him, was the Head of Graduate Studies for the Economics Department at

Georgetown University. He had been the Assistant Dean of the Business School when Dylan attended, but a propensity for giving female graduate students a little too much attention had killed any hope of eventually becoming the Dean, along with his second marriage. Dylan had stayed in touch with him over the years.

Dylan was desperate. With Caroline dead, he had to find someone else who could help him figure out what was going on with the employment data. Petro had the knowledge, experience, and, as a Washington insider, a unique perspective. He had called Petro this morning hoping to get some insight on the BLS's data collection process.

"Professor, thank you for returning my call," Dylan said. "I'm well, and how are you?"

"Fabulous! I've been enjoying reading your research emails. I quoted one at a recent dinner with one of the President's economic advisors. I started a little trouble, but it was wonderful. What can I do for you, my friend?"

"As I mentioned in my message, I wanted to see if you had some time to go through the April employment report and the BLS data collection process with me. There's something wrong with the data. I'm sure of it, but I need a stronger resource to help me break it down. You came to mind immediately."

"Thank you for the compliment. Yes, the data was definitely anomalous—actually, quite remarkable. As it so happens, your timing is very good. I have a Ph.D. student and a couple of undergraduates working on the next edition of my macroeconomics text book. I can have them look at any data you would like."

"That's great, Professor. Thank you. Would you have time for a visit to discuss the data?"

"Yes, I would love that. I'm leaving for Europe tomorrow. I'll be there all of next week meeting with the ECB and some finance ministers, but I'll be back on Saturday. How is the following Monday or Tuesday, May 21 or 22?"

"Monday, the twenty-first, would be perfect."

"Excellent. Maybe we can have dinner Sunday night. You can meet my new friend. She's about your age."

"My age?"

"She's quite intelligent," Petro replied.

"I believe you, Professor, and yes, I'd like that. Can I ask you one more thing?"

"Of course."

"Do you think someone could be playing with the data, or am I being paranoid?"

Petro was silent for several seconds. Then he said, "Dylan, any economist you speak to around the world would tell you that the integrity of U.S. economic data is better protected than the President. So, if you really want to have this discussion, you will need to be mindful of two important protocols. First, no one of any significance gets to toss around the suggestion that the most important economic data infrastructure in the world is being manipulated. Second, no one to whom this first protocol applies ever discusses it over the phone. Now, Dylan, I am truly looking forward to your visit."

"Likewise, Professor."

Dylan knew Petro was the person of significance, not him.

CHAPTER 13
Friday, May 11, 2012

BLAIR ARMSTRONG was an alpha woman in an alpha man's business.

As one of the few women at the helm of a large hedge fund, she was an icon, of sorts. In the 1990s, she had been a top corporate bond trader at Morgan Stanley. She blew up in the wake of the Enron and WorldCom bankruptcies, supposedly losing two hundred million dollars. She left in 2002 to start her own hedge fund, Differential Capital Management. Her aggressive trading style during the boom years generated huge returns, growing Differential to $20 billion under management by the time the financial crisis hit.

Hedge funds proliferated during the mid-2000s, fueled by easy access to credit, booming financial markets, and a glut of money searching for double digit returns in single digit growth economies. They helped fuel the excesses that led to the financial crisis but weathered its devastation much better than the rest of the world. Dylan considered them inevitable mutations of an economy addicted to debt and consumption.

Now, after the financial crisis, Differential was a third the size it had been at its peak, but it still traded billions of dollars worth of bonds every month with Wall Street firms, although not FTS. For

Andrew Cantor, a good meeting today with Blair Armstrong and her team could ensure success for the rest of his career. That was why he had left all the work to Dylan.

Dylan and Cantor were ten minutes late because they couldn't get a taxi on a busy Friday afternoon in Manhattan and had to walk. The sandwiches that Cantor ordered had already been delivered to the conference room in Differential's office when they walked in. A group of people were sitting around a long meeting table eating.

"Hi, I'm Rick Jones," a small, slightly round man said as he walked up to them. In his late thirties with a scruffy beard, Jones was wearing nice slacks, an expensive looking pink dress shirt without a tie, and loafers with no socks. He shook hands with Dylan first, then Cantor.

"You're late," a husky, stern woman's voice declared from behind them.

Blair Armstrong strode quickly to the other end of the long table and sat in the empty seat that had been reserved for her. Medium height and somewhat thin, with short, bleached blond hair and sharp features, Armstrong was attractive in a glaring, neon type way. She wore a stylish, black leather skirt and a tight, white blouse, accompanied by a black onyx necklace and large, matching earrings. Dylan guessed she was in her early forties.

"I'm always early," Armstrong said as Rick Jones sat down to her right. "I expect anyone who does business with us to be early too. My first impression is not particularly strong, Dylan, and first impressions matter. We're decisive at Differential." Armstrong stopped talking abruptly, her face intense as she waited for a response.

The meeting was about him, Dylan realized, not Andrew Cantor or FTS. He didn't know why, and he wasn't going to ask. Whatever he said next would set the tone for the meeting and determine its success or failure.

"My apologies for our tardiness. No excuses, since I only believe in results. My presentation is in front of you. To start, April's jobs number is bad data—an error, maybe even manipulation, if you want to be paranoid. Either way, it will be revised down in coming months. Despite that, it's put support under all financial markets except Treasuries. The economy is structurally much weaker than the jobs data suggests. This rally in risky assets will continue for the next few weeks, but I expect a major selloff going into month-end and the next employment report. More volatility can be expected as we approach the Presidential election and the battle around tax increases and sequester spending cuts slated for 2013."

Dylan looked at Armstrong and thought he detected a slight smile.

"What are your top three trades for the rest of the month?" Armstrong snapped.

"One, buy high yield bonds, including Greek and Spanish debt. Two, short Treasuries, and three, buy agricultural commodities, particularly corn and rice."

Armstrong sat back in her chair, maintaining her intense, steely expression. It was a signal to Rick Jones and the rest of the team, he understood. She was done feeding, and now everyone else could jump on his carcass. Rick Jones and a few other people around the table launched into questions while Armstrong looked on.

After fifteen minutes, Armstrong stood up and walked out. Dylan noticed a distressed look on Cantor's face. The rest of the Differential team grilled him for an hour and a half before the meeting ended.

On their way out, Armstrong's assistant stopped Dylan and said that Armstrong wanted to have dinner with him the next Wednesday. He knew it wasn't a request.

As they rode down the elevator, Cantor asked him, "Any reason you didn't tell her you wanted me to go with you to dinner?"

"Armstrong didn't want you there."

"How do you know that?" Cantor whined.

"She's decisive, remember."

"Are you saying she doesn't like me?"

"No, I'm saying today's meeting went very well, and she wants to follow up with me."

"Fuck you, the meeting went well," Cantor exclaimed. "They mauled you."

They stepped off the elevator and walked out the building to Sixth Avenue. Dylan stopped, turned to Cantor and calmly said, "If the meeting hadn't gone well, we would have been out of there in twenty minutes instead of two hours. I'm guessing you'll have a couple of big trade orders waiting from Differential when we get back."

Three large trade orders from Differential were waiting for Cantor when they walked into the office. Cantor paraded around as if he had just returned from a kill with enough meat to feed the entire FTS clan. Dylan hadn't bothered to mention to Cantor that Rick Jones told him after their meeting that the trades would be waiting when they returned. He wanted Cantor to sweat a little if he was going to take all the credit for his work.

Dylan sat at his desk late Friday afternoon analyzing the April unemployment data as he waited for Compliance to approve his weekly strategy note so he could email it out to clients.

In addition to the number of new jobs created each month, the BLS's monthly employment report also published the results of a household survey which included the unemployment rate, or the percentage of the workforce without jobs. It was a less reliable indicator of employment trends than job creation, but markets watched it closely as a corroborating economic statistic.

Despite the lagging tendency of the unemployment rate, Dylan was examining the current and historical data to try to identify anything he might have missed that would have hinted at the potential for April's incredible job growth. But he had yet to uncover even one data point that suggested the possibility of robust job growth, never mind 483,000 new jobs.

Meanwhile, financial markets around the world continued to behave like April's data was real. Everyone wanted to believe the number, except him. But he couldn't be this wrong.

Dylan leaned back in his chair and glanced around the nearly empty trading floor. Then his Blackberry rang. It was MG. He hesitated but decided to answer.

"It's Dylan . . ."

"It's Mary, and I know you know it's me when I call. Did you get my message yesterday?"

"Sorry, I've had a busy couple of days."

"I understand. Did you watch my segment? It's getting a lot of buzz, especially your conspiracy angle."

"No, not yet."

"Okay, well, have you decided if you're going to help me? You'll get a lot of publicity out of it. And it will be fun to work together."

For the first time in four years, MG wanted something from him. The feeling of being affectionately manipulated was familiar. She thought she could work him the way she used to when they were engaged. She was more skillful now, but he was also a different person.

"Alright," he said, "but there'll have to be some ground rules so I don't get in trouble with compliance." He was willing to risk almost anything to escape FTS—even trusting MG again.

"I understand," she said. "Can you meet Monday night?"

"Yeah, Monday's fine. How about the Oyster Bar in Grand Central at seven?"

"That's great. I loved that place when you took me there that time."

He had only taken her there once, early when they were first dating. They slept together for the first time afterwards, he remembered. He assumed she didn't.

"I have to go," he said, even though he didn't.

"Okay, thank you, Dylan. I'm really looking forward to this. Bye."

Dylan hung up, took a deep breath and released it slowly. *What am I doing?*

He sat up and went to the ICIN website on his computer. The video of MG's news segment appeared immediately, and he clicked to play it.

The camera panned a circle around MG standing on the corner of Park Avenue and 48th Street, her head back and hair flowing, gazing up at the sapphire sky, a short, bright green sheath dress fitted tightly to her exquisite body, her long, toned legs spread apart. Angled metal and glass buildings stretched high, narrowing as they approached the blue expanse above her. She brought her head forward and looked into the camera, then raised the microphone suggestively to her lips and started:

"If you close your eyes, you can feel it, hear it, and even smell it—money! It lives and thrives here in this revered and reviled center of capitalism. Trillions of every major currency flow over electronic wires each day between financial titans like JPMorgan behind me. But what if that electronic river of money was drying up, and with it, the jobs, incomes, and global influence that feed this nation, once the economic superpower of the world?"

The camera turned and faded out to capture the length of Park Avenue stretching north behind her, office buildings lining both sides like canyon walls, hovering over an endless stream of yellow taxi cabs.

"It's not just a scare tactic to get you to watch—that's what this dress is for. It's really happening. No jobs, no money, no spending—the telltale signs of a slowly dying economy. Politicians and business executives are terrified you'll figure it out and do something this election season to change it, at their expense."

She walked towards the camera, forcing a close up of her face and chest.

"So, finish doing whatever you're doing to yourself and pay attention. For the next four weeks, ICIN will present a special series on the upcoming Presidential and Congressional elections and the roles that you and the economy will play in their outcomes. Our first segment will look at the state of the job market for young people. Last week's employment report said things are much better than anyone knew. But what if I told you the government was playing with the data to make you think that? We have someone who might be able to prove it. But you'll have to stick around through this commercial break to learn how you and this economy are being manipulated. I'm Mary Gannon, body and news, for ICIN!"

Andrew Cantor walked by on his way out, presumably headed to Annie Moore's for Friday night drinks. Dylan paused MG's video as Cantor stopped and looked over his shoulder.

"You used to date that?" Cantor remarked with admiration.

Billy McDonald walked up behind Cantor and quipped, "Yeah, but then she got the LASIK surgery, looked at him and cut her losses."

Without turning around to look at McDonald, Dylan asked, "How much are you up this week, Billy?" He knew that asking a trader how much money he had made was the equivalent of asking how big a dick he had.

"Enough to buy the beers, no thanks to you," McDonald quipped, walking away. He shouted back to Cantor, "Hey, let's go man. I'm thirsty."

Cantor slapped Dylan on the shoulder as he left and said, "Thanks for the help with Differential today. I'll make sure Joe knows."

Cantor and McDonald walked around the corner laughing. Dylan gritted his teeth. He knew Cantor would take all the credit for Differential's business when he spoke to Joe Brooks. FTS was a sales driven firm, Brooks had told Dylan when he first interviewed for the position. On his first day on the job, Brooks called to remind him that he wasn't a salesman.

On warm nights, the outdoor section of The Beer Bar near Grand Central Terminal swelled with young working professionals looking to grab a drink, sneak a cigarette, and examine each other after a long day of living the modern American Dream.

Dylan had promised to take Duke, the new, young woman in Compliance, out for a drink at the famous Beer Bar if she stayed late to approve his strategy note. Because it was a provocative piece, specifically discussing the possibility that the jobs data had been inflated to make the economy appear stronger leading up to the elections, he didn't want to risk having a senior Compliance person review and reject it.

"So, this is the famous New York City Beer Bar!" he shouted to Duke as they maneuvered to a tall metal table in the outside patio. She was from Kentucky. He figured she'd believe him.

Duke stared at all the people who might be famous in this famous place.

Dylan politely interrupted the waitress servicing the next table and asked if they could order when she was ready. The waitress looked at him, annoyed, and turned back to the other table.

A minute later, the waitress turned to him and said, "Okay, go ahead."

"Long day, huh?" Dylan said.

She glanced up. He immediately noticed her hazel eyes, prominent cheeks, and gently sloped nose. Her full lips were colored purple. Her medium length, dark brown hair was wavy, streaked with the same color purple, and her skin was a shade of olive. She had an attractive, athletic figure, with a small tattoo of a crucifix on her left wrist. She was different.

"Sorry, long day for me too," he added, smiling as he focused on her eyes.

Her look softened. "Yeah, definitely. What can I get you?"

Duke was half way through her fifth beer as Dylan took the last sip of his second. He couldn't remember what Duke had been talking about for the past fifty minutes, but she was starting to act a little drunk and standing closer to him with each chug of beer.

"Didn't you used to date that gorgeous ICIN reporter," Duke blurted, taking a step closer.

"Yeah, we were engaged, but she broke it off."

"You know we have the same eyes?" Duke said, moving closer. "Not me and her—me and you. But I have blond hair . . ."

He stepped back, laughed, and said, "I know. How about you? Any boyfriends? If not, I can announce that you're looking right now. I'm sure a long line will start forming."

"Stooooop!" she shouted, not realizing how loud she was. "Dylan, you're so baaad!" Her face suddenly turned white. "I have to go to the ladies room. Do you know where it is?"

The waitress showed up and directed Duke inside to the restaurant.

"Your friend's a little drunk," the waitress said after Duke hurried off.

"I know. I'm going to put her in a taxi," he replied, looking at her in a way that prompted a smile. They had already exchanged several moments of staring briefly in each other's eyes. "I'm Dylan," he said and offered his hand.

"Lina," she said and shook his hand.

"That's a nice name," he said. "Well, I guess you can bring me the check."

She returned quickly with the check. Dylan paid with a generous tip. She thanked him, smiled, and placed a napkin next to his beer with her name and phone number written on it.

"Lina Sabatini," he recited softly and watched her as she hurried off to service another table.

Duke came back still looking white and said she needed to leave. Dylan walked her over to 43rd Street and Vanderbilt, put her in a taxi, and gave the driver a twenty to take her home.

After the taxi drove away, he looked across Vanderbilt, trying to catch a glimpse of Lina amidst the throng of people overflowing the famous Beer Bar patio. He thought he heard his name called . . . He looked and saw a large man in a suit waving to him from the crowd.

"Tom Sygowski," Dylan muttered angrily and headed for the subway.

CHAPTER 14
Saturday, May 12, 2012

AT 8:13 a.m., Saturday, Senator Murphy opened the heavy metal door of the small conference room on the second floor of the old, nondescript government building in Washington.

Randolph Boatman, the Republican Majority Leader of the House of Representatives, stood behind him. Boatman was from Texas, average height and shaped like a block, the forty extra pounds from thirty years of government service distributed proportionately. His thinning, artificially dark hair seemed to have been painted in streaks over his scalp.

Both men sported blazers—navy blue for Murphy and brown for Boatman—pink polo shirts and khakis.

A tall, wiry woman wearing a navy blue blazer, white button-down shirt and jeans stood on the far side of a small, round meeting table scrolling through messages on her Blackberry. She could have been in her early or late forties, with short dark hair and angular features. She looked up at them, revealing her intense, glassy blue eyes and a faded scar on the left side of her neck.

"Patricia, you know Randy," Murphy said, stepping into the room and closing the door after Boatman walked in.

She nodded, then sat down. Murphy and Boatman followed.

"Thank you for accommodating us on such short—" Murphy started.

"Senator, could we dispense with the pleasantries?" she interrupted in a strong, deep voice. "You insisted on this meeting. You know it's not protocol. So, please get to the point?"

"Okay, Patricia. What the hell is going on with that jobs number?" Murphy snapped. "Where did 483,000 come from? Aren't you supposed to be monitoring this?"

"I'm not responsible for monitoring that or any other data," she shot back. "We're not administrators. If I'm responsible for anything, it's making sure Senators and Representatives don't stick their politics where they don't belong."

"Now Patricia," Boatman said with a noticeable Southern drawl, "you may not like us asking to meet with you like this, but that number was extraordinary. Much higher than anyone expected. It's going to affect confidence, which is politics, like it or not. It could turn key elections, possibly the Presidency. That wasn't part of the deal. My people want some assurances—"

"The only assurance I'll give you is that we're looking into it," she interrupted.

"You'd better look into it pretty damn quickly," Murphy sneered. "That ICIN rag is all over this story now. They're hell bent on pumping up a conspiracy theory. That type of attention will be bad for everyone . . . including you."

Boatman asked, "Are you saying you don't have any information for us, Patricia?"

She was silent for several seconds, examining them like they might be infectious. She finally said, "We know that a rogue BLS employee was responsible."

"A rogue employee?" Murphy replied. "What are you doing about him?"

"Nothing. *She* is dead."

Murphy's eyes widened. "Dead?" he repeated. "A woman? Who was—"

"Congressmen," she interrupted, looking back and forth between them, "it's obvious that you think you have some special access here, but with all due respect, stay out of this. It's my problem now. Your agendas are political, but this—"

Boatman cut her off. "The rest of the group is just as concerned, especially Mitch."

She paused at the mention of the name, her eyes revealing her deference. "Well, even he has an agenda, but until he calls me, I'll assume he intends to respect the process, as you should."

"The process is at risk of being exposed," Murphy shot back. "What are you going to do?"

"If you're talking about ICIN and that reporter, Mary Gannon, we aren't going to do anything," she said firmly. "She's just trying to create a story. It would be a serious error to give her any reason to think she has one. But we're monitor—"

"I'm talking about the Wall Street strategist who's feeding her all that bullshit—Dylan Regan," Murphy snapped.

"We're aware of him," she said. "He's insignificant. Why are you so worried about him?"

"Because important people are starting to notice what he's saying," Murphy replied.

"And he's got that reporter churning up all the young people, trying to get them to vote everyone out," Boatman added. "This thing blows up in the press and it could crush the economy. No one gets reelected then."

"Exactly what do you expect me to do about that?" she asked.

"Whatever you can to get him to back away," Murphy answered. "Then Gannon will have nothing to work with."

"We're not going there unless it's absolutely necessary," she said.

"Mitch wants something done," Boatman said. "And the rest of the group agrees."

She stared at them for several seconds, then said, "Tell him to call me if he's that worried."

"Patricia, you should be careful," Murphy said. "You're new to this role. No matter how fast your star is rising, there are very significant people and interests involved that you need to appreciate. I wouldn't want you to miscalculate . . . for the sake of your career, I mean."

"I'll take that as friendly advice, Senator. I'll update the appropriate people as soon as we know something. You'll hear from them. Now, you should probably leave first." She stared at them coldly.

Murphy stood up, his frustration obvious. He left quickly, with Boatman following.

After several minutes, she picked up her Blackberry and dialed a number.

"It's Patricia. . . . Yeah, they were pissed. I have to talk to the Director. . . . No, he wants regular updates. I want you to find this Dylan Regan and shake him down a little. . . . He knew Caroline Brenner? . . . Alright, but don't give him any reason to suspect anything. We have to contain this. That's all."

CHAPTER 15
Saturday, May 12, 2012

DYLAN LOOKED out the window of his Upper East Side apartment onto 96th Street below. A few rain drops were just starting to fall. Traffic was light, even for a Saturday morning. The mosque across the street was quiet, although he couldn't remember ever seeing it busy.

He took a sip of his coffee, made a face and spit it back in the cup. "What the . . ." he said and walked to his kitchen. He looked at his coffee maker and saw that the grind setting for the coffee beans and the brew level were both too low. That's why it tasted like dirty water. "Cleaning lady," he muttered.

He started to make a new pot of coffee when his Blackberry rang. It was Brad.

"Hey Brad. You okay?"

"Surviving . . ."

"How was it?"

Brad's voice was somber and distant. "She was in a box . . . a damn box. I couldn't say goodbye. She wasn't there . . ."

Dylan didn't know what to say, so he just listened.

After a long silence, Brad said, "I think she was murdered."

"What?"

"It wasn't an accident. I think her ex-boyfriend killed her. I'm not sure, but I know she was murdered. I'm going to find who did it, and I'm going to kill him."

"Brad, hold on. What do you mean, she was murdered? Is that what the police report said?"

"It's the Medical Examiner's report. I got a copy from the police department."

"And it said the cause of death was murder?"

Brad took a deep breath and exhaled. "No, the cause of death was brain trauma. I'm talking about the manner of death. It's classified as either natural, accident, homicide, suicide, undetermined or pending. They labeled Caroline's death 'pending'."

"But she was killed in a hit-and-run. That's a homicide, right? Or at least an accident. How can it be pending?"

"Because they don't know what they're goddamn talking about!" Brad exclaimed.

Dylan didn't respond. He heard Brad take several deep breaths.

Brad continued: "It's pending because the ME doesn't know if Caroline was killed by accident or if it was some sort of negligent homicide like drunk driving. The report said they were awaiting additional evidence to determine which it was. Until then, it's pending."

"So they think it might have been an accident?"

"I told you it wasn't an accident!" Brad snapped. "She was murdered!"

"Okay . . . but how do you know?"

After a long silence, Brad said, "Caroline always parked her car on her street. It's short, with a turn at the beginning. She wouldn't get hit by surprise there. A car would never get up enough speed to hit her as hard as the report says, unless it was intentional. And how could a second car run her over without knowing? There just isn't that much traffic. It's too much of a coincidence that she breaks up with this guy and then gets hit by a car."

"Brad, that's not a lot to—"

"I know she was murdered," Brad insisted. "Her note said she had a problem that she needed my help with. It had to be her ex-boyfriend. He was probably really upset when she dumped him."

"That's a long way from murder," Dylan said. "Maybe it was a work problem—"

"I don't care. I'm going to find whoever did this, and . . ."

"Jesus, Brad, I know you're upset, but you're not going to kill anyone."

After a few seconds of silence, Brad said, his voice quivering, "You don't understand . . . You didn't see the pictures, her body . . ."

"I'm sorry, Brad. But if you really think someone hit her intentionally, shouldn't you share that with the police?"

"I tried, but they're assuming it was a hit-and-run, probably a drunk driver. Not intentional. It's routine to them." Brad paused, breathing quickly. "Do you know the statistics on mistakes by medical examiners doing autopsies? They're wrong all the time!"

"But if you really believe Caroline was murdered, you have to figure out a way to get the police to listen. You have to have a plan. You can't just go around saying you're going to kill someone. That won't help. It sounds crazy. You know that, right?"

"I have a plan," Brad said.

"You do?"

"I have some friends in the police department. They agreed to look at the ME's report for me. I trust them. And I'm going to talk to Caroline's sister, Jackie, and Shannon Dunn, her friend at the BLS. I'll get all the information the police and the ME haven't tracked down."

"I guess you do have a plan. That's a lot of work, though. Do you need any help?"

"This helps, listening to me rant."

"Well, I'm here for whatever you need. You know that, right?"

"I know. Thanks. I have to go. I'll call you in a few days." Brad hung up.

Dylan looked out the window at the rain falling hard now onto 96th Street. He tried to remember how he had felt when Kyle died. Kyle was everything to him—his big brother. He couldn't feel Brad's loss, but he knew it was immeasurable. He wanted to help. Brad was his friend—the only good thing in his life that hadn't been destroyed over the past four years.

His Blackberry vibrated. He walked over to the coffee table and picked it up. It was a text message from Tom Sygowski: "Bro, that was me last night at the beer bar. Sent u a few messages. Need to talk. Urgent. Have great opportunity for u. Tom"

Dylan deleted the message and threw his phone onto the couch. He needed to go for a run.

The overcast sky was only spitting a few droplets now as Dylan stretched outside his apartment building on 95th Street. He rotated his right ankle to loosen it, feeling a tendon snap across the calcium deposits he had built up from tearing so many ligaments playing basketball. He winced at the loud crack it made.

Dylan finished stretching and took off running, darting across Third Avenue, headed for Central Park. He was on the dirt path that circled the reservoir in no time, running faster, growing angrier with every pace.

Tom Sygowski . . . never forget . . .

The steady rhythm of his breathing was hypnotic. His mind drifted back to May 2002.

Dylan had completed the first year of his MBA at Georgetown's McDonough Business School and had just started a summer internship in Merrill Lynch's corporate bond research group. Enron, an energy company that had filed the largest bankruptcy in U.S. history six months earlier because of an accounting fraud, had sent every Wall Street firm searching to identify what other corporations might be filing false financial statements. Dylan's first assignment was to screen all the major corporate bond issuers for any hints that their financial statements were suspect. He flagged WorldCom, a large and rapidly growing telecommunications company.

WorldCom generated millions in fees for Wall Street firms like Merrill Lynch. Dylan knew that suggesting one of the firm's largest investment banking clients was committing fraud was not a smart strategy if he wanted to be offered a job when he graduated. So, he cornered Tom Sygowski at a local bar instead. Sygowski was the Merrill Lynch bond trader responsible for the telecommunications sector, including WorldCom.

The morning after Sygowski had listened over several beers to Dylan explain how WorldCom's financial statements were inscrutable and its business model unsustainable, he started selling the three hundred million dollars of WorldCom bonds Merrill Lynch owned. Two weeks later, WorldCom announced a massive accounting fraud that would eventually lead it to file the largest ever U.S. bankruptcy, surpassing Enron. Sygowski was a hero, and he used his influence to make sure Dylan was offered a position in Merrill's corporate bond strategy group when he graduated from Georgetown in the spring of 2003.

Over the next five years while Dylan was at Merrill Lynch, the U.S. and world economies changed dramatically. Wall Street did as well. The large brokerage firms like Merrill Lynch, Goldman Sachs, Morgan Stanley, and Lehman Brothers that had dominated financial markets for decades steadily yielded to "universal banks" like Citigroup, JPMorgan, BankAmerica, UBS, and Deutsche Bank. U.S. politicians and regulators capitulated to the banks' growing economic power by throwing out long standing safeguards aimed at limiting their risk taking ability. These banks became the pillars of a financial services driven economy and, ultimately, too big to fail.

The Federal Reserve flooded the U.S. economy with easy credit during this period, enabling anyone and everyone to have it all, today, by borrowing from tomorrow. In this spirit, politicians promoted ever increasing home ownership, regardless of financial means. The result was a historic housing bubble funded by unprecedented and unsustainable consumer debt.

Dylan rose to become the number two person on Merrill's corporate bond strategy team, earning $750,000 in 2007. But the seeds of the financial crisis had already sprouted by the start of 2008. The U.S. and most developed economies were in recession. Then the housing bubble started to burst, triggering the collapse of Bear Stearns, a midsized Wall Street firm that specialized in mortgage-backed securities. The Federal Reserve came to the economy's rescue by lowering interest rates dramatically, flushing financial markets with even more easy credit, the same drug that had gotten the world into its dire predicament.

By August 2008, Lehman Brothers, a large, aggressive Wall Street firm with a significant mortgage bond business, was rumored to be in trouble. Speculation swirled and confidence evaporated, leaving it in desperate need of a government bailout.

But the U.S. was in the final leg of a bruising Presidential election pitting a liberal Democrat, Barack Obama, against a conservative Republican, John McCain. Government involvement in the economy was a contentious election issue. Bailing out any profligate financial institution might incite a major voter backlash that could change the course of the Presidential election. The stage was set for a decision that would ignite a global financial crisis worse than anything since the Great Depression. On the verge of collapse, Lehman Brothers would not be bailed out.

It was Tuesday night, September 9, 2008, and a financial tsunami was headed towards the world, but few investors, economists, strategists, politicians, or business leaders realized it. Dylan was drinking a Sam Adams and waiting for MG at the bar at 10 Downing, a contemporary American restaurant in the West Village. A large, strong hand slapped him on the shoulder.

"Just the man I'm looking for," declared Tom Sygowski, grinning as he worked his six foot, two inch, two hundred fifty pound frame in between two bar stools. "I tried to grab you before you left. I thought you worked until midnight?"

"Hah, every other night. Dinner with my fiancée tonight."

Dylan knew Sygowski wanted something. Sygowski had taken over trading bank and finance company bonds earlier that year and had been leaning on him for help ever since.

"You got a minute? It's urgent," Sygowski said in a low, serious voice as he signaled to the bartender to bring him a beer.

"Yeah, what's up?"

"Listen, I had to take down a block of sixty million Lehman bonds."

"You serious?"

"Yeah, and I can't hedge them. No one's making a fucking market in anything. Bro, I know you hate everything here, but I need your help." Sygowski stared at Dylan with a desperate look for a few seconds, then grabbed his beer and guzzled half of it.

"Shit, Tom. What do you need?"

"I need you to recommend buying Lehman bonds, just for a short-term trade." Sygowski saw Dylan's eyes widen and quickly added, "Hey, you don't need to pound the table. Just suggest they're oversold. You got a lot of credibility now. If you say this selloff is overdone, some fast money asshole will have to cover his Lehman short and buy my bonds."

"What about getting a client to buy them—an insurance company or pension fund?" Dylan suggested, trying to dance around the request. He didn't like Lehman bonds, not even for a short-term trade. And he knew talking to Sygowski about recommending them was violating every rule in the compliance manual.

"Clients are loaded to the gills with Lehman and other financials. They won't add more unless someone like you recommends them. The credit hedge funds smell blood, and it's my fucking blood!"

"But aren't you short financials? Haven't you been hedging your positions?"

"Hey, sometimes I gotta buy bonds I hate in order to keep our clients happy," Sygowski replied. "You know that. And markets don't go straight down. They always bounce. This market is due."

"You made a bet financials would rally, didn't you? Jesus Christ, Tom—"

"I got you this fucking job, Dylan! I've been your biggest supporter, even when the other traders complain you're not helping them enough. You gonna hang me out to dry now? You owe me!" Sygowski's face was red.

"Screw the other traders! They make all the money, and I lose it all, right?" Dylan paused and glared at Sygowski. "How much are you down?"

"Don't ask."

"Is this going to be a threesome?" a tall, thin and uncommonly beautiful woman with short brunette hair asked playfully as she leaned over to kiss Dylan on the cheek.

Dylan still remembered MG clearly that evening—the sensual smell of her floral perfume and the mini, fitted navy blue skirt and suit jacket she wore, a snug white blouse underneath, and her long, shapely legs flowing down to navy blue heals. He recalled it all—the last serene image before his world imploded.

"Tom, you remember my fiancée, MG," he said, then looked at her and smiled. "Tom and I were just strategizing on how to save Merrill . . . and ourselves while we're at it."

"Well, you are *The Strategist*," she remarked, rolling her big brown eyes.

"Nice to see you again, MG," Sygowski said. "I was just leaving to go work out." He reached to grab money out of his pocket to pay for his beer.

"I got it, Tom," Dylan said. "I'll get something out on that in the morning. We'll figure it out, okay? I'll talk to you tomorrow."

Sygowski's eyes brightened. "That's great, buddy! I owe you." He took out a hundred dollar bill and ushered to the bartender. "Anything they drink is on me."

Dylan was breathing hard as he approached the end of his third lap around the reservoir, his Georgetown T-shirt soaked, the humid air seeming to drip down his face and neck. He had run nearly five miles. He sprinted to the park exit on 94th Street and stopped. He put his hands on his hips, closed his eyes and walked slowly as he leaned his head back, gasping for air.

Dylan recalled pausing that Wednesday in September 2008 to question what he was doing before sending out his note to clients recommending they buy Lehman bonds. By the time Sunday came, he already knew Lehman was going to file bankruptcy the next day—the biggest in U.S. history. He and Sygowski were fired that week. Whether or not another spark would have ignited the global financial meltdown had Lehman been bailed out was academic from a historical standpoint. But it wasn't to him. Lehman had destroyed his career—maybe his life.

CHAPTER 16
Saturday, May 12, 2012

MARY HAD never heard of The Saint Thomas Moore Cerebral Palsy Center until Jeff asked her to accompany him to a fund raiser Saturday night at the New York Waldorf-Astoria Hotel. Senator Murphy had recently been named a trustee, which made Jeff's presence mandatory. The Center was located in McLean, Virginia, just outside Washington, D.C.

She chose her dress to be a provocative transition from the grand era long past that she associated with the Waldorf-Astoria to the sexual glamour of ICIN. It was a simple black satin, sweetheart cocktail dress with a slanted hemline that peaked high on her left thigh, accented by silver metal rings around her upper arms and wrists, and black and silver high heels. As she strolled into the Grand Ballroom looking for Jeff, she sensed the many eyes upon her.

A young, male waiter moved quickly to offer her a glass of white wine. She took one from the tray and then noticed a short, paunchy, older man with an annoyed look standing to the side of the cocktail bar. It was Rothstein—brown suit, loose tie, bottle of beer, and everything else that made him Rothstein. He saw her, and raised his bottle in acknowledgement.

Mary knew he was out of his element. She was curious and tempted. She strolled over to him, attracting stares from various aged men standing and talking at a table nearby.

"Hello boss. You lost?" she asked with understated glee.

"Isn't that your boss over there, sucking up to Murphy and Hayes?" Rothstein replied, looking over her shoulder.

Mary turned around quickly. Jeff was on the other side of the room in a circle, talking with four men and a tall, attractive black woman. She recognized Senator Murphy, former Governor Hayes, and John Wiley, ICIN's founder and owner. The fourth man, thin and angular with white hair, and the woman, she didn't know.

She turned back and asked, "What is Hayes doing here, and who are you calling my boss?"

"What are you doing here, and isn't that short, skinny guy with the curly hair your new boss?" Rothstein shot back, then took a swig of his beer.

"So, you know I'm dating Jeff Schwinn. I'm sure you also know he's Senator Murphy's Chief of Staff. He would take umbrage to you calling him my boss . . . and he's taller than you," she replied, looking down at him mockingly.

"Taller than short isn't fucking tall," Rothstein quipped, then shuffled over to the bar for another beer. He returned and resumed: "Hayes is here pretending to help raise funds for the CP Center, but he's really in town to lock down financing for an independent Presidential run. He's giving a policy speech Tuesday at NYU as a trial balloon. He's spending time with Murphy this weekend to see if a moderate Republican and a moderate Democrat can actually add up to one legitimate candidate. If it does, they'll look to announce a run in a few weeks."

Rothstein paused and gulped some more beer. "The white haired guy with them is Donald Granger, the big money manager who has enough money and friends to get them financed and launched quickly. Wiley's in the mix because he knows Murphy and wants to keep his connections up. Murphy and Hayes think they can use Wiley to harness ICIN and get them attention faster than any other media strategy. The black woman's probably a hooker."

Mary's mind started to race. If Rothstein was right about Governor Hayes working on an independent Presidential run with Senator Murphy, she'd be first in line through Jeff for the hottest story on the planet. But why hadn't he told her about it? . . . *That woman isn't a hooker.*

"What do you mean harnessing ICIN?" Mary asked. "Wiley wouldn't allow us to be used like that."

"You just make sure your fucking boss doesn't try to use you that way. I'll handle Wiley."

"Boyfriend, not boss," Mary snapped.

"Semantics," Rothstein muttered.

The lights dimmed briefly, and the Master of Ceremonies asked everyone to take their seats so dinner could be served and the evening's program could start.

"I've got to go get tortured," Rothstein grumbled and shuffled off towards a table where John Wiley was now sitting with his wife.

Mary walked over to the table where Schwinn was sitting along with Senator Murphy, Murphy's wife, Governor Hayes, and a refined, older woman Mary assumed was Mrs. Hayes. Donald Granger was also at the table, sitting next to an attractive Asian woman about Mary's age who looked several months pregnant. The tall, black woman Rothstein said was a hooker was there too, with an empty chair next to her.

Schwinn stood up and gave Mary a light kiss on the cheek before she sat down.

"Since I seem to be the one who knows everyone," Schwinn started with a self-deprecating smile, "I'd like to introduce my friend, Mary Gannon. Some of you may have seen her on that sensational news network, ICIN." He gestured towards the Governor and said, "Mary, this is our special guest speaker tonight, Governor Hayes, and his charming wife, Dorothy."

"It's a pleasure, Governor Hayes, Mrs. Hayes," Mary said.

"Please, call me Dorothy," Mrs. Hayes said and smiled. "That is quite a young man you've captured there."

"Thank you, Dorothy," Mary replied, smiling politely. She didn't appreciate the suggestion that she was the fortunate one. Men pursued her.

"You've probably heard of Donald Granger, the founder of Macro-Quantitative Advisors," Schwinn continued.

"Of course, the money manager up in Connecticut with all the math models and great returns," Mary said. "Is it true you don't talk to the press?"

"You are as charming as Jeff has claimed," Donald Granger replied with a slight bow of his head. "May I introduce my wife, Hui."

"It's nice to meet you," Mary said.

"Very nice to meet you, Ms. Gannon," Hui Granger said in perfect English. "You are somewhat of a celebrity in China, although you are edited significantly since your work can be a bit provocative. However, I enjoy it very much."

"Thank you. ICIN is trying to launch its own network there," Mary replied. "I'd love to get your thoughts—"

Schwinn interrupted. "Mary, you remember Senator Murphy and his wife, Karen."

"Of course,' Mary replied and smiled warmly. "Hello, Senator . . . Karen."

Senator Murphy nodded in acknowledgement and said, "Mary . . ."

Mary added, "I love your dress, Karen."

"Thank you," Karen Murphy replied. "I wish I could still wear what you do."

Mary feigned a smile, then turned her eyes to the attractive, black woman across from her.

Schwinn said, "And this is Julie Watson. Julie is on the board of the Elizabeth Granger Foundation, the primary sponsor of this event. And she's why we have such a good table."

"Now Jeff, you know it's really Donald's generosity," Watson replied, then smiled at Mary. "I watch you all the time on ICIN. I love your work."

Mary was about to respond when the Master of Ceremonies walked over to the table. He was large and round, in his late fifties, and balding, with patches of white hair around his ears. He sat down next to Julie Watson.

"Oh, and this is Peter Zimmer," Schwinn said, "our host and Trustee extraordinaire of the CP Center. Peter, this is Mary Gannon."

"Jeff, everyone knows who Mary is, even me," Zimmer replied and laughed. "It's really a thrill for me, Mary. My teenagers are going to be so jealous when I tell them I met you. Thank you for coming and supporting us."

"That's very kind of you," Mary said. "It's a special cause. I'm honored to be here." She paused, then looked at Julie Watson and asked, "So, Ms. Watson, how do you know Jeff?"

"Please, call me Julie," Watson replied, "and I—"

Schwinn interrupted and said, "I'm in politics, Mary. I have to know everyone, especially friends of Donald Granger." He nodded in deference to Granger, then turned and smiled gratuitously at Watson.

Watson returned the smile.

Mary smiled at Jeff, then glanced at Watson, and then Zimmer. She wondered if Watson and Zimmer were there together. "So, Peter, are you in politics too?" she asked.

"Hah, God no," Zimmer answered, "but I do work for the government. I got involved with the Center because my daughter has CP. She's a patient here. It's made a real difference in her life. Mine too."

"That's really a heartwarming story," Mary said.

"Well, it wouldn't be possible without the generous donations Julie gives us from Donald's foundation," Zimmer said.

Mary smiled and asked, "So, where in the government do you work?"

"I'm an Associate Commissioner for the Bureau of Labor Statistics," Zimmer answered.

"Oh, you work for the BLS?" Mary replied.

"Going on twenty years," Zimmer said.

"Did you know Caroline Brenner? She was the economist there who was killed in a hit-and-run a little over a week ago. I knew her."

An anguished expression crossed Zimmer's face. He shook his head slowly and said, "Yes, everyone knew Caroline. She was such a wonderful person. It's just so awful, and the driver didn't even stop. Everyone at the BLS is still upset." After several seconds of silence, Zimmer said, "Well, they're serving the salad, which is my cue to start the program. Please excuse me." He stood up and walked over to the stairs that led up to the stage.

As they ate their salads, Governor Hayes looked up and said, "So, Mary, you're the remarkable young reporter for ICIN I've heard so much about from nearly everyone, including my daughter. Are we on the record, or can we relax tonight?"

"Of course you can relax, Governor. It's only on the record if you say something worth reporting." Mary smiled playfully, and everyone at the table laughed.

"Fortunately, Ms. Gannon, I never say anything I don't really believe," Hayes replied. "The media can report what they want. I trust the American people to see the truth."

"It sounds like you think the media is to blame for the toxic political discourse today," Mary responded.

"Not at all," Hayes countered, "but I do think our political leaders now worry more about their images than the job they should be doing, just so they appear to be electable. And look at what that's done. This country's a mess, and no one's to blame, no one takes responsibility, especially in Washington. Ms. Gannon, your profession is no more responsible than my profession, but we are all responsible. What are you going to do to make things better? I intend to change this absurd system." Hayes smiled and added, "But I might need a few votes to do it."

"You have mine, Governor," Schwinn volunteered quickly.

"Thank you, Jeff. How about you, Ms. Gannon?"

"Until I know you're actually running for office, I can't say. Are you running, Governor?"

"Look at that. I think I'm being called up for my speech," Hayes said, smiled and stood up. He walked to the stage while the others at the table laughed.

"How about you, Senator Murphy?" Mary asked. "Care to share your plans?"

"As soon as Jeff decides what I'm doing, I'm sure I'll be the second person to know . . . right after you," Murphy replied.

Schwinn forced a smile, looked at Mary and said, "Maybe we could all take a break from our work and—"

Just then, the room erupted in applause as Governor Hayes strolled onto the stage. He gave an impassioned speech on compassion, responsibility, and public service, tying them back to the mission of the Cerebral Palsy Center. It was a speech bordering on political opportunism, but he received a standing ovation.

The rest of the evening was taken up by an endless stream of speeches and a charity auction run by Peter Zimmer. Most of the items had been donated by Donald Granger and his wife.

After the event was over, Mary was standing outside the Grand Ballroom waiting for Jeff to finish making his rounds when Donald Granger approached her.

"Ms. Gannon, thank you for the entertaining evening," Granger said. "I wanted to tell you how much I enjoy your reporting. You are really an exceptional journalist."

"Thank you, Mr. Granger. May I ask you a question?"

"I'm sure you will, regardless of my answer," Granger replied, smiling slightly.

"You're correct," she said. "So, I've heard rumors that you may be backing Governor Hayes when he announces his candidacy for the Presidency. Care to comment?"

"Charming, Ms. Gannon, but we both know the answer to that question. Now, may I ask you a question?"

"Certainly," Mary answered.

"I would expect that someone with your talent and drive would like to ultimately be awarded a Pulitzer or something of that magnitude to validate your credentials as a journalist."

Mary raised her eyebrows. "Is that your question, Mr. Granger?"

"Just a working assumption," Granger replied, a barely perceptible smile on his face. "Why would someone who wants to be taken seriously as a journalist promote a wild conspiracy theory about the employment data being manipulated when there are so many important and urgent issues in this economy and this election season to report on? That is my question, Ms. Gannon."

Mary felt her face flush as blood sped to her head. She pressed her lips, but stopped as soon as she realized she was projecting anger. She took a quick deep breath through her nose, smiled wryly and said, "If you'll answer my question, I'll answer yours . . . since I asked first."

"Clever and charming," Granger replied, the same barely perceptible smile on his face.

Granger's wife walked up to them and said, "Excuse me, Ms. Gannon. Donald, I will be waiting in the car." She bowed slightly to Mary, then walked towards two large men in navy blue suits who were waiting to escort her.

Mary looked back at Granger and asked, "Why does my story bother you so much?"

Granger stared at her for several seconds, then smiled more noticeably. "Very few things truly bother me, Ms. Gannon. Wasted talent is one of them."

Before Mary could respond, Schwinn walked up, touched her lightly on her lower back and asked, "Are you ready to leave? I'm exhausted."

Mary turned slightly, smiled at Jeff and said, "Hi there. Sure."

"Good night, Ms. Gannon . . . Jeff," Granger said and walked away, quickly accompanied by another two large men in blue suits.

"What were you discussing with Donald?" Schwinn asked as they walked outside.

"Nothing, really. He's quite evasive and secretive. Speaking of secretive, how do you know Julie Watson?"

"From the CP Center," Schwinn answered.

"She was very friendly towards you, or was I imagining it?"

"Hah, that's just her personality."

"My producer thinks she's a hooker." Mary looked at him with a quizzical smile.

"A hooker? Maybe I should go back and find out," Schwinn replied as he waved for a taxi.

"Wouldn't you rather pay me?" Mary asked, pretending to be hurt.

"I would, but I could never afford you," Schwinn answered, squeezing her close as a taxi pulled up to the curb. "I'll just have to depend on your charity." He moved to kiss her.

"It's not charity if you deserve it," she said softly as she opened her lips.

"No one deserves you . . ."

"I know, but you'll do," she said and closed her eyes as their lips touched.

CHAPTER 17
Sunday, May 13, 2012

A HEAVY rain pounded the sill outside Brad's apartment window late Sunday morning. He sat at his kitchen table staring at the first page of his notebook. He picked up his pen and wrote the word "WHY" in the margin and underlined it.

It now read: "<u>WHY</u> DID CHRIS SMITH KILL CAROLINE?"

Smith must have been devastated when Caroline broke up with him, Brad figured. Murder was purposeful, usually personal. Smith was the only person he knew of with a strong personal motive. And he was a lawyer, which didn't mean anything other than he was a scumbag.

Brad picked up his cell phone and called Jackie, Caroline's sister. They had scheduled an eleven o'clock call.

"Hello?" a woman's voice answered.

"Jackie, it's Brad. Is now good?"

"Brad, yes, just let me close the study door. I'm still at my parents' house. Are you okay?"

"I'm okay. How are you doing?"

"Well, you know, I just keep thinking about when Caroline and I were kids and would fight all the time. I remember being so jealous of her. She was my big sister and seemed to have everything. But as we got older, we became best friends. I guess I grew up, and Caroline never really let any of that stuff bother her. She always forgave me. That's how she was."

Brad could hear her sniffling from crying. "I know," he said. He wanted to believe Caroline had forgiven him too. "Jackie, I need to know how Chris Smith reacted when Caroline broke up with him."

"Okay, but why? You don't think he had anything to do with Caroline's death, do you?"

"No, I don't think so. It's just I never talked to her after she told him, and I want to make sure he didn't give her a hard time. You understand . . ."

"I do," Jackie said and cleared her throat. "Um, she told him the Friday before she was . . . before she died. I talked to her that night. She said he was upset but he'd been expecting it. To be honest, I don't think she ever took the relationship that seriously. He was just fun to hang out with. She was really waiting until you two got back together. I think that's why she broke up with him. She thought you were going to ask her. Was she right, Brad?"

"Yes, she was." He was more certain every time he said it.

"That makes me so happy. I just wish . . ." She stopped and wept for a moment.

"Jackie, Caroline left a note under my apartment door the day she was killed saying she had a problem that she needed my help with. Do you know anything about that?"

"Um, she did call me that morning. I guess you guys had an argument the night before. She realized she was a little rough on you. I asked her why she was upset, but she didn't want to talk about it. I told her not to worry, because you would forgive her for anything, because you loved her . . . I'm sorry, Brad. Is it okay that I tell you that?"

"Yes. It's true."

"Well, that's all I know about whatever was bothering her. I never talked to her again . . ." She started to cry.

Brad was silent until he thought she had stopped. He said, "Lindsey Cho said Caroline was close to taking a job in New York City, but she thought she had turned it down. Do you know anything about that?"

Jackie cleared her throat again and said, "Oh, yes, she was so excited about that, maybe a month or so ago. I asked her about it when she called to tell me she broke up with Chris, since I was wondering how it would work if you two were really getting back together. She said the job wasn't what she thought it was and then changed the subject."

"Did she tell you the firm?" Brad asked.

"No, I'm sorry. I guess I'm not being very helpful."

"You are, Jackie," Brad replied. "How about her work. Was anything going on there?"

"Um, she didn't talk much about her job, at least not to me. Wait, she did tell me that her boss died suddenly. That was about six months ago now. I don't think she liked him very much. But nothing else really since then."

"Okay, well, were there any other boyfriends before Chris?"

"Yes, maybe three or four," Jackie answered. "You know how beautiful she was. After you two broke up, guys were always asking her out. She was a little too nice, but she ended things pretty quickly with all of them. None of them were ever serious, not even Chris."

"Would you have their names and contact information?"

"Uh, probably, but why do you want them? Is there something going on, Brad?"

"No, I'm just checking everything out to make certain the person who killed her is caught."

"Do you think someone killed her on purpose, like an ex-boyfriend? If you do—"

"Jackie, I don't have any information. It was probably a drunk driver, and the police will catch him, or her, but I can't just sit on my hands doing nothing."

"I'm sorry, Brad. Just the thought of someone hurting Caroline intentionally . . ."

"I know. Can you email me that information as soon as you track it down?"

"Sure, but promise you'll let me know if you learn anything new, okay?"

"Of course. Thank you, Jackie. Take care of yourself."

Brad hung up and looked at his notebook. He hadn't learned anything about why Chris Smith killed Caroline. He was going to have to talk to Smith himself. But first, he wanted to speak with Shannon Dunn, Caroline's friend at the BLS who had called to tell him she was dead.

On Brad's third call, Shannon Dunn finally answered.

"Shannon, this is Brad Johnson. Sorry for calling on a Sunday, but do you have a few minutes to talk about Caroline?"

"Oh, Brad . . ." Shannon replied, seeming surprised. "I thought you were someone else. I can't really talk right now. My daughter's waking up from her nap. Can I call—"

"I only need a minute, Shannon. I just have a couple of quick questions."

"Brad, I can't really talk to you about Caroline."

"Why is that?"

"Everyone in my group at the BLS—the group Caroline was in—everyone was told not to talk about anything involving Caroline except to the police and FBI."

"Who told you that? And why?" Brad demanded.

"Brad, please understand. I could get in trouble," she said.

"I'm sorry, Shannon. It's just that you were Caroline's best friend at the BLS. I only want to know what was going on with her there, before she died. Why is that a problem?"

"I'm just doing what I was told, Brad. I can't afford to lose my job. I think it's only until the investigation is over. I'll talk to you all you want after that. I have to go—"

"Wait . . . Can you at least tell me what you know about her ex-boyfriend, Chris Smith? He doesn't have anything to do with the BLS. It shouldn't violate anything."

Brad heard Shannon sigh and then silence.

After several seconds, Shannon said, "Okay, but it has to be quick."

"Thank you. Um, how did they meet? Did she talk about him? Did she mention how he reacted when she broke it off?"

Shannon said, "Well, she met him a few months ago, at Third Edition over in Georgetown. You probably know it. A bunch of us went out for a drink there after work one night. Chris was there and started flirting with Caroline. Before I knew it, she was meeting him there most Monday nights. I asked her about him, and she said he was just fun company, nothing serious."

"Did she tell you anything else about him? What kind of guy he is?"

"You know he's a securities lawyer, right?"

"Yes. What else?"

"Well, just that he likes to party, and he's supposedly funny. Caroline was just biding time with him until you two got back together. She said she was honest with Chris about that."

"Did Caroline say how he reacted when she ended it?"

"She said he was disappointed, but that's all. Brad, I really have—"

"Just one last question. Caroline supposedly had a job offer in New York. Did you—"

"That's all I can tell you, Brad. I have to go," Shannon said.

"Okay. You said Chris Smith hangs out at Thirds most Mondays?"

"Yes," Shannon replied. "You're not thinking of doing anything, are you?"

"No. It's just for my notes," Brad answered. "Thank you, Shannon."

"I wish I could have been at the funeral, but I didn't have anyone to watch my daughter."

"You were a good friend. That's what matters."

"I miss her so much," Shannon said, choking up. "When it's safe, I'll help however I can."

"What do you mean?" Brad asked.

"I mean when the investigation is over. Take care, Brad," she said and hung up.

CHAPTER 18
Monday, May 14, 2012

NOTHING MUCH had happened in the world over the weekend, so Dylan attributed the severe bond market selloff underway early Monday morning to the growing confidence that the U.S. economy had finally risen from the ashes of the financial crisis. Stock market futures were pointing to a two percent higher opening.

As Dylan stared vacantly at his Bloomberg screens, Bob Berkley, the salesman he had gone to dinner with at Del Frisco's, sauntered over. Berkley was a "medium" in every way, except his compensation. He was the top producing bond salesmen. FTS had lured him over from Citibank with a two-by-two contract—two million dollars a year guaranteed for two years—just before the onset of the financial crisis, making him look like one of the smartest rats to flee the sinking Wall Street banks.

"Hey buddy," Berkley said casually. "You know I've been trying to get into MQA, right?"

"Yeah, anything going on?" Dylan replied, barely acknowledging him since he assumed there wasn't.

"Well, I've been sending them your strategy stuff, and they seem to like it. I got them to agree to a meeting. You know they don't even talk to some of the top sellside firms."

Dylan sat up and turned his chair to look at Berkley.

With a trillion dollars in client assets, Macro-Quantitative Advisors, or MQA, was one of the most successful and secretive firms in the investment management business. It specialized in quantitative analysis, a style of investing that used mathematical models to predict changes in the economy and markets. It had supposedly averaged twenty percent a year in investment returns over its thirty-year history. Meeting with MQA was a dream he had stopped having long ago.

"When do they want to meet?" Dylan asked, trying to conceal his eagerness.

"Short notice—tomorrow. I'm going to try to get them out for drinks afterwards. They could be a two million dollar account for me. You gotta be on the top of your game, buddy."

"Don't worry. I will."

Dylan knew MQA had no interest in a relationship with FTS, Bob Berkley or Berkley's professional female friends. MQA wanted something, something that could help them. He found it hard to believe it was his strategy advice. But he wasn't going to question it too much, since he may have just been handed the keys to his FTS cell.

Dylan saw her walk through the dark oak saloon doors of the Oyster Bar in Grand Central Terminal, as if he was the camera in an old movie. She wore a knee-length blue slit skirt with a white short-sleeved tapered blouse and a single strand pearl necklace. Her suit jacket was flung over her shoulder, held by one finger, a flexible leather brief case in her other hand.

Mary saw him and indicated to a disappointed maitre d' that she didn't need his help.

"Sorry I'm late," she said and sat down. "How are you doing? You look good. Your hair's wet. Were you working out?"

"Yeah, I went for a run."

Mary leaned her elbows on the table, rested her chin on her clasped hands and parted her lips slightly. She looked at him with sincerity he didn't trust but wanted to.

"Dylan, I really appreciate your help. This is my first major series at ICIN. I know your research will help me make it something special."

New tactics, Dylan thought. Honesty to gain his trust, compliments to stroke his ego, and vulnerability to make him want to help—all in ten seconds. She was better than he remembered.

"And the publicity should be good for you," Mary continued. "It could help you get out of FTS . . . You know what I mean."

He knew all too well. "Let's order and get some work done," he said.

Dylan spent the next hour sharing his views on the state of the U.S. economy, explaining how any confidence boosting data like the strong April jobs number could drive increased consumer and business spending, which might influence the outcome of the Presidential election. He wove his views into a motivation and scenario for manipulating the employment data. Mary took constant notes.

After the waiter cleared their plates and delivered two espressos, Mary said, "It sounds like a no brainer for the Democrats to try to inflate the data. Do you think they've done it before?"

"First, if there really is a conspiracy, it's probably a joint one with Republicans since it's unlikely that one party would ever let the other get away with manipulating the data on its own. Still, if they're willing to conspire together, why not just work together to run the government better? That would really drive confidence higher, but we know that's not happening."

"Are you saying you don't really think there is a conspiracy?" she asked.

"Well, something's definitely wrong with the data, but I'm not really sure what or why."

"But you keep suggesting in your research that there's a conspiracy behind it."

"That's part of being a sellside strategist. I have to be provocative or no one will read my stuff, especially at FTS. You know that. But I'm convinced the data is bad, and writing about it does focus attention on the problem."

"I get it," Mary said. "So, could it be some rogue group of Democrats playing with the data to boost the President's reelection chances, and Republicans haven't caught on yet?"

"Anything's possible, but from everything I know, it's extremely hard to get access to the data, never mind manipulate it without anyone realizing. I think it would have to be systemic, something that's been in place for a while, which gets me back to the problem with my conspiracy theory."

"Which is?" Mary asked.

"Which is how could a longstanding practice of manipulating the data stay concealed? It's more likely that the BLS just fucked up—pardon my French."

"How do you spell that?" she asked as she continued to write notes.

"Funny," Dylan replied. "Anyway, to answer your question, I've looked at the historical data, but I can't tell if it's been manipulated. I didn't find anything like April's number. It's almost too big. No one would be that obvious. It looks like either the BLS made a really big data error or it's real, and I don't believe it's real. The details behind the number are too contradictory and inconsistent as well."

Mary asked, "Isn't it suspiciously serendipitous for the BLS to make such a big data error in a positive direction for the economy at such a crucial time for the elections? I know you don't believe in serendipitous coincidences."

The comment caught Dylan off guard, and he smiled to disguise his reaction. When they first met, he had used that line to insist it had been fate and not coincidence.

Whatever game MG was playing, her point was still a good one. A BLS data error was too serendipitous. Caroline's death was also a strange coincidence, especially if it was murder as Brad believed. His paranoia started to grow. He wondered if the jobs data and Caroline's death could somehow be connected.

Mary noticed Dylan's expression and asked, "Is there something else?"

"No, it's nothing."

She examined him for a few seconds, then said, "Well, what else should I cover to make my series exceptional?"

Dylan thought for a moment, then said, "The growing unemployment problem among graduating high school and college kids is the biggest crisis facing this country. There's a generation of young people who are unlikely to ever have a career because there are no jobs for as far as the eye can see. This lost generation will be forty before they get a steady job, but it'll be too late to start a career by then. And the generation after that will have it even worse. That's when you'll see discontent and upheaval, maybe even violence. It's a number of years out, but that's the real cost of three decades of borrowing against the future so everyone could have it all today. It's this lost generation who will ultimately pay, not the people who borrowed trillions and spent it on nothing."

"That's pretty dire," Mary said, "but a great focus for my series. Well, it's getting late. I have to go, but I'd love to continue this. Does next week work?"

"Uh . . . sure," Dylan said, then added, "You should also check out this grassroots movement that a bunch of unemployed and underemployed college grads have started. They're growing it through social media, but it's not like *Occupy Wall Street*. The focus is on finding jobs rather than protesting. It could get really big, especially if someone like you highlights it. I think they're calling it 'The Lost Revolution'."

"Catchy. Sounds interesting. Thanks." She hesitated, then asked, "Do you mind if I pay?"

"It is *your career* we're working on."

"True . . ." she said, "but you could luck out with this and get a job offer from a real firm."

Her comment stung, but Dylan just smiled and waited silently while she paid. They walked out the back door of the Oyster Bar to a still bustling Grand Central Terminal.

As Mary turned to say goodbye, her cell phone rang. She looked at it, and her eyes brightened. "Hi there," she answered. "Just leaving. See you at my place. Bye."

Dylan assumed she was talking to Jeff Schwinn.

She hung up, looked at Dylan and said, "Thanks again. I'm going to grab a cab."

"MG," Dylan said as she turned to leave, "use my cell number when you call. I have to be careful about Compliance. And make sure you talk to me before you reference me or FTS in anything. You understand?"

Her excited expression turned scornful. "I understand, and it's Mary, not MG. You understand?" She walked away without waiting for a response.

CHAPTER 19
Monday, May 14, 2012

BRAD WALKED into Third Edition on Wisconsin Avenue in Georgetown shortly after eight Monday night. "Thirds", as it was called, was a pub club that catered to the barely twenty-one college crowd. He'd been there plenty of times before, with Dylan, when they overlapped for a year at business school. It was quiet, with only a handful of people in the bar area.

Brad recognized Chris Smith standing at one of the tall wooden tables talking to a young woman and another man. He was shorter than he remembered from Caroline's funeral but otherwise the same—blond, bland and unimpressive.

What did Caroline see in him? Jackie said he was funny. Caroline did like funny men. He remembered her telling him if he wasn't so sexy, she'd dump him because he wasn't funny enough. He was going to find out just how funny Chris Smith was.

Brad went to the end of the bar near a sign that read "Rest Rooms" and ordered a Budweiser. If Smith came there regularly on Mondays, he probably drank a lot. And if he drank a lot, he probably went to the men's room frequently. Brad waited, sipping his Budweiser.

After ten minutes, Smith headed for the sign pointing to the rest rooms. Brad stepped in front of him and walked ahead down the hallway. He opened the door to the men's room, then held it for Smith. Smith stepped in and hurriedly unzipped his pants. Brad quickly checked to see if anyone else was in the men's room—no one.

When the door closed, Brad grabbed Smith's shirt and hair from behind, yanked him away from the urinal and threw him hard against the door. Smith turned, wide-eyed and pale, to face Brad. Brad clenched Smith's neck with his left hand, held him up against the door, and then grabbed Smith's left wrist and bent it back over his forearm.

Smith screamed in pain, his eyes bulging in fear at this six foot two, two hundred pound black man in a gray business suit pinning him up against the men's room door.

"What do you want?" Smith cried.

"I want you to tell me everything you know about Caroline Brenner's murder. If I think you're lying, I'll hit you until you spit blood." He banged Smith against the door again to make his point, then let go of Smith's neck and wrist and stepped back.

Smith's eyes narrowed as he recognized Caroline's name and realized he wasn't going to be mugged or raped. "Are you with the police? The FBI? I just talked to—" Smith suddenly seemed to figure something out. "You're Brad Johnson, Caroline's old boyfriend. I—"

"Tell me everything you know about Caroline's murder!" Brad snapped.

Smith was more confident now. "I told the police and FBI everything I know. Talk to them. I think I'll talk to them too. I'm a lawyer—"

Brad whipped his left arm around, forming a fist in a fraction of a second, and hit Smith in the side, just below his kidney. Smith groaned, and his legs buckled. Brad grabbed his shirt, pulled him up and slammed him against the door. He stepped back, keeping his fists clenched.

"Tell me what you know!" Brad yelled.

"What do you want to know?" Smith cried.

"Everything, and make it quick."

"Uh, we dated, but she wasn't serious about it. I liked her a lot, but she said she hoped to get back together with you." Smith paused and caught his breath. He straightened up. "About a month ago, she told me she was going to break up with me because she thought you guys were getting back together soon. I said I understood and hoped she would be happy. She was a great person, beautiful and—"

"Shut up! Just tell me what you know about her murder!"

"Murder? What—I didn't do it, if that's what you're asking. I was in Bermuda. The police already checked me out. I wouldn't hurt her. I mean, look at me . . . We were just friends. I was already seeing someone else when she dumped—"

"What do you know about another job she was looking at?"

"Uh, she interviewed with a firm up in New York and—"

"What firm?"

"I don't know. She didn't want to tell me. I just know she had some concerns about it."

"What concerns?"

"She didn't say. I assumed it was being away from you."

Brad was silent, breathing from his nose like a bull deciding if he would attack. He didn't want to admit that Chris Smith didn't look or act like someone who could have killed Caroline.

"If you didn't do it, you know who did," Brad sneered.

"I don't, I swear. I just know she was pretty tense the last month."

"About what?"

"I think her job, but she never really talked about it," Smith replied.

"Why do you think it was her job?"

"Because she seemed to be working late all the time the month before she died."

"What else?"

"Uh, you should talk to the research guy up in New York she used to help sometimes. The FBI asked me all about him. His name's Reagan, or something like that."

"Why was the FBI involved?" Brad asked.

"I don't know. They said they were working with the police."

Brad glared at Smith for a minute without saying anything, then reached for him. Smith flinched. Brad guided him away from the door and opened it.

"I'm not going to say anything to the police," Smith said as Brad started to walk out.

Brad stopped, hovered over him and said, "I know you're not." He glanced down at the long wet stain on the leg of Smith's unzipped khakis, then left and let the door close.

As Brad hurried down the hallway, he heard Smith exclaim, "Shit!"

CHAPTER 20
Tuesday, May 15, 2012

THE INITIALS "MQA" were affixed prominently at the top of a tall, neo-modern, glass, metal, and stone office building overlooking I-95 and the Long Island Sound in Stamford, Connecticut. It housed the headquarters of Macro-Quantitative Advisors.

Dylan and Bob Berkley arrived just in time for their three o'clock meeting and were met at the visitor's check-in by a young, attractive and well spoken woman of Indian heritage.

"Mr. Regan, I'm Mr. Granger's assistant," she said with a slight British accent, ignoring Berkley. "Please follow me."

Donald Granger was the co-founder and Chief Investment Officer of MQA. He enjoyed an almost mythical status in the investment management industry. Dylan was surprised that his assistant had greeted them, but he didn't believe Granger would actually attend their meeting. *That* would be unheard of.

Granger's assistant bypassed the extensive security for routine visitors and brought them to a roped off elevator attended by a security guard. There was only one stop on the elevator. It shot up and opened to an expansive lobby decorated in international décor with various pieces of Asian, African and European art distributed throughout like a museum.

Two young men in suits were waiting on a blue leather couch by the window. Granger's assistant introduced them as portfolio managers who would accompany Berkley back down to the lobby and entertain him in the Starbucks while Dylan attended the meeting. Berkley walked to the regular elevator bank with the two young men, a dejected look on his face.

Granger's assistant directed him to a set of wide glass doors. She typed in a code on a keypad, and they slid back, disappearing into the walls. He followed her into a small area with two wide bright metal doors before them. The glass doors closed behind them. She pressed her thumb on a blank pad against the wall and looked into a retinal scan. The two metal doors slid back into the walls, revealing a very large, modern office. The south and west facing walls were all tinted windows overlooking Stamford Harbor and I-95.

They stepped in, and she gestured him to the left where four men and one woman stood around a set of glass and metal tables shaped like parentheses. A large flat LCD screen was supported by a flexible metal arm at one end, and a separate, small rectangular glass desk top with a black leather chair sat at the other end. Three touch screen terminals were imbedded in each of the parenthetical tables, accompanied by a blue leather chair.

I don't believe it. This is Donald Granger's office.

Dylan had heard rumors that it was designed by Granger himself to give the impression that you were part of a mathematical equation. Quickly glancing around, he could see it was true.

A thin, angular man, slightly taller than average, with short, white hair, moved from the side of the black leather chair and walked over to greet Dylan. He could have been in his early or late fifties. He wore a simple green tie and a powder blue dress shirt, black belt, black shoes, and pleated navy blue herring bone slacks. His suit jacket was nowhere in sight. His attire looked expensive but otherwise similar in style to Dylan's—corporate and innocuous.

"Mr. Regan, I'm Donald Granger."

"It's a pleasure to meet you, Mr. Granger. Please call me Dylan." He extended his hand.

"Thank you, Dylan. Call me Donald," Granger said and shook his hand, neither limp nor strong. Granger turned to the three men and one woman standing around the tables. "This is Ms. Lee, Mr. Schwartz, Mr. Royce, and Mr. Bhatia."

Dylan shook each of their hands but sensed it was not the time to try to exchange business cards. They knew who he was and probably didn't care if he knew who they were.

Granger directed him to a blue leather chair in the middle of one parenthetical table, then went to his chair at the head. Granger looked at his assistant, and she left. An older Asian man in a white jacket brought in some coffee, tea, and other drinks, along with a plate of cheese and crackers, and some grapes. Granger poured coffee for Dylan and himself. The others followed.

It was Dunkin coffee, Dylan knew immediately.

"Yes, it's Dunkin," Granger said, reading his reaction. "It's my favorite as well. Starbucks is too bitter for me. Life can be so bitter. Why should your coffee accentuate it?"

Granger smiled, while Ms. Lee and Mr. Schwartz laughed softly. They all seemed to have the same persona, like a disciplined army that knew how to work together on the battle field.

"It's good. Thank you," Dylan said, wondering how Granger knew he drank Dunkin coffee.

After sitting silently for several minutes examining him, Granger finally spoke. "I enjoyed your recent article analyzing historical correlations of economic indicators to the employment figures. The case you make for a possible government data error was especially compelling." Granger stopped and looked expectantly at him.

Dylan interpreted this as a signal to start. "Would you like me to go through my analysis?" he asked as he reached for the presentations in his leather bag.

"Presentations are not necessary," Granger said. "But before you discuss your work, please tell us something about your framework for looking at the markets."

"Um, certainly," Dylan said. "Well, my framework is a hybrid approach that combines the best of the two basic styles of investing—fundamental research and quantitative analysis. I focus on where we are in the economic cycle, what factors will likely drive the economy, and—this is the key—what structural changes are occurring that could cause the economy to behave differently than in the past. Most investors missed this during the financial crisis. They assumed historical economic relationships would persist. But they didn't understand that the massive borrowing over the past three decades was unsustainable. When it all started to collapse, it was like a seismic shift. Most investors, business leaders and politicians didn't realize what was happening. They still don't."

Dylan paused to see if there were any questions.

Mr. Bhatia raised his hand slightly. "Should we infer that you believe macroeconomic modeling—what we do here—is only successful during relatively stable periods?"

"Not exactly, but let me explain with an example. The behavior of the economy and markets during the eighties and nineties was almost all momentum, with predictable reversals within historical boundaries. Most investors just followed the trend and did well. Now look at the past decade. The failure of such an approach when there is structural change is painfully obvious. To be successful, any approach has to account for the possibility of such change."

"But Mr. Regan," Ms. Lee interjected, "are you saying that the quantitative modeling approach we employ at MQA could not, by itself, have successfully anticipated the global financial crisis—an earthquake by your analogy?"

"Yes, that's correct," Dylan answered.

"Well, you obviously haven't done your homework," Mr. Bhatia quipped. "Our performance through the crisis was phenomenal."

"But that just tells me you did something different this time," Dylan argued. "I would still insist that relying entirely on mathematical models that assume the economy will behave the same way it always has is not only wishful thinking for today's world, but wishful modeling."

No one laughed at his pun. His career in economic comedy was over before it had started.

"What specific examples do you have to support your approach?" Mr. Schwartz asked.

"My own success," Dylan replied.

"But your last two jobs forecasts were very wrong," Mr. Royce piped in. "I understand economic data can be revised, but your degree of error has to prompt doubt, does it not?"

Dylan paused, then said, "That's why the data is wrong."

"Excellent," Granger interjected, smiling. "We have a good understanding of your framework. Now, please walk us through your analysis of why the employment data is wrong. Don't hold back. This is what we are good at."

Dylan spent the next thirty minutes explaining his work on the employment data, answering questions, and presenting a picture of a jobs number that was too contradictory and historically unprecedented to be correct, predicting the BLS would eventually revise the data lower.

When Dylan finished, Mr. Bhatia said, "I don't understand. You clearly suggested in your strategy note that there was a conspiracy to manipulate the data for political purposes. You now sound more convinced that it was a BLS error. Which do you believe it was?"

"Well—"

Granger interrupted: "Unfortunately, Dylan, we've exceeded our time. We need to return to the challenge of making our trend following models work in a trendless and unpredictable economy. Please do not take that the wrong way. We truly appreciate your keen insights."

Ms. Lee, Mr. Schwartz, Mr. Royce, and Mr. Bhatia shook hands with Dylan and left.

After the metal doors slid shut, Granger turned to Dylan and said, "I enjoyed our meeting. I would like to get together once a week for the next three weeks so we can discuss this challenging economy in greater detail. Are you available?"

"Yes, of course. Thank you." Dylan was surprised at the request since he hadn't sensed particularly positive body language from the others, and Granger was inscrutable.

"Very good," Granger replied. "Mr. Berkley's presence is not needed. My assistant will arrange the details."

As if choreographed, Granger's assistant appeared and escorted Dylan down to the main lobby and through security. She said a car would pick him up next Tuesday at two and then left.

Bob Berkley was standing by the building doors talking on his cell phone. He hung up and walked over to Dylan. "I feel like some Indian food," Berkley snickered, staring at Granger's assistant walking to the elevator.

Dylan shook his head. "Are we going out for drinks with any portfolio managers?"

"No, they said they don't do that stuff with small firms like FTS," Berkley replied. "What the fuck kind of way is that to treat someone who drove three hours to help you?"

"They didn't get where they are by making big mistakes," Dylan remarked.

"Well, they're assholes. So, did they say anything about doing trades with me?"

"No, but Granger wants me to come back to meet with them for the next few weeks."

"Buddy, that's awesome! They have to give us some business to pay for that!"

"Sorry, Bob, but Granger said you don't need to attend. I'm sure we'll still get something out of it. They understand the business."

"They sure do," Berkley said, a big smile crossing his face as he looked up from his IPhone. "They sent a couple of huge fucking trades through our desk while we were here. That prick McDonald better make sure he credits me with the commissions."

CHAPTER 21
Tuesday, May 15, 2012

"GANNON!" THE wall behind Mary bellowed.

Without knocking, Mary opened Rothstein's office door and walked in. Jane Reyes, ICIN's senior producer, was standing behind Rothstein looking over his shoulder at the video of Mary's next segment.

Half Puerto Rican and half Irish, Jane Reyes was in her late forties, short and athletic, with a soft, intelligent face. She had worked with Rothstein for twenty years. She was his audience and his filter, and sometimes his brains, but he never conceded that. She whispered something to him, then walked around and sat down in one of the two chairs in front of his desk.

Without being offered, Mary sat down in the other chair and opened her notebook. Rothstein glanced at her to let her know she was being presumptuous. She raised her eyebrows in response, as if to say, "I've been waiting forty-five minutes."

Rothstein leaned back and said, "Alright, run me through your piece."

"Well, the focus of this segment is the economic state of young voters and the potential ramifications on the Presidential election," Mary began. "I start out in the bedroom of this young man who graduated from college a year ago and hasn't been able to find a job. I follow him from one menial job interview to another, starting with a fast food restaurant. There's even a bouncer job at a strip club where we have a little fun. That may get edited.

"From there, I review the horrible job market statistics for young people, highlighting that college graduates can't find jobs where they can earn enough to live on their own and make their school loan payments. I flash to parts of interviews with Speaker Levy, Senator Murphy, and two CEOs. Then I interview several young veterans in front of the Vietnam Memorial who are working at minimum wage jobs and ask if military service is now a prerequisite for such jobs.

"I finish the segment in front of the White House. I briefly analyze the voting power of the youth demographic and interview two of the organizers of this grassroots movement of unemployed recent college grads that's gaining traction in social media circles. It's called 'The Lost Revolution' and is sort of an advocacy group to combat the youth unemployment crisis.

"So, I finish by asking how far politicians and policy makers might be willing to go to restore confidence and mitigate the impact on the elections of this emerging lost generation of young people who may never have meaningful jobs because the future of this economy has been mortgaged. That's obviously a setup for the next segment, which will examine the possibility that the employment data is being manipulated."

Mary stopped and waited for Rothstein to criticize her.

Rothstein glanced out the window and then looked at Reyes to signal for her to speak.

"This is good, Mary," Reyes said. "I already told you it's too long. I'll work with you to cut it back. You need to add more from the unemployed college grads and vets. Really pull out how bleak the future is to them. Also, try to get a provocative comment out of someone in the White House, even the press staff, to make the political angle more controversial. It's good, but it needs more emotion on the issues you highlight."

Mary nodded and then looked at Rothstein.

"It's decent," Rothstein grumbled, "but not good enough to get young viewers to really listen. You've got the sex, the looks, the personality—they'll all be watching you for that. But as soon as they're finished jerking off or playing with their dildoes, they'll go back to their iWorlds and block out this infected grown-up world you're showing them. They don't want to hear where their lives are really headed. But they have to know. Your piece doesn't do it."

Mary thought for a moment, then said, "Okay, so you want me to do more to get viewers to understand the truth about their future."

"People make their own fucking truths," Rothstein snapped. "They don't need you or ICIN for that. Your job is to get them the ingredients. News is information—the stuff people can't get on their own. If we don't give them the information to make their own truths, someone else will make the truth and feed it to them. Or worse, force feed it. Fucking politicians, dictators and CEOs are in the business of making the truth for people. That's a bad fucking business, unless you're one of them."

Mary smiled tolerantly, gripping her pen tightly as she listened to Rothstein's lecture.

Rothstein sat up and leaned forward. "Listen, Gannon. Most people can't recognize real news from crap. But once someone is allowed to start telling people what their truths are, generations will be pissed away before anyone grows the balls to challenge him. Your job is to find those ingredients and figure out how to get people to want them. That's why you dress up like a hooker or a regular working class grunt or whatever it takes to get people to consume the news. Once we feed it to them, they can make whatever truth or bullshit they want to believe out of it. That's fucking freedom."

Mary looked at Rothstein and replied, calm and deliberate, "So, you want me to do whatever it takes to get real news and then whatever it takes to get people to listen. One out of two isn't good enough."

"Not bad," Rothstein muttered, a hint of a smile vanishing like a twitch.

"I'll get people to listen," Mary added, "but what am I missing for news?"

Rothstein's eyes narrowed. "Find out if there's a real conspiracy and who the fuck is behind it. That's real news." He glanced at Reyes, then back at Mary. "I'm done. Get out."

Reyes accompanied Mary to the elevator and stopped her before she got on.

"You realize he hasn't gotten this involved with anything on the production side in a couple of years," Reyes said. "He sees something in this story. Don't get discouraged and don't get complacent. Most of all, don't make the mistake of thinking you're bigger than the story. You understand?"

Mary nodded.

Reyes turned and walked back to Rothstein's office.

CHAPTER 22

Wednesday, May 16, 2012

DYLAN WASN'T sure he heard the man correctly. It was only 6:45 Tuesday morning, and he was just walking out of Dunkin Donuts with a cup of coffee.

"Mr. Regan, did you hear me? I'm Special Agent Cole with the FBI. This is Special Agent Ricci. We'd like to talk to you about Caroline Brenner."

Dylan quickly scanned the man and woman—similar gray suits, serious, authoritative. Why did the FBI want to talk to him about Caroline? And there and now? Were they really FBI agents? He looked for their guns but couldn't see them. Maybe he was being paranoid, but this was too strange.

A young business woman wanted to enter the store. Dylan stepped away from the door to let her pass. The man and woman moved with him. The man was a little taller than him, similar build, but older by fifteen years. The woman was short and athletic, Hispanic, about his age.

"Mr. Regan," the man said, pulling out a small black leather case and flipping it open to show an FBI badge, "all we want is to ask you some questions and grab some coffee."

The woman pulled out her badge as well. Dylan squinted to examine both. They looked official, but he had never seen an FBI badge before.

"If you don't want to talk now, we can come back later and bring you downtown to our offices," the man said. "That will be a longer discussion, with bad coffee. What do you say? Want to grab some coffee with us, Mr. Regan?"

Dylan asked, "Is this normal FBI procedure—grabbing coffee while questioning someone?"

"It's a little out of the ordinary," the man replied, "but so is leaving a voice message for a murdered government employee saying you think something is corrupt in her office. You don't have an alibi for the night Ms. Brenner was killed. But we don't like to assume guilt before we actually question someone. It's the American way. Now, we'd like some coffee. You going to join us?"

Dylan scrutinized the man again. A slight smile was pasted on his face. The woman was expressionless. They weren't trying to intimidate him, and they seemed to know things only the authorities would know. More importantly, Agent Cole had said Caroline was murdered.

"Agent Cole is it? Okay, you have my attention."

Dylan and Cole went downstairs while Agent Ricci ordered coffee. They sat in the corner he usually occupied when he needed to think. The green sweat suit lady was at her usual table. Agent Ricci joined them a minute later.

"That's good coffee," Cole remarked after taking a sip. "Now, you seem pretty nervous, Mr. Regan. Any particular reason?"

Dylan took a sip of his coffee, then said, "No, I get accosted all the time at Dunkin Donuts by FBI agents wanting to talk and have coffee with me. They usually order jelly donuts, though. That's why I'm a little suspicious."

Cole feigned a smile on top of the one that seemed stuck on his face and started to respond.

Dylan interrupted: "Before you ask me any questions, you said Caroline was murdered. The last I heard, the cause of death was still pending. Did the police catch the driver?"

Cole replied, "No, but we have reason to believe it was a homicide."

"What reason?"

"I can't share that with you, Mr. Regan. It's an ongoing investigation."

"Well, have you talked to Brad Johnson?" Dylan asked.

"We're talking to you," Cole replied. "That's all you need to be concerned with right now."

"Alright," Dylan said, his muscles tensing, "then what do you want?"

"Where were you Wednesday night, May 2?" Cole asked.

"Am I a suspect?"

"Not as long as you confirm what we already know," Cole replied.

"I worked late that night. I remember because I was having dinner the next night with a client and needed to get some work done beforehand. I left around nine. When I got home, I ordered Chinese take-out. You should be able to check all that."

"We already have," Cole said as Agent Ricci took notes. "You left a voice message for Ms. Brenner at her office the Friday following her murder saying you thought something was wrong with the employment data, that it might be corrupt. What did you mean by that?"

"The April jobs number came out much stronger than anyone expected. It was too good to believe, and I called her to talk about it. I thought the BLS might have made a data error. That's what I meant."

"Was there something going on between you and Ms. Brenner?" Cole asked.

"What? No, that's crazy. She was in love with Brad Johnson. She just helped me when I had questions about economic data."

"In your last research report, you suggested there's a government conspiracy behind the jobs report," Cole said. "Why do you think that?"

Dylan stared at Cole for a moment, wondering why he was asking these questions. He said, "It's just a theory I've developed since the April jobs number came out."

"Why are you so confident the data is bad?" Cole asked.

"If you read my strategy note, you already know why."

"Did Ms. Brenner tell you anything before she was killed?"

Dylan paused, glanced at Agent Ricci, and then back at Cole. He asked, "Are you suggesting there's a connection between the data and Caroline's murder?"

Cole replied, "I'm asking if Ms. Brenner shared information with you before she died?"

"What?" Dylan snapped. "You're suggesting Caroline was giving me inside information? She wasn't, but if she was, why would I kill her?"

"Did you kill her?" Cole asked calmly, the slight smile still pasted on his face.

Dylan clenched his jaw, glared at Cole and sneered, "No."

"Were you betting on the markets with inside information on the employment report, Mr. Regan? Did Ms. Brenner find out about it?" Cole took a sip of coffee.

Dylan eased back in his chair. He didn't respond.

"Or maybe Ms. Brenner was upset over you feeding information to your former girlfriend at ICIN," Cole continued. "Maybe Ms. Brenner was jealous and you two argued."

Dylan asked stoically, "Why would I draw attention to myself by talking about a government conspiracy if I was involved in insider trading with the data?"

Cole said, "That's what we're asking you, Mr. Regan."

"So, this is the good cop, mute cop routine I've heard about," Dylan quipped and shot a look at Agent Ricci.

"We have to ask these questions," Cole replied.

"Is that right? You have to grill me about things that should have nothing to do with Caroline's death. Why is that? Unless someone really is playing around with the data. Isn't a local hit-and-run a matter for the Washington police?"

Cole took another sip of coffee and then said, "The FBI always gets involved when a government employee in a high profile agency is murdered. And it's standard procedure to work with the local police. Now, I know you're upset at all these questions, but—"

"You're wrong, Agent," Dylan interrupted. "Your questions don't upset me. It's your lack of answers. You're not telling me anything, but you're insinuating a lot, and most of it doesn't make any sense." Dylan stared at Agent Ricci and said, "What about you? You have any answers for me, or are you just the short, silent type?"

"Don't be an asshole," Ricci snapped. "You don't want to make enemies of us."

Dylan nodded slowly and said, "That's true, Agent Ricci, but could you tell me exactly why I would *be* your enemy?"

"That's enough for now," Cole interjected. "We'll be in touch, Mr. Regan. Enjoy your coffee."

Cole stood up and walked towards the steps. Ricci followed, glaring at Dylan.

Dylan waited until they were out of sight and muttered, "What the fuck was that?"

The green sweat suit lady in the corner heard him, looked up and mumbled something back.

CHAPTER 23
Wednesday, May 16, 2012

AFTER BLAIR Armstrong's reprimand for being ten minutes late to their meeting last week, Dylan wanted to be early for his 7:30 dinner with her at Avra, a trendy Greek restaurant on 48th Street and Lexington Avenue. His head was still spinning from his meeting this morning with the FBI, or whatever it really was.

He arrived at 7:05. Blair Armstrong was already at the bar waiting.

Her black, sleeveless, scoop-necked dress flowed smoothly over her medium framed body to a few inches above her knees. She wore an ostentatious double strand pearl necklace he assumed was real, gold and pearl earrings, and three-inch black heels. With her short, bleached blond hair, she was the image of a Wall Street power woman.

As he approached the bar, Armstrong picked up her black sequined clutch and short black jacket, walked towards him and said, "You learn fast. That's good. Let's go to our table."

Armstrong took the wine list from the hostess as they sat down, asked Dylan if he was fine with white, and ordered a bottle of Malagousia before he could respond. She asked for some sparkling water, placed her cell phone on the table and turned her attention to him.

"My apologies if I seem in a rush. I really don't have much patience for the slow service at these expensive restaurants."

He had been warned of her intense personality, but something else seemed off. Her sensitivity to the price point of the restaurant revealed a sense of value that her appearance blatantly contradicted.

She continued: "I'd like to get to know you better, Dylan. I want to understand what you're looking to do, and see if we might be able to do it together at Differential."

She was even more aggressive than her reputation. But he was given a reprieve from the pace of their conversation when the waiter brought the wine and took his time opening it.

"Just pour, please." Armstrong instructed him. "I don't need to taste it. We'll be ready to order in five minutes."

"It's very good," Dylan said after tasting the wine, just to finally say something.

"I order it every time I come here." She stared intensely at him and asked, "What is it you're looking for, Dylan? What do you want with your career?"

It felt like an interview, but it could have been an interrogation. Dylan knew it wasn't the time to be humble. He said, "I want to be the best at what I do. I want to drive the success of the firm I'm working for. I want to work with smart, talented people. I want to make a lot of money. And I want to work for a real firm—one that wants to be the best, like me."

"Differential is real, Dylan," Armstrong said. "And I'm real." Her clear, green eyes accentuated her intensity.

Once again, the waiter gave him a reprieve as he came over to take their orders.

"The New Zealand Snapper, cooked well, not watery, and nothing to start," Armstrong said.

"The American Snapper, please," Dylan said. "Nothing to start as well. Thank you."

Armstrong examined him for a moment, then said, "You know FTS isn't real. You're too smart not to. It's an insignificant sellside firm trying to skim the buyside whenever and however it can. Why are you still there?"

Punching him in the nose wouldn't have been any more aggressive. Her question didn't shock him, since he woke up every day asking himself the same thing, but he was starting to feel intimidated, and he didn't like it.

"There are realities in life that even the smartest people can't avoid, like bills," he said. "Sometimes, you have to move backwards to be successful. FTS is a detour for me, not a roadblock." He stared back at Armstrong, feigning a smile, and then took a sip of wine.

"Why not turn a backwards strategy into a successful strategy and come work for me at Differential?" she asked, a suggestive smile appearing as she leaned forward slightly for effect.

This time, he was shocked. He wasn't expecting a job offer. Everything about this dinner was fast. She seemed more sexual to him now than intense, almost like MG.

He didn't have an immediate response, so he took a sip of wine. Then he grabbed a slice of bread and started buttering it. *Why's she moving so fast? She wants something. But what?*

The waiter's timing proved impeccable once again as he showed up with their dinner.

"Why don't you think about it while you eat. You don't want to make such an important decision on an empty stomach," Armstrong said, clearly pleased with her own attempt at humor.

It was an uncomfortable fifteen minutes. He felt like he had to eat as fast as her. The waiter cleared the table as soon as they were finished.

After their espressos were delivered, Armstrong said, "I'm decisive, Dylan. Are you?"

He sipped his espresso to give himself time to think. "Yes, I am," he answered, "but I always do my homework first, to make sure I have all the information I need to be right."

"Didn't you do your homework before you came here?" Armstrong asked.

He smiled at her attempt to use his own words to intimidate him. "If that's a real offer your making, then I'm interested, but to be candid, I don't really understand where it's coming from. You barely know me or my work."

"The offer is real, Dylan, and it's now. I've done my homework on you. I always do. But you need to decide if you really want this. There are a thousand qualified candidates out there who would kill for this opportunity. Think about it, and let's meet next week to discuss it in detail. I want to move fast with you or move on."

He nodded as if he agreed. "That's fair. Thank you. Should I call you?"

"Rick Jones will contact you," she replied and signaled for the check. "Sorry to rush, but I need to get to the Upper West Side. I'm meeting someone at Broadway Blues, the new jazz bar that just opened up. Have you heard of it?"

"Uh, yes, very exclusive, I hear."

Armstrong signed the check and said, "It's more expensive than I prefer, but this man is trying to impress me so I'll sleep with him. You sleeping with anyone, Dylan?"

He had started to stand to say goodbye but stopped, caught off guard again.

"Don't get up," she said. "Finish your coffee. I'm only teasing. I can be funny when I want." She left without shaking hands.

Dylan sat back down, not sure what game they had just played, but sensing he had lost.

Armstrong's question sat in Dylan's mind like a bad meal as he walked up Park Avenue after dinner. He wasn't sleeping with anyone and hadn't in a while. He thought of Lina Sabatini, the waitress at The Beer Bar last week. The folded napkin with her number was still in his money clip. He had meant to call her to see if she was interested in grabbing dinner. She was different. Right now, that's what he wanted.

A text message would avoid any awkwardness if she didn't remember him: "Lina, hi, it's Dylan from last Friday. Want to grab dinner some night? Let me know."

In today's world, he knew a week without sending a text was a light year. He had probably waited too long to show an interest. Then his Blackberry vibrated. It was her.

"Dylan, love to. How is Friday? Where?"

"Friday is great. Anywhere you want is good for me."

"The Place on W4th at 8pm. I know the hostess and will get res."

"Done. See you there."

"Done done. Ciao. L-"

She had to be Italian—his favorite food and wine and bankrupt European country.

CHAPTER 24
Thursday, May 17, 2012

"MANNER OF Death: Homicide."

Brad quickly read on and stopped at the last sentence on the page: *The victim was likely hit and run over by a single vehicle three separate times, two in the forward direction and one in the backing-up direction, at speeds estimated to be approximately twenty to forty miles per hour.*

He leaned over, closed his eyes and squeezed the report. *Nooo . . .*

"You okay over there?" a male police officer asked from behind the window of the visitor's desk at the Third District police station.

Brad nodded, wiped his eyes and continued reading the updated Medical Examiner's report on Caroline's autopsy. He had received a call late yesterday afternoon that it would be available this morning. There was more information than the first report, but head trauma was still the cause of death. The Medical Examiner could not determine which strike had likely killed her.

He closed his eyes again. *Who would do this?*

"Mr. Johnson . . ."

Brad opened his eyes and looked up. "Uh, Detective Garcia . . . Are you ready for me?"

"Are you ready?" Garcia replied.

Brad stood up. "Yes."

Garcia brought him to a small conference room in the back of the precinct. Garcia sat down in a chair on one side of a small metal table. Brad sat down in a chair on the other side.

"So, Mr. Johnson, before you ask me any questions, I'd like to know what strings you pulled to get the ME's office to review its autopsy and issue a new report, in a week. I've never seen a turnaround like that in twenty years. You must know someone important."

"Does that matter?" Brad snapped. "Caroline was murdered. Shouldn't you be worrying about that instead of who I know?"

Garcia's jaw tightened. "I don't like being yelled at, Mr. Johnson. This meeting is a courtesy, because I was asked to accommodate you, but watch that temper. I might start to think you killed her, and this is all just a clever game to hide it."

Brad took a deep breath, exhaled slowly and said, "I'm sorry, Detective. It's just learning she was murdered . . . the way she was . . . I just want to find who did this."

Garcia stared at him for a few seconds. His expression relaxed and he said, "Okay, I understand. You feel like you have to do something yourself. It's natural. But trust me. We know what we're doing. We'll find this guy."

"I believe you," Brad said. "Can you tell me where you are in the investigation?"

"Well, it's still ongoing, and we don't—"

"Detective, it won't go beyond this room. Please?"

Garcia paused, then said, "Well, I'll probably be giving you the information tomorrow anyways, with your contacts. May as well save myself some time."

"Thank you," Brad said and forced a slight smile.

"Alright, Ms. Brenner was apparently heading to her office that night. Her parking pass registered in the garage underneath the BLS office building. And the garage camera shows her car entering and leaving within a fifteen minute time span. She never checked in at security, though. So she either forgot something, maybe her I.D., or she changed her mind. She looked like she was in a hurry to leave, but that might be the way she drove."

"It wasn't," Brad responded quickly. "The report said the vehicle that hit her was likely a black SUV, probably an Explorer. Did you see any SUVs go in or out around the same time?"

"That's a smart question," Garcia replied. "And yes, we checked, but no SUVs or other vehicles showed up on the surveillance cameras."

"Are there other cameras in the garage, or the elevators?"

Garcia answered, "The elevator has one, but it was out of service that night. The elevator, I mean. Most government building garages only have cameras in a few spots. We checked them all and there was no other recording of her or anyone else suspicious. But . . ."

"But what?" Brad said.

"Well, there was an attempted rape in a building garage a block away about a week earlier. We don't have anything to connect Ms. Brenner's death to that, but we're looking at it to make sure we cover all possibilities."

Brad said, "The ME's report said her blood was on the seat of her car, and she had a long, thin cut on her right forearm."

"What's your point?"

"I had dinner with her the night before, and she didn't have that cut on her arm. Caroline was meticulously neat. If there was blood in her car, then it had to have just happened. Maybe she was attacked in the garage by someone with a knife and got away."

"Interesting," Garcia replied. "But then why didn't she go straight to the police, or even the hospital? It doesn't really make sense that a mugger would follow her all the way to her apartment. And the garage cameras don't show anything."

"She had to have gotten that cut somehow," Brad insisted.

"Maybe she cut herself cooking, or it's from the vehicle that hit her," Garcia said. "I don't know, but we're looking into everything. Trust me, Mr. Johnson."

"What about Chris Smith, her ex-boyfriend?"

"Well, I can't really discuss suspects, but I can tell you he wasn't even in the country when Ms. Brenner was killed. He was in Bermuda, with another woman."

Brad paused, then asked, "What about the list of other boyfriends I sent you?"

"Yeah, right. Thanks for that," Garcia said. "We've checked them all out. Nothing."

"Have you talked to the people at the BLS that she worked with?"

Garcia sighed. "Mr. Johnson, I know how to do my job. This still looks like a drunk driver hit her, or someone who was going too fast and didn't see her."

"But why would the person drive over her three times?"

"If I had all the answers, the guy would be in custody," Garcia answered. "It was dark. Maybe he drove back to see what he had hit and ran over her again, then panicked. Maybe he was a she. I don't know, but we'll figure it out. You need to let us do our job. Please?"

Brad stared at Garcia for several seconds. He nodded. "Okay, thank you, Detective." He stood up and asked, "Is the FBI helping out on this?"

Garcia stood up and gave Brad a quizzical look. "Why would they? We don't need them screwing up our cases."

A light rain was falling when Brad left the station. He stopped and sat down on the same bench as he had the last time. It was wet, and he was late for work, but he didn't care. He closed his eyes. They began to water, blending with the rain.

Brad opened his eyes and stood up suddenly. He started walking quickly, then jogging. He pulled out his cell phone and dialed information. "The Bureau of Labor Statistics, please?"

When the BLS operator picked up, he said, "Office of Statistics, Shannon Dunn, please?"

"You mean the Office of Employment and Unemployment Statistics?" the operator asked.

"Yes . . . Shannon Dunn," he replied.

Brad's mind was racing as he hurried towards the Metro. He needed to get a look at Caroline's laptop. She tracked everything in her life on it. Whatever the problem was that she needed his help with, she would have recorded it on her laptop. Now that her death was officially a homicide, the police would confiscate it. He needed to go through it first.

"Hello, this is Shannon Dunn."

"Shannon, it's Brad Johnson."

"Brad, what are you doing calling me at work? I told you I can't talk to you about Caroline. Please, I could get in real—"

"Shannon, I just wanted to see if Caroline's laptop is in her office somewhere."

"Brad—"

"Please, can you just take a quick look?"

Shannon sighed and said, "Hold on." After a minute, she picked up again. "I didn't see it. I even checked in her desk drawers. I have to go, Brad."

"Thank you, Shannon." He hung up and walked down the steps to the Metro. He didn't expect it to be in her office since Caroline seldom took it to work. But he wanted to make sure before he broke into her apartment.

Brad calculated that someone would likely be expecting a delivery, visitor or repairman sometime this morning. The first two buttons he pressed on the wall outside the door to Caroline's apartment building prompted skeptical greetings over the intercom, to which he replied, "Sorry, wrong apartment."

After the third try, he heard a buzzing sound and the door unlocked. He pushed it open and walked quickly to the stairwell around the corner, bypassing the elevator. He climbed the three floors to Caroline's apartment. He was familiar with the layout.

Brad pulled out a multi-purpose hand tool from his suit coat pocket and popped the main lock on Caroline's apartment door. This was why he had installed the double bolt when she first moved in there. But he had counted on it not being engaged, hoping her parents had stopped by after identifying her body and forgotten. He was right.

Caroline usually kept her laptop on the desk in her living room, but it wasn't there. He looked everywhere, but it was nowhere to be found. Caroline almost never took it out of her apartment except occasionally when she traveled. Her life was organized and logical. The only thing she ever lost track of was her cell phone. It was a genetic defect, she used to tell him.

He stopped searching. Maybe her sister or parents had taken it. He'd call them and find out.

He glanced around at her apartment. Except for some different fabrics on the furniture and paint on the walls, everything was the same as when he had last been there. She had kept all the pictures of them in the same places. He looked at the one by her bed of them eating cupcakes outside Georgetown Cupcake. It was her favorite.

The apartment suddenly felt hot and dense. He couldn't stay.

Brad found the accordion folder that she kept her bills in, grabbed the old mail sitting on the table, and took the mailbox key from the kitchen counter. He opened the door to leave—a stocky man with a shaved head was standing there.

Brad looked in the man's bloodshot eyes and caught a faint whiff of cigarette smoke. He knew the man wasn't the police or FBI. Then he heard the click of a switchblade . . .

Brad threw the folder and bills in the man's face, lifted his leg and rammed his shoe into the man's stomach, sending him slamming against the hallway wall. Brad turned quickly to a fighting stance, crouching as he pulled the hand tool out of his pocket, fumbling to extract its short blade.

The man recovered immediately, raised his knife and sneered something in a foreign language. He stepped towards Brad, but then took off down the hallway towards the stairs.

Brad hesitated and then went after him. The man was fast and already down two flights by the time Brad got to the stairwell. He knew he wasn't going to catch him, but he might get a glimpse of the man's car and license plate.

A silver Ford Explorer was disappearing around the corner when Brad shoved the front door of the building open. He couldn't see its plate. "Damn," he muttered.

His heart was racing and his left arm trembling. He looked down. Blood was flowing from a slice across the top of his hand. He wrapped a handkerchief around it and ran back upstairs. He picked up Caroline's bills, locked her apartment and took the elevator to the foyer. Then he opened her mailbox, grabbed everything in it and left.

Brad thought about calling Detective Garcia, but he decided to wait, since he'd have to explain why he was there. He wanted to try to find Caroline's laptop first, so he could look at it before the police. Whatever problem she wanted his help with had gotten her killed. He was sure of it now.

CHAPTER 25
Friday, May 18, 2012

JEFF SCHWINN sat in Senator Murphy's Washington office late Friday afternoon discussing the Senator's agenda for the next week.

"Last thing," Schwinn said. "Donald Granger is available for a call at three on Tuesday."

"Finally," Murphy said. "I'm starting to wonder if he even wants to support Hayes' Presidential bid. Maybe he just doesn't want me as VP."

"I talked to Donald at the fundraiser last weekend," Schwinn said. "He was very supportive of you as VP if Governor Hayes decides to run as an independent. But if you don't mind me asking, why aren't you considering running for President as an independent yourself? You're the stronger leader and candidate."

"Thanks for the vote of confidence, but it's too risky to run outright against Obama right now. Yes, he's vulnerable, but that employment number is going to help him. If I run as the Governor's VP and we lose, I should be in an even better position for the Democratic nomination in 2016. The party leaders won't want to risk me splitting the vote as an independent. Of course, if we win, I can live with being the Vice President of the United States."

"Smart," Schwinn said. "You know that Speaker Levy will probably be the Republican nominee in 2016 if the President wins a second term. He'll be tough."

"That's why I have to be careful not to alienate the party too much. But everything depends on this economy. Speaking of which, I caught Mary's news segment. I don't know what was more provocative—pumping up that ridiculous conspiracy theory, promoting that Lost Revolution group, or those outfits she wore. I'm sorry, Jeff, but that strip joint thing was over the top. I didn't think my interview with her would be part of something like that."

"I apologize for that," Schwinn replied. "She truly believes she's helping you with the youth vote by highlighting you in those segments. As for the conspiracy stuff, that's her ex-boyfriend influencing her. I already talked to her about that, but I'll speak to her again."

"Well, you tell her—" Murphy started but was interrupted by his secretary opening the door.

"Excuse me, sir. Representative Boatman is here for your four o'clock," she said.

"Okay, show him in," Murphy replied, then looked at Schwinn. "I'll see you Monday."

Senator Murphy handed a glass of Midleton Irish Whiskey to Representative Boatman who was sitting in a leather chair, his legs stretched out and shoes off.

"Enjoy it, Randy. I'm getting low," Murphy said as he settled into his leather couch. "It's twenty years old. I used to get a bottle every year from the Bank of Ireland when I visited Dublin, but everyone I knew there has been fired since the government took them over."

"That's what you get for lending a hundred-twenty cents on the euro to build houses on potato farms," Boatman remarked with a strong Southern drawl.

"We did the same thing here, just in dollars," Murphy replied.

"If you say so. Anyway, did you talk to Patricia?"

"Yes, but she said she didn't have any new information she could share with us."

"Cunt," Boatman quipped.

Murphy snorted. "Republican language . . . but my sentiment exactly."

"My people are seething," Boatman said. "That bullshit jobs number could turn the Presidential election. It's gotta be fixed. And it can't happen again."

"Well, Patricia did say she sent someone to give that strategist, Dylan Regan, a hard time."

"Really?" Boatman replied. "I thought she wasn't going to help us with him. Did it work?"

"She wouldn't tell me anything else," Murphy said. "She plays as many games as Mitch."

"Speaking of Mitch, he won't be too happy if this thing blows up in the press because of ICIN and your boy's girlfriend. I thought you said he could control her."

Murphy said, "Regan's the real problem. Without him, she doesn't have any info or story."

"But without her, nobody cares about him," Boatman shot back. "My guys think we're taking the White House back. Anything about the group gets out and no one gets reelected . . . Democrats or Republicans."

"I know, Randy . . . I know," Murphy said and took a gulp of whiskey.

"We need to discuss it with Mitch," Boatman said.

"I was supposed to meet with him today, but he rescheduled," Murphy said. "He wants to wait to see if Patricia accomplishes something first, before we discuss other options."

"Then when does he want to meet?"

"Next week, at his place. Can you believe him? Memorial Day weekend. And he wants you there too."

"Okay, I don't have any plans. But I'm surprised he's being so patient," Boatman said. "I thought he'd want this taken care of quickly. And he hates Patricia."

Murphy took another gulp of whiskey. "Regardless, we should call a meeting of the whole group to discuss it. Mitch will have to show up and talk about it then."

"The whole group?" Boatman repeated. "Mitch hates those meetings. And you know he doesn't give a damn what Nancy or Harvey thinks. He barely tolerates us. No, I say let's wait and see what Mitch has to say next week first."

Murphy gulped down the rest of his whiskey, then stared at Boatman for a few seconds. "Do you and Mitch know something you're not telling me?"

Boatman finished his whiskey, stared back at Murphy and smiled. "I was going to ask you the same thing."

CHAPTER 26
Friday, May 18, 2012

DYLAN'S LEGS were stiff as he walked down the steps to the coffee cave. He had run six miles last night and then lifted weights, knowing he wouldn't get a chance to work out tonight. Tonight was dinner with Lina Sabatini. That's why he had resisted the jelly donut.

The middle-aged woman in the faded, dirty green sweat suit was at her usual table. Some tourists who sounded like they were speaking German had taken his spot, so he settled into a small table near the steps. The coffee was decent for a Friday afternoon.

Before he had a chance to start thinking about everything that had happened this week, his Blackberry rang. "This is Dylan . . ."

"Hi, Mr. Regan. It's Ron Pahlavi. We met at the Bridgeport American Legion."

"Oh, hi Ron. Call me Dylan. I'm not an old man yet."

"Uh, sorry."

"Just joking. How's it going?"

"Um, pretty good," Pahlavi replied. "Do you have a minute?"

"Yeah, sure."

"Great. Okay, first, thank you for setting up those informational interviews with JPMorgan and Goldman Sachs. I learned a lot."

"Did anything come of them?"

"Well, not really," Pahlavi replied. "That's why I'm calling. I wanted to ask if you had time to go over my resume and my pitch with me. I'm not really clicking with these people."

"Yes, of course. Can you shoot me an email so I can look at my schedule?"

"Yes, okay, I'll do that. Thank you very much, Mr.—I mean, Dylan."

"No problem, Ron. Listen, if Wall Street is what you really want, don't give up."

"I'm not," Pahlavi said. "This is nothing compared to losing a hand. Thanks again. Bye."

Dylan hung up and took a sip of coffee. He thought about Ron Pahlavi's determination and optimism. He was like that when he first started at Merrill, before he blew up with Lehman. He wanted to warn Pahlavi that Wall Street wasn't so different from Afghanistan. Just another battlefield. But Pahlavi had to learn that for himself. All he could do was try to prepare him, so his whole life didn't blow up, like his had done.

Dylan glanced up and saw a tall, thin and well dressed black man walking down the steps. The man stopped at the bottom and looked around for a seat. He took the small corner table across from the green sweat suit lady. Dylan watched the man sip his coffee and check his messages at the same time—talented. The man looked like he might be unemployed, maybe going to an interview. Probably a salesman. Too well dressed to be a strategist. You didn't hang out in the coffee cave unless you were miserable or unemployed . . . or a German tourist.

Dylan's Blackberry rang. It was Brad.

"Hey Brad, you okay? I called you a couple of times. I need to tell you something."

"Sorry. It's been busy at work. We're crunching to get the *Flow of Funds Report* out in a couple of weeks."

Dylan knew the report well. It was a massive compilation of data on all financial flows in the U.S. economy put out quarterly by the Federal Reserve. Brad headed a small team responsible for coordinating a part of the data aggregation process.

"Don't worry about it," Dylan said. "Listen, two FBI agents accosted me the other morning when I was getting coffee. They wanted to talk about Caroline. They said she was murdered."

"The FBI? What did they want with you?"

"They grilled me like I was a suspect. Do you know anything about Caroline's death being labeled a murder?"

"Yes," Brad answered. "The Medical Examiner's Office reissued its report and labeled it a homicide. I picked up a copy yesterday."

"Jesus . . . What else did it say?"

Brad's voice trembled. "She was . . ." He stopped, cleared his throat and continued: "She was run over three times by an SUV. It wasn't an accident. She was murdered."

"So, the police must think it was intentional then. What are they—"

"No, they're still not sure. They think it might have been a drunk or someone who didn't see her and made the mistake of running her over again when they went back to check. But I know it was intentional."

Dylan asked, "How do you know that?"

"Because I ran into the guy who killed her, at her apartment."

"What?" Dylan exclaimed.

"I don't have time to explain now. I'm late for a meeting. I called to see if I could come up tomorrow, maybe spend the night, go through everything with you. I need your help . . ."

"Yeah, of course, Brad. But how—"

"I have to go, Dylan. I'll tell you everything tomorrow. Thank you." Brad hung up.

Dylan had never eaten at The Place, but the West Village restaurant fit the image he had of Lina Sabatini—warm and intimate, stylish but not fancy, with something very alluring that he couldn't quite describe. When he saw her walk through the door wearing a one shoulder, black sequin and blue lace dress, painted across her exquisite figure, generously revealing her shapely legs, he figured the something he couldn't describe was pure sexuality. When she kissed him on the cheek and her dark, wavy hair that smelled of coconut lightly caressed his face, he realized it was something more. She was different, but real. It scared him a little.

"You look incredible," he said, surprised at how natural the words sounded.

"Thank you," Lina replied, sitting down at the small table for two by the window. "I made this dress myself."

"Really? Is that what you do for a . . . I mean—"

"Hah, you're smooth," she said and smiled effortlessly. "The money is very good at The Beer Bar. That's why I work there, but I have a creative writing degree from Hunter College. I want to be a writer, but it's a tough profession to break into. Making clothes is just a hobby."

"Well, from what I see, you're really good at it," he said and smiled.

"It's a rip-off of a design by a top fashion house. It was cheaper than paying five hundred dollars for one." She paused, smiled effortlessly again and said, "You look okay too."

Dylan laughed. "I buy all my own clothes. I bought this blazer, just for tonight. The woman at the store said I would look like I knew something about fashion. Did she lie?"

Lina leaned over the table, looked him up and down and said with a coy smile, "I'll tell you later, after I decide if I like you better in it or out of it."

He stared at her, an obvious look of consternation on his face. She started to giggle and then laugh. He smiled and then laughed too. It felt strange to laugh so freely. But it was also vaguely familiar, as if he'd felt this way before, a long time ago.

A tingling sensation flowed up his legs through his arms, towards his head. He glanced around the small restaurant with its oak beamed ceiling and stone fireplace, seeming dark and cold now as a wave of anxiety raced through his body. Caroline's murder, the FBI, and FTS all flashed through his mind. The world wasn't this safe, this serene.

Then he felt Lina touch his hand. He moved his gaze to her large, hazel eyes. Light streamed back, and the warmth of the lit fireplace rushed over him.

Maybe it was . . . for now.

CHAPTER 27
Saturday, May 19, 2012

THE DOORMAN didn't know what to do. He was large, but this guy in the lobby was big, muscular. The guy was dressed nicely but carrying a black duffle bag and acting suspicious. He had walked in several minutes ago and gone straight to the side of the window, leaned against the wall and started looking out as if he was hiding from someone . . . and he was black.

"Uh, excuse me, can I help you, sir?" the doorman asked.

"No, thank you," the guy said, continuing to stare out the large picture window.

The doorman glanced over at a Hispanic woman behind the concierge's desk who was watching anxiously. He took a deep breath, looked at the guy and said, "Sir, do you live here, or are you visiting someone? If not—"

"Apartment 7M, Dylan Regan," Brad said, turning to look at the round, pasty white, six foot four doorman. "He's expecting me."

Dylan stepped off the elevator of 215 Normandie Court, one of four buildings in the massive rental complex on 95th Street that covered the entire block between Second and Third Avenues. He saw Brad standing by the concierge's desk in the main lobby and walked towards him.

"Hey, you causing trouble again?" he hailed to Brad to get his attention.

Brad turned and gave Dylan a quick, wry smile. "I'm not the one who always gets in fights with guys twice my size."

"Ah, those weren't real fights," Dylan said and smiled warmly. "Those guys just didn't like being shown up on the court by a white guy. You know the feeling."

They shook hands and embraced briefly.

Dylan said, "It's good to see you, Brad. How you holding up?"

"Alright, I guess," Brad answered. "Thanks for letting me visit."

"Anytime. You know that," Dylan replied. "Hold on a second. I just have to ask these guys something before we go up to my apartment." He stepped over to the desk counter, got the Hispanic woman's attention and said, "Excuse me. I pay for the building cleaning service to come every two weeks. They came a week ago and showed up again this morning, so I sent them away. I just want to make sure I don't get charged for it."

"Mr. Regan, correct? Apartment 7M?" she asked as she typed something into the computer.

"Yes."

"Um . . . I don't show anyone cleaning your apartment the previous week . . . or a charge for it . . . Just today and two weeks ago," she said, scrutinizing her computer. "They have to check in with the apartments they're going to clean. Are you sure they did yours last week?"

"Well, I didn't actually see them," Dylan answered, "but someone messed up my coffee machine last week. I just assumed it was the cleaning ladies."

"Ernie . . ." she called to the big, heavy doorman who had tried to confront Brad. He walked over quickly. She asked, "Do you remember if there were any maintenance checks in building 215 the last week or so? Mr. Regan says he thinks someone was in his apartment and disrupted his coffee maker. He's in 7M."

"Oh, hello, Mr. Regan," the doorman said. "Uh, no, nothing in the past two weeks in 215. They're working on 225 this month, but that wouldn't affect you."

"Hmm," Dylan said. "I guess I'm going to have a dirty apartment for two weeks. Okay, thanks." He turned back to Brad. "Let's go upstairs. Want to clean my bathroom?"

Brad feigned a smile, then glanced out at 95th Street as they walked to the elevator.

Dylan opened the door to his one bedroom apartment, stepped in and said, "Welcome to my McMansion. I pay extra for the panoramic views of Spanish Harlem and the mosque."

Brad walked to the middle of the small living room and looked around. "It's nice . . . modern. Do you like it here?"

"Yeah, for the most part. It's a lot cheaper than the Village."

"Do you miss your old place?"

"I don't dwell on it. No pun intended. I was fortunate to sell when I did. It was probably a good thing MG moved out after Merrill fired me. If I had waited any longer, I would have had to file bankruptcy." Dylan paused, thinking about it, but then caught Brad looking at him. "Anyway, this complex is great. There's a health club on top, with a pool and a sun deck that has tremendous views, *especially* in the warm weather." Dylan smiled but Brad didn't respond. "So, the couch is a convertible. It's made up already. Nothing but the best for you. Don't try to sneak in my bed tonight, though."

Brad forced a smile.

"You want something to drink or eat?" Dylan asked.

Brad put his bag down by the couch and said, "Yeah, food would be good, but do you mind if I go for a quick run before we eat?"

"No, go ahead," Dylan replied. "I already ran this morning."

"That's okay. I can go by myself."

"You know your way around?"

"Yes. The Central Park Reservoir is west from here, right?"

"Yeah, on Fifth Avenue," Dylan answered.

Brad quickly changed into his running clothes, then asked, "Is there a back way out?"

"Go down to the basement level, by the laundry room, out to 96th Street. Why?"

"I'll explain when I get back." Brad opened the door, then turned and said, "Oh, I called Mary on the way up. She's going to stop by later tonight if that's okay."

Dylan frowned and said, "Fine. Before you go, sushi or Italian takeout?"

"Since when do you eat sushi?" Brad asked.

"I know you like it," Dylan replied and threw Brad his key card. "Use that to get back in."

"Thanks. Sushi's good," Brad said and left.

Dylan walked over to his living room window and looked out. The mosque's minaret cast a long shadow down 96th Street in the bright, late day sun. After a few minutes, he saw Brad dart across the street and turn towards Second Avenue. *Where are you going, Brad?*

He heard his Blackberry vibrate on the coffee table. He picked it up—a text from Lina: "Hey, you left early. Assume you made it home safe. L-"

Dylan smiled, remembering leaving Lina's apartment just after six this morning. She stirred but didn't open her eyes as he kissed her cheek. She grabbed him around his neck and pulled him towards her, moving her lips across his chin to find his mouth. Her hair still smelled like coconut, and her dark, smooth body was especially alluring in the faint, early light from her bedroom window.

He texted: "Didn't want to leave but you said your roommate would be back early. Really enjoyed last night. Want to try again?"

She responded: "Yes, but were you the investment banker or lawyer?"

"Poorer—the strategist," he sent back.

"Now I remember. The big, tough guy with warm hands. I liked you!" she texted.

"Ditto! In DC tomorrow and Monday. Tuesday night work?" he sent back.

"Yes and I know a hot new place," she responded.

"Where?" he texted.

She shot back: "Your apartment!"

He laughed and texted: "Hear that place is expensive!"

"Hope so! 8pm good?" she responded.

He texted: "Done."

"Done done. Ciao! L-"

Brad was already in the shower when Dylan returned with the sushi. He set the food out on his kitchen table, which was tucked under the opening that looked into the galley kitchen. It was also his dining room table when he entertained, which he had yet to do. Lina would be the first. He put on some Bruce Springsteen music, opened two bottles of Sam Adams, and sat down.

A minute later, Brad stepped out of the bathroom and walked over to the side of the living room window. He peeked out onto 96th Street, then turned to Dylan and asked, "Mind if I turn down *The Boss?*"

"No, go ahead," Dylan answered.

Brad turned the music lower and then sat down across from Dylan. He grabbed one of the bottles of beer and said, "Sushi and Sam Adams—my favorite meal. Thank you."

They ate in silence for ten minutes. Then Dylan looked up and asked, "Are you going to tell me what's going on?"

Brad stared at Dylan for a moment, then put his chopsticks down and sat back. He said, "I was followed driving up here. Someone in a silver Explorer. I thought I was being paranoid when it disappeared after I came out of the Lincoln Tunnel, but then I saw it again on the corner of 95th and Third. It had Virginia plates, but I couldn't make out the number. So, I parked in a garage two blocks away and walked here. That's why I went running. To see if I could sneak up on whoever it was. But they were gone."

Dylan said, "There are a million silver Explorers out there. Why do—"

"I know when I'm being followed," Brad snapped.

"Okay . . . then you must know who it was," Dylan replied. Brad was silent. Dylan said, "You can say her name, you know."

"I know."

"Well, then say—"

"Caroline!" Brad yelled and slammed his fist on the table. "Is that what you want to hear?"

Dylan startled and sat back, putting his hands on the table to steady it. He glared at Brad and pressed his lips tight. Then he took a deep breath and said, "I'm sorry, Brad. I wasn't—"

"It's not your fault," Brad interrupted and bowed his head. "I just don't know what to do. I can't accept she's dead . . . until I find her killer." Brad looked up, his eyes desperate and pained. "I need your help . . ."

Dylan had seen that look before, when he was twelve, in his father's eyes after his taxi business failed. It was only a year after Kyle's death. Dylan remembered feeling helpless and angry as he watched his father suffer. Nine months later, his father was dead from a drunk driving accident. His father was flawed, maybe even weak, but he had always told him and Kyle to look out for one another, to fight for each other. Brad was his friend—the closest thing to a brother he had now. He wasn't helpless anymore.

He looked in Brad's eyes and said, "I'll do anything you need me to do."

Brad said, "Thank you."

"So, how can I help?"

"I want to talk through everything, see if you have any ideas or suggestions. I have to figure out who killed Caroline. I don't think I can do it by myself."

"Okay. We'll do it together," Dylan said and paused. After a few seconds, he added, "But if this is going to work, I have to be able to be brutally honest with you."

"I understand."

"Starting with the fact that we may never find who killed Caroline."

"Until it's over, however it ends, I can't stop," Brad said.

Dylan stared at Brad for a moment, wondering what he was getting himself into. Then he stood up and walked over to his coat closet. He pulled out a collapsible easel with a large drawing pad and set it up in front of his flat screen television in the living room, ten feet from the kitchen table. He grabbed a blue marker out of a clear plastic bag of markers, took the top off, and turned to Brad.

He said, "Well, let's get started."

CHAPTER 28
Saturday, May 19, 2012

DYLAN WHIPPED around, and Brad leapt off the couch. The loud banging repeated. Dylan moved quickly to the side of his apartment door. Brad followed several steps behind.

"Who is it?" Dylan asked loudly.

"The paparazzi! We heard Brad Johnson's in there!"

Dylan shook his head. It was MG.

"How'd you get up here?" Dylan asked her as he opened his apartment door. "I thought I was paying for a doorman building."

Mary strolled in and said, "Ernie at the concierge recognized me from ICIN. I told him I was your girlfriend."

"Very funny. You're early," Dylan replied, sneaking a quick scan of her body. She was wearing red, cropped skinny jeans with a blue stretch, V-neck silk top and denim jacket.

"I have plans later," Mary replied, then walked over to Brad and gave him a warm hug. "It's really good to see you," she said, her eyes wet as she pulled away.

"You too, Mary," Brad said. "You look terrific, as usual."

"You're nice . . . I don't know what to say. I'm so sorry about Caroline." She brushed away a tear as it rolled down her cheek.

Brad nodded and looked down, retreating into his anguish for a moment.

Mary glanced at Dylan. Then she noticed the leftovers on the kitchen table. "Sushi and beer. You guys on a date?"

Brad looked up and laughed lightly. "Yes, Dylan's trying to seduce me."

Dylan half laughed too. It was the first time Brad had loosened up all night. MG was good for something, he thought. He asked her, "Want something to drink?"

"Yes, water, please."

Mary and Brad sat on the couch. Dylan brought her a bottle of water and then sat down in his lounge chair. He watched and listed to them talk. The conversation inevitably came back to her work.

Mary noticed Dylan staring at her and stopped talking for a moment. She looked around the apartment and said, "So, this is your new place? It's nice . . . cozy."

Dylan smiled, but didn't respond.

Mary turned back to Brad and asked, "Have the police found the drunk driver yet?"

Brad sat up straight and looked down at the floor, his jaw tightening.

Mary darted a look at Dylan and then asked Brad, "What's wrong? Is it something I said?"

Brad looked up and replied, "Caroline wasn't killed by a drunk driver. She was murdered."

"Murdered?" Mary exclaimed, glancing at Dylan again. "What do you mean?"

Brad cleared his throat and replied, "She was run over three times. It was intentional."

Mary's eyes widened and her mouth opened, but nothing came out. She looked at Dylan, then back at Brad and asked, choking up, "Who would do that to her?"

Dylan interjected, "The police are still investigating. That's all we know right now."

"I'm sorry, Brad," she said. "I didn't know."

"It's okay," Brad replied. He sat back on the couch and stared into space.

Everyone was silent. Dylan watched MG while she watched Brad, an empathetic look of pain on her face. He saw her notice the easel and then read the page of notes written in blue marker on the large drawing pad.

Mary's lips tightened. "What are you planning?" she asked, turning and looking at Dylan.

"Nothing," he answered. *Jesus, that's pathetic.*

"I recognize that easel," she said. "It's obvious you're working on something. And I'm guessing it has to do with Caroline's death. I might be able to help."

"Mary, it's—" Brad started.

"Brad," Dylan interrupted, telling him with his look that he didn't want to bring her in.

"Mary," Brad continued, "Dylan and I need to talk about some things first, okay?"

Her eyes narrowed, darting back and forth between them. She said, "I can help, and I want to. But it's your decision. I have to get going." She stood up and looked at Brad. "It's good to see you, Brad. And I'm sorry again about Caroline."

Brad stood up and walked her to the door. "I'll call you in the morning," he said.

She hugged him and left without saying anything to Dylan.

Brad closed the door and walked back to the living room. He looked at Dylan and said, "I want to include Mary."

Dylan replied, "Brad, she just smells a story. She can't be trusted."

"I know she hurt you with that article she—"

"I did that to myself," Dylan interrupted. "She just exploited it."

"I trust her," Brad insisted, then took a deep breath and added, "She might be able to help."

Dylan clenched his teeth, trying to control his reaction. Brad was the one suffering, the one who had lost the person he loved. It was his call, even if it was a mistake.

Dylan said, "Okay, Brad. I told you I'd do anything to help."

The loud banging on his apartment door Sunday morning didn't startle Dylan this time. He knew it was MG. He fastened his jeans and threw on a black T-shirt as he walked out of his bedroom to answer it.

"Where's the hammer?" he asked, opening the door.

Mary stood in the hallway, holding a bag of bagels, a muscular, older man next to her.

"You never were funny in the morning," she said. "This is Hank Stewart, a private investigator who's done some work for me at ICIN. I wanted you and Brad to meet him. I think he can help." She paused, widened her big brown eyes and said, "Can we come in or are you going to just pose there all day in your sexy muscle T-shirt with your zipper down?"

Dylan stepped back to let them in and quickly pulled up his zipper.

Stewart was a little taller than him but shorter than Brad, late forties, in good shape, with a full head of closely cropped, dirty blond hair. He had greenish-blue eyes, with a faded scar under the left one and a barely noticeable kink to his otherwise straight nose, suggesting it had been broken once or twice. He wore a dark green generic polo shirt and jeans, with black sneakers. He was holding a black notebook with a pen sticking out of it, but no gun.

Dylan turned to Brad, who had walked over to get a look at Stewart. As with Mary, it was Brad's call whether to let Stewart join them. Brad nodded.

"Dylan Regan," he said and shook Stewart's hand. He turned to MG and asked, "How'd you get in this time?"

"A woman recognized me. I came up the elevator with her, but I went to Hank's apartment first. He lives here in Normandie Court, in the tower on the other side of the lobby."

Brad introduced himself to Stewart, then gave Mary a hug.

Dylan watched as Mary walked into his kitchen and started preparing a plate of bagels, lox and cream cheese. She had on white stretch flare pants, a low cut, fitted black blouse and a short, stylish lightweight black leather jacket.

Mary glanced at Dylan and said, "I see there's coffee. Could you pour some for Hank and me, please?"

Dylan stared at her and shook his head slowly in silent protest. He poured two cups of coffee and brought them over to the coffee table. He noticed Stewart examining the large sheets of paper with his notes that he had taped to the wall last night so he and Brad could review them. Brad sat on the far end of the couch, holding a cup of coffee and watching Stewart.

MG brought the bagels over and stopped to look at the wall of notes. "How late were you guys up decorating?" she asked. "I don't like the colors, but the disheveled look goes well with the rest of the apartment."

Dylan forced a smile but didn't respond.

Mary settled into Dylan's lounge chair, and Stewart sat down on the couch near her. Dylan pulled a kitchen chair over by Brad. They all drank their coffee in uncomfortable silence.

Mary finally said, "I prefer talking to mind reading, so I'll start. Hank has worked for the NYPD and the New York Attorney General's office. He's done a lot of work for me over the past six months, and I trust him. If you're trying to figure out who killed Caroline, Hank can help . . . and he's free."

Hank Stewart wasn't free, Dylan knew. MG was going to have ICIN pay his tab so he could help her break a sensationalist murder story—beautiful economist for the BLS brutally killed by someone for some reason. MG was always good at sensing the potential of a story.

Dylan looked at Brad to see if he wanted him to share everything. Brad nodded.

Dylan stood up and said, "Alright, I'll go through what we know."

He grabbed the blue marker off the coffee table and walked over to the wall of notes. He went through the details of Caroline's autopsy and what Brad had learned from Detective Garcia, her family and Chris Smith. Then he told them about Brad's search for Caroline's laptop and his confrontation with the man at her apartment. After Dylan described his own strange encounter with the FBI, he moved to the last sheet of paper taped to the wall.

Dylan said, "Finally, these are the possible scenarios we came up with to explain Caroline's murder, along with the information we need to figure out what really happened." He paused, read his notes on the sheet for a second, then continued: "So, the key seems to be the problem Caroline said in her note to Brad that she needed his help with. It's an assumption, but it pulls everything together, although we don't know quite how."

"Excuse me, Dylan," Hank Stewart said, "but am I right that you have three scenarios—a work connection, a personal connection, and it looks like a government connection?"

"That's right."

"And it looks like from your notes that they could all be related too," Stewart added.

"Correct again," Dylan said. "But the work connection is the most likely scenario, although there could also be a personal angle to go along with it."

"I see she had a job offer in New York City," Stewart said. "Anything there?"

"That's something we still have to track down," Dylan answered, "but right now, it appears no. She apparently turned it down so she could stay in Washington."

Mary asked, "What do you mean by a possible personal connection to her work?"

Dylan paused, glanced at Brad, then looked back at Mary and said, "Well, we have to allow for the possibility of a personal relationship with someone at her work that went bad. Her old boyfriends seem to have been ruled out by the police, but—"

"She wasn't having an affair," Brad interrupted. "I would have known . . . and she wasn't like that."

Dylan looked at Brad. After a long silence, he said, "I know she wasn't, Brad, but someone at the BLS might have been infatuated with her. That wouldn't be surprising. Although, it doesn't explain the guy who attacked you at her apartment."

Stewart looked up from taking notes and asked, "What about the third scenario—the government connection?"

Brad stood up and walked to the kitchen.

Dylan's eyes followed him. Then he looked at Stewart and said, "I think Caroline's murder might be related to the unexpectedly strong employment report. The FBI focused on it when they talked to me, and it's clearly connected to her job. The timing is just too coincidental."

"But . . ." Mary said, expecting Dylan to complete her sentence.

Brad did instead as he walked back into the living room. "But there's no proof other than his theory. Yes, there's probably a BLS connection, but a government conspiracy to manipulate the data is just . . ." He paused and looked at Dylan. "Anyone who knows anything about the economic data collection process knows how hard it would be to pull something like that off."

Dylan pressed his lips tightly, stared back at Brad and said, "It's still a possibility. And we both think the problem she was having had something to do with her job at the BLS. Regardless of the scenario, we have to go down the same path to figure out what happened."

Stewart looked up from his notebook again and asked, "What are your next steps?"

Dylan grabbed his coffee, took a gulp and said, "Brad's going to track down what he can about Caroline's old boss who died six months ago. Her sister suggested they didn't get along. Two deaths in six months in one group at the BLS is suspicious at the least."

"Do you know how he died?" Stewart asked.

Brad interjected, "No, but it was supposedly sudden. The problem is there's an information lock down at the BLS around Caroline, at least until the police finish their investigation."

Dylan added, "I'm going to try to talk to someone in her department at the BLS using the cover that I need help understanding the recent jobs data. It's a long shot, but I might be able to find out something about what was going on with Caroline there. I'm headed down to Washington later today too. I'm meeting with someone who can shed some light on the employment report for me."

Brad took a deep breath and said, "I'm also going to go through Caroline's bills to see if there's anything there. And I'm going to talk to her family and friends again, but I don't expect that to yield much."

"What about her laptop?" Stewart asked.

"Her family didn't take it," Brad answered. "I checked. I don't know where it is, but it seems like the guy who killed her doesn't either. Which means it's out there somewhere."

"You're sure that man was trying to get into Caroline's apartment?" Mary asked.

"Yes," Brad replied.

"But how do you know he's the one who killed her?" she asked.

Brad stuck out his left hand and showed her the thin, red slice across the top of it from the man's knife. "Caroline had an unexplained slash on her arm too. It was him. I'm certain."

"The FBI is still a question for me," Dylan interjected. "The police don't seem to know they're even involved. Isn't that strange?"

"No—" Brad and Stewart both started to say.

Brad looked at Stewart and said, "Go ahead."

Stewart continued: "No, not necessarily. They might be doing initial work before deciding how involved they want to get. But like everything, it needs clarity." He looked at Brad and said, "You were going to say something?"

"You covered it," Brad replied. "But there is one more thing. Someone in a silver Ford Explorer with Virginia plates followed me up here from Washington."

"Did you get the number?" Stewart asked.

"No."

"Any idea who it might be?" Stewart asked.

"Caroline's killer," Brad replied. "I saw a similar SUV driving away from her apartment."

Stewart nodded and everyone was silent for a few seconds.

Mary took a deep breath, turned to Stewart and asked, "So, what do you think?"

Stewart looked at her for a moment, and then Dylan, before settling on Brad. "My first instinct is to tell you to go to the police, since they're in the best position to get information and follow up. But you don't seem to have any faith they're going to pursue this in earnest."

Brad stared at Stewart, then replied, "It's been two and a half weeks. The longer Caroline's murder goes unsolved, the less effort the police will put into it. They're overloaded with cases. Labeling it a drunk driving hit-and-run makes it easy for them to wait and do nothing."

Stewart said, "So, you don't believe a mugger did this after she got away initially?"

Brad flashed the slash on his left hand again.

"I understand," Stewart said and thought for a moment. "You *do* realize there's a good chance you won't get anywhere with this? You need to keep your expectations low."

"We know that," Dylan interjected, a hint of impatience in his voice.

Stewart glanced at Mary, then looked at both Dylan and Brad. "Well, information gathering is the most important part of solving these crimes. Like your strategy work, Dylan. What you've done so far is good. I think you're on the right track. I can look into Caroline's background and the people she worked with at the BLS. Any names you can give me would help. I should also go down and meet with this Detective Garcia. I might be able to get more out of him given my background."

Mary looked at Dylan and said, "I met a gentleman from the BLS last week at a cerebral palsy charity event. He was someone senior and knew about Caroline. His name was Peter . . . Peter Zimmer. You should call him and use my name to get a conversation. It might help."

"Peter Zimmer," Dylan repeated. "Thanks."

Stewart looked at Mary. "I'm sorry, but I have to get going. I'm meeting my son downtown. You'll have to tell me where this falls on your priority list. I'll pull together a note with my recommendations and drop it off." He looked at Dylan. "I'll leave a copy under your door too. You can share it with Brad. I try not to use email for my work unless necessary."

Stewart stood up and shook hands with Brad and Dylan. Mary walked him to the elevator.

When she returned, Brad was packing up to leave. She said, "I have to get going too. I think Hank can really help on this. So, when do you guys want to get together again?"

Dylan glanced at Brad, then looked at her and replied, "Let's see how this week goes first."

Mary frowned, then looked at Brad. "I want to help however I can. Tell the strategist here to keep me in the loop. Okay? Take care of yourself, Brad." She hugged him goodbye. Her eyes were moist when she was done. She smiled at Dylan and left.

Brad finished packing and turned to Dylan. "Thanks for everything. I don't know what else to say."

"That's enough."

Brad asked, "You sure you don't want to drive down with me, instead of taking the train?"

"I'm sure. I have to finish my strategy note before I leave. Be careful driving."

Brad nodded and left.

Dylan watched from his window as Brad snuck out the back entrance, crossed 96ᵗʰ Street and headed for Second Avenue. He questioned if any of this would help Brad, or if it was just prolonging Brad's agony, since he couldn't think of a realistic scenario that didn't end badly.

CHAPTER 29
Monday, May 21, 2012

HALF-WAY up the hill on O Street, nostalgia joined Dylan as he walked towards Georgetown University Monday morning for his meeting with Professor Petropoulos. He reminisced about his two years at the McDonough Business School and the excitement and optimism he had felt towards his career prospects back then. As he walked through the Healy Gates, he thought of FTS and reminded himself it was a different world now.

Dylan had met up with Petro and his new woman friend last night for dinner at Café Milano, an exceptional but expensive Italian restaurant on Prospect Street that he could never afford when he attended Georgetown. But it wasn't the setting to ask Petro any serious questions.

Petro was sitting behind his desk in his office on the fifth floor of the Intercultural Center drinking coffee and talking to a young man when Dylan walked in. Although Petro was all of five foot six, his long, gray streaked hair and tanned Mediterranean facial features combined with his thin physique to give him a playboy air, for an economist.

Petro greeted Dylan warmly, handed him a cup of gourmet coffee and introduced him to Evan Rogers, a Ph.D. candidate who was helping update his macroeconomics textbook. Rogers was just under six feet, innocently handsome, thin, with brown curly hair. He reminded Dylan of Kyle, except Kyle had a mischievous quality to him.

Dylan settled into an old captain's chair and took out his notebook.

Petro said, "I asked Evan to take a look at your data set and analysis. He has done some very nice work on it. Evan, why don't you go through it for Dylan."

"Sure," Rogers said. "So, I looked at the unrevised employment data since the 1960s and found eight instances of surprisingly strong job growth that stuck out for the economic environment at the time. But if you just look at the final revised data, these instances don't look as dramatic. As you know, the initial release of any monthly jobs number entails a lot of estimation. The number is then revised—really updated—as the rest of the data comes in. So, it's plausible that the anomalies I found are the result of the limitations of the data collection process, or the BLS just did a poor job with the initial data collection and estimation. But as you know better than me, financial markets react to the initial data release the most and pretty much ignore revisions. If I were going to manipulate anything, I'd focus on that first data release because it has the biggest market impact, and it's the easiest to cover up later on with revisions."

"Are you saying you think there's something there, that the data's bad?" Dylan asked.

Rogers replied, "Well, something strange is going on because the eight instances I identified occurred during or at the end of very weak economic periods. Also, in all of these instances, there are a number of other months around them where the data looks pretty suspect too, just not enough to be flagged as an outlier. The subsequent downward revisions to these eight instances, as well as to the suspect months around them, look extreme compared to anything else in the data series. And the final revised data is dramatically different from the initial releases in all of these instances. Put it all together and it's hard not to think someone was either playing with the data or really screwing up during these periods. But it's impossible to prove."

Dylan said, "What about the data collection—"

Petro interrupted: "Dylan, I just wanted you to meet Evan and have him give you a quick overview of his analysis. He can email you the rest of it. I thought we'd take the remainder of our time this morning to catch up a little and let Evan get back to his work."

Dylan realized Petro wanted to talk privately. He thanked Rogers and closed Petro's office door after Rogers left.

"He's a brilliant young man," Petro said.

"Yes, he seems very smart."

"He's like you were in many ways."

Dylan smiled. "Okay, Professor, I know you want to make a point."

Petro smiled back. "You know me, of course." He put his hands together as if in prayer and seemed to contemplate for several seconds. Then he put them on his desk, looked at Dylan and said, "As you know, we take information for granted in academia. And in economics, we assume everyone has complete information—no advantages. This, of course, is unrealistic. Information is probably the most valuable resource in any economy and the cornerstone of democracy. Thus, it should be no surprise that this great nation depends on a substantial information infrastructure. Any suggestion that it has been compromised could undermine confidence in the foundation of this government. That would be bad, I think you would agree."

Dylan laughed. "Yes, that would be bad, although the government's doing a pretty good job of undermining confidence on its own."

"Unfortunately true. Now, I also think you would agree that this nation's confidence depends heavily on the economy. A stable economy is vital to our security, both from external and internal threats. No nation can remain free and strong without economic vitality."

"Spoken like a true economics professor. Yes, I agree."

Petro paused. After a long silence, he said, "We are both aware of dark periods in our history when the economy was in such dire shape that confidence was at risk of eroding completely, and with it, the stability of the government and country. If managing economic information to bolster confidence could stabilize the economy during these desperate times and ensure the survival of the government that protects our freedom, would you not at least consider it, especially if it was only temporary?"

Dylan stared at Petro in consternation. "Are you saying you know the employment data has been manipulated to boost confidence in the economy?"

"Dylan, I went to great pains not to say that."

"Okay, Professor, you didn't say it, but are you aware of it being done before or now?"

"I have no knowledge of any such thing. But I have, after so many years in this city, heard a number of things."

"And what have you heard?"

"Before we go there, as someone who genuinely cares about your best interests—as a friend—I must implore you to refrain from pursuing this topic any further after this. The information I have is all urban legend, conjecture that has fed and grown on itself."

"I'm capable of processing all that, but I need to hear it to process it."

"But are you attuned to the intense sensitivities involved in running around and suggesting that the most important economic data infrastructure in the world has been compromised? Of course it's not true, but making any such claims, particularly in this city and in this economy, could create significant problems if people were to listen . . . for both of us."

"What kind of problems?" Dylan asked.

"Well, first, assuming people gave credence to any such claims, confidence in the U.S. economy would be severely undermined. As I already suggested, the global economy would be in upheaval, and the political ramifications would be unspeakable. Second, as a historian of sorts, I can tell you that the messenger is always shot, sometimes literally, but especially when the information proves not to be true."

Dylan scrutinized Petro for several seconds. He knew Petro had no appetite for endangering his own political status within Washington. Petro was giving him a serious warning, hoping he would heed it.

"I understand," Dylan said, "but I would still like to know what you've heard over the years. Besides, who's going to pay attention to what I say?"

"Ah, it would be a mistake for anyone to underestimate you, but as you wish," Petro said with a slight bow of his head. "Again, it's all urban legend, but I have been told—by people I would expect to know such things—that the flexibility inherent in the data collection and estimation processes for some macroeconomic data has been, during times of exceptional stress, liberally exploited for brief periods to support confidence. The goal has always been to stabilize the economy, not misrepresent it, and the actual data ultimately gets fully reflected with time. It is usually a simple matter of generous estimations, never outright distortions. And the instances are supposedly extremely rare."

"But who decides this?" Dylan asked. "How does it all work? How can it work?"

"You have a two hundred and fifty year-old bureaucracy in place in this city—more than enough time for certain unspoken and widely accepted practices to be established and become entrenched. I image that long time politicians are more or less aware of this flexibility and, under extreme circumstances, know what informal buttons to press to get something done."

"Are politicians running this? I can't imagine how that wouldn't be abused?"

"Ah, I quite agree. Reliable people have suggested to me that there might be a small group of senior politicians who make recommendations to an even smaller group of long-time data bureaucrats, with a nonpolitical gatekeeper to prevent abuse. But I have no idea how the checks and balances would be maintained if all this were really true . . . which, of course, it isn't."

Petro smiled—that European smile Dylan assumed he had used one too many times with an attractive female student, the smile that said too much, the smile that had cost him becoming the Dean of the business school, and two marriages.

"You say reliable people told you all this, but have they said whether it's going on now?"

"Dylan, I couldn't and wouldn't say under any circumstances."

"But I need to know, Professor. A friend, someone who worked at the BLS, was murdered a few weeks ago, and it may have something to do with this *flexible* practice."

"Ah, you didn't tell me that was the reason you were so interested. I thought it was just you're inability to accept that you were very wrong about the employment data."

"But I don't think I was wrong, certainly not after what you just told me, but there may be something bigger here. Have you ever heard of this *group* resorting to violence?"

"Dylan, I haven't told you anything," Petro calmly corrected him.

"Fine. Is there any urban legend about this supposed group killing someone?"

"Not to my knowledge, but we are talking about national security, so anything is possible."

"Any urban legend about who's involved? The FBI, CIA?"

"I can't say, because I don't know. But as I have already said, it is quite serious business to suggest such practices are even going on. The risk to this country if financial markets and other governments were to believe such claims is unfathomable—worse than Lehman Brothers."

"But the risk of abuse—political or financial—is an even bigger threat because you won't be able to control it once it's gotten into the system. You know that, Professor."

"I can only advise you to be careful, Dylan. True or not, yelling government conspiracy in the middle of a weak economy may not be very responsible, especially if people listen."

"Neither is murder, but I hear you, and I'll be careful."

"Good. Now, what did you think of my friend last night?"

Dylan smiled. "Charming, but you said she was my age. She just graduated from college."

"Ah, but at my age, that is a rounding error."

They both laughed.

Dylan thanked Petro, and they agreed to talk again soon. As he walked back through the Healy Gates on his way to catch a taxi to the train station, he noticed a black SUV parked at the corner of 37th and O Street. He started to cross the street, and Agent Cole stepped out of the passenger side, followed by Agent Ricci on the driver's side.

"Good morning, Mr. Regan," Cole remarked. "Long walk for your morning coffee."

Dylan stopped ten feet away. "What are you doing here?"

"We're working. And you?" Cole replied nonchalantly.

Dylan examined them for a few seconds, then answered, "Taking a night class."

"In the morning?" Ricci said.

"That's when it was scheduled."

Dylan stood looking at them, and they stood looking back at him. After a minute, he understood that's all that was going to happen. It was a message—they were watching him, and he should be intimidated. He waved and walked down the hill, flagging a taxi at 35th Street.

CHAPTER 30
Monday, May 21, 2012

JUDY THOMPSON was a tall, large woman who looked like she might have been very attractive once. And she was Ben Thompson's ex-wife.

Ben Thompson was Caroline's former boss at the BLS who had died six months earlier. Brad had gotten his name from Caroline's sister Jackie and then researched him on the internet. From Thompson's obituary, Brad was able to track down Judy Thompson.

But he had lied when he called her, telling her his sister used to work for her ex-husband and had just died herself of cancer. When Judy Thompson shared with him that her son played basketball, Brad quickly made up a story, telling her that his sister had left a special basketball book for her son. Sympathy was going to get him more information than asking her if her ex-husband had something to do with Caroline's murder.

Judy Thompson worked at the National Air and Space Museum in the center of Washington. She agreed to meet Brad at the food court during her Tuesday morning break so he could give her the book.

"You didn't say you were tall, dark, and handsome," she said as Brad introduced himself.

"Thank you, Mrs. Thompson. You're younger than I thought you'd be," he replied.

They sat down at a metal table with their coffees.

"Call me Judy. I've always looked younger than my age."

"Sure, Judy. So, I'm sorry about your ex-husband's sudden death."

"Sudden?" she sneered, then caught herself and took a deep breath. "I'm surprised he didn't drop dead sooner. He had a heart condition for years but kept eating and drinking like a glutton. He was a mess and wouldn't change. That's why I divorced him."

"Did he have a heart attack?"

"Yeah, then he died on the operating table having emergency surgery. Third time, the . . ." She stopped and shook her head. "Michael's the only one who really misses him."

"Michael's your son?"

"Yeah, he's a sophomore at American University. They recruited him for basketball."

"He's playing there now?"

"Nah. There's politics on all those teams."

"I know. I guess it's been tough paying for college with his father gone."

"Michael's fine. Big Ben—that's what everyone called him—he left enough money for all of his tuition. I don't know where it came from. I got nothing for alimony when we divorced. A year later, he's living in a condominium, driving a Lincoln SUV, and I'm still getting peanuts. He made a deal with the Devil for sure. Two years of good living, Big Ben, then you're mine."

She was bitter, like the prom queen whose life hadn't turned out the way she expected.

"So he had family money?" Brad asked.

"Nooo. He was white trash from West Virginia. He just starts living it up two and a half years ago, then drops dead last November. I thought he was borrowing money, but he didn't have any debt. Something was going on. He gambled too. All I know is I never saw any of it."

"They must have paid good bonuses at the BLS," Brad said to get her to talk about his work.

"Bonuses? I never saw one when we were married. But I didn't talk to him after I sent him packing, except where Michael was concerned. I don't know what was going on at his work. Who knows. The government's throwing money at everyone these days." She sighed, then said, "I'm sorry, Brad, but I only have a few more minutes. What about your sister and this book?"

"Well, like I said on the phone, my sister just died. She used to work for Ben. She knew your son loved basketball and left this for him."

Brad slid a hard cover book towards her. It was a history of the Boston Celtics signed by the legendary coach Red Auerbach. Caroline had given it to him for his birthday, just before they broke up.

"Well, that was very sweet of her. I'm sorry to hear she died, but I don't get why she liked Big Ben so much. I heard he was a bastard to work for. He sure was a bastard to live with."

"She had a big heart and saw the good in people," Brad said, touching the book.

"Well, I can give it to Michael, but I get the feeling you're kind of attached to it. It's a nice gesture, and I'll tell him, but I'm sure he'd want you to keep it. Things like that are for the folks who are hurting when someone dies. You look like your still hurting."

He smiled at her and nodded. "It is kind of special to me . . . Okay, but if your son changes his mind, just call me."

She said goodbye and left to go back to work.

Brad stayed and finished his coffee, thinking about Big Ben Thompson. Thompson probably hadn't been murdered, but something suspicious was going on with him before he died. He was living a lavish life style, at least by his ex-wife's standards, and without debt—almost un-American. And inexplicable for a BLS employee.

CHAPTER 31
Tuesday, May 22, 2012

A STRIKINGLY attractive woman sat on a blue leather couch near the window overlooking Stamford Harbor in the reception area of Donald Granger's office. She looked tall, even sitting, with long, dark, toned legs bent to the side. She wore a form fitting, light gray suit with a white blouse opened to provide a glimpse of her impressive cleavage, a pearl necklace above it. She had sharp, angular features, and her wavy, chestnut brown hair was slightly lighter than her skin.

Dylan had just arrived at MQA for his second meeting with Donald Granger and his team. As he approached the woman, he wondered if she was a piece of Granger's art collection.

Granger's assistant accompanied him over to the seating area and said, "Mr. Regan, may I introduce Ms. Watson." Then she left.

"Nice to meet you, Ms. Watson," Dylan said as he leaned over and shook her hand.

"My pleasure, Mr. Regan, and please call me Julie."

He sat down across from her and said, "I'm Dylan. Are you with MQA, Julie?"

"No, I work for Eagle Research."

"I'm in research myself, but I don't think I've heard of Eagle."

"We're a specialty boutique with a focus on technology, communications, and defense."

Dylan asked, "Are you an independent research firm?"

"Sort of. We're what some call an expert network consulting firm. We put companies in touch with people who are authorities in a specific industry. Our clients are investment managers, hedge funds, Wall Street firms, corporations, and even governments."

Granger's assistant returned with a cup of coffee for Dylan and informed him that Granger would be ready for him in ten minutes.

Dylan took a sip—Dunkin, of course. He turned back to Watson and said, "I thought expert network firms were mostly pseudo-lobbyists. It sounds like your firm is more value added consulting." He was skeptical, but she was provocatively attractive.

"I couldn't have said it better myself," Watson replied, catching his eyes.

He hated consulting firms. Executives hired them when they needed a seemingly independent and credible voice to deflect blame for their failures, he believed. But he had never seen a consultant that looked like her.

"And what do you do at Eagle?" he asked, returning her gaze.

"I head client relationship management. And what do you do?" she replied, leaning forward and revealing more of her cleavage, smiling like she knew precisely what she was doing.

"I'm a fixed income strategist on Wall Street."

"Oh, now I recognize your name," she said. "Donald has talked a lot about you. I was a bond saleswoman myself at Bear Stearns several years ago."

Granger's assistant returned and said, "Mr. Granger will see you now, Mr. Regan. Please follow me."

Watson stood up with Dylan and shook his hand. She was as tall as he was. She stepped closer and handed him her business card, gazing directly into his eyes, a coy smile on her face as he thanked her.

No formal agenda had been communicated for the meeting, and Dylan was told no presentation was needed. He wondered who would be there. When the metal doors slid open, Granger was standing waiting for him, alone.

They shook hands, and Granger ushered him to two blue leather couches in the corner overlooking the harbor and I-95. Granger explained that he had designed his office to flow like a matrix algebra equation and that this was the objective function section. The rumor was true.

Granger gestured for Dylan to sit down on the couch facing the window and then sat down opposite him. Dunkin coffee was waiting on the table between them.

With no other pleasantries, Granger started: "Dylan, please tell me what you think about the major economies and market sectors around the world. I want to understand your framework in practice and what investment solutions you are recommending to navigate these treacherous markets. You have two hours. It is quite a challenge. If you are not prepared, please tell me."

Granger called it a challenge, and that's exactly what it was, Dylan knew. Equivocating would be the same as declining it. He guessed the meeting would end right then. Their last meeting was just an inspection, he now understood. This was the real test.

"I'm prepared," Dylan said, then took a drink of coffee and began. "I view the U.S. economy like an empire, once great and still young, but at a crossroads. Will it fade like all empires, its demise inevitable as its people continue to pursue a self-destructive belief that they can have it all today by taking from tomorrow, or will it do what's necessary today to ensure there will be an economic future for its children beyond just servicing decades of recklessly accumulated debt?"

Dylan spent the next two hours going through his framework on the U.S. and global economies and translating his views into investment strategies. He finished by raising the question of what a fading empire would be willing to do to convince its people that it was still vibrant, alluding to his suspicions that something was amiss with the employment data.

Granger said, "Ah, I see you have not relinquished your conspiracy theory. I had thought it was just a typical sellside attention grabbing technique."

Dylan tensed at Granger's condescending tone. He said, "If it was a mere theory, why would the FBI be interrogating me about it?"

Granger's eyes widened slightly. He said, "How should I respond to that?"

Dylan realized he might have set off alarms with Granger instead of establishing credibility. "If you'll bear with me, I'll explain."

Granger nodded.

Dylan shared what had happened to Caroline and then related his encounter with the FBI. He asserted that it was proof he was pressing on a government nerve and that the FBI was trying to intimidate him so he would stop writing about his theory. As he finished, he noticed Granger's amused, skeptical smile.

"I am sorry to hear of your friend's death," Granger said, "but I do not see what it has to do with the purpose of this meeting. I respect creative thinking, but I do not really have time for fantasy, which is what your theory unfortunately projects."

Before Dylan could respond, Granger's assistant walked in and said, "Excuse me, sir, but Client Two has requested an immediate meeting and is en route. They should be landing on the helipad in ten minutes."

Granger stood up. "My sincere apology, Dylan. I must abbreviate our meeting. This is one of our largest clients."

"I understand," Dylan said, stood up and started walking with Granger and his assistant.

As they walked out of his office, Granger said, "Thank you, Dylan. This was an excellent meeting. Now, do you like to sail?"

Dylan was taken aback by both the compliment and the question. "Uh, yes. My uncle took me sailing a few times off of Bridgeport when I was young. It was just a small Catalina, but I really enjoyed it."

"Excellent. Are you free this Friday for a sail around the Sound?"

"Uh, yes. When were you thinking? I can catch a train—"

Granger laughed dismissively. "My assistant will arrange for our helicopter to bring you up and back. I look forward to it."

Granger stopped in front of the couch where Julie Watson was sitting, looked down at her and smiled. She stood up. He looked at Dylan and asked, "Have you met Ms. Watson?"

"Yes, I have."

Granger looked at Watson and said, "Julie, I am sorry, but an urgent client meeting has come up. I will not be able to meet with you today."

"No problem, Donald," she said and smiled.

Granger turned to Dylan and asked, "Would you mind if Ms. Watson accompanied you back to the city with your driver? I have been rude and kept her waiting all afternoon."

"No, of course not," Dylan replied.

"Julie, we will meet tomorrow. I promise not to keep you waiting," Granger said. "Well, not too long," he added, displaying a rear moment of humor.

As soon as they were on the highway, Watson asked Dylan, "So, how was your meeting with Donald?" Her long, toned legs stretched across the divide in the middle of the floor of the backseat, almost touching his.

"Very interesting, in a good way," he replied and smiled, then changed the subject. They spent the rest of the ride talking about where each of them lived and life in New York City.

When they pulled up to her apartment building on the Upper West Side near Central Park, Watson asked, "Would you be interested in meeting to discuss how our firms might be able to work together? I know FTS is small, but you never know where it might lead."

Dylan smiled and said, "Why not?"

"Great. How about dinner this Thursday night?"

He checked his calendar on his Blackberry, then said, "Sure, that works."

She said, "I'm going to be downtown for a meeting. What about 10 Downing at 7:30?"

"Uh . . . that's fine."

"I'll make a reservation. My treat of course. It'll be fun." She caught his eyes and bit her lower lip gently. Then she smiled and stepped out of the car.

He sat back in the car and shook his head. He started to think about his dinner with Lina later on and smiled to himself.

His Blackberry rang. It was MG. He ignored it, but a minute later, she called again. He sighed and answered, "Yes?"

"Why are you in a bad mood?" she asked immediately.

"I'm not. What do you want?"

"I want to interview you tomorrow for my next segment, but I need to go through a few things with you first. Can you grab a quick drink or bite to eat tonight?"

He hesitated. An interview with MG on ICIN would give him tremendous visibility. It was why he had agreed to help her. But it was too late to reschedule with Lina. And he wanted to see her. He said, "I have plans later, but I can meet you for a quick drink at seven."

"You have a date. I can tell," she said playfully. "Seven is fine. Where?"

"Ottomanelli's on Lexington and 93rd."

"Really? Alright, see you there," she said and hung up.

As the limousine pulled up to Normandie Court, Dylan noticed he had a new voice message waiting. He thanked the driver and stepped out, then listened to the message. It was from Tom Sygowski, again asking him if he could grab a beer to talk about the opportunity he had. This time, however, Sygowski revealed what the opportunity was. His firm, Baker Cohen, was looking to hire a strategist and wanted to interview him.

Dylan thought for a moment, then saved it—you never know.

CHAPTER 32
Tuesday, May 22, 2012

DYLAN WAS pieces of a man—physical but not powerful, good looking but not handsome, smart but only occasionally brilliant, charming but arrogant, sweet but not tender, tough but not strong, driven but too often to self-destruction. He was pieces that never quite fit to make a complete man—to Mary.

Jeff was more of a complete man to her. He didn't have Dylan's strengths, but he didn't have his weaknesses either, and it was Dylan's weaknesses that had almost brought her down. Jeff wanted her to succeed, maybe more than himself. That was important—to her.

But Jeff could be controlling, even manipulative. She had tried to discuss Governor Hayes' possible Presidential bid with him again Sunday night, but he had only wanted to talk about her meeting with Dylan and Brad. She asked him if he was jealous. He smiled at the suggestion, like a teacher tolerating his pupil. That bothered her, more than it probably should, and she told him so. He apologized right away, but it wasn't sincere, she knew.

She could always tell where Dylan stood on things. She was never quite sure with Jeff. That was why he had a promising political future. And that was why he could help her.

Mary sat back in her chair at Ottomanelli's Grill and took a sip of her Pinot Grigio. Dylan was more of a man than Jeff in one respect, though—he was late. Jeff never kept her waiting.

Dylan walked into the restaurant a few minutes after seven. He looked better than he had in a while, she thought. He was fitter, and even seemed taller. His brown polo shirt with black bands down either side clung tightly to his muscular chest and arms, accentuating his trim waist. His black slacks cut smoothly along his hips and legs, muscular but not bulky. And he was wearing the black leather watch she had bought him for his birthday five years ago.

Is that intentional?

"Sorry I'm late," Dylan said, "I was working out and lost track of the time."

"Maybe you should wear a different watch," she quipped.

"Why would I do that?" he asked and took a sip of water.

His eyes were blue and intense, the way she remembered them when they had first met. By the time she broke off their engagement, his eyes had seemed to fade. Did eyes really change color with your life, she wondered. If so, he must be doing better. They were alluring again.

"Never mind," she said. "So, who's this woman you're meeting after this?"

Dylan frowned and said, "A friend."

"Obviously. And how do you know her?" she asked teasingly.

He sighed and said, "She's a waitress at The Beer Bar."

"A waitress?"

"Yeah, and an aspiring writer, and she designs her own clothes. She's a quarter Italian, Spanish, Greek, and French, and she's very good in bed, especially on the first date."

The young waitress who had just come over to their table blushed as she asked if he would like something to drink. He ordered a glass of Chianti.

"Clever, as always," Mary remarked. "Can we order quickly so I can talk to you about our interview tomorrow?"

"I told you I only have time for a quick drink."

"Yes, I forgot. You're interviewed on the hottest news networks all the time."

Before Dylan could respond, the waitress returned with his wine and asked if they would like to order dinner. Mary asked her to come back in ten minutes.

She turned back to Dylan and said, "Alright, let's hurry up so you can get to your waitress friend. So, you're the star of my next—"

"Before we discuss that," Dylan interrupted, "I want you to know I got in some hot water with Compliance last week because you mentioned me in your segment. I told you that you have to tell me beforehand if you're going to reference me or FTS in any context. If you can't do that, we can't do this."

Mary never liked being reprimanded by Dylan. He was always so critical and judgmental, even when he was wrong. She replied, clearly perturbed, "Referencing you was a hook for this week's segment. I'm confident it's helping you. It's not like everyone's clamoring to know what someone from FTS is saying."

She knew that would sting. His jaw tightened but then quickly relaxed. She was surprised that he didn't want to banter. The woman he was meeting must be special. But a waitress?

Dylan said, "Fine. Let's get this done. Tell me about the segment."

"Alright, the interview is at eleven o'clock in front of the New York Stock Exchange. You need to be there at ten-thirty. You're the star. Here's a list of the questions I plan to ask." She handed him a sheet of paper. "They focus on the economy and its likely impact on the Presidential election, your government conspiracy theory, and the youth employment crisis. You okay with them?"

Dylan finished reading the questions, then said, "They're fine, but I have to know that I won't be made to look like some crazy strategist claiming this is another Watergate conspiracy. As it is, I'm going to piss Compliance off when I go over their heads to get approval to do this. So, I'll have to see it before it airs. And I need veto rights."

"I understand your concerns, Dylan," she said with a sincerity she almost felt. "I can show you the clip before it airs, but only my boss has veto rights. Trust me. I won't let you look bad."

She noticed the intensity of his blue eyes again. He wanted to believe her, she sensed, but he was reluctant. He was remembering September 2008, she knew, and the article she wrote on the Wall Street pundits who had recommended buying Lehman Brothers stock and bonds right before it filed bankruptcy. She had gone easy on him, and it had hurt her with her editor. Dylan never understood. Someone was going to write that article, and it was better that she did. He blamed her, but he was the one who chose bond traders over his integrity. He was the one who violated a trust, not her.

Dylan suddenly straightened up and looked over her shoulder out the window. He smiled and waved to someone. He looked back at her and said, "Sorry MG, but I have to get going. Listen, I know this interview will be good for me, and I know it will be good for you, but don't try to pull what you did with your Lehman story. That won't be good for either of us."

As he stood up to leave, she said, "Dylan, you're just going to have to trust me. And it's Mary. MG doesn't exist anymore. You need to remember that. See you tomorrow. Have fun."

CHAPTER 33
Tuesday, May 22, 2012

DYLAN WALKED towards her, and the sounds of the city faded as an unassuming and eager smile greeted him.

Lina's one shoulder orange top stretched tightly across her breasts, wrapping around her like a large scarf, revealing her smooth, bare waist. She wore a black bandage skirt and low black boots. Her hair was streaked orange, her lips similarly colored.

She wasn't Wall Street or business or MG. She was different, and he liked that.

"I was headed to your apartment and saw you sitting by the window," Lina explained. "I'm early, I know, but I was going to try to surprise you. If you're still busy, I can wait."

"That's okay. I'm finished with my meeting. That was the reporter who's interviewing me tomorrow for a piece on the economy and the elections. Did you make those clothes yourself?"

"I did. So, that was a reporter? Did you tell her you had to leave to have sex?"

He laughed and didn't offer a comeback. It had been a long day, and he didn't want to joust with another woman tonight, especially one that made him feel good.

Lina slid her hand into his as they took the elevator up to his apartment. Her grip was strong but soft and cool.

He reached inside and switched on his hallway light, then stood back to let Lina in. He stepped in behind her and closed the door. As he turned to her, she put her hands on his chest and pressed firmly until his back was up against the wall. He slid his hands up her smooth, shapely hips to her bare waist and squeezed as she pressed her stomach against his belt, working her left leg in between his. She moved her hand up over his shoulder to the back of his neck, grabbed his hair and pulled his head down forcefully towards hers, stopping just in front of her eyes. She parted her lips and moved towards his, hovering just before touching, staring into his eyes, showing him her desire.

She slid her tongue over his lips and then pulled his head towards hers, moaning quietly as she closed her eyes and kissed him. She pulled her lips away slowly, moving her tongue over his chin and down around his neck, gripping his hair tighter and pressing her leg harder between his.

She jumped back suddenly, smiled and giggled.

"Text then sex," she said and laughed. "My friend told me there's a great sushi place on Second that delivers. I'll text them while you open the wine. We can talk about what you want for dessert while we wait."

"Sushi, my favorite," he said and dropped his head in resignation.

Dylan opened a bottle of Chardonnay while Lina ordered the sushi. He kept two decent bottles of white wine in his refrigerator at all times. MG had told him when they first started dating that he should always be prepared to serve a woman white wine in his apartment. If she drank it, then she was willing, although not guaranteed, to have sex with him that night. He watched Lina take a sip of wine, then smiled—a good sign.

"Can I ask you something?" she said, looking over her glass at him.

"Sure."

"It's sort of personal."

"Then no," he replied and laughed. "Of course, but I might not answer the way you want."

"That's okay," she said. "So, the reporter you were with tonight—that was Mary Gannon, wasn't it? I recognized her from the internet."

"Uh, yes, it was. Why?" he asked, sensing he wasn't going to like the answer.

"Well, you said the other night that you were engaged to a news reporter who used you to get ahead in her career and then broke it off." Lina paused. "You were different after you told me. More . . . more intense. Don't get me wrong. It was great, but you were . . . I don't know, a little dark, I guess. Anyway, I noticed, and then I realized tonight when I saw you with her. She's the reporter you were engaged to, isn't she?"

He felt guilty, but he wasn't sure why? He hadn't done anything wrong. He liked Lina. She wasn't MG, and he didn't want her to be. Why was this feeling so complicated so soon?

"Yes," he answered and clenched his jaw.

"Why didn't you just tell me?" she asked.

"Why would I?"

"Why would you? Well, it was obvious the other night you were still feeling something from when you were engaged to her. And she's gorgeous and the hottest thing on the internet. Then you went out to dinner with her tonight and didn't tell me anything about it. Didn't you go out with her last week too?"

"Why are you getting upset?" Dylan asked. "She was a long time ago. Anyway, we've only gone out once. Why would I start reporting everything to you after one date?"

"You were pretty talkative the other night," she shot back.

"Sorry, that didn't come out right," he said. "But are you really jealous? After one date?"

Her eyes softened, and she said, "Maybe I'm a little jealous, but it's because I like you, not because I should or shouldn't be after one date or fifty. Anyway, that's not why I'm upset."

"Then why? I don't understand."

"I'm upset because I think you still have feelings for her, and you don't even know it. I'm sorry. I know we just met, and I'm not looking to get serious right away, but I'm not looking to get involved with a guy who's involved with someone else either . . . especially if he doesn't even realize it."

Dylan didn't say anything for a while. He looked at her, wondering why he was having this conversation on a second date. She didn't seem so different anymore. Her eyes were still exotic, but there was more behind them now—expectations. He sighed and said, "You think all I'm looking for is sex? To forget? Or remember . . . whatever. I like you Lina—"

"Dylan," she interrupted, "do you think I kid myself when a rich investment banker hits on me at The Beer Bar? Oh, he thinks I'm special and wants to bring me home to his family in Greenwich. I know what's going on with these people. Money is something you can guess at pretty well. I know who has it and who doesn't if that's what I want to go after."

She paused and took a deep breath. "I didn't sleep with you because you're on Wall Street and make lots of money, and I don't expect anything. It could've been just one really nice night and nothing else. I wanted the other night with you, but I'm not sure you know why you slept with me. Now I'm not even sure it was me you were with . . . and that's something I need to know. You told me a strategist is someone who figures things out. Well, I think you need to figure out what you want, because I can't tell if it's me or someone else."

"What do you want from me, Lina?" he asked, frustrated and tired.

She looked at him, her eyes glistening. "Just . . . when you're sure it's me you want to be with, I'd like to do this again. I'm sorry. I'm going to go now."

Dylan didn't watch her leave. He wasn't sure what had just happened, but he realized he was experiencing that a lot lately.

CHAPTER 34
Wednesday, May 23, 2012

BRAD WAS supposed to meet Liz Winthrop at The Saint Thomas Moore Cerebral Palsy Center in McLean, Virginia at noon. Traffic was brutal because of the pouring rain. He was late, but she had waited.

"I didn't want to leave without seeing you, Brad," she said, giving him a warm hug. "It's so nice that you wanted to see Susan."

Liz Winthrop was Caroline's aunt. Brad had met her several times when he had accompanied Caroline to visit Susan, Liz Winthrop's daughter with cerebral palsy. Susan received therapy at the CP Center. Caroline used to volunteer there several days a month.

Caroline adored Susan. He remembered marveling at the endless energy she had for Susan and the other patients. Making an effort to see Susan was something Caroline would have wanted him to do, he knew.

But he also wanted to find out if Caroline had shared anything with her aunt. It was a long shot, but his only shot right now. He had already spoken to Caroline's sister and Lindsey Cho again, but neither one had anything new. He had left a message for Shannon Dunn, but she hadn't called him back, and probably wouldn't. He had no other ideas.

Brad caught up with Liz Winthrop for a few minutes, and then she brought him to see Susan, who was finishing an occupational therapy class.

"I can't believe she'll be sixteen in August," Liz Winthrop said as they watched Susan. "We're having a sweet sixteen party here at the Center. Caroline was going to attend." She looked tenderly at Brad. "I'm sorry. This must be very hard on you. How are you doing?"

"I'm still trying to make sense of it," Brad replied. "How was Susan when you told her?"

"She took it pretty hard," she said. "Whenever I tell her we're coming for a session, she cries because she knows she's not going to see Caroline. Peter Zimmer has been great with her since Caroline's death. He's really made an effort to make her feel better."

Brad recognized the name and said, "Peter Zimmer?"

"Oh, do you not know Peter?" she asked.

"The name is familiar," he answered, remembering that Mary had said she met him at a fundraiser. "Doesn't he work at the BLS?"

"Yes. He was Caroline's boss," she said.

"Her boss? What is his connection with the CP Center?"

"He's on the Board of Trustees. His daughter has CP. Did you see the new construction going on when you drove in?"

"Yes," Brad answered.

"Well, that's going to be the Jessica Zimmer Advanced Research Wing, named for his daughter," she said. "I heard he raised most of the money for it. The CP Center is truly his life's passion. In fact, this is where Caroline first met him."

"She did. When was that?"

"Early last year, I think, just after you two broke up. Caroline was working with Susan, and he stopped by to say hello. They started talking, and six months later, she's working for him."

Brad's mind started to drift. Was Caroline having an affair with Peter Zimmer? Was he the problem? Had she tried to break it off and—no, she would never have an affair with her boss.

"Brad . . . Brad," Liz Winthrop said to get his attention.

"Uh, yes?"

"You wandered off there."

"Sorry," Brad said. "So, do you know when Peter Zimmer usually visits? I'd like to introduce myself, maybe talk about Caroline a little with him."

"I understand," she said, "but you don't have to wait. That's him down the hallway there, in the suit, talking to those doctors."

She was pointing to the visitor's desk where a big, heavy man in a gray suit was standing and laughing with a few men in white jackets.

"Why don't you go ahead now," she suggested.

"Thanks. I'll be right back." Brad walked quickly down the hallway. The doctors were just leaving when he said, "Mr. Zimmer? Excuse me, I'm Brad Johnson. I was very close with Caroline Brenner. I just wanted to introduce myself."

Zimmer's smile faded for a moment, but then an empathetic expression took over. "Brad, yes, it's good to finally meet you. Caroline talked about you all the time. My condolences. Are you here to see Susan?"

Brad quickly looked Zimmer over. He was his height and large, with round folds of skin below his relatively young looking face. Probably late fifties, his bald head and white hair around the ears making him look older. *Definitely not Caroline's type.*

Brad answered, "Yes, I was just with Susan and her mother. Caroline talked about you a lot too. I've been meaning to call to see if you had time to speak with me."

"Speak to you about Caroline?" Zimmer asked.

"Yes."

"Well, I'm not really sure what I can offer, but in any event, we've been instructed by the police not to discuss anything until their investigation is over. I'm sorry, Brad."

"Please, I just want a few minutes?" Brad replied, staring in Zimmer's eyes.

Zimmer hesitated, then smiled sympathetically. "Okay, why don't you call my office and get on my schedule for next week. We can grab a cup of coffee and chat."

"I was hoping you had some time now," Brad said.

"I'm sorry, but I have to get back to my office for a meeting. Take care. It was good to finally meet you."

The receptionist handed Zimmer an umbrella, and he left through the sliding front doors.

Brad breathed quickly through his nose as he watched Zimmer leave. After a few seconds, he took a deep breath and went back to say goodbye to Liz and Susan Winthrop.

As Brad drove out of the parking lot, he pulled up behind a silver BMW 535i. In between his wipers shoving the pounding rain away, he saw Peter Zimmer at the wheel. Zimmer stared in his rearview mirror for a second, then roared away.

A sixty thousand dollar toy for a government bureaucrat . . . but it's not an Explorer.

CHAPTER 35
Wednesday, May 23, 2012

THE INSTANT message on his Bloomberg screen said, "If you are interested in working for me, meet me at The Beer Bar at 5:30. I have a table outside. Don't be late."

Dylan read it again. Blair Armstrong had just sent it.

He looked at the lower right of his computer monitor—5:09 p.m., barely enough time to be early so Armstrong didn't think he was late. He grabbed his suit coat and hurried out the door.

Since Friday was a half day in the markets because of the Memorial Day weekend, many Wall Streeters were taking Thursday off to have a five day weekend, which made tonight the real start of the holiday weekend. That was why The Beer Bar was packed.

Dylan wove through the overflow crowd until he reached the hostess. He told her that he was meeting Blair Armstrong there, and she immediately escorted him to a tall table and chairs in a corner of the outdoor patio. He didn't know it was possible to reserve a table at a frat party. Armstrong wasn't there yet.

"Sam Adams?" a familiar voice said from behind him.

He turned and saw Lina. "Uh, hi . . . no, a glass of Cabernet, please."

Lina returned promptly with his wine and a glass of water. She smiled briefly at him—that honest, unassuming smile that made him feel special—then rushed off to tend to another table. He watched her, noticing how her tight white T-shirt and short black shorts accentuated her lean, athletic figure. He cringed, remembering last night at his apartment.

At six o'clock, he had no wine or water left to sip, and he had chewed all the ice in his glass. Armstrong was still not there. Was it a tactic? She was a mass of contradictions, he realized. Could he work for her? His options were FTS or what? The answer was "yes".

"Dylan, I hope you weren't waiting long," Blair Armstrong said, seeming to appear out of nowhere. She sat down, forgoing any pleasantries. "I assumed you'd be late. I can't stay. I'm headed to my place on Martha's Vineyard. I have a plane waiting. It's not mine. I'm cheap. I lease it with four other people."

Lina stopped by and asked Armstrong, "Would you like something to drink?"

"Chardonnay, quickly, please," Armstrong replied.

Lina looked at Dylan and smiled. He raised his empty wine glass to signal another.

After Lina left, Armstrong said, "She likes you. Not really your type, though."

He managed a slight smile but didn't respond.

After several seconds of awkward silence while Armstrong stared at him, he said, "I never heard from Rick Jones about setting up a meeting. Was I supposed to call him?"

Before Armstrong could respond, Lina returned with their wine. Lina left and Armstrong said, "No, I told him I wanted to talk to you first. This is an exceptional opportunity I'm offering you, but I'm not sure you fully appreciate it."

Dylan said, "It's just that your offer seemed very quick. But I really do understand what a tremendous opportunity it would be, and I'm very interested."

Armstrong took a sip of wine, her clear, green eyes focused on him like an interrogation lamp. She asked, "Dylan, do you realize what it takes to work for me, to be successful?"

He wasn't sure what Armstrong was asking, but his instincts were always to match intensity with intensity, uncertainty with confidence. He said, "Blair, I only know how to succeed. I never stop until I do. So, yes, I understand."

She continued to scrutinize him, pressing her thin lips even tighter together. She took another sip of wine and seemed to relax somewhat.

"I believe you, Dylan," Armstrong said and then stood up quickly. "Rick Jones will call you tomorrow to set up a meeting next week between the three of us. We'll finalize everything then." She paused and gazed at him, as if flicking the interrogation lamp on and off to play with him. She started to leave, then turned back and said, "One last thing . . ."

Dylan stared at her.

She asked, "Do you know Peter Zimmer?"

He recognized the name from MG. He replied, "I know who he is. He's with the Bureau of Labor Statistics."

Armstrong pursed her lips, a sly smile seeping through for a moment, before she turned and left. She got into a black limousine that was waiting for her on Vanderbilt.

Lina hurried by, then stopped short and asked him, "Is your friend returning?"

"No."

"Well, the bill is already paid for. Do you want anything else?"

"No, thank you," he replied without looking at her.

She hesitated, as if she wanted to say something, but then left to service another table.

Dylan sat back and took a gulp of wine. He looked around. The crowd was starting to thin. He shook his head. *What kind of game is Armstrong playing? Is she offering me a job or not? And who the hell is this Peter Zimmer?*

CHAPTER 36
Wednesday, May 23, 2012

GARY ROTHSTEIN started his career forty years ago covering the Watergate hearings for The Boston Herald. He bounced around the top daily newspapers after that before landing with The New York Times as a political reporter. His right leaning views and working man style contrasted sharply with the liberal, intellectual persona of The Times. Rothstein knew he was a token, the paper's equivalent of affirmative action, and it gave him job security.

But the internet was neither politically correct nor merciful. With the collapse in newspaper circulation and the surging popularity of inexpensive internet news, well paid, old-line reporters like Rothstein became the industry's equivalent of the Oldsmobile. He was at the front of the line for layoffs by the time the financial crisis hit in 2008.

When John Wiley called him, Rothstein was unemployed, sitting in his Brooklyn apartment drinking a beer and cursing the television as he watched the 2008 Presidential election results. Wiley was a burgeoning internet billionaire and had tracked down Rothstein to discuss his latest idea—launching an internet news venture targeted at the under thirty demographic.

"Gary, how would you like to run the most original and provocative news platform in the history of the business, your way?" Wiley asked Rothstein before he could hang up on him.

Rothstein was hooked.

Wiley wanted to be a media and technology billionaire included with the likes of Jobs, Zuckerberg and Gates. Rothstein wanted to be the truck driver bringing the news to the masses—his way. Wiley gave the new venture its name, International Cable and Internet News—ICIN. Rothstein gave it its soul.

John Wiley sat in a chair drinking a bottle of beer in Gary Rothstein's office. "You know, Wednesday night's pizza night at the Wiley's. I hope you appreciate what I'm giving up."

"I hate pizza," Rothstein grumbled. "And next time you want to pull rank, bring me a real fucking beer instead of this piss." He downed the rest of his beer.

"Jesus, you're worse than when I first dragged you out of that flea bag apartment in Brooklyn," Wiley said and laughed. "How'd you know I want you to change something?"

"Because we don't socialize." Rothstein pulled his feet off the coffee table and sat up. "So, you going to stop wasting my time and tell me what you're making me do?"

Wiley smiled, took a sip of his beer and said, "Okay, Gary, your way. I want Mary Gannon to interview Governor Hayes, and I want it aired in her time slot tomorrow. It's short notice, I know, but it's an exclusive. He's going to announce his independent bid for President."

"He's a fraud."

"I don't know why you say that, but I believe you, as always. That just means he'll most likely win." Wiley paused, waiting for a response. "You'll set it up? Hayes is expecting a call."

"No."

"No?" Wiley repeated and examined Rothstein for a minute, then smiled. "Okay, what's it going to cost me?"

"Nothing, but it'll cost Hayes."

"What do you mean?"

"I'm going to expose him. That's the only way we do this interview," Rothstein said.

"No problem. It's news either way, and good for ICIN, just as long as you don't start with tomorrow's interview. I'm sending a message to Washington, and I don't want it blowing up before they get it."

"Then that will cost you."

"What . . . How much?"

"Two million for the bonus pool."

"Fuck, Gary . . . Alright, fine."

"It'll be more next time," Rothstein sneered. "No interference. That's our deal."

"This isn't interference. It's opportunity. Anyway, at least I didn't tell you to shut down Gannon's series like I'm getting pressure to do."

Rothstein's eyes widened, which he didn't like to do. "Who's pressuring you?"

"Some big politicians and financial players. They want her to stop suggesting the government's playing with the data. Not good for confidence, or their poll numbers. She must be doing a great job."

"Asshole . . . You knew I wouldn't shut her series down, so you threw them a bone and delayed it with this little game to interview Hayes."

"I love you too, Gary. The truth is I wanted Gannon interviewing Hayes. But there are additional benefits, as you point out." Wiley stood up, walked to the door and said, "A deal's a deal. Don't screw around with this. I'm serious." He opened the door and left.

Rothstein got up, walked to his desk and called Jane Reyes. "It's me. Get Gannon and come up. Change of plans."

Mary opened the door to Rothstein's office as she knocked. Reyes was already there. Mary walked over to her usual chair and sat down.

Rothstein looked at Reyes.

Reyes nodded, turned to Mary and said, "Change of plans. You have an exclusive interview with former Governor Hayes tomorrow. He's announcing he's running for President as an independent candidate. Your special series gets pushed to next week."

Mary tried to contain her excitement. She started to calculate. She was scooping all the major networks and newspapers. It would raise her stature—

"Gannon!" Rothstein barked. "Stop fucking daydreaming and start thinking about the interview. I want you to find out everything you can on Hayes, starting now. Use Stewart. And dress like whatever sixty-year old politicians fantasize about. Make him think about his cock instead of your questions so you get some real answers. You got it?"

"I don't understand," she said. "Why are we going so hard at him? This is an opportunity for ICIN to—"

"Listen to me," Rothstein snapped. "Anyone who wants to be President of this country has something wrong with him. Find it and expose him. Then let people decide for themselves."

"That could take some time. Is this a priority over my series?"

"You can't handle both?" Rothstein sneered.

Mary pressed her lips and took a deep breath through her nose. "I can," she said.

Rothstein stared at her for several seconds, then said, "I'm done. Get out."

Reyes and Mary walked to the elevator. Mary stopped and asked, "What's really going on?"

"John Wiley wants this," Reyes said. "He knows Hayes will throw a monkey wrench in the Presidential election. He wants a way to suggest he might back Hayes so he gets cooperation from the FCC and Congress on some media acquisitions he's looking at. He flexes ICIN's muscles, and the political establishment worries enough about keeping him neutral to make sure any deals he's trying to get approved slide through. Rothstein covered Hayes' early campaigns. He doesn't like him. He thinks he's a fraud. Your job is to show everyone that. Understand?"

"Yes, but what if I can't find anything?"

"Then you're not trying hard enough or you're not good enough. There's always something. If it's small, make it bigger. No politician's as good as Hayes pretends."

Mary nodded and said, "Okay. I'll find something."

"One last thing. Wiley's getting pressure from some politicians and financial players to shut down your special series. You're touching a nerve. Push harder."

CHAPTER 37
Thursday, May 24, 2012

DYLAN RELIGIOUSLY tracked the unemployment claims released every Thursday by the Department of Labor. They were the closest thing to a real-time measure of job creation available. This morning's claims data was bad again, continuing a two-month negative trend that should have raised doubts about the 483,000 jobs magically created in April.

But he knew no one cared. April's number had given everyone confidence—confidence that things could return to the way they were before the financial crisis, confidence to lie to themselves, confidence to believe. And it was this confidence that had sent stocks and all other risky securities higher for the third week in a row, while safer bond prices tanked as interest rates continued to rise.

It was fool's confidence, Dylan believed, and the next employment report would prove it.

"Hey Regan, what's your forecast for the May jobs number next week?" Billy McDonald shouted from his seat, a half eaten bacon, egg, and cheese sandwich in front of him. "I wanna know what to add a half million to so I get it right!"

Giggles and snickers rose from the trading floor. With Caroline's murder, the jobs data, and Blair Armstrong racing through his head last night, Dylan hadn't slept much. He was in no mood for Billy McDonald. He stood up, and the floor fell silent.

"You actually trading these days, Billy?" Dylan asked quizzically, staring over at McDonald. "I thought you were just stamping tickets for the salespeople."

"At least I've got a P&L," McDonald shouted, his mouth half full. "You even know what the 'P' stands for?"

"Your pussy, right?" Dylan quipped as everyone watched to see where the exchange would go. "They have operations to fix that, you know, make you a man. I'm sure you can afford it with all those trading profits of yours."

"Fuck you!" McDonald shouted. "Anytime you wanna find out how much of a man I am, you let me know!" McDonald stood up, too late to have the threatening effect of his words.

Dylan smiled and said, "Now's good . . ."

McDonald stood silent, anxiously seething. He wasn't going to do anything, but he couldn't back down without embarrassing himself.

Andrew Cantor walked over to Dylan, placed his hand on his shoulder and said, "Hey, tough guy. You have a second to talk about Differential?"

"Sure," Dylan said and sat down. He knew Cantor was trying to defuse the situation to allow McDonald an honorable retreat.

Cantor grabbed an empty chair. "So, someone saw you at The Beer Bar last night having a drink with Blair Armstrong."

"And?"

"And don't you think I should know about any meetings you're having with my clients?" Cantor replied.

Dylan pressed his lips together and took a deep breath through his nose to calm down. He said, "She called me last minute and insisted I meet her for a drink. I didn't get a chance to give you a heads up. She just wanted a quick meeting to get my read on the markets."

"Did you sleep with her?" Cantor asked with a deadpan look before a big smile crossed his face. "Differential gave me three good trade orders this morning. Then someone told me you were out with

Blair Armstrong last night. Hey, it's okay to sacrifice your body for business, buddy. And she's pretty hot, but you gotta tell me when you meet with my clients. Okay?"

Dylan didn't want a reprimand, no matter how slight. "When I'm the reason your clients are doing business with you, I don't *gotta* do anything. Okay?"

Cantor's body tensed. A forced smile appeared, and he said, "Sure, boss. Just so we're on the same page." He stood up and walked over to talk to McDonald.

Dylan turned back to his Bloomberg screen. Someone tapped him on the shoulder. He sighed and turned around, an annoyed look on his face. Lin Chang, an energetic Chinese saleswoman who covered Asian clients was standing there, smiling nervously.

"Excuse me, Dylan. Do you know anything about SCT bonds?"

He remembered that SCT, or Solar-Chemical Technology, manufactured solar energy panels. A sharp drop off in orders from China last year had sent the stock tumbling almost ninety percent. Its bonds fell to distressed levels on rumors that it was going to file bankruptcy, but the company somehow managed to limp by.

"I haven't looked at SCT in a while," he said. "What's going on?"

"I have a client who sold thirty million SCT bonds to Billy last week at a fifteen dollar price," Chang replied. "Billy said it was a good price, but now my client just said the bonds are trading at thirty. They want to know why we told them to sell. Can you help?"

Dylan remembered Bob Berkley telling him last week that MQA was looking for SCT bonds. Berkley obviously told McDonald, who convinced Lin's client to sell the bonds. The commission probably paid for Berkley's new BMW.

Dylan spun back to his Bloomberg screen and pulled up a description of the company.

"It could just be a short covering rally," he said to Chang. "Corporate bond markets are pretty illiquid right now with so many traders gone for the Memorial Day weekend. I'll do some research on it and update you Tuesday. Does that work?"

"Yes, thank you," Chang said. "Also, my client will be coming over here to visit next month. I'd like to take you to dinner with them. They like your research."

"That sounds good, Lin." He assumed no hookers would be involved.

Dylan spent the next two hours finishing his weekly strategy note, focusing on the theme of a generation of young college graduates without any real hope of landing career oriented jobs. He ended his note with the suggestion that a looming lost generation of young voters was a powerful incentive for incumbent politicians to find a way to make the economy appear stronger than it really was. It was provocative, but he knew Compliance would approve it. With all the new business he was generating, he was untouchable now. Joe Brooks had made that clear to everyone, even though he wasn't a salesman.

It was almost two in the afternoon, and he still hadn't eaten. He left to get a cup of coffee. The coffee cave was empty, except for a young couple he thought might be German tourists. He sat down at his usual table, pulled out his Blackberry and dialed a number.

"Hello, this is Atul," a man's voice with a British accent answered.

"Hey Atul, it's Dylan. Do you have a minute?"

"Always, my friend. I still owe you for that last trade idea."

Atul Rouf was a friend from business school who worked at a small hedge fund in Manhattan. He was Dylan's source of intelligence for all things hedge fund related.

"Thanks," Dylan said. "I need info on Blair Armstrong's hedge fund, Differential Capital."

"Ah . . . have you met her?"

"I have."

"She's intense, isn't she?"

"That's an understatement," Dylan said. "I think she's trying to hire me."

"You don't know?" Atul replied. "She's not known for her subtlety. How can I help?"

"I need to find out what's going on there—her investment performance, what the flows in and out of her funds have been like, and anything else you can dig up."

"I think I can do that, but are you sure Differential is the place you want to be, my friend?"

"No, but I'm certain FTS isn't where I want to be," Dylan answered.

"I hear you," Atul said. "I should be able to get you something next week."

"Thanks, Atul. Have a good holiday."

Dylan hung up and took a long drink of his coffee. He thought for a minute, then picked up his Blackberry and dialed the number he had tracked down at the BLS for Peter Zimmer.

"Hello, Peter Zimmer's office. This is Rebecca . . ."

"Yes, hello. May I speak with Peter, please," he said, acting as if he knew Zimmer.

"Can I ask who's calling?"

"Dylan Regan."

"And what is this about?" she asked.

"Mary Gannon asked me to call him," he said.

"Mary Gannon? Really?"

"Yes, we're mutual friends. Is he available, Rebecca?"

"Please hold a second," she replied. A half a minute later, she picked up and said, "I'm sorry, Mr. Regan, but Mr. Zimmer can't talk to you now. May I take your number?"

It didn't work. He gave her his number and hung up, then finished his coffee and left.

When he got back to the office, the trading floor was virtually empty, even though it was only two o'clock. The cleaning lady had started to do her rounds already.

His Blackberry vibrated—a text message from MG: "Interview pushed to next week. Mg"

"Why?" he quickly texted back.

She responded: "Breaking news. Go to ICIN."

"That sucks MG," he sent.

She texted: "You are welcome. Don't call me mg. Mg"

Dylan sat down and pulled up the ICIN website. The ICIN banner scrolled across the screen along with some pop music. Then MG appeared, sitting across from former Oklahoma Governor George Hayes, preparing to interview him.

She looked like she had dressed to invoke an updated image of the Roaring Twenties—a modern flapper—wearing a peach colored, lace halter top, closed around her neck with a long diamond slit, and a short matching skirt. Her hair was combed to the side, with a lace headband.

Despite MG's suggestive appearance, Hayes wasn't distracted, handling her aggressive questions as if he'd rehearsed. He maneuvered quickly to his announcement that he was running for the President of the United States as an independent candidate. He insisted that the country needed him now, to help the generation of young people watching ICIN take back their future—the future that Democrats and Republicans had mortgaged.

As Dylan watched, he wondered how Hayes had gotten a copy of his strategy note.

CHAPTER 38
Thursday, May 24, 2012

BRAD WAS finishing up some work on the *Flow of Funds Report* when his cell phone rang. "Hello?" he answered.

"Brad, it's Shannon Dunn."

"Shannon, thanks for calling back. Sorry to hound you, but—"

"Brad, I told you I can't talk to you. I'm taking a real risk calling."

"Shannon, you know Caroline's death has been labeled a homicide. I have to figure out who did it and why. I need your help."

"But no one in the department is supposed to talk about Caroline's death to anyone outside of the police. You have to understand. I could lose my job, and I can't afford that."

"I don't understand," Brad snapped. "You can't be fired just for talking. It's the government. They don't fire anyone. Who's telling you that?"

"Brad, I really—"

"Caroline was murdered! You were her friend!" he yelled. He took a deep breath and said, calmer, "Just tell me who's stopping you from talking, and I'll leave you alone. I promise."

After a long silence, Shannon said, "My boss, Peter Zimmer. He told everyone again in a staff meeting yesterday, but this time he hinted that we could get fired. Then he called me into his office this morning and warned me not to talk to you. He said you were too upset, and it might hurt the investigation. Brad, I'm scared out of my mind."

"Okay, okay. Thank you. Don't worry. I won't put you in the middle. Goodbye."

Brad hung up and leaned his forehead against the wall. He clenched his fist and pressed hard against the cheap, wallboard construction. A dent formed. He pulled his fist back to punch the wall, but stopped. He turned, grabbed his suit coat and walked to the elevators. He went down to the lobby, through security and out to the sidewalk. He started walking fast, towards Massachusetts Avenue and the BLS building where Caroline worked. He pulled out his cell phone and dialed Peter Zimmer.

"Hello, Peter Zimmer's office. This is Rebecca . . ."

"Rebecca, this is Brad Johnson. I left a couple of messages this morning. Could I—"

"I'm sorry, Mr. Johnson, but Mr. Zimmer is extremely busy and will call you when he has the time."

"But he told me yesterday to call and set up a meeting. That's what I'm trying to do. I just want to get on his schedule."

"I gave him your messages, Mr. Johnson. When he tells me what he wants to do, I'll—"

"I'm calling about Caroline Brenner!" Brad snapped. "He knows that!"

"Please don't yell at me. There's nothing else I can do for you. Goodbye." She hung up.

Brad stopped walking and closed his eyes, his rage drowning out the noise of people and cars swarming the streets of Washington as the government work day ended. He opened them and started running, faster, then faster again, bumping into people, cars slamming to a halt, blaring their horns. He ran and ran, his anger propelling him, until he suddenly realized he was in front of Caroline's apartment.

He stopped and stood there, breathing hard, dripping sweat. He bowed his head. *I'm sorry Caroline . . . It's my fault.*

He stood like that for several minutes. Then he lifted his cell phone and dialed.

"Third District, Officer Michaels," a man's voice answered.

"Detective Garcia, please," Brad said, his breathing slowing.

"Who's calling?"

"Brad Johnson"

"Hold on."

Brad waited, sweat rolling down his face and neck, his breathing steady now.

"Hello, Mr. Johnson. It's Detective Garcia. I have some—"

"Did you tell Peter Zimmer not to let anyone talk to me?" Brad interrupted.

"What are you talking about, Mr. Johnson?"

"No one at the BLS will talk to me about Caroline's murder. Did you do that?"

"Calm down, Mr. Johnson," Garcia said in a conciliatory voice. "No, I never told anyone at Ms. Brenner's workplace—Mr. Zimmer or anyone else—that they couldn't talk about her. I just said that they should make sure we know everything first. But it doesn't really matter now."

"What do you mean?"

Garcia said, "I was going to call you. We found the man who killed her."

CHAPTER 39
Thursday, May 24, 2012

WHEN JULIE Watson suggested dinner at 10 Downing, a superstitious chill raced down Dylan's spine. It was the bar at 10 Downing where he had agreed to try to help Tom Sygowski by putting out a recommendation to buy Lehman bonds. He had only been back there once since—when MG broke off their engagement. What else could possibly happen to him there?

He was early and went to the bar and ordered a Sam Adams. As he took his first sip, he felt a large, strong hand grab his shoulder. His muscles tensed. *It can't be.*

Dylan looked over his shoulder. Tom Sygowski was smiling down at him. He was heavier, with more gray hair, but it was him.

"Dylan Regan! What's happening, man?" Sygowski boomed.

"Tom Sygowski," Dylan said, standing to shake his hand. "How's it going?"

The memory of Sygowski trying to blame him for having bought Lehman bonds was still fresh, even after four years. It was every rat for himself the week that Lehman went under. After they were fired, Sygowski quickly landed a new job with Baker Cohen, a medium sized sellside firm. Sygowski never returned his calls while he struggled to find a job.

"It's going good, man," Sygowski said as he ordered a shot of Tequila and another beer from the young woman bartender. "Hey, you're a hard man to reach. I've been calling and sending you messages for the past three weeks. You ducking me, bro?"

"No. I've just been really busy with this crazy market."

"I got you, man. No problem. So, I hear you're doing good at FTS. You know, I talk to Billy McDonald all the time."

"You know Billy McDonald?" Dylan replied.

"Yeah, I talked to him this morning. Told him I saw you last night at The Beer Bar with Blair Armstrong. You left before I could talk to you. She's something, isn't she? Hot, rich and crazy. Imagine that in bed!" Sygowski laughed at his own joke, then downed the Tequila shot. "So, McDonald says you're doing lots of business with her. You fucking her? Just joking, man." Then he leaned towards Dylan and said quieter, "You took my business, you know."

"What are you talking about, Tom?"

"Aah, you know what I'm talking about. Differential's doing lots of business with FTS and nothing with me anymore. I know. McDonald tells me. He says it's because of you. I know the traders at Differential, and they say that too. You know McDonald hates you?"

"It's mutual," Dylan said. "So, did Differential cut you off or something?"

"Yeah, Blair fucking shut me down, after I couldn't help her any-more. We were killing it together. Now, you're helping her, ain't you buddy?" Sygowski swayed slightly and pointed his finger at Dylan.

"If you say so," Dylan said, leaning back.

"Hey, you go to Thompson's funeral?" Sygowski asked, then gulped some of his beer. "I didn't. I only met him once. Fat prick."

"Who's Thompson?"

"Come on, man," Sygowski exclaimed. "Okay, act like that . . . but don't pretend you don't know what's her name, the woman who worked for him, 'cause I know you do."

"What woman?"

"Shit, what's her name? I'm having a brain freeze. Thompson told Vaughn she knows you and likes you. That's how you got Blair in your pocket, right? Through her?"

"Who's Vaughn?" Dylan asked, hoping Julie Watson would show up soon and rescue him.

"Now I know you're bullshitting me," Sygowski said and laughed. "Walter Vaughn? The head of sales for Baker Cohen? He's like a legend, man."

Dylan recognized the name. "Oh, yeah, I've heard of him, but I've never met him."

"Hah, I knew you were pulling my leg. I need another shot. You want one? You gotta have one. Toast the Merrill days."

"No thanks. Beer's good for me."

Sygowski ordered another shot of Tequila, downed it and gulped some beer. He stared at Dylan, his eyes wide and glassy. "I'm why Blair knows about you. You owe me, bro."

"Want to explain that, Tom, because I still think you owe me from Merrill."

"Fuck that . . . ancient history. Anyways, I got an opportunity for you if you think I owe you. We're looking for a strategist. We're growing, man. It's a good seat, much better than FTS. We'd be working together again, man!" Sygowski chugged the rest of his beer and waved to the bartender for another. "Yeah, Blair would have to start trading with me again. You watch out for her. She's fucking brutal, a real cunt."

The young woman bartender was just delivering Sygowski's beer. She looked down to avoid his gaze as she grabbed his empty glass.

"Sorry about that," Sygowski said to her. "I was talking about my dog. She crapped all over my house today. You like dogs? You look like a dog lover . . . You know, they say beautiful woman love dogs, not cats."

She forced a smile, glanced up at Dylan and then went to the other end of the bar.

"I see you still got it, Tom," Dylan remarked. "So, what's this opportunity?"

"She's cute . . . Oh, hey, listen. I can help you with Blair, you know. Uh, Walter can tell you about the position. You know Walter, right?"

"No."

"No? That's him, down at the end of the bar," Sygowski said, pointing to a short, trim, balding man in a blue pinstripe suit, talking to a couple of other Wall Street types. "Hey, Walter! Come over here, man! There's someone you gotta meet!"

Walter Vaughn sauntered towards them, relaxed and arrogant, a bottle of Budweiser in his hand. He was in his late fifties and wore stylish black rimmed glasses. Dylan recognized the self assurance of a man who made a lot of money but didn't work very hard for it. He saw them every day at FTS.

"Walter, this is Dylan Regan, the guy I told you about from Merrill," Sygowski said loudly, spraying spit as he did.

"Nice to meet you," Dylan said and shook Vaughn's hand. He had a limp handshake, European, Dylan guessed.

"Ah, Tom's told me a lot about you," Vaughn said with a distinct Boston accent. "You're the strategist at FTS, right? I've read your stuff. I like it."

"Thanks," Dylan said, assuming Vaughn had never read anything he'd written.

Vaughn continued: "Tom said he was going to talk to you about the strategist role we're looking to fill. It's a high priority for us. I would definitely like to discuss—"

"Dylan," Sygowski interrupted, "you gotta come work with me and Walter . . ."

Vaughn smiled tolerantly at Sygowski's interruption, then said, "Here's my card, Dylan. I'll give you a call Tuesday morning. We're anxious to fill this role. You'd be a good fit."

Dylan took Vaughn's card and then caught Julie Watson out of the corner of his eye.

She strolled towards him like a model on a catwalk, wearing a bright red cocktail dress with halter straps that crossed just under her neck, revealing more than enough of her generous breasts. Her dress stopped several inches above her knees, with red heels at the end of her long, toned legs.

"Sorry I'm late," she said and kissed him on the cheek. "Have you been waiting long?"

"Any wait was worth it," he replied.

"Why, thank you. You look quite dapper," she said, smiling flirtatiously.

Dylan turned to introduce her. "Julie Watson, this is Tom Sygowski and Walter Vaughn. They're with Baker Cohen."

Watson said, "A pleasure to meet you both."

Sygowski slurred his hello with a dirty grin as he stared at her chest. She towered over Vaughn as he shook her hand. Then the hostess came over and told Watson their table was ready. She followed the hostess while Dylan waited to pay for his beer.

"I got it, man," Sygowski bellowed, then lowered his voice and whispered, "Tell me if those are real, okay?" He laughed and slapped Dylan on the back.

"Thanks, Tom," Dylan said, then looked at Vaughn. "It was good to meet you, Walter. I'll give you a call."

Vaughn replied, "I look forward to it."

Dylan walked to the table where Julie Watson was waiting. She gestured for him to sit in the chair next to her. He noticed her watching him as he sat down and unfolded his napkin.

Watson leaned her elbows on the table, crossed her hands, and rested her chin on them. She asked softy, "Dylan, what do you really want?" Her large, brown eyes twinkled.

"Well, what are my options?"

"Anything you can imagine. Or do you just accept the choices in front of you?"

"The choices in front of me look pretty appealing," he replied with a sly grin.

She opened her lips slightly, bit her lower lip gently, and started to smile when the waiter showed up and asked if they would like to order something to drink. Since they were both ordering fish, they agreed on a nice bottle of Sauvignon Blanc.

"So, seriously," Watson said, relaxing now, "what is it you would like for your career if you could have anything?"

Dylan paused, reluctant to discuss his real dreams with her, but then said, "Well, ideally, I'd like my own investment management firm. But that takes a track record and a substantial network, neither of which I have. So, starting a hedge fund is probably more realistic since I could launch with a much smaller amount of capital."

The waiter delivered the wine and poured a taste in Watson's glass. She sipped it and then lifted her glass to Dylan's mouth and said, "Try this. It's lovely."

He took a sip and agreed, aroused by the suggestiveness of her gesture.

The waiter poured a glass for each of them and then took their dinner orders.

They spent the next hour sharing each other's stories. He learned that she had been a model in high school, then gone to Stanford University, and then onto Northwestern Business School for her MBA. She had worked for Microsoft and Yahoo afterwards, and then as a saleswoman for Bear Stearns, before joining Eagle Research to head up client relationship management.

As they drank double espressos after dinner, Watson said, "Dylan, you must have realized by now that Donald Granger is very high on you. I've never seen him take such interest in anyone before. He wants you to join MQA. He's more or less told me that."

"That's flattering to hear, but until he gives me an offer, I'm not going to assume anything."

"I understand, but let's assume I'm right for a moment," she said. "Why not start your buyside career with MQA? In a few years, you could launch your own firm. Donald might even seed you. By then, you could even afford to hire me. That would be fun."

"I'm sure it would be, and if Donald gave me the opportunity, I'd jump at it." He paused and then asked, "So, why aren't you working for him?"

"Well, I am, sort of. We're on retainer with MQA. I cover the account directly. If you went there, I would cover you too." She leaned forward and gazed into his eyes, biting her lip gently and smiling.

A rush of blood coursed through his body. He needed to change the subject. He said, "Let me ask you a business question. Since Eagle covers technology firms, do you know anything about SCT, Solar-Chemical Technology? They were close to bankruptcy several months ago, but their bonds and stock have shot up recently."

Watson leaned back from the table. "Well, I know the company, but I haven't followed it closely. Why do you ask?"

"Just some clients asking," he said. He had successfully killed the mood.

Watson excused herself to use the ladies room. She returned ten minutes later and said, "Would you like to get some fresh air? I've already taken care of the bill."

"Sure. Thank you for dinner," he said and stood up.

They left the restaurant and strolled for a block talking about nothing before she said she had to get going. Dylan flagged a taxi.

As the taxi pulled up to the curb, Watson moved closer and placed her hand on his chest, her knees touching his. She said, "I was going to invite you to have a drink with me, but you seem distracted, so I'll save it for another night."

She opened her full lips, leaned forward and closed her eyes. She kissed him, moving her tongue in and around his mouth slowly and gently. She pulled her lips away gradually, letting her tongue linger a little longer on his lower lip as she opened her large, brown eyes.

"This was a business dinner, right?" he said as she eased away from him.

"Aha . . . and that was my business thank you."

Her eyes clung to his as she slipped into the taxi, closed the door and drove away.

CHAPTER 40
Friday, May 25, 2012

"THE LIMIT" was her name, Dylan made out as the Boston Whaler skipped over two foot waves, speeding towards the grand gaff schooner that had to be one hundred fifty feet long. She had a sleek, white hull and teak trim adorning a long, dark blue cabin with tinted windows. She was new, but she looked classic.

A dark silhouette stood on her bow, the sun blinding from above. As they approached, Dylan could see it was Donald Granger, watching and waiting.

Granger greeted him as he climbed aboard. They walked to the stern where Granger took the wheel and steered The Limit to open water on Long Island Sound. A crew of five young men and three young women unfurled the sails, directed by an older man wearing a Captain's hat. Soon, she was cutting the waves, running east, foam and spray flying over her bow.

Granger gestured for Dylan to take the helm. He stood silent as Dylan steered, pointing at different points on the horizon for him to head towards. The early afternoon sun was hot. Dylan took off his windbreaker, feeling the rush of cold spray dance over his arms as

The Limit flew towards the open ocean, rapidly approaching but never reaching the horizon.

Just before New Haven, Granger signaled for the Captain to take the wheel and turn her about. He motioned Dylan to a seating area just before the main cabin where a light snack and drinks had been set up. A young woman crew member waited to serve them.

"I understand why you named her 'The Limit'," Dylan said after taking a drink of iced tea.

Granger smiled, clearly pleased. "It was a day like this when I first took her out that it came to me—how the sensation of racing towards the horizon and never reaching it is similar to a mathematical equation speeding towards its limit." He sipped some white wine and relaxed on a built in couch.

They sat quietly for a while, listening to her slice the waves, her sails snapping and lines whistling with every tack. Dylan sensed Granger watching him enjoying the experience.

"I read your strategy note," Granger said casually. "Very good. You seem convinced that April's jobs data will be revised down, but is that something you would bet on?"

Dylan thought for a moment. "Well, unless there is another significant upside surprise in the May jobs report next week, I think the markets have priced in a lot of good news already. Most economists are expecting about fifty thousand new jobs, but I think it'll be flat."

"I hope you are right. We have similar views and our portfolios are positioned accordingly. Are you worried that confidence is starting to build and the economy is turning up?"

"Well, that would be good, of course," Dylan said, "but I'm not seeing anything pointing to that other than April's number. That's why I'm struggling with it. The only explanation that makes sense is bad data, intentional or not."

Granger asked, "Then why isn't anyone else with credibility proposing the same explanation?"

"I think people want it to be true. And most sellside economists and strategists are paid to talk, not invest."

"If that's how you think Wall Street works, why do you stay, given your obvious abilities?"

Dylan replied, "If you're asking why I haven't moved to the buy-side, it's because I haven't found the right opportunity. Money managers, hedge funds, insurance companies—they're still not really hiring, even after almost four year since the financial crisis started."

"Are you saying you do not see an opportunity on the horizon, right now? Figuratively speaking, of course." Granger smiled briefly.

Dylan hesitated, then asked, "Are you suggesting there is one?"

Granger looked at him calmly for several seconds without responding. Then he smiled slightly and said, "You have probably speculated, at the least, that I might want to bring you onboard with MQA. I am telling you that is what I would like to do. You have tremendous potential. MQA needs new blood—your blood. Do you want this opportunity?"

Dylan's head felt light for a moment, but it wasn't the waves. In their two meetings, he had never seen Granger eager. Now, Granger seemed eager to hire him. Julie Watson was right, but this was fast, much faster than he was prepared for.

"I'm not sure what to say. Yes, I very much want the opportunity. Is there an interview process?"

Granger replied, "There is a process, but please know that this is an official offer. HR will contact you. I am anxious to see you at MQA within the next week or two at the latest."

"That soon?" Dylan replied, suddenly realizing he probably wouldn't have time to help Brad while he was starting a new job, and career.

"Is that a problem?" Granger asked, his demeanor suddenly stern.

"No . . . I just thought the process would take longer. I'd like to give FTS two weeks' notice, to be professional."

Granger stared at him, expressionless. After a long silence, he said, "I am confident they will allow you to leave immediately."

Dylan read Granger's response to mean that he would make sure FTS cooperated. Granger had that much influence, and he clearly wasn't accustomed to waiting. Dylan wondered if FTS would pay him a prorated bonus to get on his good side for when he was at MQA. He assumed Bob Berkley would invite him to dinner to meet his female friends.

Dylan said, "Thank you, Donald. I'm really excited."

Granger smiled his acknowledgement. He sat, relaxed and confident, watching Dylan, as if admiring his new possession. As The Limit pulled up to its mooring off of the Indian Harbor Yacht Club, he said, "I have arranged a quick dinner for us before you return."

"Thank you," Dylan replied, suddenly feeling sun burnt and exhausted. The strange feeling of stepping back onto land only heightened the sensation he now had of being pulled along in his life, no control, the direction dark, his destination predetermined.

They talked pleasantly about nothing over dinner, the first time Dylan had seen Granger truly relax. After they finished, Granger accompanied him to the helicopter.

"Do you like chess?" Granger asked as they waited for the pilot to complete his checklist.

"Uh, yes, but I haven't played in a while."

"Have you ever played mind chess?"

"I have. Very challenging."

"I'm looking for a new playing partner," Granger said louder as the helicopter rotators started to spin. "Are you interested?"

"Uh, sure, but I have to warn you, I'm rusty!" Dylan shouted.

"Wonderful! You will be fine! I'll be White to get it started! Pawn to d4!"

Dylan stared at Granger and realized he was serious. The air whipped around them, the rotators deafening now. "Knight to f6!" he yelled, then climbed onboard.

The helicopter lifted off and angled over the harbor towards the southwest, the sun blinding just above a line of dark cumulus clouds on the horizon, their fringes red. Dylan glanced back at Granger's fading silhouette, still watching and waiting.

Dylan walked into Normandie Court and saw a tall, thin and very attractive black woman standing at the concierge's desk. He was already hot from the sunburn he'd acquired from four hours of sailing, but the sight of Julie Watson raised his temperature a few more degrees. Her white, plunging V-neck dress hugged her body, stopping many inches above her knees.

"There you are," Watson said playfully. "Maybe my surprise won't be wasted."

"Julie . . . hello," he said, walking towards her, trying not to gawk. "What surprise?"

She met him half way, stopped and kissed him lightly on the lips while he pretended not to notice her body. Her perfume was subtle and sweet, like lilacs. He didn't know what the surprise was, but he didn't want to waste it.

She said, "I was going to buy you that drink I promised, but you look a little sunburned . . . and it's getting late."

"Yeah, I went sailing with Donald Granger."

"You did? Wow! He never invites people on his yacht. Even I haven't been on it. Did he offer you a—wait, do you have any wine in your apartment?"

"A decent bottle of Pinot Grigio . . ."

"My favorite. I could have a quick glass, and you could tell me about it. I'm guessing Donald offered you a job, or intimated it, since he seldom says anything outright. Either way, I'd love to hear about it. I can give you my thoughts since I know him pretty well. Then my surprise won't be wasted, although you'll be paying for the drinks." She smiled coyly.

"My pleasure," Dylan said and smiled, his sunburn suddenly no longer bothering him.

Watson strolled into his living room, looked around and remarked, "More or less what I expected—warm and strong."

After Dylan opened the wine, he grabbed two glasses while Watson looked out the window onto 96th Street. It was a very nice view, he mused, as he watched her from behind. He brought her a glass of wine. She took a taste, gazed at him with her big, soft brown eyes and slowly curled her lips up into a suggestive smile.

He laughed and walked to his bedroom to wash up and put on a clean shirt.

As he stepped back into the living room, he realized the lights were all off. He moved cautiously to the middle of the floor, turned and looked at Watson's silhouette figure standing facing the window. He widened his eyes to adjust to the darkness, absorbing the glare of the streetlights seeping up from 96th Street below, now illuminating her smooth, dark, bare body . . . wearing only a white thong.

She turned, faced him and said, "Surprise . . ."

CHAPTER 41
Saturday, May 26, 2012

"IF CAROLINE'S killer died in that car crash, then who followed me up here?" Brad asked Dylan, then glanced at Mary and Hank Stewart. "It was the same silver Explorer that tailed me here last weekend . . . Darryl Dwyer didn't kill Caroline."

Brad was sitting on the couch in Dylan's apartment early Saturday afternoon. He had just driven up from Washington to fill them in on what Detective Garcia had told him about the man the police believed had killed Caroline.

Dylan handed Brad a cup of black coffee and said, "I wasn't challenging you. I was just asking why you don't think this Darryl Dwyer did it. What did Detective Garcia tell you?"

Brad pressed his lips tightly and exhaled through his nose, as if releasing the pressure of his rage. He said, "Alright, early Thursday morning, the D.C. police found a black Ford Explorer flipped over and crashed into a tree along the side of I-295. It was in flames when they arrived. Darryl Dwyer was the driver. He was declared dead at the scene. A preliminary toxicology report put his blood alcohol level at almost three times the legal limit. He was burnt over half of his body, but head trauma seems to be the likely cause of death."

Stewart asked, "But what makes the police think this Darryl Dwyer did it?"

"Caroline's cell phone was in his jacket," Brad answered, "along with a switch blade they're examining for traces of blood that might match Caroline's, from the cut on her arm."

"What about the vehicle itself?" Stewart asked.

"It was reported stolen two months ago," Brad said. "The plates were taken from another vehicle recently. There were scratches and dents on the passenger side panel consistent with the damage to Caroline's car. The paint is being compared to the traces found embedded in her car. The tires also seem to match the bloody tracks left at the scene."

Stewart looked up from the notes he was taking and said, "This is compelling, Brad."

Brad stared at him for several seconds without responding, then looked down at the floor.

Mary asked, "What do the police know about Darryl Dwyer?"

Brad looked up and said, "They think they know he did it, but they're wrong."

Mary looked sympathetically at him.

Brad continued: "He was African American and a career petty thief. He hung out at a local bar called The Beltway most nights. I know the place. It's a dive, about half a mile from Caroline's apartment. Dwyer had a history of minor violence, and his license was revoked permanently for drinking and driving."

Dylan asked, "But what's his connection to Caroline? Why would he kill her?"

Brad replied, "Their theory is that Dwyer had seen her around the neighborhood and tried to mug her that night, but she got away. They think that made him angry, and he either followed her home or knew where she lived and waited for her."

"Didn't she work late that night?" Stewart asked. "Where would he have tried to mug her?"

"That's another reason it doesn't make sense," Brad said. "It wasn't Dwyer. He was a petty thief, not a murderer. The way Caroline was killed was deliberate, vicious. Not something from a local bar room lush. And Dwyer doesn't explain the guy who attacked me at her apartment. But the police have already decided they solved it."

Dylan looked at Brad and said, "I can see why they think that, but if you're right, it means whoever killed Caroline also murdered Dwyer."

Stewart added, "Which makes this a lot more dangerous."

Mary asked, "But why kill Dwyer and try to make it look like he killed Caroline?"

Dylan answered, "Because someone's getting too close to figuring out what really happened. But the police weren't close to solving it, which means it's one of us."

Stewart looked at Dylan and asked, "Then why not go after Brad, or even you?"

Dylan thought for a moment, then said, "Whoever's behind this doesn't want to attract any more attention to the case. He, *or she*, wants it to go away quietly, which is why you serve up Dwyer as the killer, nice and neat. But that means this is bigger than just Caroline's murder." Dylan stopped, seeing Brad's pained expression. "I'm sorry, Brad. That didn't come out right."

Brad glanced at him, then looked down and nodded.

After a few seconds of awkward silence, Dylan said, "Something has to have changed to trigger this move by the killer."

Stewart said, "Then we should probably go through what everyone found out this week."

Brad looked up and said, "I'll go first." He gulped down the rest of his coffee and cleared his throat. "Caroline's old boss who died six months ago, Ben Thompson, came into some—"

"Did you say Thompson?" Dylan interrupted.

"Yes, Ben Thompson," Brad replied. "Why?"

"Uh . . . continue," Dylan said. "I'll tell you afterwards."

Brad stared at Dylan for a moment, then said, "Anyway, Ben Thompson apparently started living pretty high, at least according to his ex-wife, two years before he died. No family money, and he was supposedly broke when he got divorced. Then he suddenly buys a condo and a new car on the salary of a government bureaucrat, but he had no debt and left his son a bunch of money for college."

"How did he die?" Mary asked.

"Complications from emergency surgery after a third heart attack," Brad said.

"That doesn't seem suspicious," Mary said. "And it was six months ago, long before Mary was killed. Do you really think it's connected?"

"I don't know," Brad replied. "What's strange is that Peter Zimmer, the guy you told Dylan to call, doesn't just work at the BLS. He hired Caroline and was her boss, which means he was Ben Thompson's boss too. Zimmer is a trustee at this cerebral palsy treatment place in McLean, Virginia. I met him there while I was visiting Caroline's cousin who has CP. I asked him if he would talk to me about Caroline, and he said he'd meet me for coffee. Now his secretary is stonewalling me. On top of that, Shannon Dunn finally told me he's the one who's been telling her not to talk to me. And I checked with Detective Garcia. The police have never told anyone at the BLS not to discuss the investigation."

Dylan was silent, his mind racing—Thompson, Zimmer, Sygowski, Vaughn and Blair Armstrong—all with a connection to Caroline.

Stewart asked, "Anything else, Brad?"

"Just that I went through Caroline's bills and statements, but I didn't find anything."

"How about her laptop?" Stewart asked.

"It's still missing."

Stewart wrote some notes, looked up and said, "Well, I checked out Caroline's background and the people in her group at the BLS. She—"

"You looked into Caroline's background?" Brad interrupted.

Stewart replied, "We need to know everything about her, Brad. She was keeping something from you. You already know that."

Brad clenched his jaw and nodded.

"I didn't find anything new," Stewart continued. "I also tracked down this Ben Thompson and saw that he lived pretty well for his circumstances. No debt is definitely suspicious, although I confirmed that his death wasn't. I also checked out her co-workers, particularly Shannon Dunn, but there was nothing suspicious with any of them, at least on initial screening. Dunn visits her twin sister up here in Queens a lot, but that's nothing."

"Did you check out Zimmer?" Brad asked.

"Yeah, after I learned he ran the group Caroline worked in," Stewart answered. "He graduated from the University of Chicago in '75, got his MBA there in '78, spent some time on Wall Street and then worked the last twenty years at the BLS. He has five children—three in college, one in private school, and his daughter with cerebral palsy. And he owns a vacation home on a golf course in South Carolina. I don't know yet where his finances stand, but right now, the Zimmers look like every other over-indebted, upper middle class American family."

Brad took a deep breath, exhaled and looked at Dylan. "Did you have something?"

"I'm not sure," Dylan replied. "MG, do you remember Tom Sygowski?"

Mary sighed and answered, "Yes, and it's Mary . . . please."

Dylan glanced at her, then continued: "Tom Sygowski is a bond trader I used to work with at Merrill Lynch. He's with Baker Cohen now, a mid-sized Wall Street firm. I ran into him the other night. He was drunk and started talking to me about this hedge fund manager I've been doing business with recently, Blair Armstrong. She owns Differential Capital Management. Anyway, he asked me if I went to Thompson's funeral. No first name, just Thompson. Then he starts accusing me of stealing his business from Differential because this woman who worked for Thompson knows and likes me. I didn't know what the hell he was talking about, but now—"

"You think the woman was Caroline," Brad interrupted. "But what would she or anyone else at the BLS have to do with a Wall Street firm, never mind a hedge fund?"

"Maybe Differential was the firm that gave her a job offer," Dylan replied. "I don't know, but it gets stranger. I had a drink last week with Blair Armstrong, and she asked me if I knew Peter Zimmer." He paused, then added, "Zimmer, Armstrong, Sygowski, Thompson—all knowing each other? That's some coincidence."

"And you don't believe in those types of coincidences," Mary interjected.

"That's right, I don't," Dylan replied. "Now, you're really going to think I'm crazy. I also visited with a business school professor of mine last week at Georgetown. He looked at the employment data and my analysis and then shared with me that he's aware of long standing rumors of someone in the government manipulating the data during bad economic times to boost confidence in the economy. Then—"

"So all this is coming back to your conspiracy theory?" Brad interrupted.

"Just listen, will you?" Dylan replied, then took a deep breath. "Those two FBI agents were waiting for me when I left Georgetown. But they didn't stop me or question me. They were just trying to intimidate me. Maybe Caroline's murder has nothing to do with the data, but something strange *is* going on with the data, and something strange *is* going on at the BLS."

After several seconds of silence, Brad said, "Caroline wasn't interested in working for a hedge fund. I don't know why she would bother to interview with one."

Stewart wrote something down, then looked at Dylan and said, "I think we want to first figure out if there's a connection between the BLS and that Wall Street firm or the hedge fund. I'm not sure how to verify those rumors about the Government manipulating the jobs data."

Dylan said, "I agree. I already have a plan. I'm going to call Tom Sygowski and set up a meeting. He wants something, so he might tell me what, if anything, is going on. I'm also supposed to meet with Blair Armstrong and her partner this week. She's smart, but I might be able to get her to talk about Zimmer."

"Why don't I try to talk to Peter Zimmer?" Mary suggested. "He'll probably take my call, especially if I say I want to interview him about the CP Center. I'm going to be down in Washington this week anyway."

"That's a good idea," Brad said. "The CP Center is supposedly his life's passion. He probably wouldn't turn down an opportunity to promote it."

"And once I'm in front of him," Mary continued, "I can try to get him to talk about Caroline's death. I'll shake the tree, and we can see what falls out."

Stewart said, "It's worth a try. I'll head down to D.C. this week to talk to the police about Dwyer. Hopefully, I can get some additional info from this Detective Garcia."

Brad said, "Well, I'll probably stop by The Beltway, the bar where Dwyer hung out, and see if I can find anything out. Besides that, I don't have any other ideas."

"Will you have time to meet with me while I'm down there?" Stewart asked him.

"Of course," Brad said, knowing Stewart was just trying to make him feel useful. He looked at Dylan and asked, "Could you take a look at Caroline's bills and statements? You might find something I missed. I brought them with me."

"Sure, just leave them here," Dylan said.

Stewart asked, "Brad, when are you headed back to D.C.?"

"As soon as we're done here," Brad answered.

"I could follow you part of the way to see if someone's tailing you," Stewart offered.

"That would be helpful . . . show everyone I'm not crazy."

Mary leaned forward slightly and said, "Brad, I don't think that."

Dylan said, "If you are being followed by Caroline's killer, how do we protect ourselves from someone we don't know but who clearly knows us?"

Stewart said, "If the goal really was to make it look like Dwyer killed Caroline, then whoever's behind this probably thinks it's working and doesn't feel the need to do anything, at least right now. But all of you need to be careful and take precautions."

"Why am I in danger?" Mary asked. "Whoever this killer is doesn't even know about me."

Dylan quickly countered, "I wouldn't be so sure about that."

"He's right, Mary," Stewart added. "We have to assume the killer knows about all of us."

"Mary, maybe you shouldn't approach Zimmer," Brad said. "It might be too—"

"Thank you, Brad" Mary interrupted, "but I can take care of myself. Besides, whoever's trying to cover this up isn't going to risk going after an ICIN reporter . . . especially me."

"Before everyone leaves," Stewart said, "I'd be negligent if I didn't advise you to try again to convince the police about all of this. The situation has gotten potentially very dangerous."

Brad replied, "They think they've solved Caroline's murder. They're not going to listen to us, never mind believe our theories, until we have real proof. And we don't have that yet."

"I understand," Stewart said, "but you'll have to go to them at some point, preferably before anyone else gets hurt."

Mary stood up and said, "Sorry, but I have to get going. I have dinner plans tonight, and I have to get some work done beforehand. We're basically done, right?"

Dylan nodded and stood up. Brad and Stewart followed. Mary walked over and hugged Brad. Stewart shook Dylan's hand, then told Brad that he would meet him in the lobby downstairs. Mary smiled at Dylan as she and Stewart walked out the door.

Dylan turned and saw Brad standing by his living room window. He walked over and stood next to him as they both gazed out onto 96th Street below.

"I am being followed," Brad said, still staring out the window.

"Do you need me to believe you?"

"Yes . . . otherwise there's only Caroline . . . To be honest, I'm having a little trouble telling what's real . . ."

"Then I believe you. But I need to tell you something, Brad."

Brad walked to the middle of the living room, turned and said, "Okay, tell me what you need to. Then I have to get going." His face was empty.

Dylan stepped towards him and said, "I have a job offer, from a buyside firm, MQA up in Connecticut. It's something I really want, and it gets me out of FTS. I'm dying there. You know that. I have to start in a week, two at the most." He paused. "If I don't take this now, I'll lose it. But I might not be able to continue helping you once I start . . . I said I'd be honest."

Brad stared blankly at him for a while, then said, "I understand, Dylan. You've already helped a lot. You should take the position. I'm happy for you."

"That's all you're going to say?"

Brad looked away and said, "I have to go." He started walking towards the door.

Dylan walked quickly after him, grabbed his arm and said, "Brad, that's not—"

Brad whirled around, knocking Dylan's hand away, then grabbed his neck and shirt. He drove Dylan towards the wall, knocking over an end table and lamp as he did.

"Fuck you!" Brad screamed and slammed Dylan up against the wall, sending a framed photograph crashing to the floor.

Dylan felt his head hit hard against the wall. He instinctively swung his forearms up to force Brad's hands from his neck and shirt, and then propelled his forehead into Brad's face just under his eye, knocking him off balance. He stepped quickly to Brad's side, grabbed him and swung him around, sending Brad crashing into the wall, another picture shattering on the floor.

Dylan pulled his right arm back quickly, intending to drive a short, hard punch into Brad's exposed face. It wouldn't stop Brad, Dylan knew, but it might daze him enough to make him think. Brad was bigger and stronger, but he was quicker and dirtier. The black guy had grown up in a middleclass suburb, and the white guy had grown up on the streets of Bridgeport.

As Dylan brought his fist forward, he caught Brad's eyes, blank and distant. His arms were by his side. He wasn't going to defend himself.

Dylan stopped. He let go of Brad's shirt and stepped back, dropping his arm and unclenching his fist. He saw a welt and cut above Brad's cheek, oozing blood from his head butt. Brad wasn't there, Dylan realized. He had gone somewhere—to be with Caroline.

"I'm sorry, Brad," Dylan said, breathing hard. "Are you okay?"

Brad stared into space for a few seconds, then slowly seemed to become aware of what had just happened. "Uh, are you okay, Dylan? I'm sorry. I lost it . . ."

"I'm fine. I don't think you should drive. I can clean that cut if—"

"I'm alright," Brad interrupted. "Take the job. For yourself and for me. I have to go." He pushed himself away from the wall, took three long strides to the door, opened it and left.

CHAPTER 42
Sunday, May 27, 2012

THE SHORT, red-haired, slightly overweight woman stood waiting on the subway platform. She looked about forty, but she was Irish, which meant she was at least five years younger. She'd been waiting five minutes already with no sign of a train, not even a hint on her freckled face of the air being pushed through the tunnel well ahead of the lead car, like she always felt whenever a train was approaching on the Metro back home in Washington.

But this was New York City's M Line, a Sunday afternoon, Memorial Day weekend. Shannon Dunn had waited at this stop too many times on her way to visit her twin sister in Queens to expect to feel that faint breeze coming from the tunnel anytime soon. She put her small suit case down, pulled her cell phone out from her handbag, and dialed.

"Hello . . ." a man's voice answered, seemingly out of breath.

"Hi, is this Dylan Regan?" she asked.

". . . Sorry, yes it is."

"Uh, my name's Shannon Dunn. I was a—"

"I know who you are, Shannon . . . from Brad Johnson . . ."

"Oh, good. Are you alright, Mr. Regan?"

"Yes, sorry about that. I just got back from running . . . and it's Dylan, please."

"Okay, Dylan. It's Shannon. Um, do you have a minute to talk?"

"Yes, of course . . . Could you speak a little louder, Shannon? You're a bit faint."

"Oh, sorry, sure. I'm in the subway here waiting for a train." She stepped closer to the edge of the platform to improve the signal, a trick she learned on the Metro. "Is that better?"

"It is. Are you here in New York?"

"I am," she replied. "I'm on my way to my sister's in Forest Hills, to visit my mother. She's in a nursing home nearby."

"Oh, that's nice."

"Yeah, well, my sister does most of the work taking care of her. I visit as much as I can. But anyway, I called about Caroline."

"Okay . . ."

"I don't know if you saw, or if Brad even knows, but the police found the man who killed her. He died in a drunk driving accident. He had Caroline's phone. I guess they're pretty sure it's the same car that hit her too."

"Brad does know, and he told me about it," Dylan said.

"Oh, good. Well, the reason I called—wait, did Brad share with you that I couldn't talk to him about Caroline because of the investigation?"

"He did," Dylan replied, "but that shouldn't apply anymore, right?"

"I would think so, but my boss told everyone on Friday that we still shouldn't discuss it with people outside the office, to be respectful to Caroline's family."

"Did he say you'd get in trouble?" Dylan asked.

"No, but he was looking right at me when he said it. I'm just very nervous about the whole thing. But that's why I'm calling you."

"I don't understand."

"Well, I wasn't sure if I was going to do this, since I could still get in trouble, but I just feel so guilty about not helping Brad when he asked me. Anyway, he called me a couple of weeks ago and asked me to check and see if Caroline's personal laptop was in her desk. I looked, but I couldn't find it, but then I did."

"You have it?" Dylan asked.

"Yes. I don't know why Caroline left it there, but—"

"Where did you find it?"

"Oh, I'm sorry. It was in the bottom drawer of my file cabinet next to my desk. I keep it locked because I store some personal stuff there, and one time someone stole something, the cleaning man, I think. Anyway, Caroline sometimes put her purse in there if she was going out and didn't want to carry it around. She knew where I kept the key. So, the day after Brad called, I opened it to get something, and there it was, under my stuff. I almost didn't see it."

"So, why didn't you just call Brad and tell him?"

"I know I should have, but I couldn't take the chance. My boss was watching me, and . . ."

"And what?"

"Well, there was a flash drive in an envelope taped to the top of it, with your contact information on it, like she was going to mail it to you."

"To me?"

"Yes. I don't know what's on it, but it made me even more nervous. I didn't know what to do, but then the police found the man who killed her, so I decided it was probably safe to tell someone."

"But why call me instead of Brad?"

"I'm still afraid if my boss finds out I gave something to Brad, I'll get in trouble. Caroline talked to you all the time, and your Brad's friend. I thought you could give him her laptop and take the flash drive."

"Yeah, okay, Shannon. How do I get them from you?"

She said, "I brought them up with me. I can drop them off tomorrow, if that's okay."

"I can come get them tonight, if you want," Dylan quickly offered.

"No, no. That's okay. I'm meeting some friends for lunch tomorrow not too far from where you live. It's Normandie Court on 95th Street, right?"

"That's right."

"I'll stop by around noon, if that works for you," she said. "I'm looking forward to meeting you. Caroline always said such nice things."

"Thank you. Just give me a call when you're on your way."

"I will," she said, then paused. "Um . . ."

"Is there something else?"

"Well, Brad wanted to know what was going on at work before Caroline died. I said I'd tell him everything after the investigation was over, but I don't think I can do that yet."

"Do you want to tell me, and I'll pass it along?" Dylan asked.

"That's what I was thinking, if you don't mind," she replied.

"No, I'm glad to. Was Caroline having problems at work?"

"Well, what I can tell you is that something was bothering her. She worked late all that week before she died, and she seemed very tense. I asked her what was going on, but she said it was better that I didn't know. And she was acting strange about the phones too."

"What do you mean?" Dylan asked.

"I mean, she wouldn't use her work phone or her cell to make calls at the office. She kept using mine, and then she started borrowing my cell phone too. It was weird, but she wouldn't tell me what was going on."

"That is weird," he said. "What about her boss? Anything strange there?"

"I couldn't really tell. I know she was going to meet with him that day she died. She was preparing something—" Shannon stopped, feeling a breeze caress her face and a faint rumble from the tunnel. "Oh, a train's coming. I have to go, Dylan. We can talk some more tomorrow. Thank you. Bye."

She hung up and hurriedly put her phone in her handbag. It suddenly slid off of her shoulder to the ground. She stared at it, bewildered, then noticed the strap was sliced.

"What in the—" she started to say but sensed someone behind her. Before she could turn around, two strong hands grabbed her coat, lifted her partially off the ground, and shoved her into the oncoming light—

CHAPTER 43
Monday, May 28, 2012

"I'VE NEVER been here before. This is impressive," James Murphy said as he stepped out of the black stretch limousine and gazed at the oversized beach house.

"That's because you're a Democrat," Randy Boatman quipped. "This is Mitch's war compound. Republicans only. I'm not sure he's ever invited a Democrat here before."

"I thought he was the son of a truck driver, pulled himself up by his bootstraps. How does he afford a weekend home like this?" Murphy asked as they walked across the driveway of crushed seashells.

"Wife's family has money, and I've heard he's a savvy investor," Boatman answered.

Murphy scoffed and said, "The only savvy investors in Congress are the ones who use their positions to get information before everyone else. I've heard Mitch is in with some big time financial players with ties to China. Everyone's scared to talk about him . . . including you."

Boatman just grunted. They climbed the wide wooden steps to a covered porch that flowed around the side of the eight thousand square foot house overlooking a private beach and dock on the Eastern

Shore of Chesapeake Bay. The late morning sun was struggling to burn through an overcast sky as a lone seagull cried to them from the sandy fringe of the expansive lawn.

"Mitch should be back by now," Boatman said, breathing heavily. "He was taking his family to the airport this morning."

"He'd better be," Murphy replied, looking around from the porch. "I have to catch a plane back to New York this afternoon, and we need to—"

"Gentleman," a strong, friendly voice boomed from behind them, "I hope you weren't waiting too long."

Murphy and Boatman turned around and looked down at the bottom of the steps. A tall, wiry, athletic man wearing a sweat-soaked white T-shirt, gray shorts and running sneakers stood there, panting slightly. Another shorter, but still tall, muscular black man, similarly dressed and sweaty, stood several steps behind him.

Mitchell Levy, the Republican Speaker of the House of Representatives from the State of Washington, was the tall white man. He was in his late forties but looked younger, with a full head of closely cropped, dark brown hair and hazel eyes. The other man was his bodyguard.

Levy turned and nodded to his bodyguard, then bounded up the steps two at a time, stopped in front of Murphy and Boatman, and smiled. He glanced at his IPhone, checked his messages, and looked back at them. He smiled again.

"I thought I could get a quick run in before you arrived, but it appears you beat me," Levy said. "Come on in and let's talk. Jim, I know you're on a tight schedule."

"I am, Mr. Speaker," Murphy replied. "Thank you for the invitation. Beautiful place."

"Why are you being so formal, Jim?" Levy asked as he opened the screen door to a large but charming entryway, decorated like a photo spread from *Coastal Living*.

"Alright, Mitch," Murphy replied. "Can we sit down quickly and talk in private?"

"Of course," Levy answered and directed them to a small, airy sitting room in the back of the house with bay windows looking out at the distant beach. "My wife and kids left this morning, so it's just us today. Oh, and Theresa, the housekeeper. This is private. No surveillance or anything like that to worry about, Jim. Randy knows. You can speak freely."

Before Murphy could say anything, a small, older Hispanic woman brought in a tray of iced tea and lemonade with a plate of scones and marmalade. Then she left and closed the door.

"So, Jim, I'm sorry it took so long to set up this meeting," Levy said and sat back in his floral cushion, wicker lounge chair. "Thanks for coming out here on a Sunday."

"Better late than never, I guess," Murphy remarked. "We need to talk about the mess with the process . . . and Patricia's difficult personality while we're at it."

"Hold on, Jim," Boatman said, sitting up in his chair, "Mitch, could we first talk about those last two jobs numbers. I'm getting a lot of grief from my people. You know that data could turn the election back to Obama and cost us a number of other close races."

"I hear you, Randy," Levy said and took a sip of iced tea. "First, any reason Mannino and Richards aren't here? They're part of the group."

Murphy sighed and said, "Really, Mitch? You barely tolerate Nancy. And it's the same with Harvey for me. We're never productive when we all meet. This is a problem solving session, not a vote on what we're recommending to the admins."

"You're right," Levy said, "Mannino's an idiot, and I'm aware you think the same of Richards. But they're the other members of the group. So, we can discuss problems today, but no decisions until they're consulted. I'm not going to start overriding an eighty year old process. Now, has Patricia given any more updates?"

Murphy took a deep breath and exhaled. He waited several seconds, controlling his temper, then said, "No. All we know is a rogue economist jacked up the April jobs number and then died in a hit-and-run accident. We still don't know what she knew or why she did it. The police did find the hit-and-run driver the other day dead in a drunk driving crash."

"Interesting . . ." Levy remarked slowly, then sipped some iced tea.

Boatman said, "Mitch, the upcoming jobs report will be a big problem for us if the admins just try to correct that April number by spreading it out over three months. They do that and the fucking economy will look like it's going gangbusters. You gotta say something to them."

Levy replied, "It may be the only way they can fix what that rogue economist did without bringing excessive media scrutiny that could jeopardize the process. You've got that ICIN reporter, Mary Gannon, pumping up a government conspiracy theory that's catching fire with everyone under thirty, especially the ones without jobs. And now I hear she's going to try to pump up this Lost Revolution group that's holding a rally here on Thursday."

Murphy said, "I heard that's barely a handful of protesters."

"Right now," Levy replied, "but once she flashes those tits and legs alongside their banner, the whole world will know about it. I'm sorry, Randy, but the numbers have to look consistent until the revisions next year. No one will care by then . . . unless this economy never improves."

Murphy said, "Something has to be done, Mitch, but not about Mary Gannon."

Levy smiled and replied, "Jim, you're taking Randy's side over Obama? So, the rumors about you hitching your wagon to Hayes' Presidential bid are true."

"Those job numbers aren't good for Romney or your Republican brothers either," Murphy snapped. "But maybe you don't mind if Romney loses. You could head the ticket then in 2016."

Levy sat up in his chair and placed his glass on the table. "Okay, Jim, cards up. You're willing to run as Hayes' VP and win or lose because you think you'll preserve the option either way of heading the

Democratic ticket yourself in four years. I'm trying to undo the mess this woman created with the process while keeping you, Randy and the rest of the group happy. For all I know, you had her killed. My point is, don't tell me I'm playing politics!"

Murphy was flustered and intimidated. He didn't come there to pick a fight, at least not until 2016. He slumped his shoulders in a sign of submission and said, "Mitch, I apologize. It's just that Randy and I are both worried these conspiracy claims are gaining traction in the media and the public. It's a real threat to the economy and national security. We have to contain it."

"Apology accepted, Jim," Levy said, then smiled and sat back in his chair, relaxed again. "So, you don't think Gannon is the real problem. I take it you think it's this strategist guy."

Boatman interjected, "Yeah, Dylan Regan. He's feeding Gannon all her material. Patricia was supposed to scare him off, but it hasn't worked. If this guy Regan gets any more attention for his theories, there'll be no fucking confidence left in this country. That'll hurt all of us. And it could push the election to Hayes." Boatman glanced at Murphy and said, "Nothing personal, Jim, but Hayes becoming President would be a disaster for this country."

"Worse than Bush?" Murphy quipped.

Levy said, "Isn't this Regan a Wall Street nobody who can't hit the broad side of a barn with his forecasts? Why's he such a concern?"

"He's very smart and stubborn," Murphy replied. "Without him, Gannon has nothing but her looks. These young people don't believe things are as good as the numbers say. They're buying into Gannon's crap, which is Regan's crap, even if his forecasts suck."

"So, you both want to make sure Regan doesn't bring any more attention to the process, and you both want the admins to refrain from pumping up the job numbers anymore." Levy smiled. "Now that's true bipartisanship . . . but what are you suggesting we do?"

"Use Karl Robson to send Regan a message," Boatman answered.

Levy was quiet for several seconds. He looked at Murphy. "You agree with him, Jim?"

Murphy answered, "Yes, but just to intimidate him. Scare him a little."

Levy rubbed his chin and said, "Mannino and Richards won't go along."

Boatman said, "Who cares what—"

"I'll decide that," Levy snapped, flashing a stern look at Boatman. He glanced at Murphy, then said, "I have to think about this. In the interim, Jim, talk to Patricia again. See if she can do something more. Tell her we spoke."

Levy stood up, signaling the meeting was over. Murphy and Boatman followed suit.

Levy shook Murphy's hand and said, "Jim, thanks for making the trip." He turned to Boatman, shook his hand and said, "We have to trust the admins to manage these numbers, Randy. Don't worry. Romney still has a chance."

CHAPTER 44
Tuesday, May 29, 2012

"HANK STEWART. I have a ten o'clock appointment with Detective Garcia," he said to the female officer behind the visitor's window at the Third District police station in Washington.

She typed something into the computer and then told him to take a seat.

At 10:35 a.m., Garcia opened the door, looked out and said, "Mr. Stewart?"

Stewart followed Garcia to a small conference room in the back. Garcia sat down at a small metal table. Stewart sat down across from him. Garcia said, "I don't have a lot of time, Mr. Stewart. This is a professional courtesy, seeing that you're former NYPD."

"Understood, and thank you," Stewart replied. "I'll be quick. You know I'm looking into Caroline Brenner's murder as part of an investigative series that Mary Gannon is doing." He hoped dropping Mary's name would get him some cooperation.

"She's that reporter with ICIN who does that sexy stuff on the internet. Wow, my daughter worships her." Garcia smiled, seeming to think for a moment.

Stewart said, "So, I'm trying to wrap up a few things, and I was hoping you could help me."

"Well, it's pretty straight forward."

"Could you review it for me?"

Garcia sighed and said, "This guy, Darryl Dwyer, targeted Ms. Brenner to rob her. It went bad, she got away, and he ran her down out of anger. Dwyer stole the vehicle. Long rap sheet. Then he gets drunk and drives off the road into a tree. He had her cell phone and a blade with specks of blood that matched Ms. Brenner's . . . Why is Ms. Gannon doing a story on this?"

"She was friends with Caroline Brenner. She wants to make sure the family has all the information. Anything you can share before the ME's report comes out?"

"Celebrities," Garcia muttered. "No. You'll have to wait for the report like everyone else. It should be quick, though. Another friend of hers is using some influence to speed it up."

Stewart nodded and asked, "Does Dwyer have any family I can speak with?"

"You know I'm not supposed to give that out. But you're going to find it anyways, so I'll make it easy for you." Garcia gave him the names of Dwyer's brother and estranged wife but wouldn't share their contact information. He said they both lived in Washington.

Stewart asked, "Where did Dwyer live?"

"A flop house off Rhode Island Avenue."

"Where'd he work?"

"He didn't," Garcia said. "He was on disability, for depression."

"Was he on medication?"

"Yeah, supposedly standard stuff, but toxicology hasn't come back yet. His brother checked in on him regularly. Talk to him."

"He drank too? Booze and drugs—how'd he drive straight to run someone down?"

"Practice, I assume. He was arrested several times for DUI. Lost his license."

"Why did he need money if he was on disability?"

"Who knows. Don't you want more money? Maybe he thought Ms. Brenner was pretty and that's what happened. We'll never know."

"Where'd he park the vehicle?"

"How do I know? On the street," Garcia replied, getting annoyed. He didn't have good answers, and he clearly didn't like feeling interrogated. "Listen, Stewart, maybe you have to ask all these questions, but it sounds like you're fishing for something. What is it?"

"Okay, Detective. Dwyer doesn't look right for it. He's depressed, not angry, on medication and still drinking, which would pacify him. He steals a car over a month ago and keeps it hidden without any parking tickets. He doesn't have the money to park in a garage or a lot, and he switches around the plates like a professional. No history of stalking or real violence, and he has no connection to the victim. How could a depressed, drunken, petty thief do all that?"

"You left out a few facts," Garcia replied defensively. "Dwyer had her cell phone and the knife he cut her with. And he was in the car that killed her. He lived near her and hung out at a local bar. He's a thief, and he's been arrested for assault before. It makes total sense, unless you're looking for another answer."

Stewart stared at him calmly, knowing Garcia was starting to doubt his own explanation.

Garcia sat back in his chair and tossed his hand in the air. "You've seen these cases before. None of them fit perfectly, because we never know everything. But when evidence is this strong, the perp is the obvious guy. Sensationalize it if you want, but I don't have time for that."

Stewart knew Garcia wasn't going to back down. This was one of hundreds of pending cases, and it had been solved. Why would he want to question that?

Garcia stood up. "That's all I have time for, Stewart. Now, how about a favor for me?"

Stewart stood up and said, "Sure, Detective."

"Can you send me Mary Gannon's autograph for my daughter?"

Stewart said he would and left. His next stop, The Beltway, the bar that Dwyer hung out at. If Dwyer pretty much lived there, someone would know if he was a killer.

The fragrant smell of stale beer and ammonia hit Hank Stewart as he walked into The Beltway a few minutes before noon. He paused to let his eyes adjust from the daylight outside to the dark, dimly lit bar. *Just like old times.*

No one was inside other than the bartender who was stocking beer and listening to Johnny Cash on the radio. Stewart had already walked around the outside a few times, noticing a black BMW 328i in the parking lot in back. He had taken down the plate number.

"What would you like?" the bartender asked. He was in his midtwenties, clean cut, with a slight build.

"Bud," Stewart replied as he leaned on the bar. "Is that your Beamer out back?"

"Yeah, nice, huh?" the bartender answered, clearly proud of his toy. He flipped the cap off of a bottle of Budweiser and put it on the bar in front of Stewart.

"Business must be good," Stewart said, putting ten dollars on the bar and smiling. It was a glaring inconsistency, which was always a good place to start digging.

"Not bad," the bartender said, eyeing Stewart cautiously.

"Name's Hank. What's yours?" Stewart boomed, pretending to be just a talkative customer.

"Tim."

"Tim what?"

"Tim Adams."

"How you doing, Tim? You knew Darryl Dwyer, right?" Stewart asked, still smiling.

Adams stopped what he was doing, surprised by the question. "Who are you?" he asked, moving out of Stewart's reach.

Given his nervousness, Adams probably didn't have a gun behind the bar, Stewart figured, so he smiled and glanced around. They were the only ones in the place. Adams had nowhere to run. And he was small. Cooperation was his only strategy.

Stewart took a drink of beer and said, "Don't worry, I'm not the police. Insurance investigator, just checking on a few things. Was Dwyer here the night he supposedly ran down that woman a few blocks away?"

"I don't know. Reggie worked that night. I already told the police that."

"Reggie have a last name?"

"Rodriguez."

"You must have known Dwyer," Stewart said, taking another swig of beer. "What kind of guy was he?"

"Well, he got crazy sometimes. You know, talking to himself, slamming his fist on the bar."

"Did he ever go after anyone?"

"I never saw him, but he could have. He did with that woman."

"You know something about that?"

"No, no, I don't . . . But the police said he did, so he must have, right?"

Stewart sensed Adams was holding back, but he wasn't going to get any further unless he threatened him, and it was too soon to do that. "When does Reggie work next?"

"Friday night."

"Does he drive a Beamer?" Stewart asked sarcastically.

"Uh, no. Hyundai, I think."

Stewart left the ten dollars for his half bottle of beer and left.

A light rain was coming down as Stewart climbed into his car. He took out his notebook and wrote down the names of the two bartenders. It would be easy enough to check on how Adams financed the BMW. His twenty-five years of questioning scumbags told him something didn't smell right, and it wasn't the beer and ammonia. They actually smelled good.

CHAPTER 45
Tuesday, May 29, 2012

THE BEER Bar was mostly empty early Tuesday evening when Dylan stepped inside, soaked from the torrential downpours, his small umbrella mutilated. He looked around. Tom Sygowski wasn't there yet. He asked the host for a table in the far corner.

Dylan had sent Sygowski a Bloomberg message this morning, and they had agreed to meet for a beer. Walter Vaughn called him shortly after and left a message about getting together to discuss the opportunity at Baker Cohen. He hadn't called Vaughn back yet. He didn't know Vaughn, how smart he was, whether he was a crook or a cheat—they were different—or whether he could be manipulated to give up information. But he knew Sygowski, and he knew he could get something out of him.

"Chianti or Sam Adams?" a familiar voice said.

Dylan looked up and saw Lina. "Hi . . . Sam Adams, please."

"You're a little wet. Want a towel?"

"No, that's okay. I like the rain."

"Me too," she said, smiled and left to get his beer.

He took out his Blackberry and dialed Brad. It went immediately into his voicemail.

"Hey Brad, it's me again. You really need to call me back. Shannon Dunn called me and said she has Caroline's laptop. She was going to drop it off at my place yesterday, but she never showed. I've called her several times, but I haven't heard back. I think she got cold feet, but maybe you can talk to her. Please call me."

He hung up as Lina delivered his beer. "Thank you," he said. Then his Blackberry rang.

She smiled and left.

"Hello?" he answered.

"Dylan, it's Atul."

"Hey Atul, how was your holiday?"

"Very good. I was in the Hamptons at my house. You should come out one weekend."

"I might take you up on that."

"Promises, promises. Anyway, I tracked down that information on Differential for you."

"Great. What did you find?"

"First, all their funds are down big this year. They have apparently been whipsawed the past few months, which has led to lots of client redemptions from their main fund. It's a bit surprising since they did quite well last year and brought in a lot of new money as a result. But that was after a mediocre 2010 and a very bad '08 and '09."

"That's interesting," Dylan said. "Any insight on what's going on there?"

"Just rumblings about possible key people defecting, but nothing definitive. I'm waiting on another contact to get back to me. I'll let you know if I hear anything else."

"Thanks, Atul. I really appreciate it."

"My pleasure. Now, second, I need a small favor."

"Sure, what is it?"

"I need to find out more about SCT, the solar panel manufacturer. I made a bet against their bonds a couple of weeks ago—sold a bunch of protection—and I'm getting killed."

"That's a weird coincidence. I'm looking into SCT right now. From what I can tell, the company should be in bankruptcy. So, the recent run-up in the stock and bonds is either technical or some positive news is leaking out to the market. I should know more this week. I'll give you a call when I do."

"Thank you, but please hurry before I lose my shirt. Or worse, my BMW. Cheers," Atul said and hung up.

Dylan put his Blackberry down and took a drink of beer. Then he saw Sygowski walk in holding a large umbrella with the Merrill Lynch logo on it. Sygowski shook himself off like a big dog, then waved to him and headed over to the table.

"Bro, the world's coming to an end out there." Sygowski shook his hand and slapped him on the back. "So, how's it going?"

Lina walked over quickly to take Sygowski's order. He grinned and asked for a Budweiser as his eyes rolled over her.

"Thanks for making it," Dylan replied.

Lina returned quickly with Sygowski's beer and a couple of menus. She caught Dylan's eyes briefly and left. Sygowski nodded his approval to him. "Man, I was shitfaced the other night," he blurted as he took a swig of beer. "I don't remember half of what I said to you."

Dylan knew Sygowski remembered everything. "Don't worry about it," he said. "You didn't say anything bad. You were just frustrated that Differential wasn't doing any business with you. You said it was because of me."

"Yeah, it was just frustration," Sygowski said and lifted his bottle in salute.

"But we both know it's true," Dylan replied and smiled knowingly. "That's why we're here, right? To see if there's an opportunity for us to work together again, like Merrill."

"Yeah, that's right, like Merrill. Hey, Vaughn really wants to talk to you about the strategist position we're looking to fill." Sygowski paused and eyed him. "You said it's true about why Differential's doing business with you instead of me. So, you are working with Blair?"

Dylan wasn't sure what "working with Blair" meant, but he had Sygowski nibbling. He said, "Yeah, I just couldn't talk about it there at the bar. I don't know Vaughn."

"I got you, bro. I shouldn't have put you on the spot," Sygowski said, his excitement seeping out. He took a big gulp of beer. "So, did you know Ben Thompson?"

"Yeah, but not well. Kind of a jerk. I met him once, through Caroline Brenner." He wanted to see how Sygowski would react to her name.

"Yeah, yeah, Caroline Brenner. I couldn't remember her name the other night," Sygowski said and finished his beer. "She's how you got in with Blair, isn't she?"

"Sort of," Dylan answered to cover for the fact that he didn't know what Sygowski meant. "She introduced me to Peter Zimmer. I'm working with him now. Do you know him?"

"Peter Zimmer?" Sygowski repeated. "No, but I've heard his name. He was Thompson's boss, right?"

"Yeah, then Caroline's after Thompson died."

"I didn't know he was part of this. But that makes sense. Wow, the head guy." Sygowski waved to Lina for two more beers.

Dylan wanted to ask, "Part of what?", but if he really was working with Zimmer and Armstrong, then he was supposed to already know. Innocuous was better, he decided. "Zimmer's not the head guy. He's just an Associate Commissioner at the BLS."

"Okay, but still, if you're working with him, Blair must love you."

"I don't know if she loves me, but she's trying to hire me."

Sygowski's eyes widened. "Fuck! Blair's trying to hire you? That's smart. She's fucking smart. That would suck for me. Man, I thought we were going to work together again?"

Sygowski was hooked. But Dylan still had to figure out what they were really talking about before Sygowski realized he was lying. He had a guess, but he had to be careful. If he was wrong, he'd expose himself.

They both stopped talking as Lina delivered their beers.

After she left, Dylan said, "Listen, Tom, I'm here because I'm interested in working with you, not Blair. I trust you. I don't think I can trust her." He paused. Now he would see if his theory was true. "Peter isn't crazy about Blair either. And he'd prefer me to stay on the sellside so he can be flexible about who he shares the data with."

Dylan waited for what seemed like an hour, trying not to appear too eager, looking to see if Sygowski was skeptical or surprised or confused at anything he'd just said. None of them. He was excited and stared at Dylan like he had just been given the keys to Fort Knox.

"That's awesome!" Sygowski exclaimed and guzzled most of his beer. "Vaughn's going to want to get you onboard right away. Fuck FTS, bro. We're back in business."

Dylan was stunned. Maybe Sygowski misunderstood him. He said, "Whoa, slow down, Tom. I need to know a few things before I share anything with Vaughn, or even you. I have to be really careful."

Sygowski gulped some more beer and said, "I understand, Dylan. Me too."

"Okay, just out of curiosity, when was the last time Thompson gave you the data to give to Blair?" If Sygowski answered the way Dylan expected, his theory would be confirmed.

"The November report last year, just before he croaked."

It's true. Unbelievable! Ben Thompson had been leaking the most important economic data in the world—the U.S. employment report—through the slimy fingers of Tom Sygowski and Walter Vaughn to the dirty hands of Blair Armstrong, who was presumably using it to make billions trading anything from bonds to stocks to commodities to foreign exchange. Knowing what was in the U.S. employment report ahead of everyone else would enable you to make a successful bet on just about any market in the world.

Dylan wanted to let his mouth drop, but he just nodded, as if it all made sense. He glanced around the still mostly empty bar, a wave of paranoia sweeping through his mind and body. This must be when a bullet pierces his head and everything goes blank, or when Sygowski bursts out laughing at his gullibility, or when he wakes up. Nothing.

"Okay," Dylan said, "but Peter hasn't told me anything about how you guys worked with Thompson and Blair. I have to know everything if I'm going to join you guys."

Sygowski suddenly looked worried. The hook was coming loose.

Dylan added, "Hey, if you're not going to tell me everything, I'll just go to Blair—"

"Hold on, bro," Sygowski interrupted. "Keep your Irish down. It's just that Vaughn wants to talk to you about everything first. You know, make sure we're not being set up. He'll kill me if he finds out I told you anything." Sygowski downed the rest of his beer and signaled to Lina for two more.

"Me setting you up?" Dylan replied in consternation. "I've got the data, not you guys."

"I know that," Sygowski said, "but Vaughn doesn't trust anyone. He's smart, but it makes him paranoid sometimes."

"Listen, if I join Baker Cohen, then you and I are a team. Vaughn won't mess with us."

Lina delivered their beers, taking away Dylan's half full bottle.

"I like that," Sygowski said and tapped his bottle with Dylan's in a toast.

Dylan took a drink of his beer, then stared at Sygowski and said, "But I have to know everything, Tom."

Sygowski nodded, took a swig of beer and leaned over the table. He said in a hushed voice, "It started back at the end of 2010. Vaughn came to me and asked how I would monetize getting an early look at the jobs number every now and then. At first I thought it was a setup, and I told him to fuck off. But when I realized he was serious, I knew he'd just find someone else, so why not me. He knew Thompson from when they both worked together as bond traders in the old days. Vaughn said Thompson came up with the idea himself, but I don't really buy that. Now that I know about Peter Zimmer, I'm guessing he was the brains behind it."

"Probably," Dylan said. "So, how did Blair get involved?"

"I brought her in, to make it harder to detect that we were using the data. I was afraid we'd get caught if we tried using it directly ourselves to trade."

"Why her?"

"We worked together at Morgan Stanley before I jumped to Merrill," Sygowski answered. "I knew Differential got hammered during the crisis and was maybe going to go under. I figured she'd be receptive to an arrangement. She bit right away and agreed to do all the trading through our desk at Baker Cohen, mostly me. Boy, she was aggressive too."

Dylan was mildly impressed. Sygowski wasn't a genius, but he wasn't stupid either, despite the bumbling trader act he put on. "Why did Vaughn include you? Why not set it up himself?"

"Vaughn's a pussy," Sygowski said. "He didn't wanna get his hands dirty. So, I set it up with Blair, and he told Thompson to communicate with me when he had the data."

"How did that work?"

"Well, Thompson would send me a Bloomberg message asking how gaming bonds were doing as a signal. Then we'd go back and forth with messages that had the jobs information embedded as credit spread quotes on corporate bonds. I went down to Washington and worked it all out with him at the beginning. That's the only time I met him. He was a big, fat dude. Fatter than me, but pretty smart."

"How did you get the information to Armstrong?"

"Same way. She made me work through Rick Jones, though. Making money was easy after that, especially since Thompson seemed to know the best months to give us the data."

"He didn't give you the data every month?" Dylan asked.

"No, only five times last year, and a couple at the end of 2010. How often are you getting it?" Sygowski asked, seeming a little suspicious.

"Every month," Dylan answered.

"Really? That's awesome, man."

"What did you mean by Thompson knew the best months to give you the data?"

Sygowski replied, "Yeah, it was uncanny. Whenever he shared the jobs data, it always came in way above consensus and really surprised the markets. We made a ton of money every time. It turned things around for Blair. Differential's been sucking wind this year without it."

"So, Thompson only gave you the jobs number?"

"Yeah," Sygowski answered. "What is Zimmer giving you?"

"I'm getting the unemployment rate too."

"Fuck, the unemployment rate too?" Sygowski remarked in awe, then checked around to make sure no one was listening. He chugged most of his beer, belched and ordered two more.

"How'd you pay Thompson?" Dylan asked.

"Cash. We'd meet at one of the Atlantic City casinos after he gave me information. It's good cover for carrying lots of cash. The IRS doesn't track gambling stuff very good. It was only about half a million all in. He could have made a lot more, but he didn't know what real money was . . . and then he fucking croaked. Screwed me royally."

"What an asshole," Dylan quipped and took a sip of beer.

Sygowski grinned, finished his beer and replied, "A dead asshole."

Dylan smiled back. "So, how'd you know I was friends with Caroline?"

"Thompson told Vaughn that she talked to you all the time. Right before he died, he said he needed a bigger payout because he had to pay her now. Vaughn was pissed, but he did it."

Dylan knew Caroline would never be involved. Thompson must have been using her name to get more money out of the deal. He said, "Caroline mentioned something about that."

Sygowski laughed. "Anyway, after Thompson died, Vaughn assumed she was giving you the look instead of us. I told him I knew you, but he wouldn't let me call you. He was too nervous. Then when Blair didn't do any business with us for months, he told me to reach out to you. That's why I've been calling."

"How did Armstrong know to contact me?"

"She didn't tell you?" Sygowski asked.

"No. She just invited me to dinner a couple of times and eventually brought up Caroline."

"What a sneaky bitch," Sygowski said. "Well, after Thompson died, I told her Caroline was the man and that she was friends with you. I said I knew you and could probably set up a conversation. I thought she might start doing business with me again. Now I know why she didn't. She had her own plan."

Dylan took a gulp of beer to think. If Sygowski and Vaughn thought Caroline was part of the data leaking arrangement, why kill her? Same for Armstrong. Unless Caroline had somehow figured out what Thompson had been doing and was going to expose it. Maybe that was the problem she needed Brad's help with.

Lina delivered two more beers. Dylan smiled and handed her his half full bottle.

Sygowski gulped some beer and asked, "So, what setup do you have with Zimmer?"

Dylan replied, "I'm not going to share those details until I have an agreement with Vaughn."

"Hey, bro, I just told you everything—"

"I'm the one with something to lose here, Tom. Not you."

"Alright, I understand," Sygowski replied. "Then you better meet with Vaughn right away. We gotta get this thing going again."

"I'll talk to him tomorrow," Dylan said. He thought for a moment, then asked, "So, did you ever approach Caroline about working with you like Thompson?"

"I did," Sygowski answered. "Didn't she say anything to you?"

"No, but she probably didn't know we're friends."

"Yeah, I should have mentioned your name. Anyway, she acted like she didn't know what I was talking about or who I was. Fucking Vaughn went ballistic when I told him I asked her."

Dylan's head suddenly felt like it might explode. Sygowski had told him more than he could process while drinking. He needed time to think. He signaled to Lina for the check.

"Where you going, man? I thought we'd eat and talk some more?" Sygowski said.

"Sorry, Tom. I have a long day tomorrow. But this was really good. I'll call Vaughn in the morning. And I'll stall Armstrong until I know I'm joining Baker Cohen. Okay?"

Sygowski's face brightened. It was the same response as four years ago with Lehman, Dylan realized. Sygowski insisted on paying this time too.

The rain had stopped, Dylan noticed as he walked to the door to leave. Lina was waiting with his broken umbrella.

She said, "Call me next time it rains. I'll go walking with you." She smiled. It was real.

He wanted to stay and talk to her. He wanted to take the job with MQA. He wanted to know what was wrong with the data. He wanted to figure out who murdered Caroline. And he wanted to understand why his life seemed so fucked up all at once. But he didn't want to get killed in the process, and the information he now had might just do that.

"I will," he said and left. He looked both ways as he crossed Vanderbilt to grab a taxi.

CHAPTER 46
Wednesday, May 30, 2012

THIS WAS the site of their second date, Brad remembered, because their first one had been so bad. He had taken Caroline out to a Vietnamese restaurant on their first date, and everything that could go wrong did go wrong. But she had laughed—the easy, beautiful laugh he fell in love with. She agreed to meet him for a less ambitious date the next morning here at The C&T House, a gourmet coffee and tea shop on G Street. He could see her sitting across from him now, her blond hair shimmering in the early sun, sipping a cup of Lapsang tea, her favorite because it was sweeter than most black teas.

A low voice called his name, startling him. He looked quickly over his shoulder. It was Hank Stewart. They had agreed to meet at nine this morning.

"Sorry about that," Stewart said. "I came in the back way, like you asked. No one followed me. Nice place."

"It is," Brad said. "Caroline loved their tea. How do you know?"

Stewart sat down, holding a small plastic bag in his hand. "How do I know what?"

"How do you know no one followed you?"

Stewart smiled and handed him the bag. "I've done this before. Here, this is for you."

"What is it?"

"A surveillance detection device to check if there's a tracking bug on your car, or anything in your apartment. If you're being followed, your car's probably bugged. Directions are inside."

"Thanks," Brad said. "I was going to buy one myself. Want some coffee?"

"Sure, black."

Brad went to the counter and ordered two black coffees. He eyed everyone in the shop as he carried two steaming cups of coffee back to the table and sat down.

"You're a project manager with the Federal Reserve, right?" Stewart asked.

"Yes. Why?"

"You handle yourself differently than a government bureaucrat." Stewart took a sip of his coffee. "Don't get me wrong. That's a good thing."

Brad ignored the comment. "You said you had some information."

"I do," Stewart replied, "but first, have you talked to Dylan today?"

"No. Why?"

"He left me a voice message this morning. He met with that bond trader, Tom Sygowski, last night. He thinks he found out what was going on at the BLS, the problem that Caroline wanted your help with."

Brad's eyes widened. He put down his coffee and asked, "What was it?"

"It sounds like she uncovered an insider trading scheme using the employment data."

"What?" Brad exclaimed. "I have to talk to Dylan."

"Do you want to hear what I found out on Dwyer first?" Stewart asked.

Brad hesitated, then said, "Okay, go ahead."

Stewart recounted his conversation with Garcia. Then he added, "I also spoke with Dwyer's brother and wife. They both said he was bipolar and on medication. His condition deteriorated last year after he was laid off as a janitor. That's why his wife left him. She said he was rough with her a few times but nothing serious. But she hadn't seen him in six months. Dwyer was on disability, which brought money in. His brother checked on him once a week. He was adamant that Dwyer couldn't have killed anyone in his condition, never mind stolen a car."

Stewart then told Brad about Tim Adams and Reggie Rodriguez, the two bartenders at The Beltway. He had checked on Adams and learned that he recently bought a used BMW for $30,000, paying $10,000 in cash and financing the rest, an extravagant purchase for a bartender.

"That's a lot of tips," Stewart remarked. "Something smells there to me."

Brad asked, "You think Adams had something to do with Dwyer's death?"

"I think he knows something. I'm coming back down here on Friday to try to talk to this Rodriguez. I'll have a better read after that and decide how to get Adams to talk."

Brad sat silent, thinking for a while. Then he stood up and said, "Thanks, Hank. I need to talk to Dylan now." He paused. "You never told me if you saw anyone following me Saturday."

"I didn't see anyone, but there was a lot of traffic, so there's no way to be sure."

Brad nodded, grabbed the small plastic bag, and walked out quickly. He started to head back to his office but turned and went to the Metro station nearby. He rode it to the stop near his apartment, got off and went to the paid lot where he parked his car. He turned on the surveillance detection device Stewart had given him and scanned his car.

The device started beeping . . .

CHAPTER 47
Wednesday, May 30, 2012

BLAIR ARMSTRONG might be more than just another hedge fund manager in search of an information advantage, Dylan worried as he waited for her late Wednesday morning—she might also be a murderer. And she was late, again.

Her assistant had called this morning to tell him Armstrong wanted to meet at Cucina, a bistro in the MetLife building, at ten o'clock sharp. Rick Jones had never called last week to set up a meeting between the three of them as she said he would, so he wasn't sure what this meeting was about.

Cucina was quiet and empty, he noted as he took a sip of coffee— burnt, bitter European style, with milk, no half and half. What was the point? Just watered down espresso.

He took out his Blackberry to check his messages. Walter Vaughn had sent him a text, following up on a voice message from earlier this morning. Sygowski had obviously told him about their meeting last night. But he didn't want to talk to Vaughn until he had a plan. Vaughn was smarter than Sygowski and might figure out he was lying about Zimmer and Armstrong.

Dylan took another sip of coffee, cringed at the taste, and started to think about leaving when Armstrong entered the restaurant, dismissed the hostess and walked over to his table. She wore a stylish black suit consisting of a short jacket and knee-length skirt. Her violet blouse was opened at the neck to display an ostentatious silver necklace he assumed was real.

She had told him she was frugal and unpretentious. She had told him she was honest. She had told him she was always early. Maybe she was there to tell him she wasn't a murderer.

Armstrong sat down without offering an apology for being late. She ordered an iced tea from the waitress, then turned to him and said, "It's good to see you, Dylan. The markets are volatile today, so I can't stay long."

He nodded and said, "I understand."

"I'm surprised you could get away," she said. "It'll be different when you're working for me. Speaking of which, Rick Jones is traveling this week, which is why the three of us couldn't meet. That's why I'm taking the time to meet with you today—so you know I still want you to join us as soon as possible. We'll finalize your offer when Rick returns on Friday."

Armstrong was stalling, Dylan realized, stringing him along to believe he'd be given an offer any day but intentionally delaying it. But why, if she really wanted him?

Just then, his Blackberry rang. He pulled it out and glanced at it. It was Brad. Bad timing. He sent it to his voicemail.

"Nothing to say?" Armstrong remarked, her clear, green eyes staring at him expectantly.

He was about to respond when his Blackberry rang again, startling him. This time it was MG. He sent it to his voice mail.

Armstrong pressed her lips together and glared at him, signaling her displeasure with the interruptions.

Dylan turned his Blackberry off and put it on the table. He stared back at her, his mind racing. He decided to take a risk. "I talked to Peter Zimmer."

A slight wry smile appeared and she said, "I thought you barely knew him."

"I thought you were always early," he quipped.

She snorted a laugh and then narrowed her eyes in a mixture of suspicion and skepticism. She asked, "What did he say?"

"He said he'll support whoever I decide to go with."

She leaned forward, focusing on his eyes. "You're talking with someone else?"

Dylan nodded slightly.

The waitress stopped by to see if they wanted to order any food.

"Not now," Armstrong snapped without looking at her.

The waitress hesitated, as if she might respond, but then left in a huff.

Armstrong sat back, her jaw clenched, and continued to glare at him. After a long silence, she said in a guttural voice, her lips barely moving, "It's MQA, isn't it? You've been working with them all along."

The accusation surprised Dylan. Billy McDonald was probably bragging to everyone about the business FTS was doing with MQA. But her response also revealed something—she wasn't working with Zimmer. If she was, she wouldn't be accusing him of working with Zimmer to feed the data to MQA. That was why she wanted to hire him. She thought he could deliver Zimmer and the data. But he could tell she wasn't completely sure. And she wasn't going to take the chance on hiring him until she was.

"I'm not working with MQA. It's too big and too visible," he said and paused. "But I hear you know Tom Sygowski."

Armstrong seemed to relax, the wry smile returning. She replied, "Baker Cohen? It's a second tier firm, Dylan, barely a step up from FTS, and a dead end for anyone with your talent. And you're too smart to trust either Walter Vaughn or Tom Sygowski. You don't even trust me yet. But that's good. I don't trust you yet either. Exciting, don't you think?"

"In a strange way, I suppose . . . but I need to be able to trust you."

Her smile vanished. "You say you're not working with MQA, but now they're doing lots of business with FTS, a firm they shouldn't let shine their shoes. And at the same time, you're flirting with Baker Cohen, as well as me . . . I know what's going on, Dylan."

His body tensed, but he didn't respond.

She said, "You're still trying to figure out who to work with, aren't you? You can trust me. You know that, right?"

He loosened the grip on the spoon he was squeezing. She thought he was shopping himself around to find the best bid for the data, he realized. He wanted her to think she was right. "I need to see an offer," he said. "Then I'll decide who I can trust."

She tapped her fingers rhythmically on the table for several seconds, then said, "I like you, Dylan. I see our relationship going far. We can probably finalize this process quickly by setting up a meeting between you, me and Peter."

"Peter trusts me," he replied. "He doesn't want to meet with anyone."

Armstrong suddenly seemed annoyed. She leaned forward again. "If you want an offer, but you won't arrange for me to meet with Peter, then I need a gesture of good faith—a confirmation of your relationship with him."

She wanted this Friday's jobs number, he knew—proof that he could get the data. He had to keep her believing. He said, "Alright. If you read my last strategy note, you know I'm expecting ten thousand new jobs for May. But I really expect some combination of a large loss of jobs in May and a downward revision to April that will erase about 400,000 jobs combined." He paused. "That'll have to be enough good faith."

Armstrong's eyes widened for a moment and she started to smile but refrained and pursed her lips instead. "If you're right, I'll contact you Friday afternoon to discuss the details of your offer. I have to go to another meeting now. I'm excited, Dylan. You'll like working for me."

As she stood up, Dylan said, "I'm surprised you never mentioned Caroline Brenner."

She paused, stared blankly at him and said, "Why would I? She's dead."

She walked quickly out of Cucina. He thought he could still hear her Gucci or Givenchy or whatever expensive heels she was wearing click determinedly on the marble tiles of the MetLife lobby long after she disappeared. He asked the waitress for the check, then took out his Blackberry and turned it on. A text message was waiting from MG, along with two voicemails, which he assumed were from her and Brad.

The message read: "Shannon Dunn is dead. Call me. Mg"

CHAPTER 48
Wednesday, May 30, 2012

A STRONG, anxious breeze blew through Bryant Park behind the New York Public Library as Dylan walked towards MG. She was sitting at a round table under an umbrella, her long, shapely legs angled but still flowing from a short, white linen skirt—familiar beacons, even masked by the metal table.

Two hot dogs and two cans of Coke sat waiting in front of her. They had agreed to meet there at one o'clock. Grayish-white cumulus clouds hurried across the sky, and a few drops of rain fell every now and then as the sun struggled to stay in control.

"Ketchup and relish, right?" Mary said and pushed a hot dog and a Coke towards him as he sat down.

"Yeah, thanks, but I'm not hungry," he replied, then opened the Coke and took a sip.

"I took a chance," she said and smiled. "You used to get this all the time when we met here for lunch."

"You remembered," he said, forcing a smile. "Sorry, it's just Shannon Dunn . . . You said you had some new information."

"I do. So, no one in the subway station saw her pushed onto the tracks, not even the driver of the train, but—"

"Then how do the police know she was pushed?" he interrupted.

"I'm getting there. I talked to one of the officers on the case. Apparently, the conductor said he looked up and suddenly saw her coming towards him. He said her body was turned sideways, and she was flailing her arms like someone had thrown her—his words."

"I know she didn't jump," Dylan said, "but do they have anything else that points to someone pushing her instead of an accident?"

"No, but the turnstile camera showed two men leaving immediately after Shannon was hit by the train. Of course, everyone eventually left because the line was shut down for three hours, but these two were conspicuous by their timing."

"Did the camera catch their faces?"

"No, but one of them—a tall, grungy white guy with a black stocking hat pulled down close to his eyes—he was carrying a small suitcase that looked like the one Shannon had brought into the station. A couple of people also noticed him because he looked so strange carrying it. The other one was a shorter, stocky white man in a black leather jacket and a baseball cap."

"What are the police thinking?" Dylan asked.

"Well, they think this tall guy tried to steal her suitcase and they either struggled and she fell or he pushed her onto the tracks. Based on his appearance, they think he's probably homeless. They're trying to see if anyone recognizes his profile around the neighborhood."

"What about the other guy? He fits the description of the man who attacked Brad at Caroline's apartment."

"The police don't think he had anything to do with it," Mary replied. "Besides, that was in Washington. There are a million guys who fit that description here in New York."

"But there's only one place that Shannon was pushed in front of a train the day before she was going to give me Caroline's laptop, along with a disk full of data with my name on it."

"What?" Mary exclaimed.

"I told Brad all this. I thought you talked to him."

"Just early this morning when I first heard about Shannon. I've been scrambling to get ready for this Lost Revolution rally I'm covering in D.C. tomorrow. So, what's this about Caroline's laptop?"

Dylan went through his phone call with Shannon Dunn and then his meetings with Tom Sygowski and Blair Armstrong. He finished and said, "If Caroline did discover Thompson's data leaking arrangement, I know she would have tried to expose it. That was probably the problem she wanted Brad's help with. And I bet there was something about it on her laptop." He thought for a moment, then added, "I don't believe a homeless person killed Shannon."

Mary stared at him in consternation, her mind racing. She said, "That's incredible. So, you think someone followed Shannon and pushed her onto the tracks to get Caroline's laptop? But why kill her? Why not just steal it?"

"I don't know, and I don't know how anyone else even knew about Caroline's laptop or that Shannon had it."

Mary said, "Maybe it was someone involved with leaking the data."

"That seems obvious," Dylan said, "but I have trouble picturing Sygowski as a murderer. But him, Vaughn, Armstrong, and even Rick Jones all have a strong motive if Caroline really was going to expose their insider trading arrangement. My bet's on Armstrong."

Mary was silent as she organized in her head everything Dylan had told her. She finally said, "But there doesn't seem to be any proof that Peter Zimmer's involved."

"You're right. Only his connection to Caroline and Shannon. But that's too much of a coincidence for me." He paused as he contemplated another possibility. He shook his head and said, "Anyway, right now, there's no proof that Zimmer knows anything. And I don't know where he'd get the money to hire someone to kill Caroline and Shannon."

"Don't forget Darryl Dwyer."

Dylan nodded and said, "A lot of money and a lot of planning for a BLS employee."

She nodded back, then asked, "Did Hank tell you what he found out about Dwyer?"

"Brad did. It looks like he was right. Dwyer couldn't have killed Caroline. But if Brad's right and I'm right, that makes three murders, probably by the same person."

Mary pondered for a moment, then asked, "Do you think you should tell the police that you were on the phone with Shannon just before she was killed?"

"I'm surprised they haven't tracked me down already from her cell phone."

"It wasn't on her, or any identification," Mary said. "That's why it took the police so long to figure out who she was. They think Shannon was headed to her sister's, who was apparently away for the weekend. When she returned Monday, she realized Shannon had never showed up. So, she reported her missing. The police are assuming Shannon's purse was also stolen."

"But the camera didn't show the tall homeless guy with her purse, right?"

"No," Mary replied. "What are you getting at?"

"Well, maybe the other guy on the camera had it. Maybe the two men were together."

Mary nodded and said, "It's possible. So, are you going to talk to the police?"

Dylan shook his head. "I have to talk to Brad again first."

"Why?"

"Because I want to let him know that I think Shannon was murdered. He knew I suspected it, but after what you've told me, I'm convinced. I want to see if he thinks Detective Garcia will listen to us now. And . . ."

"And what?" Mary asked.

"And I promised to help him find Caroline's killer. It's his call how we handle this."

It was a little after five o'clock when the cleaning lady appeared and startled him. As Dylan watched her empty the trash can at the next desk, he realized that a Hispanic ninja cleaning lady made no sense. She was probably FBI, maybe CIA.

He wanted to leave and go work out, sweat all the poison thoughts and images of the past two days out of his body, at least temporarily, but he was waiting for Brad to call him back.

His Blackberry rang. It wasn't Brad. "Hello, it's Dylan . . ."

"Hello, Mr. Regan, this is Donald Granger's assistant."

"Oh, hello. How are you?"

"I am well, thank you. Mr. Granger would like to invite you to an early dinner at his home in Greenwich tomorrow evening. Are you available?"

"Yes. I'll make myself available."

"A car will pick you up at four o'clock at your office. Goodbye," she said and hung up.

He sat back in his chair, wondering why Granger wanted to meet. He was a little anxious. No one from MQA had called him yet to initiate a formal hiring process. Had Granger changed his mind? No. Why invite someone to dinner at your home to reject him? But—

His Blackberry rang again. This time it was Brad.

"Hey Brad . . ."

"Hello Dylan. Sorry for taking so long to call back. I'm swamped here at the office with the *Flow of Funds Report* going out in a week."

"Don't worry about it. Do you have time now?"

"Yes, but Dylan, aren't you starting a new job in a week? You don't really have time for this. You've helped enough already."

"Let me worry about that. I have some time still."

"I don't want you sacrificing—"

"Brad, I said I'd help, and that's what I'm going to do." He took a deep breath. "Sorry. Listen, I need to do this."

Brad was quiet for a few seconds, then he said, "Alright, for now."

"Okay, I got some more details on Shannon's death from MG. I'm convinced now that she was murdered trying to get me Caroline's laptop and whatever data was on that flash drive."

"What details?" Brad asked.

Dylan shared what Mary had told him. When he was done, he said, "Shannon told me that Caroline was paranoid about the phones at work just before she was killed, even her own cell phone. Maybe she suspected someone was listening, that they were being tapped."

"Which is how someone would know that Shannon had Caroline's laptop," Brad said. "Shannon probably talked to her sister about everything over her work phone when she was arranging her trip up there."

"That's my guess," Dylan said. "But it doesn't explain how someone would know that Caroline's laptop had incriminating information on it, assuming it did. It didn't sound like Shannon knew when she talked to me. And I suspect Caroline would have had it password protected so no one could get in."

"She always did," Brad said. "Then how did this guy, or these guys, in the subway know to go after her laptop?"

Dylan was silent for a while. He finally answered, "I don't know. Maybe she mentioned to her sister that you wanted it and whoever was listening assumed it had to be important."

"Someone assumed that if I wanted it, it was important enough to kill for? That's an aggressive assumption."

"How else would someone know about it?"

Brad asked, "Could Peter Zimmer be involved?"

"If the phones at the BLS are really being tapped, then there's a decent chance he is. But so far, nothing points to him."

Brad didn't respond.

After a long silence, Dylan asked, "You okay?"

"So, Shannon probably died because of me too," Brad said.

"That's not true, Brad. And you had nothing to do with Caroline's murder."

After another long silence, Brad said, "What's next?"

"This is getting scary. Three murders, all probably tied to the most important economic data in the world being leaked. We really need to go to the police."

"But we can't prove anything," Brad countered.

"That's the problem," Dylan said. "All we have is speculation and second hand information from a sellside bond trader who will deny everything. They'll dismiss me as trying to get attention and you as crazy with grief. And the SEC would crucify me for making such a provocative claim without evidence, especially if it got into the media."

"You can't take that risk," Brad said.

"Not if I want to stay employed, or move to this other opportunity," Dylan replied. "Do you think Shannon's death will sway Detective Garcia if we talk to him again?"

"Hank didn't get anywhere with him on Dwyer," Brad said. "I doubt he'll view Shannon's death or any of the rest of the innuendo we've uncovered as relevant. He's convinced they've solved Caroline's murder."

"What about asking Hank to approach the NYPD with what we have?" Dylan asked. "He'd probably have a better chance of getting someone there to listen to us. And it might spur the D.C. police investigation along too."

"That's worth a shot," Brad said. "Or we could go to the FBI."

"I don't trust them," Dylan shot back. "They're involved somehow."

"In Caroline's murder?" Brad replied. "Dylan, you're letting your paranoia contaminate your judgment on this. We have to stay focused on finding who killed her, not your . . ."

"Not my paranoid conspiracy theory?" Dylan finished for him. "The FBI is involved, Brad. I'm certain. I just don't know how yet."

"Fine, if you want to believe that, but I don't have time to go there with you," Brad replied, clearly angry. "I'm going to try Detective Garcia again. You can ask Hank about the NYPD. But listen, if there really have been three murders around this insider trading scheme, I don't see how we avoid going to the FBI at some point very soon."

"I'm telling you, there's something else going on here," Dylan said. "But if we can't figure it out soon, then I'll go to the FBI myself. The most important thing right now is not to be—"

"Killed?" Brad finished for him.

"Careless," Dylan corrected him and then sighed. "I don't know why whoever's behind this hasn't come after you, *or me*, but we can't assume things won't change. And we can't afford to be wrong. Be careful, Brad. I'll talk to you soon."

CHAPTER 49
Thursday, May 31, 2012

SHE WAS sitting on the far side of the round meeting table scrolling through messages on her cell phone when Senator Murphy opened the door of the small conference room.

"Good morning, Patricia," Senator Murphy said.

She looked up, her intense, glassy blue eyes processing him quickly. "Just you today?"

"Just me," Murphy replied, then closed the door and sat down.

"I told you the last time these meetings aren't a good idea. So, what is it now?"

"Yes, why waste time with pleasantries?" Murphy quipped. "But I do know the Director had a talk with you about the importance of cooperation in your role . . ."

She just stared at him, calm and unemotional.

Murphy said, "Patricia, there's no reason we can't be cordial and professional about all this. We both want what's best for this country."

She continued to stare at him without responding.

"Okay then. First, that wasn't much of an update from the Bureau of Industry and Security. They told us what we already knew. Have you figured out how that number got released and what that woman was trying to do?"

"Senator, this situation has never happened before, and updates are rare for a reason. You got the same information as everyone else. As for the economist, we suspect she was a disgruntled employee trying to make her boss look bad. She was apparently exceptional with technology and seemed to have figured out some weaknesses in the BLS's systems."

"I need to know this isn't going to happen again. There are consequences."

She replied, "There's a problem, and we're figuring it out. But we don't manage the process. You and the rest of the group make your recommendations to the admins, and they decide. We just guard the process, so people who might be tempted to overreach, don't."

"Overreach? Things are about to get out of control, and you're not doing anything."

"Explain yourself," she snapped. ". . . I'm waiting."

"Alright, Patricia. Dylan Regan, that strategist. He's making too much noise with his conspiracy claims. I'm hearing about it from people who shouldn't be listening. You were supposed to make him shut up and back away."

"We've tried, but he's more persistent than we expected. We have to be careful not to feed his conspiracy theory and provoke him even more. He's a small time player. He'll go away as soon as people stop listening to him."

"Well, you're already wrong," Murphy retorted. "With that ICIN reporter promoting everything he writes, they're risking undermining this economy."

"Won't that help your run with Governor Hayes for the White House?"

"Where did you hear—Jesus Christ . . . Destroying confidence isn't good for anyone."

"I know it's not good for your financial backers."

"And it's not good for you either, Patricia. I know that. No one wins if this gets out of control. Even Randy and his crew are worried."

She continued to stare at him without displaying any emotion. "Now that you've covered every political angle, I'll repeat what I told you the last time. Political considerations have to stay out of this process. Otherwise, you'll risk corrupting everything."

"And I told you there are people and interests involved that you need to appreciate."

"I appreciate them—"

"Mitch asked me to talk to you," Murphy interrupted, a smug look in his eyes.

She pressed her lips tightly for a moment. "What does the Speaker want?"

"He wants to know if you can make a better effort to contain Regan."

She stared at Murphy, a slight wrinkle between her intense eyes, the rest of her face stoic. The faint scar on the left of her neck brightened as blood flowed to it. After a long silence, she said, "I'll discuss with my people what else we can do. Now, you should leave before me."

Murphy hesitated, a meek symbol of defiance, and then stood up. "Okay, Patricia, but don't take too long. People are getting anxious, including Mitch."

CHAPTER 50
Thursday, May 31, 2012

"LOST! LOST children, lost men, lost women, lost jobs, lost homes, lost potential, lost futures, lost hope, lost lives . . . a lost generation! Look around us! Thousands of lost people, mostly young, but all lost. Look around you! They are everywhere! They are The Lost Generation! And the only way these lost know how to find their way, to pull some hope from the barren, dead soil of the American economy and political system, is to wage a revolution of the lost, by the lost, and for the lost! Here, in the capital of the greatest, fastest fading empire in the history of the world, hundreds of thousands of people have come to start The Lost Revolution! I'm Mary Gannon with ICIN, and we are live, here in Washington, D.C., to bring you this historic event."

It was sunny and warm, a perfect day for a revolution. Organized by a loose network of unemployed and underemployed recent college graduates communicating through social media, The Lost Revolution rally was originally expected to attract ten thousand participants. By noon, it had exploded to three hundred thousand people. Local authorities were unprepared for the turnout. Washington was in chaos.

As of last night, the rally was so disorganized that there was no stage or scheduled speakers for the event. Mary, along with Jane Reyes, cut a deal with the rally's leaders to use ICIN's stage and equipment to run the event. Because ICIN was the only media firm that had taken the rally seriously, other major networks were clamoring to tap into its coverage.

Mary had chosen her wardrobe to match the theme, wearing tight, brown American Revolution styled pants and a blue stretch halter top. Brown leather forearm bands with white ruffles around her wrists imitated colonial garb.

By early afternoon, Mary had interviewed several of the event's key organizers, along with a number of politicians and activists. The crowd had grown to half a million, and law enforcement helicopters were constantly buzzing over the throng of participants, creating an air of tension for an otherwise peaceful rally. As she stood on stage with two rally organizers, waiting for Governor Hayes to appear for an interview, the crowd started to chant, "We want Hayes! We want Hayes! We want Hayes . . ."

On cue, Governor Hayes appeared next to Reyes at the bottom of the stage steps with his security detail and entourage. One of Hayes' assistants started to explain to Reyes how he wanted the interview to be run, but she quickly put him in his place, then told the Governor to follow her direction or lose the opportunity.

Hayes responded, "Of course. You're in charge."

Reyes signaled to him, and Hayes walked on stage to a roar from the crowd. Mary handed him the microphone to make some introductory comments.

Hayes gave an impassioned speech aimed squarely at the young, college educated crowd. He finished by telling them, "This great country was founded on the ideal of independence! Now, the Democratic and Republican parties have created a crisis of political independence. They have mortgaged your future and refused to work together to allow you to reclaim it. Your only hope to have the same opportunities as previous generations is to demand political independence of your leaders. Take back your government and take back your future! Vote and vote Independent!"

The crowd erupted as Hayes raised both fists in the air, a symbol he had adopted for his campaign. The cheering subsided, and Mary walked back on stage. The crowd erupted again in applause, cheers and cackles.

"Governor Hayes, that was a great speech," Mary said to him, turning half way towards the crowd, "but this is a revolution, not a campaign. So, I have a few questions that I think these young people would like to have answered."

"And I have a few answers I think they would like to hear," Hayes replied. "These young people have a right to know who they're trusting with their future."

"Well said, Governor. Now, how exactly are you going to give control of their futures back to the millions of unemployed and underemployed college graduates out there?"

Hayes looked out over the crowd and said, "I intend to implement a college graduate jobs program targeted at goods producing and non-financial services industries. It will be like a farm team system for our economy. They will not get paid much but they will get the skills and training needed in a global economy. I will be coming out with the details soon."

"And how will you pay for this program?" Mary shot back.

"Through spending cuts, many of which will be in this city and the pet programs of the crony politicians who thrive in it," Hayes replied to loud applause.

"How will you reduce the deficit?"

"Spending cuts and revenue increases."

"That sounds like the same rhetoric as every other politician, but what does it mean? What cuts and are you proposing to raise taxes?"

"My plan sounds like everyone else's because it is. The problem is clear—we can't keep spending like we have, and we have to pay off our debt now so it doesn't burden these young people. Therefore, the steps are also clear—cut spending now and raise revenue now. It's really a problem of leadership, not strategy. And right now, we have no leaders. The next President has to be able and willing to do the right thing—now, not tomorrow!"

The crowd cheered every answer the Governor gave. Mary continued, bombarding Hayes with a series of questions from healthcare to abortion to immigration to free trade. He handled them easily—too easily, Mary thought, just like her last interview of him.

Hayes finished by saying, "Remember, you may once have been lost, but your future can be found if you vote and vote Independent!" He raised his two fists and strode off the stage.

Mary turned and stood before the crowd, still applauding and cheering. It was for her, not Hayes, she knew. She was their representative, their leader, their goddess. For a moment, she felt the same intoxicating sense of power she sensed in Hayes. She understood now why politicians craved it so.

As she felt the crowd lift her, the image of Caroline's bloody body suddenly appeared in her mind. Then Shannon Dunn, and Darryl Dwyer. And then the unemployed young veterans she had interviewed, and the desperate, lost nineteen year-olds with no future.

She closed her eyes and stopped listening to the crowd. She wasn't a politician, and she wanted to be more than a celebrity. She couldn't bask in the radiance of the same sun they worshiped, if she wanted to be real.

You're a journalist . . . I'm a journalist . . .

CHAPTER 51
Thursday, May 31, 2012

THE GLOBAL financial crisis had tarnished Greenwich, Connecticut, but it was still the home of financial titans and people with money who wanted to be near other people with money. Money congregated. Big money congregated here, and it made no apologies.

Donald Granger lived on a twenty acre estate in Greenwich overlooking Long Island Sound. Dylan could only make out parts of it through the trees as the limousine drove down the long driveway. He saw several tennis courts, a large indoor and outdoor pool area, and what might have been a gym. The house was at least fifteen thousand square feet—a neo-classic design of stone, wood, and glass that evoked the image of a modern castle.

A middle-aged American woman escorted him through the house to a relatively small room in the rear with book-lined shelves and bay windows that looked southwest over the water. An antique looking round table was set up for dinner for two. A simple chess set sat on a small square table under a window with black leather and wood Captain's chairs on either side.

The woman said Granger would be with him shortly, then bowed slightly and left. He walked over to look at the chess set.

"Good evening, Dylan," a voice said, startling him.

He turned and saw Granger standing by the doorway next to an attractive Asian woman in a stylish, red, knee-length cheongsam with a mandarin collar. She was two or maybe seven months pregnant. He couldn't tell. For his part, Granger sported an expensive looking blue suit, blue shirt and red tie. Other than the obvious cost difference and Dylan's white shirt, they were mirror images, again.

"Hello, Donald," Dylan said and walked over to them.

Granger shook his hand, neither limp nor strong, and said, "I am so pleased that you could make it tonight. This is my wife, Hui."

Dylan shook her hand and bowed slightly, a formality he had picked up from his trips to Asia when he worked for Merrill Lynch. He said, "It's nice to meet you."

"Likewise, Mr. Regan," she said in perfect English with no accent. "My husband speaks very highly of you. Welcome to our home. I look forward to seeing you more in the future." She looked at Granger and said, "I will see you tonight." She bowed towards Dylan and left.

Dylan looked at Granger, offered a deferential smile and said, "Your wife is very nice. Where did you meet?"

Granger stared at him for a moment, a slight smile on his face, then answered, "I was giving a speech at an alumni dinner for the University of Chicago Business School. She earned her MBA and Ph.D. there." He gestured towards the small table. "Please . . ."

They sat down. Granger picked up a bottle of red wine that had already been opened and asked, "Chianti?"

"Yes, thank you," Dylan answered. He assumed Granger knew it was his favorite.

Granger poured them each some wine, then raised his glass in toast and said, "Pawn to c4."

Dylan had expected Granger to continue their mind chess game and was prepared. "Pawn to e6," he replied.

A small smile appeared on Granger's face. He took a sip of wine, swallowed slowly and said, "Thank you for taking me seriously. Like the body, exercising the mind is essential to maintain its vitality."

"I agree, but I have to warn you again that I am out of shape for this."

Granger offered a perfunctory smile. "I am sure you will be a worthy opponent."

An older Indian man in a white jacket delivered two bowls of New England clam chowder and informed them that the main course would be veal parmesan with angel hair pasta and marinara saurce.

Chianti, Clam chowder, Italian food—all his favorites and Granger knew it. Dylan realized he was there for more than just a chess game.

"Knight to f3," Granger said casually as he picked up his spoon.

"Pawn to c5," Dylan countered immediately.

Granger's stare seemed more intense. Dylan worried that he'd made a mistake already. It was only his third move, he told himself and took a sip of wine to hide his nervousness.

"What are you thinking about the employment report tomorrow?" Granger asked.

"I think you know that I'm expecting 10,000 new jobs and a significant downward revision to last month's number."

Granger said, "I do. Pawn to d5. And how do you think investors are really positioned?"

Dylan wasn't sure how to respond. Granger wanted to eat, carry on a conversation and play mind chess all at the same time. He made Granger's move on the image of the board in his head and froze it. The he took a taste of clam chowder, quickly sipped his wine, and replied, "The consensus forecast has moved up to a gain of 75,000 jobs. Investors are definitely more optimistic. None of the major data this month supports that optimism, though. But even if the May jobs data comes in as I expect, markets probably won't react much unless April's number is revised away. Everyone wants to believe this economy is getting better quickly, because that's what they need to believe . . . Pawn takes d5."

"As you know, MQA holds similar views to yours," Granger said and stared coldly at Dylan. After a long silence, Granger blinked and seemed about to announce a move when the older Indian man appeared and served the main course. Granger motioned for Dylan to start.

The veal was superb, and the sauce exceptional—light, a little sweet, with some zest. Could Granger really know how he liked his sauce, Dylan wondered. He wasn't even sure himself.

After eating half of his veal, Granger sat back in his chair, signaling that he was done, and asked, "How was your dinner with Julie Watson last week?"

Dylan wiped his mouth as he processed that Julie Watson must have talked to Granger. He assumed she hadn't said anything about the white wine in his apartment. Or he hoped. He replied, "It was very nice. She's impressive, and Eagle's business model is interesting."

"Yes, she is impressive," Granger remarked, a hint of a smile appearing. "Of course, there is a way you could work with her regularly."

Dylan took a slow drink of water, then said, "I'm not sure what you mean."

The older Indian man suddenly appeared, holding a manila envelope. He handed it to Granger, then cleared away their dinner plates and left.

Granger placed the envelope in front of Dylan and said, "This is your offer of employment with MQA. Please review it and call me with any questions tomorrow. I expect your answer Monday morning. Assuming you wish to work for MQA, you will need to resign from FTS immediately. Close of day Monday will suffice. I am very much looking forward to you joining us, Dylan . . . Pawn takes d5."

Dylan was stunned but tried to conceal it. Making a chess move while offering him a job and telling him he had the weekend to accept it and resign from FTS was simply astounding. He took another long drink of water. He noticed Granger's steady stare and slight, inscrutable smile, watching him, judging him. It was all a game to Granger, he realized—not just the chess. He had to concentrate. He froze Granger's move in his mind and extended his own decision tree out several more moves ahead. He said, "Pawn to d6."

The Indian man delivered two double espressos.

Granger remarked, "Impressive . . . I mean your ability to concentrate. I truly am excited over the prospect of working with you, Dylan. Do you have any questions? Knight to c3."

Dylan felt like Granger was playing with him. Was it another test? Or a tactic to divert his concentration, to win? Both, or neither? The only thing he knew for sure was that Granger valued results. But he wasn't going to give Granger the one he wanted for their chess game. He froze Granger's move in his mind again, picturing the chess board, and replied, "No, no questions right now. Pawn to g6."

Granger paused briefly, then said, "Knight to d2."

Dylan squinched his eyes for a second as he thought about Granger's move. He said, "Knight on b to d7."

Granger stared at Dylan for a while, the same slight smile on his face. He finally said, "If you do not have any questions regarding your offer, I have one more item to discuss with you."

Dylan welcomed the reprieve from their game, but Granger's solemn tone made him apprehensive. "Sure, okay," he replied.

Granger said, "Since I expect you to join us in a few days, I need to explain our investment philosophy. It's the one thing you must understand and follow without exception from your first day with MQA."

Dylan nodded.

Granger continued: "Our investment philosophy is grounded in risk management, a simple concept that most firms fail miserably at. Ideally, we would have better information than everyone else and be able to invest more successfully based on that, but information advantages are few and fleeting. To be successful, we have to be able to process the same information as everyone else, but better than everyone else. That's the essence of risk management—understanding and processing information optimally. It's why we need people like you, Dylan."

Granger paused and took a sip of wine.

"Most people think risk management is complicated, mathematically driven, but it's really quite simple. An example will illustrate my point. A while back, I was returning from China on our jet with the head economist for Bear Stearns when we encountered some turbulence. He said he wasn't worried because statistics showed that plane travel was less risky than automobiles. His comment crystallized both the principle of risk management and its failure in practice. He didn't appreciate that he could not afford to be wrong—that the probability of dying if our plane crashed was effectively one hundred percent. At MQA, risk management is focused as much on whether we can afford to be wrong as the probability of being wrong. Unfortunately, Bear Stearns would eventually learn the importance of this approach all too well."

Dylan sensed an opportunity to interject and asked, "Then why fly at all?"

"Ah, that is the correct question. You fly because in life, as in markets, you can never avoid risk. Risk must be managed. And the more you want from life, the more risk you must take. But to be successful, you have to manage risk intelligently, with fanatical discipline."

"But risk is just the yet-to-be realized future. Sometimes it's random, not in your control."

"Excellent point," Granger responded. "Let us say you take a risk and it goes wrong, maybe because you miscalculated or because life is just inherently incalculable. What do you do? Simple. You cut your losses immediately, brutally, and without emotion. You do not hope, you do not rationalize, and you do not wait. You live to risk another day."

Dylan nodded slowly, then said, "So, the key is to understand your risk better than your competition, and if randomness gets in the way—say an unprecedented financial crisis ravages the global economy—then minimize the consequences, optimize the results, and move on."

Granger smiled and replied, "Precisely."

The meeting was over, Dylan knew. He wasn't sure if Granger's words were a warning, a guideline, or an anecdote, but he understood that if he did anything to endanger MQA, he would become a loss to be cut immediately, brutally, and without emotion.

Granger walked him to the front door, shook his hand and said, "I truly appreciate your indulgence with our chess game. I am looking forward to continuing it when you officially join MQA next week."

Dylan waited until the limousine was on I-95 before he opened the envelope with the details of his job offer. There was one piece of paper with no header and only six typed lines on it:

Date: May 31, 2012

Employee Name: Dylan Regan

Position: Strategist

Base Salary: $400,000

Minimum 2012 Annual Incentive Award: $1,000,000

Start Date: Immediate

CHAPTER 52
Friday, June 1, 2012

276,000!

"Fuck . . ." Dylan muttered. Blood rushed to his head and the FTS trading floor started spinning. *How can I be this wrong again?*

The consensus forecast for May job growth was 75,000. His was 10,000. The creation of 276,000 new jobs in May would convince the world that April's jobs number was real, he knew. He looked and saw that global bond markets were already selling off sharply and stock markets were soaring.

Revisions . . . He pulled up the summary of the May report on Bloomberg. April's number was revised down to 261,000 from 483,000. That would vindicate him somewhat. Then he saw that March job growth was increased by 175,000, offsetting most of April's downward revision.

"Shit!" he said loud enough for sales people around him to glance up for a moment from their excited phone calls to clients.

With the revisions, the average job growth for the past three months was 260,000. The trend in job creation now looked credible, instead of a one month mistake or fabrication. And all the other major components of the report had come in slightly better than expected, including the unemployment rate. It was strong data no matter how he looked at it—unless the past three months had been manipulated. But claiming that would make him look fanatical.

He leaned his elbows on his desk, closed his eyes and rubbed his temples with his fingers. Would this affect the offer Donald Granger had given him last night? How could it not? Dead wrong for three straight months. But he'd been right for so long. And now, Blair Armstrong would know he was lying . . .

"Don't get too excited, folks!" Billy McDonald shouted from his seat. "It's a conspiracy! The government counted all those lost socialists in Washington yesterday as employed, but they'll be revised away next month. Isn't that right, Regan?"

Snickers and giggles rose from pockets of traders and salespeople like hyenas signaling to the clan about a wounded prey.

Dylan stood up, glared at McDonald and yelled, "Why don't you shut the fuck up and do some real trading!"

The floor immediately fell silent. People paused what they were doing. McDonald stared back, his mouth slightly open, shocked and intimidated.

"What?" McDonald replied meekly.

"Hey, lighten up, Dylan!" Andrew Cantor shouted from his seat several desks away. "It's a joke. What do you expect with three bad calls in a row? Just get us some color, will you?"

Dylan glared at McDonald for a few more seconds, then sat down. He typed up a quick email on the May employment report, saying the strong three month trend in job creation would keep the rally in risky assets going while continuing to pressure rates higher and bonds lower. He didn't dispute the numbers other than to suggest they were likely due to the same temporary factors that had created a bounce in job growth last spring before hiring slowed sharply again.

He sent the email out to clients, then picked up his Blackberry and called Petro. He got his voicemail and said, "Professor, it's Dylan

Regan. I'm sure you saw the employment report. Could you give me a call to discuss it? I'd really appreciate it. Thank you."

Now he needed a cup of coffee and some time alone in the coffee cave.

As he stood up, his turret phone rang. "This is Dylan . . ."

"What the fuck is going on, Dylan?" a man shouted through the phone.

"Is that you, Tom?" he asked, recognizing Sygowski's voice.

"Yeah, it's me!"

"Why are you yelling?"

"Did you know your friend's dead? Did you?"

"What friend?"

"Your friend at the BLS who worked for Ben Thompson!" Sygowski answered.

"Caroline Brenner?"

"Yeah, her! Walter Vaughn just told me there was a news story on ICIN about that woman who was pushed onto the subway tracks and how she worked at the BLS with another woman who was killed in a hit-and-run—Caroline Brenner! He looked her up and found out she died a month ago. Did you fucking know that, Dylan?"

"You didn't know she was dead?" Dylan asked in disbelief, then looked around the trading floor to see if anyone was listening.

"Fuck, no," Sygowski answered. "You said you're working with Peter Zimmer, but you didn't tell me it's because she's dead. Vaughn thinks you're screwing with us."

"Vaughn didn't know either?"

"Neither of us knew," Sygowski replied. "Are you pulling something, Dylan? You gotta tell me. Vaughn's spooked. He wants to drop the whole thing."

Dylan's mind started racing. If neither Sygowski nor Vaughn knew Caroline was dead, then neither of them killed her. But Armstrong knew . . .

"I have to call you back," Dylan said and hung up.

Dylan put his coffee on the table, sat down in his usual seat and looked around. The coffee cave was empty, not a miserable or unemployed or German soul in the place. He took the lid off of his coffee and sipped it.

"Shit," he exclaimed as he burnt his mouth on the steaming coffee.

He pulled out his Blackberry and started to dial Brad, but then stopped and put it down. What was he going to tell him—Sygowski and Vaughn were crooks but not murderers? That Armstrong probably had Caroline killed? Dwyer and Shannon too? But he wouldn't be able to help figure it all out because Donald Granger expected him to start next week?

He took another sip of coffee, then closed his eyes and started to drift. A diagram began to form in his mind, with nodes. Caroline's name was in the first one. Lines grew from it, connecting to other nodes—Thompson, Armstrong, Sygowski, Vaughn . . . and then Darryl Dwyer and Shannon Dunn . . . then one with the number "483" in it . . . and then the FBI . . . then Zimmer . . . and Brad . . . and then—

Dylan's Blackberry rang, startling him. He knocked his coffee over. "Fuck," he exclaimed and threw a paper napkin on the spill. He grabbed his Blackberry. "Hello . . ."

"Ah, I am so glad I caught you, Dylan," a man's voice with an indistinguishable European accent said.

"Professor, thanks for calling me back," Dylan said as he wiped up his spilled coffee.

"My pleasure," Petro said. "I thought you might be out protesting with that beautiful young reporter from ICIN. Remember, you promised to introduce me to her."

"I remember. Do you have time now to talk, Professor?"

"I have a minute or so."

"Okay, I'll make it quick. You saw the May jobs number and the revisions. There are still too many inconsistencies, so I wanted to bounce some thoughts off of you and maybe see if I could use Evan, your research assistant, for a little more work."

"Dylan, it was so good to see you when you came down," Petro said. "We must do it again soon, here or up there. I love New York." Petro paused, then said, "Evan is very busy, and I don't have any time right now either. Maybe in a few months, when things settle down."

"Is there something wrong, Professor?"

"Oh no, it's just—" Petro started, then paused again. "Ah, how to explain... When you visited, Dylan, we talked about the shadow history of the government estimating economic data using liberal techniques that might be viewed by some as self serving, or even manipulation."

"That's right. That's why I'm calling."

"And we discussed how it is all urban legend. There is no real proof."

"I remember," Dylan replied. "That's why I'm following up with you."

"And you should also remember the strong words of caution I gave you as well. This is Washington, not New York. Political influence is the currency in this city. Here, if someone comes to you and suggests that you might want to stay out of a matter in order to preserve access to certain select circles, you take that suggestion seriously. Am I making myself clear?"

"I think so," Dylan said slowly. He realized that someone had advised Petro not to help him anymore—someone with influence. Petro's Washington insider status was almost as dear to him as his life. Petro wouldn't jeopardize it for him, he knew.

"That's wonderful then," Petro said. "Now, I hope you understand how important your friendship is to me, even if there are times when it cannot be my first consideration."

"I'll have to take your word on that."

"I understand, but I would very much like to remain friends."

Dylan was silent for a few seconds. "Then you'll have to pay for dinner next time."

"In New York, when I am next there," Petro quickly offered.

"Agreed Professor. Thanks for your time. Goodbye."

Dylan hung up, frustrated. Someone in the government with influence and power had gotten to Petro. The FBI had to be involved. He was certain.

But if he was right, there were two conspiracies—one to leak and trade off of the employment data, and another to manipulate it. They had to be related. Stumbling onto two conspiracies involving the jobs data couldn't be a coincidence. But he didn't have an explanation that connected them. More importantly, he was running out of time to figure out which one had gotten Caroline killed.

Dylan walked into the Normandie Court lobby, still breathing heavy, and saw her standing at the concierge desk. He was soaked from running five miles in a light, warm rain. He had left the office early, hoping to forget the day's events and sweat out the throbbing behind his eyes. And now, Julie Watson was there to help.

She strutted towards him in her purple, fitted, scoop neck dress and stopped a few inches away. She scanned his sweat soaked body, then leaned forward and kissed him, easing her tongue slightly in between his lips. She pulled her lips back slowly, looked in his eyes and said softly, "I like the look."

"Then the five miles was worth it," he said, refusing to question why a beautiful woman had just French kissed him as he dripped a mixture of sweat and rain at her feet. He was tired of questioning everything . . . but he had to. "To what do I owe this pleasure?"

"I was remembering the other night," she replied and smiled coyly. "I never did buy you that drink. So, I took a chance and thought you might like to get a glass of wine . . ."

She was there to rescue him, he told himself, whether she knew it or not. "I'd like that," he said. "I just have to take a quick shower. Excuse me while I grab my key."

The big, round, young man behind the desk handed Dylan his key, then leaned over and whispered, "You're dating her and Mary Gannon? I want to be you, man."

Dylan feigned a smile, grabbed his key and walked with Julie Watson to the elevator bank.

The hot, hard water pelted Dylan's head and drenched his body. He felt the anguish and frustration from the day wash away, for the moment. He closed his eyes and listened to the water burst through the holes in the shower head above him. As everything was cleansed from his mind, he started to remember the last time he had seen Julie Watson. The image of her naked body in the darkness grew clearer, and the shower water got hotter. He lifted his face and let it pound his forehead, rolling down his cheeks and over his chin like a waterfall.

He felt a draft of cool air and heard a noise. He opened his eyes and turned his head.

She was standing with the shower door half open, one long leg in, her dark, naked body splattered with tiny water droplets that had bounced off of him, now rolling down her large, firm breasts to her thin, taut stomach . . . and lower.

"We only had time for one drink the other night," she said as she stepped in and closed the shower door. "The second is even better."

CHAPTER 53
Friday, June 1, 2012

MARY HAD never been to Centolire before, but Friday night after a long week was not meant for moderately priced Italian food, especially on the Upper East Side. Jeff had asked her to join him for dinner with two other couples, and now she was regretting her answer.

On the ride to the restaurant, she had asked Jeff again how much he had prepped Governor Hayes for her interviews. He insisted again that he had not helped him and then dismissed her concerns. She didn't like either response. If she couldn't trust him, he couldn't help her.

She was picking at her dinner, politely answering questions about ICIN from the two other couples, when she saw Dylan walk into the restaurant. He was wearing a blue blazer, nicely tailored and surprisingly stylish, over a light gray, crew neck shirt. With his pleated khaki slacks, he looked almost fashionable, and in great shape. His hair was wet and slightly curled in the front. She guessed he had just showered after working out.

A striking looking black woman in a short, tight, purple cocktail dress seemed to be with him. Mary recognized her. It was Julie Watson from the CP Center fund raiser a few weeks ago. As the hostess escorted them to a window table, she noticed Jeff staring at Watson before catching himself.

Rothstein had suggested Watson was a hooker, Mary remembered. She certainly dressed like one. Jeff said he knew her through Donald Granger. And she seemed to know Peter Zimmer pretty well, too. Now, it looked like she knew Dylan—very well. It was too much of a coincidence. She decided she'd have Hank Stewart check Watson out, just to be sure.

Why dress like a hooker if you're not a hooker?

Mary was silent during the cab ride back to her apartment after dinner, pondering Dylan's comment from their lunch in Bryant Park that Peter Zimmer's connection to both Caroline and Shannon Dunn was too much of a coincidence. What would he say if he knew Julie Watson was connected to Zimmer?

"You seem distracted," Schwinn said as they walked into her living room. "You barely talked to my friends at dinner."

"All they wanted to do was ask me about my work," she replied and strolled over to the refrigerator to grab a bottle of water.

"Well, you are a celebrity. But it seems like something else is on your mind. Is that woman's death bothering you, the one who was pushed onto the subway tracks that Brad Johnson knew?"

"I'm a journalist, not a celebrity, and I'm fine," she said, then walked over and sat down on her couch.

"Alright, you're a celebrity journalist. I still think you should talk about it," Schwinn said tenderly and sat down next to her.

She forced a smile but didn't say anything.

Schwinn smiled back and said, "How about this—you tell me what's bothering you, and then I'll tell you some important news I just learned about Governor Hayes' campaign?"

She looked at him and raised her eyebrows, interested but skeptical. His manipulative tactics were transparent, but she would have to play along to hear his news. She moved closer to him and put her elbow on his shoulder, then gazed in his eyes seductively and said, "I'll tell you what's bothering me, but first you have to tell me your news."

"As you wish, my lady," Schwinn replied, bowing his head slightly. "Governor Hayes is going to announce Senator Murphy as his running mate at The Lost Revolution rally in Manhattan next week. And I suggested they have an exclusive interview with you afterwards."

Mary's eyes widened and her lips parted, curling into an excited smile. It was a major story, and she was going to break it. Maybe she could trust him. Maybe he could help her.

She ran her hand through Jeff's hair and moved her lips slowly towards his, caressing them with her tongue, then kissing him softly. She placed her leg over his knees, working it gradually higher until she was on top of him. She kissed him on his neck and worked her way around to his ear and his forehead and then back to his lips as she rocked gently on his lap. She unbuttoned his shirt and rubbed her hands across his chest. She noticed how thin he was. He wasn't Dylan, but right now, she liked that.

CHAPTER 54
Friday, June 1, 2012

HANK STEWART'S instincts told him to bring his Smith & Wesson M&P when he went to speak with Reggie Rodriguez. He didn't take unnecessary chances. Going to The Beltway alone tonight to discuss a murder without protection would have been one.

Rodriguez had been bartending the night Caroline was murdered. Stewart planned to find out what he knew about Darryl Dwyer. He slipped in the back entrance and stepped up to the bar. It was quiet for 9:30 on a Friday night.

A short, round, two-hundred plus pound, smiling young Hispanic man came over. Stewart guessed it was Rodriguez. Tim Adams was down the other end flirting with an attractive young Hispanic woman and a slightly older, heavy, red headed white woman.

"Hey man, what can I get you?" Rodriguez asked jovially.

"A Bud and some of that popcorn," Stewart replied.

Stewart saw Adams turn and notice him. As Rodriguez grabbed a Budweiser out of the cooler, Adams whispered something to him. Rodriguez looked over at him, then back at Adams and shrugged his shoulders.

"Five bucks, man, unless you wanna run a tab," Rodriguez said as he slid the Bud and a bowl of popcorn in front of Stewart. "I hear you wanna ask me about that guy Dwyer who used to come in here." He looked at Stewart with a relaxed smile.

Stewart threw ten dollars on the bar, took a quick sip of his beer, and said, "Yeah. Was Dwyer here the night he supposedly ran down that woman?"

"Who are you, man?" Rodriguez asked.

"Insurance investigator. I need to make sure you guys didn't get this Darryl Dwyer too drunk. You could be liable."

"Hey, man," Rodriguez said, leaning forward on the bar to make his point, "that dude walked in the front door every night and stumbled out the front door every night. He never drove here or home. No way. If he was in a car when he died or that woman died, he wasn't driving. He couldn't. I'll bet on that."

"Was he here the night the woman was killed?"

"Like I told the police, I don't remember seeing him that night, but it was busy. I was by myself, and it was crazy with a bunch of George Washington students celebrating something. I could have missed him."

"Did you usually notice him when he came in?"

"Yeah, I felt a little sorry for the guy. He wasn't a bad dude. Just messed up in the head."

"How about the night he died?" Stewart asked.

"Same story. Never saw him, but I would have if he was in because it was slow that night. You want change, man?"

"No, keep it," Stewart said. He believed Rodriguez. There was no pretense or nervousness, unlike Adams. "Just one last question. Anyone else around here you think is capable of running that woman down? Anyone really violent, or suspicious?"

"Man, this is a neighborhood bar, with good people. I ain't gonna talk about my customers. But the answer is no. Thanks for the tip."

Stewart nodded, then grabbed a handful of pop corn, threw it in his mouth and washed it down with a couple of swigs of beer. He could make it back to New York in four hours if he left now. He slipped out the back door.

A light rain was falling. It was dark, and the metal steps from the back entrance felt slick. He stepped carefully down the stairs to the pavement, then sensed someone behind him . . .

He grabbed his M&P from inside his jacket and spun around, whipping his arm and striking something with the butt of his gun as he did. He heard a deep grunt and then felt a sharp, excruciating pain in his right side.

He instinctively jumped back, tripping on a stoop. As he fell, his back hit the edge of the building foundation, knocking the wind out of him. He looked up and saw a stocky, medium height man scramble up from the ground, a knife in his hand. Stewart's vision blurred, and the night suddenly sounded hollow.

"Fucking asshole," the man said, deep and intense, followed by something guttural in a foreign language and accent.

The sound of the man's voice rushed to Stewart's head as his vision cleared. He lifted his right arm in what felt like slow motion to point the M&P at the stocky figure. He started to squeeze the trigger, but the figure was gone. He heard running, fading in the direction of the street, mingling with the sound of rushing traffic somewhere in the night.

Stewart leaned on his left hand, feeling tightness on the right side of his stomach. He needed to get to his car, chase the man down. He lifted himself and then stood up, his back aching. His lower right side felt like glass was sticking in it. He touched it—moist.

He stumbled towards his car, the single light post illuminating his figure from above. He turned to let the light shine on his right side as large rain drops fell from the darkness. His shirt and pants were red, soaked with blood.

He lifted his shirt to look at his side, then wiped away the blood with his jacket sleeve. A five inch slice just above his pants was visible for a moment before blood oozed out again and obscured it. He couldn't tell how deep it was, but it felt like he'd been filleted.

Calling 911 would create a scene and a long process of explaining to the police what happened. He didn't want that, if he could avoid it, especially since he wasn't sure his gun license was up-to-date in D.C.

The guy was a professional—white, stocky, maybe eastern European, liked knives—but sloppy. He should have used a gun if he wanted to be sure he killed him. Maybe he was just warning him. No, the guy liked the feeling of killing. That's the only reason you used a knife.

Stewart knew he'd be dead now if he hadn't brought his M&P. He might die anyway. His mind started to wander. He got in his car, grabbed a shirt from his travel bag on the passenger seat and pressed hard on his right side to try to stop the bleeding. Then he drove to where he thought Brad lived.

CHAPTER 55
Friday, June 1, 2012

BRAD SAT at his kitchen table staring at his notebook, the names "BLAIR ARMSTRONG" and "PETER ZIMMER" written across the top of the page in front of him. Rain drops splattered loudly in the dark outside his window. His coffee was cold.

It was almost eleven o'clock, but he couldn't sleep. Not yet. He had to hear Caroline's voice first. Then he would sleep.

His cell phone rang, and he jumped, banging his knee under the table. He groaned, then looked and saw it was Hank. "Hank, everything okay?"

"I'm outside in my car. I'm bleeding . . ."

"I'll be right down. Stay on the phone."

Brad grabbed his first-aid kit and ran downstairs. He found Stewart's car parked half a block from his building, the engine off but the headlights still on. He opened the door, and Stewart looked up at him.

"You don't look so hot," Stewart said weakly, managing a smile.

"Neither do you," Brad said, leaning over Stewart to look at his blood soaked right side. He unbuckled the seatbelt. "I need to get you out of the car so I can look at that. Okay?"

"Yeah. Help me out."

Stewart put his arm on Brad's shoulder. Brad helped him out of the car and eased him down onto the wet asphalt. Stewart leaned back against the rear passenger door. It was only sprinkling now. Brad took out a small flashlight, some gauze pads and antibacterial spray. He lifted Stewart's shirt and cleared some of the blood from his wound. He sprayed some antibiotic on the wound and his hands, then cleared some more blood away and pulled up gently on the sliced skin. He shone the light inside the wound to see how deep it was. More blood oozed out.

Stewart grimaced. "What kind of fucking curbside manner is that, Doc?"

"You're not funny. It's deep, but it looks clean. Just muscle and fat. You're lucky. I'm going to butterfly it and then call 911."

"No cops," Stewart said through clenched teeth. "It'll make things too difficult. Just butterfly it and take me to the emergency room."

"Alright, but who did this?" Brad asked as he set up a butterfly bandage.

"Probably the guy who killed Caroline and attacked you."

Brad paused. "Did you get a look at him?"

"Quick one . . . similar to your description, with an accent, maybe eastern European."

"Where'd he attack you?"

"The Beltway, as I was leaving—" Stewart grimaced again as Brad taped his wound closed.

"Okay, that's as good as I can do. Let's get you in the car." Brad helped Stewart into the back seat, then said, "What story are you going to use at the hospital, so we're consistent?"

"You sound like you've done this—" Stewart started but then passed out.

338

After two hours sitting in the emergency room at the Washington Hospital Center, Brad heard his name called. He stood up as a tall, thin woman with blond hair and wearing all white walked towards him. She reminded him of Caroline, but not as pretty.

"Mr. Johnson, I'm Doctor Reynolds," she said. "Mr. Stewart will be okay. He has a nasty cut, but we cleaned it and stitched him up. He lost some blood, so we're going to keep him overnight for observation, but he should be fine to leave in the morning."

"That's good news. Thank you," Brad said and gazed in her blue eyes.

She realized he was staring at her and smiled. "So, how did you say he got that cut again?"

"He slipped and sliced himself on a piece of sheet metal sticking out of garbage can," Brad answered and smiled back.

"Really?" she said, smiling more now. "Well, I don't believe either of you. Your friend's a cop. I've seen enough of them to know. And that's a knife wound if I ever saw one. But you're probably sticking with that story, right?"

Brad just smiled and continued to stare at her.

She blushed and said, "I have to go, Mr. Johnson. Have a good night."

He watched her walk away, then closed his eyes and smelled the aroma of the hospital. An image started to form in his mind . . . Caroline, lying on a table in a white room with bright lights, a sheet covering her to the shoulders, her blond hair matted around her head. Slices opened up in the skin on her face, and blood began to ooze . . . Her eyes suddenly opened—

"What?" Brad exclaimed, opening his eyes and stepping back.

"Are you alright, Mr. Johnson?" Dr. Reynolds asked, standing a couple of feet in front of him. "You're pale."

"Uh, yes, fine . . . just tired."

She smiled sympathetically and said, "You should go home and get some sleep. This is my card if you want to call me for any reason." She touched him gently on the arm and left.

It was past two o'clock in the morning when he got back to his apartment. He lay across his bed, his clothes still on, and started to drift.

"Was that you?" he asked quietly as he fell asleep.

CHAPTER 56
Saturday, June 2, 2012

BRAD PULLED his Impala into the small lot behind The Beltway shortly after ten o'clock Saturday morning. A black BMW was the only other car there. He got out and walked to the back entrance. The door suddenly opened, and a thin, clean cut man in his mid-twenties came out with a couple of empty beer boxes. Brad assumed it was Tim Adams.

Adams startled, seeing a big black man standing at the bottom of the metal steps.

Brad had intentionally dressed to look unthreatening, wearing a light blue polo shirt, khakis, and white sneakers. "Oh, hi there," he said. "I'm meeting a friend here, but I think I'm early. What time do you open?" He smiled and took a step up the stairs.

"Eleven," Adams answered cautiously.

"You mind if I use your bathroom while I wait?" Brad asked, taking another step up the stairs. Only two more before he could grab Adams.

"Sorry, owner doesn't allow it," Adams replied, then threw the boxes over the railing into a small dumpster. He quickly stepped back inside and started to close the door.

Brad leapt the two last steps and grabbed the edge of the door with his two hands before it closed. Adams pulled hard, almost slamming Brad's fingers, but he managed to yank it open, dragging Adams halfway outside. He grabbed Adams' shirt, then throat, lifted him up and drove him into the cheap paneled wall just inside the back entrance. He pulled Adams away from the wall and then slammed him into it again, cracking the paneling.

Adams gasped for breath, his eyes wide with fear, holding Brad's wrists in a futile gesture to loosen his grip. "Take the money! Don't hurt me!"

"Tell me about Darryl Dwyer!" Brad snapped.

"I can't breathe . . ."

Brad loosened his grip. "Talk!"

"What do you want to know?" Adams cried.

"Who killed Dwyer?"

"No one. He died in—"

Brad tightened his hold around Adams' throat and yelled, "Someone put him in that car. Tell me, or—"

"I had nothing—"

Brad squeezed Adams' windpipe until the color started to leave his face. Killing him would be easy, Brad thought, but he needed information. He let up.

Adams wheezed as he struggled to catch his breath, his eyes watering. He gagged and nearly threw up. He recovered and said, "Okay . . . a guy came in a few weeks ago, hung out a couple of nights and then offered me some money to find out everything I could about Dwyer."

"Why?"

"He didn't say, and I didn't ask."

"How much did he pay you?"

"Fifteen thousand."

"What did you tell him?"

"I . . . I talked to Dwyer, since he was here most nights. I told the guy everything he told me. It was just his story. You know, his problems and stuff like that."

"What did this guy look like?" Brad asked.

"Uh, tall white guy, short brown hair, thin, but strong looking."

Brad thought for a moment. "What about the man who was stabbed outside here last night?"

"What?" Adams replied. "I don't know about anybody being stabbed last night."

"The man who was in here asking questions about Dwyer."

"The insurance investigator? I never saw him after he left . . . I swear," Adams pleaded.

"Did you tell that tall guy about him?"

Adams hesitated. Brad gripped his neck tighter and shoved him up against the wall again.

"I did," Adams gasped. "He came by with the last payment the other day. I told him an insurance investigator was here asking questions. He got angry, said if I talked to anyone again, he'd kill me . . ." Adams' eyes widened, fearing this was a test. "Please, don't kill—"

"Shut up!" Brad snapped and threw Adams hard to the ground. "If you're lying, I'll find you and finish this."

Brad left, got in his car, drove a block down the street from The Beltway and pulled over. After a couple of minutes, he saw the black BMW screech out of the lot and speed off.

Brad kept an eye out for silver Explorers as he drove on I-95 to Manhattan, Hank Stewart fast asleep in the passenger seat next to him. Just past Newark, New Jersey, Stewart woke up.

"How you feeling?" Brad asked, keeping his eyes on the road.

"Okay," Stewart answered, then glanced out the window to gauge where they were. He looked at Brad and said, "Sorry for zonking out. I guess these pain killers are pretty strong."

"Don't worry about it."

"Thanks again for driving me and my car back."

"It gave me an excuse to check out your souped-up Taurus," Brad said.

Stewart replied, "It's not souped-up."

Brad shot him a quick smile, then looked back at the road and asked, "Is there someone who can look in on you over the next couple of days?"

"My girlfriend and my sons."

"You divorced?"

"Yeah, five years."

"How many kids?" Brad asked. He sensed it was a painful question and said, "Sorry."

"It's okay. I have a son who's going to be a senior at Columbia and a younger one starting at Cornell this fall. I had a daughter in between. She was killed in a car accident six years ago."

After a long silence, Stewart looked at Brad and said, "We need to talk to Tim Adams, the other bartender. I think he had something to do with that guy waiting for me."

"I spoke with him this morning."

"Really? And how did that go?"

Brad told him what Adams said, glossing over the details of how he got him to talk.

"You must have been pretty persuasive to get all that out of him," Stewart remarked.

"I used my charm."

Stewart laughed briefly, then winced as a sharp pain shot up his side.

Brad glanced in his rearview mirror.

Stewart noticed and asked, "Someone following us?"

"No, just checking."

"Like you checked my car for a surveillance bug before we left?"

Brad ignored the remark and said, "The guy who paid Tim Adams and the one who stabbed you fit the descriptions of the two men leaving the subway after Shannon Dunn was pushed onto the tracks, as well as the guy at Caroline's apartment."

"I know," Stewart said. "That's not a coincidence."

"But why try to kill you? It's sloppy."

Stewart examined Brad for a few seconds, then he said, "My guess is they figured out who I was and wanted to make it look like I was stabbed in a fight, typical violence for a local dive."

Brad asked, "Why go after you and not me?"

"I know, it doesn't make sense," Stewart answered. "I haven't figured that out. But we know there's at least two of them, which means whoever hired them has some money."

Brad was silent, watching the road and checking his mirrors while he tried to connect all the pieces in his mind.

Stewart said, "Mary left me a voice message, so I know you talked to her, but have you talked to Dylan?"

"Just quickly this morning to let him know what happened. I'm going to stop by his apartment after I drop you off."

"So, you guys are back on speaking terms?"

Brad flashed him a quick, surprised look.

Stewart saw it and said, "I figured that bump on your cheek last week wasn't an accident." After a few seconds of silence, he added, "Sorry, it's none of my—"

"He's starting a new job soon, maybe this week," Brad interrupted. "He's probably not going to be able to help for much longer."

Stewart said, "That's too bad."

Brad continued to stare at the traffic in front of him, stoic and silent.

As they approached the exit for the Lincoln Tunnel and Manhattan, Stewart asked, "Did you talk to Garcia?"

"Yes."

"Did you get anywhere?"

Brad took a deep breath, exhaled slowly and replied, "Garcia didn't want to hear anything about Shannon Dunn or our theories. He said the NYPD was convinced a homeless man did it, and that was good enough for him. He also said the ME's report on Dwyer's death pretty much confirmed that he killed Caroline. It was her blood on the SUV and the knife, and his fingerprints on her cell phone."

"And did Garcia say why a barely functional, bipolar drunk would do this?" Stewart asked.

"He still thinks Dwyer killed her in a fit of rage because she got away when he tried to rob her." Brad shook his head and added, "He said they solved her murder, like he had promised."

"Did you tell him there might be an insider trading plot using the jobs data?"

Brad clenched his jaw, nodded and said, "He asked for proof. I told him what we had, and he said he wasn't going to challenge the NYPD or his own people based on a Wall Street analyst's speculation and an ex-boyfriend's grief. Then he suggested I talk to the SEC."

"So, three bodies aren't enough for him," Stewart said.

Brad didn't respond. He accelerated as they headed into the Lincoln Tunnel, his knuckles white from squeezing the steering wheel, just like he had squeezed Tim Adams' throat.

CHAPTER 57
Saturday, June 2, 2012

THE LOUD, rapid banging startled them, but Dylan quickly realized it had to be MG. He glanced at Brad, stood up from his kitchen table and walked to the door.

"Is Brad here?" Mary asked as soon as he opened his apartment door, then added impatiently, "May I come in?"

Obnoxious and in her grunge look—black cropped jeans, low on her waist, with a white, sweetheart halter top—she was still striking. Dylan stepped to the side and replied calmly, "We've been waiting for you."

Mary walked quickly over to Brad, who stood up. She asked, "Why did you text me to come here? Is Hank okay?"

"He's fine," Brad answered. "He was asleep in his apartment, so I thought it was better to meet here. His girlfriend and son are with him. He just has to rest and let his wound heal."

"You want some coffee?" Dylan asked her as he walked into the kitchen.

"Yes, thank you," she said and sat down at the table, seeming relieved.

Dylan poured three cups of coffee, grabbed the half-and-half and a few packets of Equal, and then joined them at his kitchen table.

Brad proceeded to tell them everything that had happened with Hank. When he was done, Dylan recounted his conversation with Tom Sygowski yesterday.

"Sygowski and Vaughn are crooks," Dylan said, "but I don't think they're murderers. Blair Armstrong had the most to lose from Caroline revealing the data leaking arrangement. And she has the money to hire as many killers as she needs."

Brad replied, "But what about Peter Zimmer? He had to have known what Thompson was doing with the data."

Dylan said, "I know that makes sense, but Sygowski doesn't know him, and Vaughn wouldn't have been so eager to hire me if he was already in with Zimmer. The only thing that implicates Zimmer is the fact that he was Caroline's boss and she was stressed about something at work according to Shannon Dunn."

"Who is dead," Brad said.

"Well, Peter Zimmer is definitely avoiding all of us," Mary said. "He didn't even nibble at my offer to interview him to promote the CP Center. I tried to set up a meeting with him, but he said he had to run it by the CP Center Board first. I haven't heard back from him."

Dylan said, "I'm not surprised. In his position, would you talk to an ex-boyfriend of a dead employee, or anyone from Wall Street, or a reporter known for her provocative style?"

Mary raised her eyebrows slightly and replied, "So, he's as paranoid as you?"

Brad said, "Maybe Thompson was just a conduit for Zimmer, and now that he's dead, Zimmer is working directly with Blair Armstrong."

"Maybe," Dylan said and paused to think.

"But?" Mary asked.

"But Armstrong was even more anxious to hire me than Vaughn, which means she probably isn't getting the data now. Her bad returns suggest that too. And she's obsessed with how well I know Zimmer.

So, either she doesn't know him or, if he really was working with Thompson, he shut it all down, possibly because Caroline found out about it."

Mary said, "Or he could have had a falling out with her, maybe over money."

Dylan replied, "Whatever the circumstances, Armstrong wants in, or back in, and she thinks I might be the key."

Brad said, "Even now, after the bad forecast you gave her?"

"I don't know," Dylan said. "I haven't heard from her."

They were all quiet for a while, drinking their coffee and thinking.

Dylan broke the silence. "I might be able to get Armstrong to meet with me again."

"How?" Mary asked.

"I'll tell her I'm going to arrange a meeting with Peter Zimmer."

Brad asked, "Won't you risk taunting her?"

"Probably, but I'll arrange it for a public place."

"What if she doesn't go for it?" Mary asked. "Or if she does, what happens when Zimmer isn't there?"

"I haven't figured that out yet," Dylan answered. "But we have to try something."

They were all quiet again for a while.

Brad broke the silence this time. He asked Dylan, "Did you get a chance to go through Caroline's bills?"

"I'm halfway through."

"Find anything?" Brad asked.

"Maybe, but I'm not sure if it's significant. I should be done soon."

Brad asked, "Will you have time to finish before you start your new job?"

"What?" Mary exclaimed. "You're starting a new job?"

Dylan shot an exasperated look at Brad.

"Sorry, I thought she knew," Brad responded.

"Where are you going?" Mary demanded.

"Macro-Quantitative Advisors. It's up in—"

"I know who they are," she interrupted. "Why didn't you say something?"

Dylan stared at her, a slight look of consternation on his face. "To you?"

She started to respond but stopped. After a few seconds, she said, "So, that's it? You're just going to stop helping us?"

Dylan pressed his lips tightly and glared at her.

Mary stared back at him with a look of disappointment and anger.

Brad interjected, "Mary, Dylan's helped much more than I ever asked. And he still has a little time, so we should make the most of it."

Dylan looked down and said, "I'll finish going through Caroline's stuff tomorrow."

"Thanks," Brad said.

Mary sighed, looked at Brad and said, "I'm going to talk to my boss about airing this whole story. Maybe if I can shed some light on it, something might break."

Brad asked, "Do you think he'll let you do a story with what we have?"

"Legal will be all over me, but I've already laid the groundwork with my special series, and he's been pushing me to find out if Dylan's conspiracy claims are real or not. So, tying it into everything else might get him to agree to it."

Brad nodded, then said, "The only idea I have is the FBI. I think it's time we talk to them."

Dylan looked up quickly and said, "What?"

Brad replied, "I didn't get anywhere with Detective Garcia, and now Hank is lying in his bed with a knife wound from the same guy that probably killed Caroline. I'm not going to wait until you or Mary is killed."

"I think Brad's right," Mary said.

Dylan stood up, walked to the middle of the living room and stopped, his back to them. He turned and said, "Just wait until I've had a chance to meet with Blair Armstrong again."

Brad stood up and said, "What's going to change? We'll have to go to the FBI either way."

Dylan replied, "I don't know, but I want to find out before you talk to the FBI. And I want to see if Hank knows anyone in the NYPD who can help."

Mary said, "So, you want us to just wait until you have to leave for your new job?"

Dylan stared at her, his jaw clenched, breathing quickly through his nose. He turned to Brad and said, "There's something more going on here. There has to be, because—"

"Because you can't accept coincidences," Mary interrupted.

"No!" Dylan snapped. "Because it's the only explanation for why none of us are dead yet!"

After a long silence, Brad said, "Alright, Dylan. I'll wait until you've had a chance to meet with Armstrong. Is there anything else?"

"No," Dylan answered.

Brad said, "Alright, I have to catch my train back to Washington."

Dylan said, "I'll go with you to the station."

"Me too," Mary added, standing up.

"Thanks, but I'd rather go alone," Brad replied.

CHAPTER 58
Sunday, June 3, 2012

THE WOMAN who answered the door could have been in her mid-thirties or late forties, Dylan thought. She was pretty, if not beautiful, medium height, thin and athletic looking in her workout clothes, with auburn hair and tanned skin.

"You must be Dylan," she said and offered her hand. "I'm Sandy. Hank's waiting for you."

"Nice to meet you," he replied and shook her hand. Her grip was strong, but relaxed. He added, "If this is a bad time—"

"No, of course not," she interrupted, stepping out to the hallway. "I'm going for a run, and Hank's getting antsy to do some work anyway, even though he's supposed to be resting. But you only have an hour. Then he's mine." She smiled and walked to the elevator.

Hank Stewart was sitting with his legs on the couch, leaning against a pillow when Dylan walked in. Stewart smiled and swung his legs around to the floor, wincing slightly as he did.

"Don't get up," Dylan said and walked over to shake his hand. "You look pretty good, for an old man with a slice in his side."

"You should see me after I've been shot."

Dylan widened his eyes as he sat down in a leather lounge chair, putting the folder he had brought with him on the coffee table. "You've been shot?"

"Twice," Stewart replied.

"I'm impressed. I've only ripped the ligaments off both ankles playing basketball. Painful as hell, but no scars and definitely not life threatening. Is that how you got such a beautiful girlfriend?"

"Sort of," Stewart answered.

"What does she do?"

"She's a lawyer."

"Ah," Dylan said. "Probably a partner in a high powered firm too, I'm guessing."

"You've already figured out she was my divorce lawyer, right?" Stewart said.

Dylan just smiled.

"That's quick," Stewart said. "How'd you know?"

"Well, not too many women who come across like her are dating ex-cop private detectives living in a one bedroom apartment in Normandie Court. She must have had the opportunity to get to know you pretty well first. Brad told me you're divorced. You have to spend a lot of time with your divorce lawyer."

Stewart smiled and said, "Mary told me you could be brilliant, when you weren't being stubborn and stupid."

Dylan laughed for several seconds. "Fair enough. If you don't mind me asking, how'd you afford such an expensive divorce lawyer?"

"You make a lot of enemies *and friends* in the New York AG's Office. I called in a favor. I'm guessing that's what you wanted to talk about."

"The first thing, yes," Dylan answered. "How'd you know?"

"Not as clever as you. Mary stopped by and told me you were going to ask about an alternative to going to the FBI. I don't think the NYPD can help, but I put in a few calls to some old contacts in the AG's Office. They'll love the chance to one-up the FBI. But I have to say I agree with Brad. This has gotten out of control. You should talk to the FBI."

"Well, call it being stubborn and stupid," Dylan said, "but the FBI is too focused on me and my data manipulation theory. I have an ego, but not that big. I know who I work for, and I have an idea of what the FBI is supposed to be working on. Neither one justifies the attention they've given me. And I'm pretty sure they intimidated my old business school professor into not talking to me."

Stewart replied, "That's not stupid, but unless you're convinced there's a connection between your theory and Caroline's murder, you are being stubborn by not going to the FBI for help. They can protect you and Mary and Brad."

"I'm not convinced, but I sense something. I just need a little more time and information to figure it out. That's the second reason I'm here."

"Is the second reason in that folder?" Stewart asked.

"Yeah, these are some of Caroline's old bills and statements. I wanted to go through what I found and see what you think."

"Go ahead."

"Okay, it took me a while to see anything wrong," Dylan said, "but there are three days in April where it looks like Caroline flew to New York."

"What do you mean, looks like?" Stewart asked.

"She didn't pay for her flights with a credit card because there's nothing on her statements. So, it probably wasn't for her job since she would have charged those expenses."

"Then how do you know she flew anywhere?"

"Well, early on April 4th, she took money out of an ATM at Ronald Reagan National Airport in Washington. That was a Wednesday, so I doubt she was heading to New York to visit friends. And if she was, why not take the train? Anyway, two hours later, there's a record of her making a call from her cell phone to a toll-free number. I tried the number and got some polite woman who asked me my name. When I asked her who I had called, she said I had the wrong number and hung up. But she had a distinct Long Island accent. I'm thinking it had to be a car service, assuming Caroline flew somewhere. Of course, the accent suggests New York."

"That's a leap just based on a phone call and an accent," Stewart said.

"Not when you put it together with the other two days," Dylan countered. "On April 12th, she had two credit card transactions at LaGuardia Airport—one around eight in the morning and another at six at night. The first was probably when she arrived and the second when she was leaving. She has no record of outgoing cell calls that day or the next. I thought it was strange, but then I remembered how she always misplaced her cell phone. So, I think the early morning credit card charge was probably for a phone call to a car service in New York, maybe the same one as before. The second one at night I could tell was food."

"Assuming you're right, then someone else paid for her flights," Stewart said. "So, who was she visiting?"

"Caroline supposedly had a job offer here in New York around that time. Whatever firm she interviewed with likely paid for all of her transportation."

"That makes sense. Okay, what about the third day?"

"That's the interesting one," Dylan said. "She had another early morning ATM withdrawal at Reagan National on April 17th and a credit card charge a little later, which I assume was a phone call to a car service in New York again since her phone bill shows no cell calls for two days. The next day, she charged something at Saks Fifth Avenue and a Duane Reade here in the city. She must have stayed overnight, but there was no hotel charge on her credit card bill."

"Okay, so she misplaced her cell phone again, and she stayed overnight," Stewart said, thinking aloud. "She could have stayed with that friend of hers in the city."

"You mean Lindsey Cho. I thought of that, but Lindsey never mentioned it to Brad. I'm still going to ask him to check with her, but my bet is she stayed in a hotel paid for by whoever she was interviewing with. The Duane Reade was on 52nd and Madison. The hotel is probably in that vicinity."

Stewart thought for a moment, then said, "Probably an expensive hotel too if it services corporate clients who have their own accounts. I'll get someone to check out the major hotels in that area."

"No legitimate hotel is going to give you information on their clientele," Dylan replied.

A slight smile appeared on Stewart's face. "If she stayed in a hotel, I'll find it."

Dylan sat at his table late Sunday night with his eyes closed, only the light in his galley kitchen on to illuminate the notebook and the half empty bottle of Sam Adams sitting in front of him. The notebook page was empty. He hadn't written anything down, not even any doodling.

He scrolled through the numerous unanswered questions he had stored in his mind, trying to figure out the common thread. *Someone knew Caroline knew something . . . Someone knew about her laptop . . . Someone knew Shannon had it . . . But how?*

His eyes shot open . . . *Someone was listening to Caroline, to Shannon . . . to me . . .*

He whipped his head around and stared at his coffee maker.

CHAPTER 59
Monday, June 4, 2012

DYLAN WAS tired and in a bad mood as he waited in line at Dunkin Donuts for his first cup of coffee early Monday morning. He had been up until two o'clock searching his apartment for anything that looked like a listening bug. The carcasses of a few dead roaches were all he'd found. And now, the same nicely dressed, two hundred pound woman he often saw when he got his second cup of coffee was ahead of him ordering several specialty drinks.

After fifteen minutes, he finally got his coffee, along with a jelly donut, and started to leave. He looked up and saw a man and a woman in similar looking light gray suits walk in. He shook his head. *It just keeps getting better.*

"Mr. Regan, could we have fifteen minutes of your time?" Special Agent Cole asked him, forcing a smile. Special Agent Ricci was her usual martinet self.

"I know, I know," Dylan said. "There's a 'Buy One Gray Suit, Get One Free' sale at the Men's Warehouse." He paused for effect, then added, "They look nice on you two . . . really."

Cole's smile diminished to a look of tolerance, while Ricci glared at him, or smiled—he couldn't distinguish. He apparently still didn't have a career in comedy.

"Downstairs," Cole replied, clearly annoyed.

Dylan hesitated, but after his conversation with Petro, he was curious. And he was pretty sure they wouldn't shoot him there, even if they wanted to. He led them down to the coffee cave and over to his usual table. The green sweat suit lady wasn't there, but the tall, thin, well dressed black man was, sipping coffee and checking messages. It was too early for German tourists.

Cole tasted his coffee, then said, "So, we were in the neighborhood and wanted to check to make sure you knew the police confirmed that Darryl Dwyer killed Caroline Brenner. The investigation is closed. It's a tragedy, but you and Mr. Johnson can hopefully move on now."

"Does that mean you won't be following me anymore?"

"You must be imagining things again," Cole replied. "By the way, how is your night class going down at Georgetown?"

"I keep sleeping through it."

Cole feigned a smile. "And how is Professor Petropoulos?"

"You know him?"

"We have some friends in common. Washington is a small place."

Dylan now understood the purpose of the meeting. In case Petro hadn't been clear, they were there to make sure he got the message—any effort he made to pursue his data manipulation theory would be blocked. He couldn't tell if they were threatening him or just informing him. Either way, they confirmed what he'd already believed—whatever was being done with the employment data, the FBI knew about it.

Dylan smiled and asked, "Do these Washington friends like to manipulate economic data?"

Cole scrutinized him for a moment, then replied in a harsh tone, "Your paranoid conspiracy theories only serve to reinforce your lack of credibility, Mr. Regan. Hardly a smart strategy to advance your career as a strategist."

"Touché," Dylan said. "Question for you . . . Does the FBI contract out its killings?"

Cole's stare grew more intense. "Ms. Brenner's murder is solved. There's nothing else for you to concern yourself with."

Cole stood up, and Ricci followed. She glared at Dylan and said, "We're the good guys. Remember that."

"I'll miss our long talks, Agent," Dylan quipped as they started to leave. "But we'll always have Dunkin Donuts."

Ricci stopped and turned. Cole quickly put his hand on her arm, then looked down at Dylan and said, "You're a funny guy, Mr. Regan. Ever consider a career in comedy instead of strategy? You might be better at it."

Dylan stared at his Bloomberg screen, watching stock markets and interest rates around the globe continue to grind higher in response to the May employment report. Right now, though, he didn't care.

He knew he should call Donald Granger and accept his offer, assuming it was still good, but all he could think about was his encounter with the FBI this morning and the possibility that his apartment was bugged. It would explain a lot—how the killers knew about Caroline's laptop and what was on it, how they knew Shannon Dunn was going to drop it off with him, how they knew that Hank wasn't an insurance investigator, and maybe even why Peter Zimmer was avoiding all of them.

But he hadn't found one. And Blair Armstrong would be acting like she knew more if she had actually been listening in on the meetings in his apartment. So would the FBI. But someone had to be listening. It was the only explanation for a lot of things.

His cell phone rang. "Hello, it's Dylan . . ."

"Atul here. Do you have a moment?"

"Oh . . . sure," he answered.

"Don't sound so happy," Atul replied.

"Sorry, there's a lot going on."

"Is that why you forgot to call me about SCT last week?"

"Shit," Dylan muttered. "Sorry. Do you have time now?"

"Then you haven't noticed all the options activity in SCT the past two days?"

"No, I haven't been following it."

"Well, SCT call option buying spiked Friday and again today," Atul said. "Someone thinks the stock is going up a lot and soon."

"Who's behind it?"

"Some big names are rumored, including your friends at MQA. I called to see what you think. I closed out my shorts on the bonds and stock, but I'm wondering if it's too late to get long now. I don't want to get whipsawed."

Dylan paused to think. He knew MQA had been buying SCT bonds pretty aggressively, and now they were supposedly involved in SCT's call options. He'd never heard of MQA gambling on a situation and being dead wrong. They knew something, and they expected it to pay off big.

Dylan said, "Okay, I'll give you my best read, but it's all speculation based on the price action and who you say is involved. I don't want you blaming me if it doesn't work out."

"But isn't that what a strategist is for? Hah, only joking, my friend. I understand."

"I don't think I like Indian humor any more than Indian food," Dylan quipped. "Anyway, this is how I see it. SCT should be in bankruptcy but it isn't, and now the stock and bonds are shooting higher. There are two things that could be driving it. It's either in the process of filing a major patent or someone is on the verge of acquiring it. Either one could send the stock and bonds up fifty percent from here. I would get in now, but be ready to sell immediately if the news doesn't pan out. If I'm right, the bonds are the place to be since their upside is almost as much as the stock."

"Fabulous! Right in line with my thinking. Thank you, Dylan. I owe you one, again."

"I'll call us even if you do something for me."

Atul replied, "Anything, so long as it is legal."

"It is. I'd like you to meet with this young veteran I'm trying to help find a job. He just graduated from UConn. He's smart, eager and tough."

"Any experience?" Atul asked.

"Does Afghanistan count? He's seen the worst of people. He should fit right in with a hedge fund."

"Who said you're not a salesman? Have him call me."

"One last thing . . ."

"I thought we were even?" Atul replied. "My Indian humor again. Go ahead."

"Can you track down what MQA's returns have been since the start of the financial crisis?"

Atul was silent for a few seconds, then said, "That will be difficult, since they are so secretive, but I might be able to. Is something going on?"

"Just doing my homework. Thanks."

"Sure. My pleasure, my friend. Cheers," Atul said and hung up.

Dylan sent Ron Pahlavi an email with Atul's contact details and then leaned back in his chair to think about SCT. If hedge fund traders were just learning about the options activity, then he knew no one at FTS had a clue about it yet. The call option buying, along with MQA's involvement, told him something big was going to be announced soon. One way or another, he knew he wouldn't be at FTS much longer. This was an opportunity to say goodbye to his favorite co-workers.

He walked over to Bob Berkley and said, "Hey Bob, I just got off the phone with MQA. They're thinking about selling their SCT bonds. Have you talked to them today?"

"No," Berkley replied, clicking out of a real estate website as he stood up. "I don't like to bug them unless I have a good trade idea. You think they're looking to dump SCT?"

"It sounded like they plan to book some profits with the bonds running up so much recently. And you know when they sell, they sell a lot. Check with them to make sure before you tell McDonald. Okay?"

"Yeah, okay. That's awesome, buddy. I'll call them and see what's going on."

Dylan went back to his desk and sat down. Ten minutes later, he noticed Berkley pick up his phone. Then Billy McDonald's line lit up on the phone turret. Dylan knew Berkley was calling McDonald to hide the fact that he was giving him the information about SCT immediately. He assumed they were planning on how to exploit the expected massive sale of SCT bonds by MQA, probably by shorting them in advance.

But MQA had no intention of selling their SCT bonds. In fact, Dylan anticipated an announcement soon that would likely drive SCT bonds and stock higher. When that happened, McDonald would lose a lot of money, and he'd only have Berkley to blame. It was a simple and elegant manipulation, Dylan mused, without anyone being killed.

Dylan waited a few minutes, then walked over to Lin Chang. "Hi, Lin," he greeted.

She stood up immediately in a sign of respect. "Yes, Dylan."

"Lin, regarding SCT, you should tell your clients who sold their bonds to try to buy them back. I think there's some good news coming soon. Billy would probably short some bonds to your clients, but don't tell him I told you that. Try to buy them as soon as possible, before the price runs up too much. Okay?"

"Yes, Dylan. Thank you." She was excited.

Dylan walked back to his desk, sat down and watched as Lin Chang diligently called her clients. A half hour later, she stood up and walked over to Billy McDonald. They took a minute to agree on a price that her clients would buy SCT bonds from him. After she went back to her seat, Dylan saw McDonald pick up his phone and Berkley's line light up.

CHAPTER 60
Monday, June 4, 2012

"GANNON!" SHE heard Rothstein bellow just as she pushed his office door open. She looked over her shoulder and startled briefly. Jane Reyes was right behind her.

Rothstein had commanded them to come to his office for a lunch meeting. He was sitting in one of the two leather lounge chairs around his coffee table, eating a fried egg, bacon and cheese sandwich, a large cup of very light coffee on the table. Two small salads in plastic containers with two bottles of water were at the other end of the table. Reyes sat down on the couch, opened her salad and started eating.

Mary stood there, looking down. *Is this lunch?* She sat in the other lounge chair, picked up her bottle of water and said, "I prefer sparkling."

Rothstein was chewing a mouthful of sandwich, so he couldn't say anything, but his expression, as always, spoke for him. He gulped down half of his coffee like it was water, sat back in his chair and grumbled, "What do you got?"

Mary put down her water and grabbed her notebook. "Okay, Governor Hayes is going to announce Senator Murphy as his running mate at the Lost Revolution rally."

"Bullshit," Rothstein barked.

"It's true, and I'm going to have an exclusive with the two of them afterwards."

"Bullshit isn't my opinion," Rothstein snapped. "It's a fact, like you being so naïve and full of yourself that you didn't stop to question this fucking joke being pulled on you."

Mary felt like she had just dropped the twenty floors from his office to the ground. She was missing something, she realized. "Why is it bullshit?"

Rothstein looked at her as if debating whether he should waste his time. He finally said, "Hayes won't make any announcement about anyone but himself during that protest, or rally, whatever. He's not going to compete for attention while all those kids are screaming about jobs. He'd come across like just another political opportunist, which is what he is, but that's what you're supposed to be showing people."

She saw it now. It made sense. Why had Jeff told her Hayes was going to announce it at the rally? He needed to explain himself—again.

"Okay, I'm naïve for thinking he'd do it during the rally," she replied, "but he's going to announce it soon, and I'll have the exclusive."

"That's not why you're fucking naïve," Rothstein snapped. "That's why you're full of yourself. You only looked at what this bogus story meant for you. Get your head out of that pretty little ass and question everything if you want to be a real journalist."

Mary pressed her lips, then replied, "Alright, then why am I naïve?"

"You're naïve because you believed that suck-up boyfriend of yours that Hayes would make the announcement this week. What did he get for playing with you like that?"

She was stunned that Rothstein knew Jeff had given her the information, but she quickly realized it was logical. Then she was furious, but more at herself. She glared at him and said, "You're an asshole."

"Old news," Rothstein shot back. "What about this revolution or rally or whatever?"

Mary recovered quickly and replied, "The next Lost Revolution rally is Wednesday here in Manhattan, but the movement is taking on a new angle that should be big. Jane and I have arranged preferred coverage for helping them organize last week's rally."

Reyes looked up from her notebook at Rothstein and said, "It'll be good. You'll like it."

Rothstein contorted his face as if he'd just swallowed something awful. He glanced out the window for a few seconds. He looked back at Mary and said, "Listen, this Lost Revolution *thing* is going to die unless you find a couple of credible faces in those kids running it and highlight them as the leaders. Right now, everyone's watching because of you and ICIN, but if this movement—or whatever you're calling it—if it can't fly on its own, it'll burn out quickly, just like that *Occupy Wall Street* bullshit."

"But—" Mary started.

"Is that how you listen, you talk?" Rothstein growled. "There's something real here, including a story, but unless you can get this two-second attention span, shit for brains generation to listen, it'll die. Hayes got something right last week. The goddamn politicians are confiscating these kids' futures. It'll be too late soon to do anything about it. When that happens, violence will be the only way to change anything. That'll be a real revolution."

"But won't we just be orchestrating the story to keep it alive?" Mary challenged. "How does that fit with your lecture about people making their own truths out of the news?"

Rothstein stared at her as if he wanted to smile, but didn't. "Just pick the faces of this thing. And make sure they look and sound good. No one likes ugly revolutionaries."

Mary pressed her lips and thought for a while. "Fine. I know who they should be."

Rothstein sat up and finished his coffee. "You got anything new on Regan's conspiracy story? Friday's employment report made him look bad. You too."

She ignored his dig and replied, "Yes, the story's getting even more interesting. It looks like this woman economist at the BLS might have been murdered to cover up a data leaking arrangement with a Wall Street firm and a large hedge fund. I actually knew her. And there are two other murders that may be related too. One of them is that woman who was pushed onto the subway tracks."

Rothstein's eyes widened slightly. "That's a real story, but how's it related to Regan's conspiracy theory?"

"Well, he's convinced they're connected and thinks the FBI is involved too. He doesn't believe three murders and two conspiracies involving the BLS can be a coincidence. I agree."

Rothstein replied, "You're assuming there are two conspiracies. He might just be hyping his theory to get attention and distract from his bad forecasts."

"He wouldn't do that," Mary said.

"So you say," Rothstein shot back. "I told you not—"

Reyes interrupted, "There's a real story here."

Rothstein's face contorted again as he shot a look at Reyes. He glanced out the window for a moment, then looked back at Mary and asked, "What do you want to do?"

Mary leaned forward in her chair and said, "I'm going to raise questions about the BLS and these three murders in my next segment. I want to use that as a segue into a special piece on the BLS and the data leaking scheme we've uncovered . . . and Dylan's data manipulation theory."

"That all?" Rothstein quipped. "You got any proof to highlight?"

"Besides three bodies, just 'he said, she said' stuff right now. I'm betting that raising some suspicions will shake something out."

Rothstein stared at her as if he'd never seen her before. "You're talking about linking three murders and an insider trading scheme to the BLS, implicating the FBI, and suggesting the most important economic series in the world is being manipulated . . . without any real proof . . ."

"I know how it sounds and the lawyers will—"

"Fuck the lawyers," Rothstein snapped. "I make those calls." He glared at her briefly, then looked down at his feet and snorted. After a long silence, he said, "Without some proof, none of this is real news. It's too fantastic."

Mary waited a moment, then said, "Whatever you think of my history with Dylan, I know this—when he senses something's wrong, he's usually right. If he says something's going on with the jobs data and it's connected to these murders, I believe there's something there. It's the truth, even if we can't prove it . . . and people need to know."

Rothstein looked up at her and said, "Keep talking like that and you're going to have to stop wearing those hooker outfits . . . Okay, cover the murders in your next segment, but I want something more before you go ahead with a focus piece on the BLS—enough for me to tell the lawyers to screw themselves."

Reyes looked at Mary and said, "Don't worry, that's not a lot."

Mary nodded, trying to control the adrenaline gushing through her body.

"What about Hayes?" Rothstein demanded. "You should have something on him by now."

Mary took a deep breath to calm down. She flipped back in her notebook, then looked up and said, "Well, Hank's found several shady financial deals that Hayes was involved with over his career as Governor, but no smoking gun. The SEC has investigated him a few times too, but no charges were ever filed. There are a few possible affairs too. We're still digging."

"That's every fucking politician in this country," Rothstein sneered. "Dig faster before he becomes the next President. I'm done. Get out."

CHAPTER 61
Monday, June 4, 2012

DYLAN WAS typing up a draft resignation email to Joe Brooks and Andrew Cantor just after lunch when his Blackberry rang. "Hello, this is Dylan . . ."

"Mr. Regan, this is Donald Granger's assistant."

"Yes, hello . . ."

"Mr. Granger asked me to call to request your answer."

Dylan hesitated, taken aback. He knew what she meant, but he replied, "My answer?"

"Yes, to your offer of employment."

"Oh . . . yes. My answer is 'yes'."

"Very good. I am sure he will be pleased. Cheers," she said and hung up.

Dylan bowed his head and breathed out heavily. He didn't know why it didn't feel good. Maybe he was too accustomed to the abuse at FTS. Maybe it was Granger's pressure tactics. Maybe it was because he felt he was leaving Brad behind. But it was the best decision for his career. He knew that.

His Blackberry rang again and he jumped. He grabbed it angrily and looked at the number. He didn't recognize it. "Yes?" he answered.

"Dylan, it's Hank."

"Hank . . . uh, how are you feeling?"

"Better, thanks. Listen, I found the hotel where Caroline stayed—the Palace on Madison."

"Uh, that's great," Dylan said, trying to focus. "Were you able to find anything else out?"

"Yeah, she apparently didn't have her cell phone with her since she used her room phone to make two calls. One was to the same toll-free number as the first time—the car service, if you're right. The second was to a personal cell. I called it an hour ago."

"Who was it?" Dylan asked.

"Rick Jones, Blair Armstrong's right hand man."

"What?" Dylan exclaimed, then glanced around the trading floor to see if anyone had heard him. "Are you sure?"

"I'm sure. I got his voice mail and hung up."

Dylan was silent, processing what Stewart had told him.

Stewart eventually asked, "What are you thinking?"

"I'm thinking I need to meet with Blair Armstrong."

"You sure that's a good idea? If she's behind these murders, do you really want her to know you're on to her?"

"That's the problem."

"What do you mean?"

"Whoever killed Caroline also attacked you, and if they know about you, then they know about me and Brad. But then why not try to kill me too, and Brad?"

Stewart replied, "Maybe Armstrong still thinks you can help her."

"That's why I have to meet with her. I have to find out."

"Well, if you do set up a meeting with her, let me know where and when, and I'll send someone to watch out for you. Don't worry, you'll never see him."

"Okay, thanks. I'll text you. This isn't your cell, is it?"

"No. I'm calling from Sandy's apartment on the West Side," Stewart replied.

"I guess you are feeling better."

"Hah, not that much better. I stayed over last night because she was a little anxious."

"About you?"

"No. A couple of women were attacked in her neighborhood the past week. It's been all over the news."

"Really?" Dylan replied. "I haven't been following the local news."

"Yeah, a woman was nearly raped last night outside a building across the street from here. It's a high rent district too. Sandy was pretty upset. She'll be okay. I'll make sure of it."

"With a slice in your side?"

"I brought my friend with me," Stewart said.

"Your friend?" Dylan replied.

"My gun."

"Oh . . ."

"Anyway," Stewart continued, "I'm still working on identifying the firm with that toll-free number. Be careful with Armstrong."

"I will," Dylan said and hung up. He turned to his Bloomberg screen, put his fingers on the keyboard and typed an instant message to Blair Armstrong: "Peter wants to meet."

Five minutes later, an instant message crossed his Bloomberg screen from Armstrong: "Beer Bar tonight at 5:30. Don't be late."

She took the bait. But it was a strange venue to discuss leaking the most important economic data in the world. At least it was an unlikely place to try to kill him.

Dylan was early, even though he figured Blair Armstrong would be late. It was 5:10 p.m., and he had already been standing on the other side of Vanderbilt Avenue for thirty minutes watching The Beer Bar.

He crossed Vanderbilt, walked through the entrance to the outdoor patio and claimed a tall table with a good angle to see Armstrong when she came in. It was surprisingly busy for a Monday night. He saw Lina on the other side of the patio waiting on a loud group of financial market manikins. He recognized a few of them—JPMorgan traders and salespeople. That was him four years ago, when he had it all, before the world changed . . . and his imploded. That would be him again soon, once he joined MQA. But he had to wait one more day, to try to help Brad. Then he'd resign.

His Blackberry rang. "Hello, this is Dylan . . ."

"Mr. Regan, this is Donald Granger's assistant."

"Oh, hello again. How are you?"

"Fine. Mr. Granger would like to invite you to dinner tomorrow night at his home in Greenwich to celebrate you joining MQA. Can you attend?"

"Uh . . . yes, of course."

"Should the car pick you up at FTS or Normandie Court?" she asked.

"Um . . . FTS, please." He realized she assumed he had already resigned.

"Very good. It will be there at four-thirty. Thank you." She hung up.

Dylan bowed his head and closed his eyes. He moaned softly. Maybe Granger wouldn't know he hadn't resigned yet. No, Granger seemed to know everything.

He sensed someone near him and opened his eyes. Two shapely legs rose from the ground in front of him. He followed them up to a short, white leather skirt, to a light blue blouse under a short white leather jacket, and then to an attractive, angular face with piercing green eyes and short bleached blond hair—Blair Armstrong, tan and intense.

A large, very white man in a loose fitting navy blue suit stood behind her. He was maybe six foot four, and maybe under three hundred fifty pounds, crew cut, late twenties, and almost intimidating, but not quite. He appeared to be her bodyguard. If he had a gun, it was hidden under one of his many rolls.

"Hello, Dylan," she said, her piercing eyes fixated on his. "When does Peter want to meet?"

Dylan hinted at a smile to suggest he wasn't nervous, but he could feel his shirt sticking to his back under his suit jacket. He answered, "When you and I have agreed on the details of our working relationship. The sooner we do that, the sooner we all meet."

She stepped closer, a subtle, seductive smile slowly appearing. Her knee touched his as she placed her hand on his chest, stood on her toes and leaned towards him. He froze as her lips parted and she kissed him, her firm tongue moving into his mouth slightly, then stopping. It wasn't passionate, or sexual, or even friendly. It was cold and threatening, like no kiss he'd ever experienced.

Armstrong stepped back, her lips separating from his quickly. She played with his tie and said calmly, without smiling, "If you wanted to fuck me, you should have just asked. You could have had the real thing. Now, you'll never work at a real firm in this city again. I promise . . . and you know I always keep my promises."

Armstrong turned and started to walk away.

Dylan didn't know what had just happened, but he sensed he was about to lose any opportunity to ever get her to talk. He had to say something to stop her from leaving. "So, you want me to tell Peter you have no interest in working with him," he asked in as casual a tone as he could fake.

She stopped, turned and walked back to the table, signaling to her bodyguard to hang back. She smiled—the tolerant, haughty smile of someone who knows the answer but is forced to explain it to someone who doesn't. She said, "You don't *know* Peter Zimmer, Dylan. You never have. I suspected as much from the start. I just had to be certain. You were never going to work for me. I would never hire a third-rate strategist from a no-name firm."

He didn't have time to feel insulted. He had to figure out if she was guessing or if Zimmer had told her. "Not bad," he replied. "Accuse me of not knowing Peter to get me to prove it, all to hide the fact that you don't know Peter and never have. I know because he told me."

"Hmm, you are smart, Dylan—the one thing I like about you. But I don't need to know Peter Zimmer to know you're not working with him, even if you might know him."

He had her talking. She couldn't help herself, he knew. She had to show she was smarter, in control. He said, "Interesting. You don't know Peter, but somehow you know I'm not working with him."

A scornful smile crossed her face. "I know because no one with real information would ever make themselves look as bad as you have with your forecasts, even as a cover. And no one with real information would hang out in that cesspool you work at unless he had to. Peter Zimmer isn't going to ignore me for the likes of you. You can't do anything for him. You've probably been trying to play both of us." She paused and glared at him. "You actually thought you could manipulate me?" She snorted and turned to leave.

"And you actually thought you could get away with murder?" Dylan replied, then glanced around to see if anyone had heard him.

She stopped and turned back to him. She looked around cautiously, like he had. The patio had gotten more crowded and louder. She took a step closer, a bemused expression on her face, but she didn't respond.

Dylan continued: "You offered Caroline Brenner a job, but she found out about your arrangement with Ben Thompson and threatened to expose it. Then you had her killed."

Armstrong stepped slowly towards him, revelation on her face. "So, this is about your girlfriend at the BLS, the one who was killed in a hit-and-run . . . You have it backwards. People kill to work for Differential. People kill to work for me. Why would I offer her a job? She had no experience and no information. Even *you* are more qualified than she was."

"Touché, but I know Rick Jones called her while she was up here two weeks before she was murdered. Is that when she said she was going to expose you?"

Armstrong pressed her lips and breathed slowly through her nose—a bull deciding if she would attack or ignore this nuisance. "Rick spoke to her once. So what? She wouldn't even meet with him. But that didn't matter. I never would have wasted my time on her. It was obvious she didn't have anything I wanted . . . just like you." She paused, realizing she was talking too much. "Clever . . . very clever. I know the police found the man who killed your girlfriend. I'm not sure what game you're playing, Dylan, but it's over."

She turned and strode away, her bodyguard clearing a path to a waiting black limousine.

CHAPTER 62
Tuesday, June 5, 2012

DYLAN STOOD outside his office building on Madison Avenue late Tuesday afternoon watching the streams of people racing to get by each other, so they could get by the next person and the next and the next. He looked at his watch—five minutes until the car picked him up to go to Donald Granger's house for dinner.

He was anxious, and his stomach was in knots. He hadn't resigned yet, and he was certain Granger knew it. Would Granger rescind his offer? But how could he start at MQA tomorrow? Or even this week?

Blair Armstrong hadn't arranged Caroline's murder. He was sure of that now after their meeting. She never even thought Caroline was part of Thompson's data leaking arrangement. And Armstrong wasn't working with Peter Zimmer either. She didn't even know him.

Armstrong might be lying, but he believed her. It made sense. Caroline never would have confronted her with what she knew. The only way Armstrong would have known what Caroline had figured out is if she had another contact inside the BLS. But If Armstrong did have another contact, then she probably would have been getting the jobs data all along, and her investment returns wouldn't have tanked after Thompson died. No, Thompson was her only contact.

Like Sygowski and Vaughn, Armstrong was a crook, but she wasn't a murderer.

But if Armstrong wasn't behind Caroline's murder, then she wasn't involved in Darryl Dwyer's or Shannon Dunn's murder either. There had to be someone else, and he couldn't leave Brad behind to figure it out by himself, to maybe be killed, while he made one and a half million dollars at MQA.

He just needed a little time, a week, before he started. He was risking a once in a lifetime opportunity—his career. You didn't make Granger wait. But Brad needed his help.

He had called Brad this morning to tell him about his meeting with Armstrong. Brad insisted it was time to go to the FBI. He argued with Brad. If Armstrong wasn't a killer, then the only other people involved with enough money and resources to arrange three murders was the FBI. But Brad refused to believe they had anything to do with Caroline's murder. He convinced Brad to wait and talk later.

The car was late. Dylan leaned against his office building. His mind drifted back to Caroline. She was very smart, maybe brilliant. She must have figured out that Thompson was leaking the jobs data. Even if she hadn't, she discovered something that had gotten her killed, and it likely had something to do with the BLS. But how did the murderer know what she knew? She probably would have gone to the authorities as soon as she was certain . . . unless . . .

Dylan pulled his Blackberry out and dialed Brad. He got his voicemail and said, "Brad, it's Dylan. Listen, if Caroline discovered Thompson's data leaking scheme, then the first person she would have gone was her boss, Peter Zimmer. We have to find a way to get to him. I have an idea. Call me."

The limousine pulled up to the curb just as he hung up. The same driver as always stepped out and opened the door for him. He slid into the back seat and they headed for Greenwich.

When they got to the FDR Drive, traffic was bumper-to-bumper. Dylan leaned forward from the backseat to catch the driver's eye and said, "Looks like we're going to be here a while. We've done this a few times now, but I don't know your name. I'm Dylan Regan."

"John Morris. Nice to meet you, sir," the middle-aged man replied.

"How long have you been driving for MQA, John?"

"I work for a private firm, not MQA, but I drive exclusively for them."

"So, how long have you been doing that?"

"A while, sir."

"That long . . . So, what do you think of MQA?"

"It's a great company, sir."

Dylan smiled. Morris wasn't even an MQA employee and he was inscrutable. Probably part of the training. Information was valuable. Never share it outside the company. Wall Street was the opposite of that culture. Dylan knew he would have to adjust.

After crawling in traffic for an hour, they merged onto I-95 and started to pick up speed. Dylan's Blackberry rang. It was Atul. "Hey Atul," he answered.

"Cheers," Atul replied. "You sound like you're in a car."

"I am. On my way to have dinner with Donald Granger at his home."

"Dinner? At his home? I'm quite impressed."

"Thanks. Do you have something for me?"

"Yes, I do, but it wasn't easy, so now you owe me."

"Better to owe you than to cheat you out of it, my father always said."

"I don't like American humor anymore than American food," Atul quipped. "Alright, MQA's returns have been spectacular the past three years, especially given that most quantitative investment managers have been horrendous since the start of the financial crisis. But MQA's returns were not so good before that. They were decimated by the crisis in '07 and '08. They supposedly lost over half of their assets by early 2009."

"Really? So, what changed?"

"I don't know," Atul replied, "but they've been killing it since mid-2009. MQA takes large, concentrated bets. They either pay off big or they lose big. This last jobs report is a perfect example. They supposedly bet huge on the number coming in above consensus, and it paid off."

The information surprised Dylan. Granger said MQA had similar views to his. He asked, "Are you sure about that?"

"Very sure," Atul answered. "I piggy-backed off a number of the trades that I learned they were doing from my contacts. It's been a very good month for me because it's been a very good one for them. And, thanks to you, reversing my position in SCT bonds has made it even better."

"Unbelievable," Dylan muttered, then glanced at John Morris to see if he was listening. Dylan took a deep breath and said, "Anything else, Atul?"

"That's it my friend, but you sound upset. What is this about?"

Dylan lowered his voice to make sure Morris couldn't hear him. "Donald Granger offered me a job. I'm supposed to start this week, but I haven't resigned from FTS yet. I need to take care of something first."

"I am truly impressed, Dylan, but are you sure MQA is the right place for you? No one works for Donald Granger. You serve him. He has a brutal reputation. There are even rumors that his wife's death in a boating accident was suspicious. I heard he married his current wife only three months later. She's Chinese and supposedly very connected to the political bureaucracy over there, which, as you know, controls the business community. Is this what you really want?"

"I appreciate your concern, Atul, but staying at FTS isn't an option. This is a phenomenal opportunity, however long it lasts. I'll be able to go anywhere afterwards."

"If you've already decided, why do you need to know MQA's investment returns?"

"I told you. I always do my homework," Dylan answered. "I'm at Granger's. I have to go. Thanks for the info, Atul."

The same nondescript American woman greeted Dylan and escorted him to the same small room in the rear of Granger's house. She said Granger would be with him shortly, bowed and left.

The round table was set up for two once again, but with only wine glasses, a platter of cheese and fruit, and an opened bottle of Chianti. He wondered if they were eating dinner somewhere else.

Dylan walked over to look out the window and glanced down at the generic chess set. The pieces were moved around. He looked closer. After a few seconds, he realized it was their game. Granger was tracking their mind chess match on an actual board. He was cheating.

Dylan suddenly felt a presence behind him and whipped around . . . Donald Granger stood two feet away, the same slight, inscrutable smile on his face.

"Hello, Dylan," Granger said and extended his hand. "Thank you for coming."

Dylan released the breath trapped in his throat, shook Granger's hand and replied, "Thank you for the invitation."

"Please, sit down," Granger said and gestured to the small table.

They sat down, and the same older Indian man in a white jacket entered the room. He poured them each a glass of Chianti and sparkling water, placed some fruit, crackers, and a selection of cheeses on two plates, and then set the plates in front of them. He asked Granger if there was anything else they wanted. Granger said no and the man left.

Granger took his wine glass, raised it in toast and said, "Here's to your first day with MQA."

Dylan hesitated, realizing Granger didn't know he hadn't resigned. He lifted his glass, forced a smile, more of relief than celebration, and took a long drink.

Granger sipped his wine, smiled a little more and said, "Pawn to e4."

The tension evaporated from Dylan's body. He nodded, smiled and replied, "Bishop to g7."

"Bishop to e2," Granger countered immediately, revealing that he had already thought through Dylan's likely move.

Dylan paused, then said, "Castle short."

"Castle short," Granger responded.

Dylan realized that Granger had mapped out more than a few moves. This was as close to a challenge as he had experienced from Granger. It felt almost physical. He froze the board in his head, then went through each of his possible moves and its path several moves ahead, building a decision tree until he detected a superior branch. He finally said, "Rook to e8."

"Queen to c2," Granger replied with a hint of impatience.

"Knight to h5," Dylan said.

Granger appeared surprised for a moment, then said, "Bishop takes knight on h5."

Was Granger actually nervous, Dylan wondered. Or was it a tactic? He decided to speed up the game to see how Granger reacted under pressure.

"Pawn takes bishop on h5," Dylan said.

Granger replied, "Knight to c4."

"Knight to e5."

Granger responded, "Knight to e3."

"Queen to h4."

Granger countered, "Bishop to d2."

"Knight to g4."

Granger said, "Knight takes knight on g4."

Dylan paused, detecting a weakness in Granger's positioning that he would be able to exploit several moves out. He closed his eyes and walked through his next five potential moves, eliminating the options one by one to produce his optimal path. What was he missing?

Nothing, he decided, and opened his eyes. "Pawn takes knight on g4," he said calmly, looking at Granger.

Granger sat back, swished his wine around slowly and took a sip. He smiled and said, "I have been meaning to ask you, Dylan, what do you think of the MQA building?"

It was a tactic, Dylan knew, to give Granger time to think. The pace had revealed something—Granger relied on diversion when he was in trouble. Dylan smiled and answered, "It's very impressive."

"I imagined that building while I struggled building MQA. I wanted it, and I eventually gave it to myself." Granger paused, then asked, "Now, what do you think about The Limit?"

"She's great. Sailing on her was incredible," Dylan replied. *Where is he going with this?*

"I imagined her after I won my first major client. I designed her myself. Most wealthy people buy their toys, but The Limit is not a toy. She is an achievement. I wanted her, and I gave her to myself." Granger paused again. "And what is your impression of this house?"

Dylan hesitated, then said, "It feels like a real home. I guess that's what strikes me the most. It's grand, but also warm. And your property is like a sanctuary."

Granger seemed pleased. "Thank you. That is exactly what I tried to achieve. I designed it when I passed my first billion in assets under management, and then I gave it to myself."

Dylan understood now. When Granger imagined something—when he wanted something—he found a way to get it. Granger wanted him, and now he had him. But Granger also seemed to be suggesting that he could have it all too, now that he had joined MQA. But he hadn't. Not yet.

Granger paused, as if contemplating the next example of his achievements he would highlight. "And have you had the opportunity to spend any time with Julie Watson recently?" Granger took a sip of wine, staring into Dylan's eyes all the while.

The room suddenly felt very warm to Dylan. Was it the rush of half a glass of red wine, or had Granger just revealed that he had given Watson to him—another example of the many luxuries he could have now that he had joined MQA? No—Julie Watson had a real job with a real firm . . . a real job with a real firm on retainer with MQA.

"Yes," Dylan answered slowly, realizing what her job really was.

Granger examined Dylan for a while, then took a sip of wine and nodded towards the chess set. He said, "I see that you noticed our game set up over there."

Dylan felt the tension ease, at least in him. "Yes, I did."

Granger said, "That is the actual Jaques of London Staunton chess set used in the third game of Bobby Fischer and Boris Spassky's 1972 match."

Dylan didn't expect Granger to explain why he was recording their mind chess game on an actual board. It was cheating, but Granger clearly wanted him to know. Maybe that was the point—Granger was controlling everything. It wasn't cheating. It was winning.

"It must have been expensive," Dylan said because he didn't know what else to say.

"No, not really," Granger replied. "You see, Dylan, expensive is a relative term to convey a sense of something's value versus its cost. I wanted it, and I gave it to myself, like everything else we have discussed. The only cost to me would have been if I could not have it—zero or one. It is not relative, so it is not expensive."

"I think I understand," Dylan said. Granger was quantitative, binomial—he either won or lost, got what he wanted or failed. There was no price too high if Granger wanted something.

But Dylan was still confused. Granger was sending him a message, but why?

Granger said, "I apologize that I only have time for some wine and cheese. I now have other dinner plans."

"Oh . . . I understand," Dylan said.

"I do not think you do," Granger replied and leaned forward slightly. "You were expecting that we would be having dinner tonight, correct?"

"Uh, yes," Dylan replied, the room feeling very warm again.

"That was my intention," Granger said, his eyes fixated on Dylan's. "I had hoped to celebrate the launch of your career with MQA, but that is difficult to do when you have yet to resign from FTS."

Dylan was stunned, and his expression showed it. Granger knew he hadn't resigned from FTS yet . . . Granger was playing with him all along.

Beads of sweat broke out on Dylan's forehead and the back of his neck. The room started to spin. His mouth felt dry and swollen. He took a drink of water, then quickly calculated his response and said, "I apologize, Donald. I just needed another day to take care of something. I am resigning first thing in the morning."

Granger stood up. His slight smile returned. "Then I look forward to dinner with you tomorrow evening."

Dylan stood up and said, "Thank you, Donald."

The middle-aged American woman walked in on cue to escort Dylan out.

Granger shook Dylan's hand and said, "After tomorrow, there is no offer. It would be a tragic waste of your tremendous talent if we cannot have dinner together. Good night, Dylan."

Dylan leaned his head back against the leather seat as the limousine sped along I-95 towards Manhattan. He closed his eyes. He was going to have to resign tomorrow . . . Maybe he could still help Brad after he started at MQA . . .

What? Dylan woke up and looked out the car window. They were on the Bruckner Expressway. He must have been sleeping for a while. His Blackberry was ringing. "Hello . . ."

"Dylan, it's Hank. Can you talk?"

"Uh, yes," Dylan answered and blinked his eyes a few times.

"I found the company Caroline called when she was in New York."

"Who is it?"

"Are you in a car?"

"Yeah, why?"

"Is it MQA's limo service?"

"Yeah . . ."

"Then you know who it is," Stewart said. "It doesn't even have a name, it's so secretive. It's a transportation and security service for the exclusive use of MQA."

Dylan's eyes darted towards John Morris. Caroline had interviewed with a New York firm, but it wasn't in New York. He said, "Thanks Hank. I have to go."

Pulling information out of Morris wouldn't be easy, Dylan knew. He would have to be creative to get Morris to reveal anything. He leaned forward from the backseat to get Morris' attention and said, "Excuse me, John. I found a cell phone wedged in the seat cushion back here. Do you remember who was the last passenger that you drove to MQA before me?"

Morris glanced in the rear view mirror nervously and said, "I'll take it and make sure it gets returned." Morris started to reach back for the phone.

"Wait," Dylan said, looking at his own cell phone and pretending it was the one he had found. "The owner's name is Caroline Brenner. I recognize the area code. It's Washington, D.C. You must have taken her to or from the airport recently. Do you remember?"

Morris seemed flustered. "I can't really talk about people I drive, okay? If you give it to me, I'll make sure she gets it back."

"Oh, look, she sent a text in case someone picked it up," Dylan said, pretending to read a message. "Please return this phone as soon as possible. Confidential information on it."

Morris was visibly upset now and said, "Please, Mr. Regan, can I have the phone? She clearly wants it back right away. I'll make sure she gets it."

"I should call her and let her know I have it," Dylan said and pretended to dial. "It's ringing . . . Hello, is this Caroline Brenner? . . . My name is Dylan Regan. I found your phone in the back of a limousine used by MQA. . . . Yes, John Morris is the driver. I'm sorry. . . ." Dylan put his hand over the microphone and said to Morris, "She's furious. She said she left it there two weeks ago and has been trying to call you since to see if you had it. She wants to talk to your supervisor."

"What!" Morris exclaimed. "I never got any calls. Let me talk to her . . ."

"Ms. Brenner, he says he never got any calls. . . . Okay, hold on." Dylan continued to pretend he was talking to a furious Caroline Brenner. He covered the phone again. "She said she doesn't want to talk to you. She wants to know when she was last in your car so she can report it. She thinks it was two weeks ago when she was at MQA interviewing."

"She's crazy," Morris said, exasperated. He typed something into an electronic log pad between the two front seats and pulled up a calendar. He pointed at it and said, "Look there. She was last in this car April 17 to see Mr. Granger, and April 12 and 4 before that—two months ago. Please, let me talk to her so I can straighten this out."

"Shit, the battery died," Dylan said. "I guess it was sitting here for a while. Listen, she sounded upset. I'll call her back later to smooth everything over."

"Thank you, but I should take that and turn it in," Morris said. "You know, since you found it in my car."

"I insist, John. I don't want to have to talk to Donald Granger about this. I'll make sure she gets her phone back and that she's not mad at you. Trust me."

"Okay, Mr. Regan. Whatever you want."

Morris didn't say anything else for the rest of the ride. Dylan knew he would report what had happened as soon as he could.

CHAPTER 63
Wednesday, June 6, 2012

"HOLD ON! Let me get to a quieter spot!" Mary shouted into her cell phone. She walked around the corner to the side of the New York Public Library at Bryant Park in midtown Manhattan. It was 10:45 Wednesday morning, and The Lost Revolution rally was about to begin. "Okay, Hank, I can hear you now. Go ahead."

"I said her breasts aren't—"

"I got that, Hank. Continue . . ."

"Okay, Julie Watson is really Joanne Washburn from Pomona, California. She's thirty-two and graduated from Riverside City College. She worked her way through school as a stripper and has one bust for prostitution that was dismissed. She changed her name along the way and somehow managed to get into Northwestern Business School. Got her MBA and did a couple of marketing stints at high tech firms. She worked for Bear Stearns before going to Eagle Research. Eagle is one of those expert network consulting firms. Their primary client is MQA, Donald Granger's firm. The breasts and nose were added seven years ago, with an update two years ago. They probably have a five-year warranty."

"Cute," Mary said. "How'd you find that out?"

"You don't want to know. Where does she fit in?"

"I met her at the CP Center fund raiser. She was with Peter Zimmer, and then I saw her out with Dylan last week. She's not his type." She didn't mention that Watson knew Jeff as well.

Stewart asked, "You always investigate the girlfriends of your ex-fiancé?"

"You always annoy your clients before submitting your expenses?"

"I guess these pain killers are impairing my judgment," Stewart quipped. "So, you also wanted to know about her connection to Peter Zimmer."

"Yes, but make it quick," Mary shouted as the noise from the rally grew.

"She chairs the committee that doles out the money for the Elizabeth Granger Foundation. That's Donald Granger's do-good vehicle, named after his first wife who died a few years ago. Anyway, the Foundation has given a boatload to the CP Center. It's funding the construction of the new research wing named for Zimmer's daughter."

"Any special relationship between Zimmer and Watson?" Mary yelled.

"If you're asking are they sleeping together, I don't know. Could just be standard big money philanthropy. But I did find one person she's probably sleeping with . . ."

"You mean Dylan?"

"No, I didn't know about him until you just told me," Stewart replied.

"Then who?"

"I had Watson followed. She's met Governor Hayes in a hotel twice since he's been in the city. I doubt he was asking for her vote."

Mary tried to suppress her reaction. Julie Watson was sleeping with Governor Hayes, and maybe Peter Zimmer, and probably Dylan. And she knew Jeff . . .

"You still there?" Stewart asked.

"Yes," Mary shouted. "If Watson really is sleeping with Hayes, it will end his Presidential bid. Rothstein will be ecstatic, but we need proof."

"Gannon!" Jane Reyes boomed from twenty yards away, sounding like Rothstein.

"Hank, I have to go. I'll call you later," Mary yelled and hung up. She started to head back to the park, then turned and walked in the other direction to get away from the noise. She stopped and called Brad's cell phone.

"This is Brad . . ."

"Brad, it's Mary. Do you have a second?"

"Mary, I'm sorry, but I'm heading into a meeting."

"It's about Peter Zimmer."

Brad was silent for a moment, then he said, "Okay, go ahead."

After Mary related what Stewart had told her about Julie Watson, she said, "Dylan needs to know about her, but I don't think I'm the best one to tell him."

"Okay, I understand," Brad said. "I'll call him after my meeting. Can you tell me where this Julie Watson lives and what she looks like?"

"You're not thinking of trying to talk to her?"

"No, I'm swamped here at work. I don't have time to head up there for that. But you know I have some friends in the D. C. police department. I'm going to ask them to check her out, in case Hank missed anything."

"That's a good idea," Mary said and then gave him Watson's contact information.

"Thanks, Mary. I have to go now," Brad said and hung up.

Mary walked up the steps to the ICIN stage in Bryant Park where Jane Reyes was standing. Next to her were Jack Sewall and Amy O'Brien, the two rally organizers Mary had drafted to be the All-American faces of The Lost Revolution, per Rothstein.

Jack Sewall was a good looking twenty-three-year-old who had graduated from the University of Michigan last year but had yet to find the high paying consulting position he thought he had bought for two hundred thousand dollars in loans. Amy O'Brien was a striking looking, half Irish and half Chinese-American twenty-two-year-old who had just graduated from Emory University with an English degree and no job interviews. She wanted to be Mary.

Mary had prepped both of them on how they needed to present themselves. She had told Sewall he was looking to get in on the ground level of American manufacturing. O'Brien was told she wanted to be a teacher in the inner city to give back something to this great country.

Sewall and O'Brien were scheduled to interview Governor Hayes to start the rally. But Mary knew they had planned a surprise to shock the political world—a declaration that could affect the outcome of the November elections and possibly determine the next President of the United States.

Before they interviewed Hayes, Sewall and O'Brien were going to announce that the Lost Revolution was being transformed into a political advocacy organization to represent the interests of young, voting aged people—students, high school and college graduates, workers, the unemployed—anyone under thirty. Its goal would be to change the political balance of power in favor of the youth whose futures had been mortgaged by the self-entitled generations preceding them. The Lost Revolution would now have a clear identity to go along with its clean-cut leaders. The political establishment would have to listen to them.

Mary waited on the stage, exhilarated, the host of this potential watershed moment in history, looking out on the hundreds of thousands of young people eager for the rally to commence. She wore all white—a collared vinyl vest and tie, with skinny cropped vinyl pants and matching heels—the color befitting the organization's virgin birth. As the ICIN music and banner appeared on the large screens around the park, she reminded herself that she wasn't the star. *I'm a journalist . . .*

CHAPTER 64
Wednesday, June 6, 2012

"AAH," DYLAN groaned as he banged his knee under his kitchen table, startled by the pounding on his apartment door. *MG...*

"What's so urgent that I had to rush over here at eight o'clock?" Mary asked when he opened the door.

"I said *important*, not *urgent*, and I sent that text two hours ago."

"I just picked it up," Mary replied. "I've been a little busy with a half a million people in the middle of Manhattan, in case you hadn't noticed."

Dylan sighed, stepped aside and said, "Come in. Want something to drink?"

"Water, please," she said, strolling into the middle of his living room.

"So, how'd you get in this time?" he asked as he handed her a bottle of water, glancing at her white, long-sleeve, sheer blouse and black leather pants.

"Ernie, of course," she answered, settling down on his couch.

"Who's Ernie?"

"Your doorman?"

"Oh, that Ernie," he replied, sitting down in his lounge chair. "I only know his friend, Bert, the guy who actually checks visitors before letting them in the building."

She rolled her eyes and then noticed his brown leather travel bag on the floor under the window. "Going somewhere?" she asked.

"Yeah, that's why I needed to talk to you. I think Brad's right. Peter Zimmer has to know about whatever Caroline discovered that got her killed."

"Why are you suddenly so convinced?"

Dylan told her about his meeting with Blair Armstrong and explained his reasoning for why Armstrong likely had nothing to do with Caroline's murder. Then he said, "What bothers me is that Caroline was too smart to let anyone she didn't trust know about what she had uncovered at the BLS. The fact that the killers didn't seem to know about her laptop supports that."

Mary said, "But whoever's behind these murders had to have known Caroline figured something out. Why kill her otherwise?"

"I know. So, she probably told someone who ultimately exposed her, either intentionally or inadvertently. And the first person she would have gone to with whatever she found out, even before the authorities, was—"

"Peter Zimmer," Mary finished for him. "He was her boss. He hired her, and he was close to her through the CP Center. She probably trusted him."

"That's right. It explains why he insisted everyone in Caroline's department not talk about her death, especially to Brad. And why he's avoided Brad and me. He knows something."

"But why would he avoid me?" Mary asked. "He doesn't know I'm working with you."

"Unless someone told him."

"You think he's involved in Caroline's murder?"

"He might have gone to the FBI with what Caroline told him. I don't know, but I have to find out."

Mary thought for a moment, then asked, "How did the killers find out about Caroline's laptop? And that Shannon Dunn was going to give it to you?"

Dylan paused, then said, "At first, I thought my apartment might have been bugged, and that's how they found out. But I was outside on my cell when Shannon called to tell me about Caroline's laptop. And I scoured my apartment. I didn't find anything."

Mary looked around and said, "Are you sure?"

"Yeah. And a listening bug in here doesn't explain how they knew to go to Caroline's apartment to look for her laptop. Brad went there on his own, before telling any of us about it. They had to have found out another way."

"Then how?" Mary asked.

"Either someone told them, or the phones at the BLS are bugged. Maybe cell phones too. Caroline was paranoid that someone was listening to her calls before she was killed. It explains how they knew what she and Shannon were doing . . . The FBI could get access to the BLS."

Mary asked, "Could Peter Zimmer have bugged their phones?"

"Not by himself. If the FBI is behind this, it's possible he doesn't even know about it. But I bet Caroline went to him as soon as she discovered something. That's probably how she was exposed before she could go to the police. Zimmer has to be either complicit or too afraid to tell what he knows. Either way, we have to get him to talk."

"So, what's your plan? You just going to walk up and ask him?"

"Basically."

"And he's going to tell you?"

"He is, because I'm going to threaten to bring down the CP Center if he doesn't. I'm going to tell him that we'll air a story about his involvement in everything—the three murders, the data leaking and insider trading scheme, maybe even the data manipulation—unless he tells me what he knows."

Mary said, "I assume the 'we' is me and ICIN. That's why you needed to talk to me, right?"

"Well, yes," Dylan replied. "Who's going to pay attention to a story out of FTS, even if I was allowed to publish it, which I won't be? Zimmer knows if you and ICIN break the story, it will get national attention. It will devastate the CP Center's image."

Mary nodded. "And since the CP Center is the most important thing in Zimmer's life, he'll do anything to protect it, including talking to you."

"Even if that doesn't convince him, he's smart enough to realize the publicity will force the authorities to investigate, which will likely destroy his career and the CP Center."

Mary thought for a moment, then said, "So, if your plan doesn't work, we fail, and you head off to MQA, while Brad tries to figure out a way to move on with his life."

Dylan clenched his jaw and glared at her. He took a deep breath, then said, "I'm giving up my opportunity with MQA as we speak. I had to resign today or forfeit the offer."

Mary's eyes widened. "You're giving up the job offer?"

"You sound surprised," Dylan said, then sighed and shook his head. "Donald Granger gave me an ultimatum. I was going to resign today, but then I learned that MQA was probably the firm that offered Caroline a job."

Mary's eyes widened again. "It was MQA, not Differential?"

"Yeah, but I don't know if it means anything. Caroline was incredibly talented, a perfect fit for any investment firm, especially a quantitative one like MQA. But it's just too much of—"

"A coincidence?" Mary interjected.

Dylan nodded. "It doesn't feel right . . . but if it ends up being just a coincidence, I'll probably try to explain to Granger what was going on, if I can."

Mary looked at him sympathetically. "I'm sorry, Dylan. I know how hard it must have been to turn it down."

Dylan stared into space and muttered, "But it still doesn't make sense . . ."

Mary leaned towards him and said, "You know, Julie Watson isn't just connected to Peter Zimmer. She has a close working relationship with MQA too."

"Who?" Dylan asked, a confused expression on his face.

"Julie Watson," Mary repeated. "Didn't Brad call you?"

"No. I've left two messages on his voicemail. What do you know about Julie Watson?"

Mary took a deep breath, realizing she had screwed up, then related the information that Hank had given her.

"Why did you have Hank check out Julie Watson?" Dylan asked angrily.

"Because she's close to Peter Zimmer."

"Yeah, right," Dylan shot back skeptically, then looked away. He had assumed he wasn't the first man that Watson had seduced so Granger could get what he wanted. But using her to manipulate the potential next President of the Unites States was aggressive.

Mary stared at Dylan, her lips pressed tightly together. She stood up suddenly and said, "I should probably go."

Dylan didn't respond. As she moved towards the door, he got up and said, "Wait . . ." He walked over to her. "I'm headed down to Washington tomorrow to confront Zimmer."

She looked at him for a few seconds, then asked, "How are you going to do that?"

"I called up the CP Center and pretended I wanted to check it out for my son. The woman told me they're having a carnival for families and patients tomorrow and all the trustees will be there. So, I set up an appointment. Once I'm in, I'll find a way to get Zimmer alone."

"Pretty smart," Mary said. "How can I help?"

"I'm not sure yet. Be ready with the story, I guess. But I'll let you know."

"I'm already working on it. Have you talked to Hank about your plan?"

"Yeah. He gave me a wireless tape recorder in case I do get Zimmer talking. He also offered to send someone with me to help, but I won't need it. Everything will be in public view. I'm actually more worried about Brad."

"What do you mean?" Mary asked.

"Besides the obvious fact that someone might try to kill him, he's become adamant about going to the FBI. I don't know how much longer he'll go along with this."

"You really think going to the FBI is such a bad idea?"

"If the FBI had anything to do with the murders, it's not just a bad idea, it's a dangerous one. I'm more convinced than ever they're somehow part of this."

Mary focused on Dylan's eyes and said, "If you feel that strongly, I believe you." She paused, then added, "I should get going. Hank made me promise to get back to my place early."

"Why?" Dylan asked.

"He's all worried about some muggings."

"You mean the ones in his girlfriend's neighborhood?"

"It's my neighborhood too."

"I didn't realize that," Dylan said. "Do you want me to go with you?"

She smiled warmly at him and said, "Thank you, but I can take care of myself."

She always had, he knew.

CHAPTER 65
Wednesday, June 6, 2012

"THAT LOOKS like a financial statement," the woman said to Brad.

She was tall, thin and shapely, with sharp facial features, and breasts barely too big for her frame. Her chestnut hair blended well with her medium brown skin, providing a striking contrast to her vivid yellow, surplice dress. Julie Watson, Brad assumed.

He had left work right after hanging up with Mary and drove six hours in traffic to where Julie Watson lived on the Upper West Side of Manhattan. If Dylan was right that Blair Armstrong hadn't killed Caroline, then Peter Zimmer had to know something. And if Watson was sleeping with Zimmer, then she had to know something too. He was going to find out.

Two hundred dollars and an elaborate story of how he used to date Watson in high school got her doorman to tell him she frequented the Stone Rose Lounge in Columbus Circle near Central Park. It was a swank cocktail bar around the corner from her apartment building.

Being tall, black and muscular had always gotten him stares from women in bars. He was counting on that, along with wearing a navy blue suit and reading an annual report, to attract Watson if she came in for a drink. She took the hook without him even jiggling it.

Brad closed the report, looked at her and smiled. "You aren't supposed to notice that."

"Well, then you shouldn't have brought it in here, especially looking so handsome," she replied, biting her lower lip and smiling back. "At least if you didn't want me to notice you."

"All out of my control," he said, turning towards her. "I have to complete this deal by next week, and my mother always insisted I look presentable when I went out . . . in case I met a beautiful woman."

"I like your mother already. Are there any other women in your life?"

"Other women?"

"You know, wife, girlfriend . . ."

"Oh . . . well, I broke up with my girlfriend two weeks ago."

"I'd say I'm sorry to hear that, but it wouldn't be true."

"An honest woman. I like that," Brad said and offered his hand. "I'm Bill Jenner."

"Julie Watson," she replied and shook his hand.

"Can I buy you a drink?"

"Yes, I'd love a glass of Chardonnay." After he had ordered, she asked, "So, Bill, what do you do? I'm guessing you're in the financial industry."

"Good guess. Investment banking with Goldman Sachs. I focus on the defense industry."

"That's an amazing coincidence. I work for a consulting firm and defense is one of the industries we specialize in."

"That is amazing. You sure you're not a spy?"

"Well, I can be anything you want me to be," she said and moved closer to him. "But first you have to tell me more about yourself."

After sharing each other's backgrounds for an hour, Watson said, "I have a fabulous bottle of Bordeaux in my apartment that I've been waiting to open for a special occasion. I think meeting you tonight qualifies. Are you interested? My apartment is right around the corner."

"You really must be a spy. How did you know Bordeaux is my favorite?"

She smiled and said, "You'll have to interrogate me at my apartment to find out."

Watson lived in a large, modern two bedroom apartment on the 29th floor of a new building with views of both Central Park and the Hudson River. She put on some jazz music, then brought the bottle of wine and a cork screw over to Brad and asked him to open it.

"So, tell me what was wrong with your ex-girlfriend," she said, smiling seductively and biting her lower lip again. "I want to be sure not to make the same mistakes."

"She was wonderful," Brad said, staring in Watson's eyes. "Just not aggressive enough."

"Another amazing coincidence. Most men think I'm too aggressive."

"I don't believe in coincidence, or that a woman can be too aggressive."

Brad put the bottle and corkscrew down on the coffee table and stepped towards her. She smiled and placed her arms on his chest, anticipating he wanted to kiss her. He grasped her right wrist gently with his left hand and bent her arm around behind her, pulling her closer as he did. She gasped slightly, smiled eagerly, and grabbed his shirt with her left hand. As she started to say something, he squeezed her body against his, lifted her up with his left arm, then spun her violently and threw her face down onto her couch.

She screamed a mix of fear and excitement, aroused but unsure what he was doing.

Brad stuck his knee into her back and bent her arm up high near her shoulder blade. She screamed in pain. He pulled a switch blade out of his blazer pocket and shoved her face into a cushion to muffle her voice. He leaned over so she could see his eyes with her peripheral vision and said, "You scream, and I'll slit your throat. You understand?"

She nodded, fear and tears in her eyes.

He flicked the blade open in front of her. She tried to recoil, but he pushed her down harder into the couch. He leaned closer to her eyes and said in a low, intense voice, "I'm going to ask you some questions and you're going to answer them, honestly and completely. If I think you haven't, if I think you made a mistake, if I think you forgot something, or I just don't like what I hear, I'll cut you and watch you die. You understand?"

She nodded, tears rolling down her eyes. He released her arm, then grabbed her hair and yanked her to a sitting position, his right leg crossed over both of hers so she couldn't kick. He held the blade loosely, several inches from her throat.

"First question," he said. "What do you know about Caroline Brenner?"

Watson's eyes widened in fear, and she began to cry. "I've never heard that name before. I swear. Please don't kill me. I'm telling you the truth."

He yanked her head back by her hair and put the blade up to her throat. "Tell me!"

"I don't know her! I don't know her . . ." she sobbed. "Don't kill me. Please . . ."

He believed her. "Then tell me about you and Peter Zimmer!" he yelled.

Her eyes widened again. "Uh, Peter's a trustee for a cerebral palsy hospital down in Washington . . . He works for the government too."

"Are you sleeping with him?"

"No . . . no, I'm not," she cried. "I'm on a charitable foundation with him. I just allocate money to his hospital."

"I don't believe you!" Brad snapped and put the blade closer to her neck.

"I'm not sleeping with him! I swear!"

He pulled the blade back and sneered, "How do you know Donald Granger?"

She caught her breath and stopped sobbing. "Donald? What do you want to—"

"Tell me everything!" he demanded, twisting the blade up and down near her chin.

"Okay, please don't . . ." she pleaded, her voice quivering. "I met him in California. I was working for . . . for an escort service. He took an interest in me, and set me up. Helped me remake myself. He put me through business school too. Then he got me some marketing jobs and helped me get my career going. It's his foundation that Peter and I are on. And he's a client of my company—"

"You're lying! You do more than that!"

"Please, alright," she cried. "Donald sometimes asks me to help recruit people, men—"

"By sleeping with them, right?"

"Yes, but only for special situations."

"What about Dylan Regan?"

Watson looked surprised. "Uh . . . Donald wanted to hire him. So, he set me up with him. Donald told me Dylan just accepted his offer. We had some fun. That's all."

"Were you spying on Dylan?"

"Spying?"

"Yes, for Zimmer."

"For Peter? Why—no, it was just for Donald, so Dylan would join his firm."

Brad glared at her. He wasn't learning anything. "Tell me about Blair Armstrong and Rick Jones!"

"I don't know either of them," she said, still scared but calmer.

Brad was frustrated. She only seemed to be working for Donald Granger. "Who else have you recruited for Granger?"

She hesitated and Brad moved the knife closer to her throat again. She stammered, "I . . . I'm talking to Governor Hayes right now . . . He's the—"

"I know who he is," Brad snapped. "Who else?"

"Uh . . . before Dylan, there was a man from Beijing. I can't pronounce his name. Before him was this guy, Jeff Schwinn. And before—"

"Jeff Schwinn?" Brad repeated. "The one who works for Senator Murphy?"

"Uh . . . yes."

"Why him?" Brad demanded.

"Donald never tells me, but I think he wanted someone on the inside with Senator Murphy. It was two years ago, though. Do you—"

"Shut up!" Brad snapped. He breathed quickly through his nose, trying to calm down and think. He hadn't learned what he had hoped. Watson didn't seem to be working with Zimmer. And she didn't know anything. Not even who Caroline was. All he'd learned was that Donald Granger used his money to buy influence, like most powerful business people, and Jeff Schwinn was on his payroll. Someone had to tell Mary. He needed to talk to Dylan.

Brad let Watson go, stood up and stepped away. He closed the knife and put it in his pocket.

Watson looked up at him, realizing he wasn't going to hurt her. She wiped her eyes and said, "This is about that woman, Caroline Brenner, isn't it? Who is she?"

"Someone you'll never be," Brad said, then turned and left, hurrying to the elevator and out the building in case Watson decided to call the police. He jogged five blocks until he was on the other side of Central Park, stopped and started walking up Fifth Avenue. It was just after eleven o'clock when he called Dylan.

"Brad," Dylan answered, "I've been calling you all day. You okay? Where are you?"

"I'm outside on 96th Street. We need to talk."

CHAPTER 66
Thursday, June 7, 2012

"SCT FILES Breakthrough Patent, To Be Acquired By Chinese Competitor For $20 Billion," read the headline on Dylan's Bloomberg screen.

It was 7:30 a.m., and Dylan was still the only one in the office. He pulled up the story.

After filing what it described as a "revolutionary patent" for a new solar panel technology, SCT announced that it had agreed to be bought by a Chinese conglomerate and competitor for three times what it had been trading at. SCT's stock and bonds were up dramatically this morning already.

This was the news behind the surge in trading of SCT call options, he realized. Someone knew about the deal and had been trading ahead of the announcement.

Dylan looked up and saw Andrew Cantor and Billy McDonald hurrying into the large conference room. They closed the door. He watched a red faced Cantor yell silently behind the glass windows at an agitated McDonald. Bob Berkley soon joined the meeting. Then all three of them sat down and appeared to be listening to someone on the speaker phone.

Dylan sensed someone behind him and spun his chair around. It was Breck, the receptionist.

"Excuse me, Dylan," she said. "Joe wants you to join the meeting in the conference room."

"Me?"

"Yes."

Dylan walked to the conference room and eased the door open. Everyone stopped talking.

"Is Dylan in the room?" a voice with a slight Southern drawl asked from the speaker phone.

"I'm here, Joe," Dylan announced as he closed the conference room door.

"Dylan, I need you to clarify something for me," Joe Brooks said. "What did you tell Bob and Billy the other day about MQA selling SCT bonds?"

Dylan knew it would come to this. Berkley and McDonald were trying to point fingers at him for whatever loss they had incurred short selling SCT bonds. He answered, "I told Bob that MQA was thinking of selling some SCT bonds and that he should check with them. He said he would. I never talked to Billy. Is something wrong, Joe?"

Brooks ignored Dylan's question and said, "Bob, is that what you heard?"

"Well, he gave me the impression they were going to dump all their SCT bonds," Berkley replied. "That's why I told Billy about it."

"I never said anything like that," Dylan interjected. "But even if you think you heard that, you were supposed to check with MQA first. Did you talk to them?"

"I tried but they never called me back," Berkley whined.

Dylan said, "Bob, how can you tell Billy that a client is dumping bonds without confirming it? But I still don't understand the problem. Doesn't Billy own SCT bonds?"

McDonald blurted out, "Joe, I wouldn't have shorted the bonds if Dylan hadn't said that MQA was dumping all of theirs."

"You shorted SCT bonds?" Dylan exclaimed, looking at McDonald. "It doesn't matter what I said. We don't make bets like that at FTS? What we're you thinking?"

"Fuck—" McDonald started to yell.

"I've heard enough," Brooks snapped. "Dylan, you can go. Everyone else stay."

Dylan went back to his desk and grabbed his leather bag. He still had to pick up his rental car before heading down to Washington. As he left, he heard muffled yelling leaking from the conference room. He didn't know how much McDonald had lost, but if it was big enough, someone would take the fall. He remembered Atul saying that's what a strategist was for.

CHAPTER 67
Thursday, June 7, 2012

THE RECEPTIONIST pointed to a tall, heavy, pasty white and bald man in his fifties, wearing a blue suit. "That's Peter Zimmer, with those children in wheel chairs," she said to Dylan.

"Would you mind introducing me?" Dylan asked.

"Of course," she said and escorted him to the middle of the outdoor courtyard of The Saint Thomas Moore Cerebral Palsy Center in McLean, Virginia. The courtyard was decorated like a small circus and filled with families and children enjoying a myriad of activities.

"Excuse me, Peter," the woman said. "This is Daniel Bigelow, the father I spoke to you about?" She turned back to Dylan. "Daniel, Peter is one of our Trustees and is responsible for our new research wing that's being built. You probably noticed it on your way in."

Dylan nodded, smiled and extended his hand. "Nice to meet you, Mr. Zimmer."

The woman excused herself and left.

"Call me Peter," Zimmer replied, shaking his hand. "Don't believe everything you hear about me. Our supporters deserve the credit. You have a son, is that right?"

"Yes, a three-year-old with CP. My wife and I want to get him the best therapy possible."

"Well, as upsetting as I'm sure it was to learn of your son's disability, we emphasize the richness of life with CP here at the Center," Zimmer explained. "We view CP as a challenge, part of life. Not a road block, and not an excuse. It's a special place, Daniel."

"I like your philosophy," Dylan said. "It sounds like the Center is very important to you."

"It is. My daughter is treated here. With her and everything I've helped to build, the Center has become my life's passion, maybe even obsession."

"Do you work here full-time, Peter?" Dylan asked.

"I wish I did," Zimmer replied. "No, I do have a full-time job."

"What do you do?"

"I work for the Bureau of Labor Statistics."

"You do?" Dylan said. "I know someone who works there."

"Oh, who is that?" Zimmer asked.

"Caroline Brenner," Dylan said and smiled as he stared into Zimmer's eyes.

Zimmer looked stunned for a moment, then started to say, "Who are—" He stopped, looked around, and lowered his voice. "Who the hell are you?"

"Dylan Regan. Recognize my name?"

Zimmer's brow furled. "The strategist . . . What do you want?"

"You're going to talk to me about Caroline Brenner's murder and what's going on at the BLS," Dylan said, continuing to smile.

"Why would I talk to you?" Zimmer asked in a low, angry voice, then smiled at some parents walking by. "Leave now, or I'll have you thrown out of here."

"First," Dylan said, still smiling, "you'll talk to me because you don't want to make a scene in front of all these children. And second, because I've arranged to have ICIN air the story of your involvement with Caroline Brenner's murder and the leaking of the employment data. You and the Center will be destroyed. Talk to me or the story gets released today. It's your call."

Zimmer glared at him, his lips pressed tight, perspiration forming on his large forehead. He said, "You can't prove anything."

"Your lawyer can debate that with the authorities," Dylan said.

Zimmer glanced around nervously, then said, "Why should I talk to you if you're going to eventually release the story anyway?"

That was his opening—Zimmer wanted something in return. Dylan smiled a little more. "I have a deal with the reporter, Mary Gannon. You know who she is."

Zimmer's eyes widened. "How does that help me, or the Center?"

"Any mention of the Center will be taken out if you tell me everything you know," Dylan replied, then stopped smiling. "Otherwise, it all gets told, today. You can bring the Center down with you, or you can save it."

Dylan waited, watching Zimmer calculate his options, his mind almost transparent behind the growing beads of sweat on his forehead. It was hard to picture Zimmer—a saint to all these handicapped children and their families—as a killer, Dylan thought. But Zimmer had just confirmed he knew something about Caroline's murder.

After several seconds, Dylan added, "You already caused the death of one person who trusted you. You going to do the same to all these kids and their families?"

A pained look flashed across Zimmer's face. "I can't talk here," he said in a low voice.

"Then goodbye," Dylan replied and turned to leave.

"Wait . . ." Zimmer pleaded.

Dylan stopped and turned back.

Zimmer said, "Four o'clock, at The Daily Grill in Georgetown. But you have to agree to keep the Center and my family out of it."

"You won't show," Dylan said and turned again to leave.

"Please, I'll be there. You'll destroy everything . . ."

Dylan walked back to Zimmer, gently grabbed his upper arm like they were having fun, then squeezed it tightly and said, "If you're not there, you'll be the one who destroys everything."

He patted Zimmer's arm, smiled, and walked away.

CHAPTER 68
Thursday, June 7, 2012

THE DAILY Grill was the restaurant attached to the Georgetown Inn on Wisconsin Avenue. Dylan spent an hour watching the entrance from a coffee shop across the street before going in forty minutes early. He wasn't going to take any chances.

Peter Zimmer showed up twenty minutes later. As the hostess escorted him over, Dylan turned on the recorder hooked on the back of his belt under his suit coat, felt the microphone under his tie, and stood up. The hostess smiled and left the two of them standing and staring at each other. Dylan gestured for Zimmer to sit down, and then he followed.

"I see you like to be early," Zimmer remarked.

"I like to be prepared," Dylan said. "So I don't get run over."

Zimmer scowled and replied, "Yes, well, before we start, I must insist that we turn off all electronic devices and place them on the table. You never know who might be listening."

Zimmer took out a cell phone, turned it off and placed it on the table. Then he took out another small device and put it down next to him. A red light was flashing on it.

"What is that?" Dylan asked, nodding at the device as he turned off his Blackberry and laid it on the table.

Zimmer smiled and said, "That is a surveillance detector, and that light says there is a device nearby, probably to record our conversation. Do you think I'm stupid, Mr. Regan?"

Dylan hesitated, then snapped, "You going to talk or play games? I'm ready to release the story . . . Well?"

Zimmer was taken aback by Dylan's aggressiveness. "I . . . I have no intention of talking to you if I'm going to be recorded."

Dylan glared at Zimmer for several seconds, then reached around his back, unhooked the recorder and placed it on the table. He saw the red light on the surveillance detector turn green.

A waiter showed up to take their drink orders. Zimmer ordered tea with lemon, and Dylan ordered coffee with cream.

The waiter left. Zimmer looked at Dylan and said, "Thank you. Now, the deal is my family and the Center won't be mentioned in any way. If that's still good, I'll answer your questions, if I can."

Dylan realized that Zimmer wasn't going to volunteer anything. Zimmer was scared, but not enough. "You have thirty minutes to tell me everything you know," Dylan demanded in a low, threatening voice. "If I'm not satisfied, the story will be released on ICIN tonight. I'm losing my patience. You don't have time to play games."

Zimmer looked panicked. "What? But where should I start? What do you know?"

"I know enough. Start with who murdered Caroline."

"I . . . I'm not sure," Zimmer stammered. "It wasn't me . . ."

Dylan leaned forward and sneered, "You know who's behind it."

Zimmer sat back, intimidated and flustered. He glanced around the mostly empty restaurant, then looked back at Dylan and said, "I just have to think . . ."

Dylan knew he had to get Zimmer talking before whoever he was scared of gave him cold feet and he backed out. "Start with Ben Thompson's data leaking deal with Baker Cohen."

Zimmer sighed and shook his head in disgust. "I didn't learn what he had been doing until Caroline discovered it after he died. I had given his responsibilities to her—"

"You didn't know what Thompson was doing?" Dylan said in disbelief.

"No, not until Caroline came to me," Zimmer said. "She found some spreadsheets Ben had hidden on his laptop and figured out everything he'd been doing with Baker Cohen."

"What about Blair Armstrong? Did you know about her?"

Zimmer looked confused. "The hedge fund woman?"

"Yeah, Differential Capital."

"Until now, I had no idea she was involved," Zimmer said. "I don't think Caroline knew anything about her either. At least she never told me."

Zimmer paused while the waiter delivered their drinks and then left. He took a sip of tea and continued: "I couldn't believe Ben had documented everything. He was supposed to be just the go-between, a buffer for me, in case anything blew up. But he decided to free lance. I warned him about trying something like that. I think the stress over the whole thing killed him."

Something else was going on besides Thompson's data leaking scheme, Dylan realized. He had to keep Zimmer talking. "So, Caroline didn't know what you were doing when she came to you with what she discovered about Thompson?"

"Of course not," Zimmer replied. "She never would have told me anything. But I knew it was only a matter of time before she delved deeper and put it all together. Unfortunately, I was right. She truly was brilliant."

If Zimmer wasn't behind Thompson's data leaking arrangement, then he had to be referring to the data manipulation, Dylan figured. He said, "So, that's why you had her killed? Because she figured out what you were doing?"

Zimmer flashed a pained look at Dylan. "I told you, I didn't have anything to do with it. I was very fond of her."

"Too late for a conscience," Dylan quipped.

"I just panicked," Zimmer shot back. "I told Donald and—"

"Donald?" Dylan interrupted, his eyes widening. "Donald Granger?"

Zimmer's face turned whiter than it already was. "I've said enough . . ."

"Alright, if that's the way you want it," Dylan sneered. "Watch ICIN tonight to hear about your family and the Center." He started to get up.

"Don't go," Zimmer pleaded. "Sit . . . please?" He sighed and said, "What do you want to know?"

Dylan sat back down. "How is Donald Granger involved?"

Zimmer flashed a quizzical smile. "I thought you had figured it all out, after you found out Caroline interviewed with him."

Dylan stopped breathing. Granger already knew about the trick he'd pulled on the limo driver, John Morris. Dylan's mind raced. *How did I miss it?*

Dylan finally released his breath, focused on Zimmer's eyes and said, "You've been leaking the jobs data to Granger, haven't you? Thompson was your messenger, but he decided to cut a side deal with Baker Cohen, right? Then Caroline discovered Thompson's deal after he died and went to you. And you told Granger, didn't you?"

Zimmer stared back, somber and guilty, but didn't respond.

Dylan snapped, "What did Granger do?"

Zimmer startled, then looked around. The few people in the restaurant weren't listening. He turned his eyes back to Dylan and said, "Donald told me to stall Caroline while he reached out and tried to hire her. If she left the BLS thinking I was going to take care of it, I thought everything would be fine, and she'd be better off too."

"What happened?" Dylan demanded in a low, threatening voice.

Zimmer shook his head. "She didn't want to leave Washington, because of Brad Johnson. When Donald started to pressure her, she sensed something was wrong. Then she got suspicious about me dragging my feet on reporting Ben's arrangement with Baker Cohen."

The waiter appeared again to see if they wanted to order something to eat. Dylan asked him to come back in ten minutes. He looked back at Zimmer and said, "Caroline confronted you, didn't she? She gave you a chance to come clean, because she couldn't believe someone who helped handicapped children could be that bad."

Zimmer nodded. "But first she noticed that the jobs data always came in above consensus whenever Ben had leaked it. She started to suspect something bigger was going on, that the data was being inflated. That's when she put—"

"What?" Dylan exclaimed. "The jobs data is being inflated?" He looked around to see if anyone had heard him. Again, no one seemed to be listening.

Zimmer sat back, a puzzled look on his face. "You've been claiming that in your research articles for the past month. I assumed you had figured it out . . . You've been bluffing?"

Dylan recovered quickly, leaned forward and said, "The story with you, your family and the Center is waiting and ready to be aired tonight unless I call Mary Gannon first. These details will just make it bigger. Now, how does it all work? And don't say you can't tell me. Your thirty minutes is up, so you'd better talk fast."

Zimmer stared back at Dylan for a while, then took a deep breath and said, "It's over for me anyway." He paused and glanced around the restaurant. "This is confidential—I mean national security confidential. The President supposedly doesn't even know. You'll never be able to prove anything. And if you try to go public with it . . . well, I'll just say don't try."

"Talk," Dylan sneered.

Zimmer sighed, took another sip of tea and looked around the restaurant again. "I only know my part. And yes, sometimes the data is managed, but only when it's vital to boost confidence in the economy. At least that's what I've been told. I don't know who decides what, but it's been going on for a long time. You need to understand, the data is eventually revised back to where it should have been to start. The management is only temporary."

Over coffee at an unassuming restaurant in Georgetown, Dylan had just learned that someone in the U.S. government was manipulating the employment data to boost confidence in the economy, and had been doing it for years. No secret code, no clandestine meeting site, no stolen microfilm—nothing to give the proper sense of proportion to this incredible revelation. His conspiracy theory had just been confirmed, but nothing had changed. It was anticlimactic.

He asked, "What other economic data is being manipulated?"

"I don't know about any other indicators," Zimmer replied. "But it's not like the data is completely fabricated. It's just smoothed out. Other countries make up their data. Look at China, India, Japan . . . even some countries in Europe. Our system has more integrity than any in the world, but we have to manage it sometimes—to get through difficult times and preserve our way of life . . . like these past few years . . . like now."

Dylan shook his head slowly, then asked, "Is the FBI involved?"

"I only know about my boss. No one else. That's how it works. I'm just an admin."

"Just an admin," Dylan repeated. "Does Granger know about the data manipulation?"

"Data management, and yes, of course. He wanted the data every month, but I told him it was too risky. Someone would notice. But he was insistent. So I told him about the data being managed. This was in early 2009. With how bad the economy was, I knew the data would likely be managed for a couple of years. But it's gone on longer than anyone expected. Donald understood immediately the potential from knowing the data."

"How about Walter Vaughn and Tom Sygowski?" Dylan asked.

"The two from Baker Cohen?" Zimmer replied. "How would they know anything? Ben didn't know. I knew he couldn't be trusted."

"But you and Granger could?"

"I never put this country at risk," Zimmer insisted.

Dylan glared at Zimmer, the patriot, then asked, "Was Caroline murdered because she figured out the data was being inflated or because she found out you were leaking it to Granger?"

Zimmer started to answer but stopped. After a few seconds, he said, "I don't know."

"What do you mean, you don't know?"

"I just know that she figured most of it out and confronted me the day she died. She told me it would be better for me if I went to the authorities before she did. I pleaded with her to work with me, that we could blame it on Ben, but she wouldn't have anything to do with it. She gave me two days, until the April employment report, or else she was going to tell the authorities."

"Did you tell Granger all this?" Dylan asked.

"No, but I didn't have to. He already sensed she was suspicious of him. When she turned down his offer, I knew how he would view it. If he can't manage a risk, he eliminates it."

"Did Granger tell you he had Caroline killed?"

"No, he doesn't tell me anything unless he has to. And I'm smart enough not to ask. I learned about Caroline when everyone else did. I've never talked to Donald about it."

"Could Granger be working with someone involved in manipulating the data?"

"Managing the data," Zimmer corrected him again. "I don't know. I told you, I'm just an admin for this process."

"Yeah, you said that already. Could someone in the government have killed Caroline instead of Granger—the FBI or whoever's *managing* the data?"

"I don't know. It's possible. Do you realize what would happen if it ever got out? It would undermine the U.S. economy, maybe devastate the global economy. That's why I'm warning you not to even try."

The waiter returned, and Dylan sent him away again. Dylan stared at Zimmer for a while, then asked, "Why was the April jobs number so outsized if you and these so-called admins were smoothing out the data?"

"Caroline," Zimmer answered. "She did something to the data aggregation so the number came out almost twice what we were targeting. It was too late to change it by the time I realized . . . and she was already dead. I didn't want anyone to connect her death to the report by delaying its release. So, I went with it. We started to adjust it back with May's report."

"So, that's why the revisions were so outsized," Dylan said. "But why did Caroline change the number to be so big?"

Zimmer looked down at his nearly empty tea cup. "I don't think she believed I would go to the authorities and confess. And she probably thought it would force the issue out in the open. I know she thought what we were doing with the data was wrong. My guess is she wanted to shock the markets . . . force attention on the data, to let everyone know." Zimmer looked up. "She was right. I wasn't going do anything. I was just going to tell my boss and hope he could convince her not to talk. But she was killed before I had to tell him."

Dylan shook his head, fighting the urge to feel sorry for Zimmer, or to strangle him. He asked, "Why won't Granger kill you too? You're the biggest risk to him now."

Zimmer looked up, a faint smile on his face. "I set up my protection when this all started. Anything happens to me and a package gets delivered to a few key people. Donald knows this."

Dylan glared at Zimmer. "You thought Granger might kill you, but you couldn't anticipate that he would kill Caroline?"

Zimmer stared back, resignation in his eyes. "Maybe I could have saved her, but I didn't. I know I have to pay for that, but the Center and my family shouldn't be destroyed because of my weakness. Caroline wouldn't want that either. That sounds manipulative, I know, but it's true."

Dylan fumed at Zimmer's self-serving plea, wanting to slam his face into the table. He snapped, "Did you tell Granger about this meeting?"

"Of course," Zimmer replied. "Donald's had someone following me for weeks, ever since he learned you were focused on me. He called right after you left the Center today."

"What?"

"I had to tell him everything," Zimmer said. "You don't lie to Donald. He'd hurt my family if I did."

"What was his reaction?"

"He didn't react," Zimmer answered. "He just wants me to call him after this."

"Someone's waiting for me outside, right?" Dylan said.

"I don't think so," Zimmer replied. "You aren't really a risk to him."

"What do you mean?"

"Who's going to listen to you?" Zimmer scoffed. "You work for a nothing firm, you've made crazy conspiracy claims, and your recent forecasts have been horrendous. You don't have any credibility, even though you've been right. But don't you already know that? Isn't that why you're using ICIN and Mary Gannon to tell the story—so people will listen?"

"I see. I'm only a risk to you," Dylan said.

"To me and this country," Zimmer replied. "If Mary Gannon reports your story, people will take it seriously. It could undermine our economy. That would be reckless, and destructive."

"So, I'm the threat to this country . . . How much did Granger pay you for your patriotism?"

Zimmer hesitated, seeming insulted, then answered, "Obviously enough."

"Obviously, and I assume the Center's new research wing was part of the deal?"

"Yes, but it's an important cause," Zimmer said. "Children are benefitting."

"Then I guess murdering Caroline was worth it."

Zimmer just bowed his head.

"Why did you do it?" Dylan asked. "How did Granger get to you?"

Zimmer looked up. "We knew each other from Chicago business school. After the financial crisis hit, I was going to lose everything—my houses, my cars. I had three college tuitions, plus private school, and the treatments for my daughter. Bankruptcy would have wrecked my family." He paused, looking for understanding. "Anyway, Donald invited me to drinks one night after a conference here in Washington. He said he'd heard I was in trouble and wanted to help, because we were friends. I knew we weren't, but I was desperate. So, I agreed. He took control after that. I think he was tracking my personal situation for a while. That's how he knew to approach me."

Dylan examined Zimmer, trying to figure out if there was anything else he needed from him. He had gotten more than he ever imagined, except a recording.

But something still wasn't right. Granger wasn't going to just watch everything play out. He was a risk manager. He had to be planning something—to minimize his risk.

"I've heard enough," Dylan said and waved to the waiter for the check.

"I'll pay," Zimmer offered. "I feel like a burden has been lifted on me."

"You'll pay eventually," Dylan replied, then stood up and threw twenty dollars on the table.

"Mr. Regan," Zimmer said as Dylan started to leave, "what I told you about the data has been going on for some time. It's a well kept and even better protected secret. Don't assume you'll just be allowed to expose it. I'm telling you this for your own protection, regardless of what you may think of me."

Dylan stared at Zimmer for a moment and then walked away. When he got to the front door, he looked out the window and recognized the black SUV with tinted windows parked across the street—Agents Cole and Ricci. Was this Zimmer's warning coming true already? Maybe they were working with Granger.

Dylan wasn't going to risk finding out. He walked through the side door into the Georgetown Inn and slipped out the back emergency exit. He made his way through the garbage receptacle area, down a short, narrow ally and out to N Street. He sprinted up the hill, cut over 33rd to M Street and hurried down to 30th where he had parked his car.

In fifteen minutes, he was sitting on I-495 in bumper-to-bumper traffic. He glanced in his rearview mirror—no Explorers or black SUVs. He closed his eyes. Granger had been ahead of him all the time. But what was Granger's next move? His eyes shot open—*MG* . . .

CHAPTER 69
Thursday, June 7, 2012

"HELLO . . ."

"Hank, it's Dylan."

"Dylan, where are you?" Stewart asked.

"Stuck in traffic on my way back from Washington. Listen, have there been any new attacks in Sandy's neighborhood?"

"Uh, yes, there was one Tuesday night," Stewart replied. "A woman was stabbed, but she got away. Why are you asking?"

"I got Peter Zimmer to tell me what he knows. I'm pretty sure Granger had Caroline killed. Probably Darryl Dwyer and Shannon Dunn too. I think he's going to try to kill MG now, to stop her from breaking the story. She lives in the same neighborhood as Sandy. I'm pretty sure the attacks were set up by Granger as a cover."

"Whoa, slow down," Stewart said. "If Granger really is behind the murders, why won't he just have you killed? Why Mary?"

"Because no one's going to listen to me, but the world will listen to Mary and ICIN."

"Okay, I see that, but how—"

"Hank, I don't have time to go through everything now. You have to find Mary. She's not answering my calls."

"Alright," Stewart said, "but I'm going to call a friend at the NYPD too."

"To check if she's already been attacked?"

"Yes. I'll call you as soon as I know anything," Stewart said and hung up.

A loud horn blared behind Dylan. His eyes darted to the rearview mirror—a gold Hyundai with Jersey plates telling him that traffic was moving again. He released the breath he was holding, then accelerated slowly, glancing down intermittently at his Blackberry to dial Brad's number. The Jersey car blared its horn again to let him know he wasn't moving fast enough.

After three rings, Brad's voicemail picked up. Dylan said, "Brad, it's Dylan. Call me as soon as you get this. It's urgent. I got Zimmer to talk. I think Granger is behind Caroline's murder, and I think he's targeting Mary next."

As Dylan hung up, the Jersey car sat on its horn and cut sharply into the speeding lane to pass him. The driver gave him the finger as he sped by.

Dylan's Blackberry vibrated—a text message. He glanced at it. It was from Hank: "No new attacks. On my way to Mary's apartment to see if she's there. Will call with update."

At nine o'clock, Dylan had just passed Newark, New Jersey, but traffic was crawling along again. It was getting dark, and he could no longer be sure he wasn't being followed amongst the multitude of headlights behind him.

His Blackberry rang. It was Hank. "Did you find Mary?" Dylan answered.

"Yes. She's okay," Stewart answered.

Dylan breathed a sigh of relief. "Where is she? Are you with her now?"

"I'm parked across the street from her apartment building. She just went inside with her boyfriend, Jeff. Looked like they were carrying some takeout. I tried calling her, but it went into her voicemail. I haven't gone in to talk to her yet. I wanted to talk to you first."

"Alright, just stay where you are until I get there," Dylan said. "If she tries to leave her building, stop her and tell her what's going on. I should be there within the hour."

"You got it," Stewart said. "Did you talk to Brad?"

"No. I've called him twice and left messages about what's going on. I'm worried."

"Why? If Granger doesn't think you matter, why would he go after Brad?"

"Brad was in the city last night and confronted Julie Watson."

"He did?" Stewart replied. "What did he find out?"

"Watson works for Granger, which I already knew. But Jeff Schwinn works for him too."

"Jeff does?"

"Yeah. He's been feeding Granger info on Senator Murphy for a couple of years."

Stewart said, "But Mary's with him now."

"She's safe inside her apartment. Jeff's not a killer."

"I don't want to take any chances," Stewart said.

"Alright, if I'm not there within the hour, go up to her apartment."

"Okay, but what about Brad?" Stewart asked. "Why are you worried about him?"

"When he came by to tell me about Julie Watson, I told him about my plan to get to Zimmer. He said he was going to the FBI, that we needed their help now because the situation had gotten too dangerous. We argued about it, and then he left."

"Maybe he hasn't talked to them yet," Stewart replied.

"Maybe, but the FBI was waiting for me after I met with Zimmer. I avoided them, but after what Zimmer told me, I'm certain they're involved. And now, I can't reach Brad after he probably talked to them. It's not a coincidence. They could even be working with Granger."

Stewart said, "Maybe Brad talked to them, and they were at the restaurant to help."

"Another maybe. We can't afford to be wrong on this, Hank. MG could die."

"Okay, I understand," Stewart said. "So, what did Zimmer tell— wait, I see someone . . ."

"Who is it?" Dylan asked as he headed into the Lincoln Tunnel. "Hank, you there?"

Silence . . . he lost the signal.

CHAPTER 70
Thursday, June 7, 2012

JEFF'S SMILE always seemed to be a deliberate effort to show you a positive reflection of yourself, Mary thought as she watched him eat. But now it felt manipulative, like he was trying to control her by making her think she needed his approval, as if he was a mirror she was supposed to please. But she was tired of feeling like she was looking in a mirror at a mirror at a mirror . . .

They were sitting at her dining room table eating a late sushi dinner. Jeff had just finished critiquing her interview of Governor Hayes during The Lost Revolution rally yesterday. Mary put her chopsticks down slowly and said, "So, I don't need your approval, but in case I'd like it, you think I conducted the interview poorly, which, if I want to get better, is a great opportunity to learn from my mistakes. Is that what you're saying?"

Jeff swished the white wine around in his glass, took a sip and swallowed slowly. He smiled at her and said, "I can see you're upset, but you know Governor Hayes will never give you another interview if he thinks you'll treat him like that again. What if he wins the election?"

Mary glared at him. "Smiling doesn't make your obvious criticism any more palatable. My work isn't something for you to manipulate.

Prepping Hayes for my interviews and telling me he was going to announce Senator Murphy as his VP made me look weak to my producer. I'm getting tired of this, Jeff."

Jeff put his wine glass down, then reached over and touched her hand. "Mary, I know you think I'm meddling in your work, and you hate that, because your work is your life, but I'm just trying to help, because I love you. You have to trust me. I'm thinking of our future."

Mary smiled, then laughed briefly, wiping away a tear. Jeff smiled and laughed similarly. She sat back from the table, looked at him and said, "So, it's not you, it's me."

The concierge bell rang. Mary stood up quickly, walked to the door and pressed the intercom button on the wall. "Yes, Raul . . ."

"Sorry to disturb you, Ms. Gannon, but there's a gentleman here who insists on speaking with you. I told him you were busy, but he said it's urgent. His name is Dylan Regan. What would you like me to tell him?"

"Mary, send him away," Jeff said and stood up. "He's interrupting our dinner."

She smiled defiantly. "Please send him up, Raul. Thank you."

Jeff said, "Fine. Obviously, you'd rather talk to him than me."

Without responding, Mary opened her apartment door. After a long silence, the elevator bell rang down the hallway. A few seconds later, Dylan appeared at her doorstep.

"Sorry for interrupting," Dylan said, "but it's urgent, and you weren't answering your phone."

"I turned it off. Come in," Mary said, then glanced coldly at Jeff.

Dylan stepped inside and stopped. Mary closed the door and walked around to stand in front of him. She stared at him, waiting.

Before Dylan could say anything, Jeff hurried over, extended his hand and said, "It's good to see you again, Dylan. How is everything at FTS?"

Dylan grabbed Jeff's hand firmly and said to Mary without looking at her, "Brad stopped by my place last night to tell me about the nice chat he had with Julie Watson."

Mary's eyes widened. "Brad talked to Julie Watson?"

"Yeah, and she told him some interesting things," Dylan replied, staring at Jeff and squeezing his hand like a vise.

Jeff's face turned white. He tried to step back. "Could you let go of my hand please?" he asked anxiously.

"You told Jeff everything about our meetings, didn't you, MG?" Dylan said, continuing to stare at him.

"What are you talking about?" Mary replied. "And don't call me—"

"You told him that we didn't believe Dwyer killed Caroline. You told him about her laptop, and that we were going to try to talk to Peter Zimmer. You told him everything we knew and everything we were thinking." Dylan glanced over at her while Jeff grimaced, trying to pull his hand away.

"What I tell Jeff is none of your business," Mary snapped. "Who do you think—"

"You told him everything, and he told Donald Granger everything."

"What?" Mary exclaimed, her eyes darting to Jeff's.

"Let go," Jeff demanded as he struggled to free his hand from Dylan's.

Dylan yanked Jeff towards him so that they were standing within a few inches of each other and said, "He's been working for Granger for years. Isn't that right, Jeff?"

Jeff's eyes widened in panic. "You're crazy!" he declared, then brought his left hand back in a fist and swung at Dylan.

Dylan whacked Jeff's fist away before the punch landed, then flung his left forearm back into Jeff's face, swinging his foot around at the same time to kick Jeff's legs out from underneath him. Jeff dropped quickly to the floor, landing on his back and screaming in pain after his head bounced off the parquet tiles. Dylan pulled Jeff's arm hard to whip him onto his stomach, kicking Jeff's right shoulder to finish the flip. Jeff now lay face down on the floor, crying in agony as Dylan pressed his foot against the joint of Jeff's arm, bent back over his shoulder.

"Stop, Dylan!" Mary shouted, stepping in front of him so he could see her.

"You need to hear this," Dylan shouted, then looked back down at Jeff and sneered, "I'll break your arm unless you tell her everything about your deal with Granger . . ."

"Aah! Stop! Please!" Jeff begged. "I'll tell you!"

"Talk!" Dylan snapped and eased the pressure on Jeff's arm.

"It's true," Jeff said, catching his breath. "I've been working for Donald for the past two years, keeping him informed about Senator Murphy. Mary, you have to understand. Everyone finds a way to make money out of Washington. You can't live if you don't. It wasn't going to be much longer. Just until the Presidential—"

"What did you tell Granger about our meetings?" Dylan demanded, twisting Jeff's arm up.

"Aah . . . I told him everything she told me."

"Why did he want to know?" Dylan yelled and twisted Jeff's arm even harder.

"Aah! Stop!" Jeff cried, tears rolling down his cheeks.

"Dylan," Mary said, "I need to hear what he has to say . . . Please?"

Dylan stared at her, and his eyes softened. He looked down at Jeff and loosened his grip. "Why did Granger want to know?"

"He didn't tell me," Jeff answered. "He never does. He just demands information. Mary, I was helping you. You were so caught up—"

"What do you know about Caroline Brenner's murder?" Dylan snapped. "Lie and I'll rip your fucking arm off!"

"I . . . I only know what Mary told me. I never met her."

"Did Granger have her killed?"

"What? I don't know. Why would—"

"Did he?" Dylan yelled and twisted Jeff's arm up.

"Aah . . . I don't know!" Jeff cried.

"What about Ben Thompson and Peter Zimmer?" Dylan snapped.

"I didn't know Thompson," Jeff answered. "I just know Peter through the CP Center."

"Is Murphy or Hayes involved with Granger?"

"The Senator isn't. That's why Donald hired me. I don't know about Governor Hayes."

"Now, tell her about Julie Watson," Dylan said, leaning down to look into Jeff's eyes.

Jeff looked up at Mary and said, "It was before I knew you. She came on to me—"

"The truth!" Dylan barked, bending Jeff's arm up more. "What was her job?"

Jeff grimaced. "We had sex . . . to get me to work for Donald, but then I met you—"

"Shut up," Dylan yelled. He looked at Mary. "Do you need any more?"

Tears ran down her cheeks. She looked down at the floor, shook her head and walked away.

Dylan reached down, grabbed the back of Jeff's collar and pulled him up. He shoved Jeff towards the door. Jeff stumbled and banged into it. As he straightened up, Dylan walked over, planted his hands against the door on either side of Jeff's head, and said, "If you say anything to Granger, I will find you and do things to you that will make you want to die."

Jeff cowered against the door. He looked at Mary across the floor. "Mary, you know—"

"Go," Mary said. "You don't exist." She turned away.

Dylan grabbed Jeff, opened the door, and shoved him into the hallway. He watched as Jeff ran to the elevator and pressed the button. The doors opened, and Jeff scrambled on.

Dylan closed Mary's apartment door. He turned and looked at her, not saying anything for several minutes. Then he walked over to her. "MG—"

"Don't," she said and turned away. She walked over to her living room window and looked out. After a long silence, she asked, her back to him, "Why do you still call me MG when you know it hurts me?"

Dylan waited a few seconds, then said, "I don't call you MG to hurt you. It's for me, my way of remembering . . . but if it hurts that much, I'll stop."

"I don't know," she said and wiped another tear from her cheek.

"I'd like to know when you do, but right now, you have to get out of here."

Mary turned and looked at him, a puzzled expression on her face. She started to respond when three hard knocks sounded on her apartment door. Her eyes darted to the door.

"That's Hank," Dylan said. "I told him to come up after ten minutes."

"Why is Hank here?" she asked, looking back at him.

"For your protection," Dylan said and walked over to the side of the door. "Who is it?"

"It's Hank," a deep voiced answered.

Dylan opened the door, and Stewart stepped in wearing a gray, zippered Cornell sweatshirt. He walked over to Mary, clearly favoring his right side, and asked, "You okay?"

"I'm fine," she answered, "but you seem like you're still in pain."

"I'm alright," Stewart replied.

Mary looked at Dylan and asked, "Why do I need protection?"

Stewart interjected, "He thinks Donald Granger arranged for the attacks on those women around here as a cover to have you killed."

"What?" Mary exclaimed. "That's crazy."

"That's why Granger did it," Dylan replied. "He's counting on everyone assuming an attack on you was just the latest in a series of violent attacks on women in your neighborhood."

Mary shook her head in disbelief. "But why does Granger want to kill me?"

Dylan said, "Peter Zimmer's been leaking the jobs data to him. Caroline figured it out, and Granger had her killed to stop her from revealing it. He can't afford to let the story get out."

Mary's eyes widened. "Zimmer told you that?"

"Just what Caroline had figured out," Dylan replied. "The rest I know because I know Granger. There's even more, but we have to get you somewhere safe first."

"Wait, I don't understand," she said. "Why not just kill you, or even Brad?"

"Because no one's going to listen to me if I tell the story, or a distraught ex-boyfriend. Granger knows that. But everyone will listen to you. He was hoping I'd take his job offer since that would have shut you down and killed the story. Killing you was probably always his backup plan in case I didn't join MQA. But he had to make it look like it wasn't related to your work. That's why he set up those attacks. I think he tried to set up Caroline's murder the same way."

Mary stared at Dylan, her eyes dazed. After a few seconds, she asked, "Does Brad know?"

"I don't know," Dylan said. "I haven't talked to him since last night. He said he was going to the FBI today to try to convince them to help us. I've left him messages telling him what's going on, but he hasn't called back. That's the other reason you have to get out of here."

"What do you mean?" she asked.

"The FBI may be working with Granger. Even if they're not, they're involved somehow. And with everything Zimmer told me, none of us are safe. I think the FBI already has Brad."

Mary started to respond, but Stewart interrupted and said, "Mary, I saw someone outside who looked like the guy that stabbed me. He was definitely casing your building. He ran when he saw me. Granger knows we're here, and he knows his setup isn't going to work."

"Which means he's desperate," Dylan interjected. "You have to get somewhere safe. I can tell you everything then so you can break the story. Once it's out there, Granger won't risk trying to kill any of us. He's too smart. He'll figure something else out, but it'll take time."

"You have to go now," Stewart insisted, "before Granger's men try to stop you."

Mary looked at Stewart, then at Dylan. "Okay, I can go to my mother's house in New Jersey. She's away. I'll finish the story there and send it to my producer in the morning."

Stewart said, "Good. I'll go with you."

"No, Hank," she said. "You can barely walk."

Dylan said, "I'll make sure she gets there safe. My rental car is downstairs in the garage. We should be able to sneak out without anyone knowing it's us."

Stewart took a deep breath, breathed out slowly and nodded. "Okay, but I'll be a decoy for you." He looked at Dylan and said, "You'll need a gun."

Mary said, "You know I don't like guns, Hank. We'll be okay. I trust Dylan."

"It's your call," Stewart said, "but you'd better get going."

Mary responded, "I just have to change and pack a few things first."

Dylan quickly replied, "We don't have time."

"I have to stay in these clothes?" she complained, glancing down at the short, gold Spanish styled jacket she was wearing over a black and gold, low cut lace camisole. A black lace skirt with a gold sash accentuated her long, shapely legs that ended in gold pumps.

Dylan quipped, "If you can make it through tonight without getting in a bull fight, I'll find you something in the morning."

Mary rolled her eyes. "Fine. I have some old stuff at my mother's I can wear. Let's go."

CHAPTER 71
Thursday, June 7, 2012

DYLAN GLANCED at Mary as they crossed the Upper Level of the George Washington Bridge and said, "I'm going to take 287 to your mother's instead of 80."

Mary looked at him and said, "I'm surprised you remember. You only went there with me once the entire time we were dating. Why the long way?"

He frowned, then answered, "It's less crowded. I'll be able to tell if we're being followed."

"You think they're following us?" Mary asked.

"No. I just want to be sure." He glanced at her again and said, "I won't let anything happen to you."

Mary caught his eyes, managed a slight smile, and then turned to look out the window.

Dylan merged onto the Palisades Parkway and settled into a steady sixty-five miles per hour as they headed north along the Hudson River. In twenty minutes, they were zipping along I-287 in little traffic. They were both silent. The night was clear but dark, with the waning crescent moon offering barely enough light to guide the multitude of stars trudging along with them.

As they passed Pompton Lakes, New Jersey, Mary pointed to a sign and said, "If you take Route 23 to Boonton Avenue, you can go the back way to my mother's house. It's a little longer, but you'll be able to see if anyone's following us."

"Okay," Dylan replied, glancing in the rearview mirror again.

Winding and dark with a single lane each way, Boonton Avenue was mostly deserted at midnight as they navigated the ridge that hugged the Fayson Lakes and Taylortown Reservoir, barely discernable as dark, flat shadows stretching between the trees below. Patches of fog hung over sections of the road, forcing Dylan to slow down.

Suddenly, they hit a deep pothole, rattling the car's suspension.

Mary sighed and said, "I forgot how much I hate this road. If you haven't lost a hubcap on Boonton, you haven't driven on Boonton."

Dylan looked at her out of the corner of his eye. "You can take the girl out of Jersey . . ."

"Hah, this girl's a long way from Jersey and never looking back. Can you say that?"

Before he could reply, an oncoming car flashed its lights and honked its horn to tell him that he should have lowered his high beams. Mary startled.

Dylan shot her a quick look and said, "Nervous?"

"You blame me?"

He didn't respond. He was watching a set of headlights in his rearview mirror approaching them fast. The car quickly closed on them and flashed its lights.

"What's that?" Mary asked, glancing over her shoulder.

"The guy behind us wants me to move over so he can pass," Dylan answered and put his right blinker on.

"That's so obnoxious," Mary remarked.

"It's New Jersey—the worst drivers in the universe," Dylan replied and eased over to the shoulder.

The car behind them pulled out to the middle of the road and sped up, its engine roaring as it passed. When it was half a length ahead, it suddenly slowed down and swerved to within a foot of them, forcing Dylan to veer over next to the guard rail. The other car's passenger window lowered.

"What the . . ." Dylan muttered and darted a look into the open window as the car sped next to them. A dark figure stared at him for a moment. Then an arm whipped out and pointed something. Dylan slammed on the breaks, lurching forward as his seatbelt tightened automatically. He heard Mary gasp and saw the front of the other car drop sharply like it had hit a Boonton pothole. A loud, quick popping sound, followed by the splintering of the window next to him, echoed faintly in his head . . .

Mary's scream seemed distant, Dylan thought and then sensed their car slowing, the brake pedal pumping automatically in response to his foot pressing down hard on it. He noticed his white knuckles on the shivering steering wheel, but he didn't feel anything as they skidded along the dirt and gravel shoulder, his body removed from his consciousness like a dream. Something warm rolled down the side of his face. They suddenly stopped, and he lurched forward again.

He turned—it seemed in slow motion—and looked at Mary. Her eyes were wide with fear, her sensual mouth contorted as she cried, trying to say something to him. But all he heard was ringing and the sound of air whooshing in his left ear. The top of his head hurt. He reached up and touched it—wet. He looked at his hand—red . . .

Past his dark red hand, through the windshield, he saw the other car in front of them. He recalled it spinning and screeching to a stop. It seemed long ago. The passenger window was still open, facing them now, their head lights illuminating an arm extending out and pointing something at them.

The ringing in Dylan's ear faded, and Mary's voice burst through—"Dylan!"

The instincts from all of his fights growing up in Bridgeport took over. "Duck!" he yelled, reaching and pushing Mary's head down.

Two quick pops pierced the silent night, immediately followed by the muffled sound of their car's front and back windshields splintering.

Dylan lifted his foot off the brake pedal and slammed down the accelerator, grabbing the steering wheel with his blood covered left hand, still holding Mary's head down with his right. The engine roared as the tires struggled to grip the gravel and dirt, finally catching hold and sending their car exploding forward. Unable to see where he was going, Dylan spun the wheel sharply left to maneuver around the other car and get onto the road.

The deafening sound of crushing and grinding metal drowned Mary's screams as they jolted to a crawl. Dylan lifted his foot from the gas pedal, turned the steering wheel all the way to the left and then stomped down on the gas pedal again. The tires screeched as the shriek of scraping metal blended in eerie symphony with the roaring engine.

Their car jumped forward, and the sound of scraping metal faded. They were clear. Dylan spun the steering wheel to straighten out. The tires grabbed the road and they bolted away.

Leaning over with his head down, Dylan tried to steer the car straight. He peeked over the dashboard and saw that they were headed towards the guardrail on the other side of Boonton Avenue. Suddenly, the rear windshield imploded, and another splintering sound popped in the front windshield. Dylan ducked, turning the steering wheel sharply to the right to get back to the middle of the road.

As they gained speed, Dylan lifted his head and glanced back at the other car sitting sideways on the shoulder, a dark figure standing next to it, both fading in the distance. He looked over the dashboard and steered their car to the right side of the road. He pulled his hand from Mary's head and asked, "Are you hurt?"

"No," Mary cried. "Can I sit up?"

"Yeah, but stay low," Dylan answered and straightened up himself. He checked the rearview mirror and saw headlights in the distance, moving up quickly. "Shit! Call 911."

A loud horn suddenly blared and bright lights burst in front of them. Dylan jerked the steering wheel hard to the right, just missing a small truck as they careered into a sharp bend in the road. He spun the wheel frantically to the left to avoid the guardrail. The left rear of their car lifted off the road, the centrifugal force pulling him towards Mary.

Dylan slammed on the brakes, but they were going too fast—they were going to flip! "Hold on!" he yelled.

The right rear of their car suddenly smashed into the guardrail, knocking it back onto all four wheels and sending them spinning around twice before coming to a stop in a patch of grass and mud on the side of the road. They were now facing the oncoming lights of the other car.

Dylan yanked the wheel hard to the right and stomped on the accelerator, spinning out of the grass and mud back onto the road. He looked at Mary, half bent over, and shouted, "You okay?"

"I dropped my phone!" she exclaimed, searching the floor. A muffled voice sounded under her seat. "I got through, but I can't reach my phone." She started to unbuckle her seatbelt.

"Don't take your seatbelt off!" Dylan snapped.

Mary stopped, then leaned over and put her head between her legs to look under her seat. She shouted, "911, this is Mary Gannon! I'm in a car on Boonton Avenue near Montville! Someone's shooting at us from another car! Can you hear me?"

The faint sound of the call disconnecting seemed to echo for several seconds, then silence. Mary lifted her head and put her hands to her face as tears rolled down her cheeks.

Dylan looked at the headlights gaining in the rearview mirror. Their car was shimmying now. They couldn't outrun the car chasing them. He wiped away some blood that had seeped into his eye. He saw a traffic light in the distance and the lights of another car far off heading towards them.

"Can you run?" he shouted over the noise of the engine and air gushing in through the blown out rear windshield, then shoved the gas pedal all the way to the floor.

"Yes. Why?" she shouted back, wiping away her tears.

"They'll be on top of us in a second. I'm going to veer into that oncoming car and try to force it into them. We'll end up in that field ahead. We'll have to run. Hold on!"

"What?" Mary exclaimed. "You'll—Dylan, the light's red!"

Dylan's head snapped back as the car chasing them slammed into their rear-end, propelling them through the dark intersection. Headlights suddenly flared through his side window—another car!

A deafening, crunching noise erupted behind them, followed by a bright flash of light and a booming explosion. A gust of heat rushed in through the shattered rear windshield. Dylan's eyes darted to the rearview mirror. He saw a car in flames flipping over and another one spinning out of control.

A horn suddenly blared! Dylan looked forward—a pair of headlights blinded him. He turned the steering wheel sharply to the right, barely missing the oncoming car, and then slammed on the brakes. They spun across the road onto the dirt shoulder, hitting a steel guardrail and stopping abruptly. The other car sped away.

"Mary! Are you alright?" he shouted.

Mary was holding her hands over her face. She nodded. "What happened?"

Dylan peered through her window at the car that had been chasing them, engulfed in flames fifty yards down on the side of the road near the intersection. The car that had crashed into it sat angled on the edge of the road closer to them. The single traffic light was now green.

"I'm not sure," Dylan answered. "The car on fire was the one chasing us. I'm going to check to see if anyone's hurt in the other one."

"But what if those men are still alive?" Mary asked, trembling.

"They're not," Dylan said. "Can you drive?"

"Uh . . . yes."

"Take the wheel," he said, unbuckling his seatbelt and popping the trunk open. "If you sense anything wrong—I mean anything—take off."

Mary got out and hurried around to the driver's side.

Dylan grabbed a tire iron out of the trunk, closed it and signaled to Mary to pull the car back onto the road. He jogged towards the other two cars. As he approached, he felt the heat of the flames leaping from the car on fire. He stopped jogging and walked slowly towards the car that had crashed into it. The right front was crushed, steam spewing from under its crumpled hood. The left headlight was still illuminated, and the driver's door was open, the inside lights on.

Dylan could see a deflated air bag hanging from the steering wheel and a dark figure sitting in the driver's seat. As he inched closer, he saw that it was a silver Impala. He looked at the license plate—*Washington, D.C.*

That's Brad's car . . .

He dropped the tire iron and ran to the car. Brad sat behind the wheel, his head back and eyes closed, streaks of blood down the left side of his face from a gash above his eye.

"Brad! Can you hear me?" Dylan shouted as he unbuckled Brad's seatbelt.

Brad opened his eyes, looked at Dylan and said, "Of course. You're yelling."

"Are you hurt?"

"I'm okay, I think. Just a bruised rib." Brad climbed out with Dylan's help, steadied himself and turned to look at the fireball twenty yards away. He asked, "Is Mary alright?"

Dylan shook his head and replied, "Yeah, just shaken up. What are you doing here?"

"You're welcome," Brad said without looking at him, then limped towards the burning car lying upside down and mangled against a steel guardrail. He got as close as he could before the heat was too much.

Dylan walked up and stood next to him. They both stared at the flames leaping from the inside of the Honda Accord. A charred and still ablaze arm hung out the broken, melted driver's side window. Dylan bent down and saw another crumpled body burning in the passenger seat.

Brad muttered, "They should have stayed with the Explorer." He limped back to his car, reached inside and grabbed something. He turned around, a gun in his hand.

Dylan tensed, stepped back and asked, "Why do you have a gun, Brad?"

"For you," Brad answered and offered it to him. "For your protection."

Dylan breathed out in relief, then said, "What the hell is going on? What are—"

"You and Mary are still in danger," Brad interrupted. "Granger can buy as many killers as it takes to keep this story from getting out. You need to leave now. Don't go to her mother's. If these guys followed you, Granger knows where you were going."

"But why are you staying?" Dylan asked. "And how did you know to be here?"

"You don't have time for questions. The police are coming. You and Mary can't be here. Trust me, Dylan. Take the gun . . ."

Dylan started to say something but stopped, shook his head and grabbed the gun. He turned to leave.

"Dylan," Brad said. Dylan stopped and looked at him. Brad said, "I told you I'd kill them."

Dylan nodded, then ran back to the car where Mary was waiting. They drove away as sirens sounded in the distance.

CHAPTER 72
Friday, June 8, 2012

THE TAYLORTOWN Inn was a run down, one story motel at the end of Boonton Avenue just north of Montville, New Jersey, with a neon sign that always flashed "No Vacancy", according to Mary. The man at the front desk offered them their choice of several unrented rooms, including the honeymoon suite for an extra twenty dollars a night. Dylan gave him two hundred dollars for two nights in the room at the end of the building farthest from the office.

"Home sweet home," Mary said, strolling into the long, thin corner room, the smell of fresh disinfectant in the air.

Two double beds occupied one half of the room. The other half was taken up by an old bureau with a television on top, two faded pink lounge chairs and a black night table and lamp. A small bathroom was tucked into the corner across from the door. A double window with a built-in seat, covered by a worn, stained pink cushion, took up most of the wall behind the door.

"You've stayed here?" Dylan asked. "Is this pink even a color?"

"I may have spent a night or two during my summers in college," Mary replied. She took off her gold jacket, placed it on the window seat and sat down next to it. She stretched her legs and leaned back, closing her eyes to bask in the glow of the room's dull yellow lights.

Dylan stared at her almost too perfect form. He took off his jacket and threw it on the bed. His blue dress shirt was stained with blood. He undid his tie and tossed it on his jacket, then walked over next to Mary and closed the blinds on the double window.

"They were supposed to kill me," Mary said, her voice quivering, her eyes still closed. "I'd be dead now if it wasn't for you."

"Brad saved both of us."

"No," she said, opening her eyes and looking up at him, "you saved me."

"It's late. You should get some sleep," he said, looking down at her.

Mary stood up and moved closer to him, trying to catch his eyes. She reached up and gently touched the top of his head where the bullet had grazed him. "Can I clean that cut first?"

He flinched, then looked into her glistening, brown eyes. He said, "Okay."

Mary went to the bathroom and came out with a couple of wet face cloths, a small towel, and a bar of soap. She put her hands on Dylan's chest and pushed him back slowly until he sat down on the window seat.

"You have to take off this bloody shirt," she said and started to unbutton it. After she helped him out of his shirt, she cleaned the small gash on his head carefully. Then she wiped the dried blood from his shoulders and chest. "Not bad for an old man," she remarked.

"I was young when all this started."

Her soft hair brushed his cheek as she reached around to wipe the dried blood from his neck and back. He breathed in her perfume, rich and sweet, while she stroked his cut lightly one last time. He winced.

"Sorry," she said and focused on his blue eyes, only a few inches away.

"For what?"

"For hurting you," she answered and glided the wet cloth slowly down his cheek, his neck, his shoulder, stopping on his chest.

Dylan knew what was happening. She knew as well, but neither of them wanted to stop. It was an experiment, to see what had changed, what was the same, if it was better or worse, and if it could last for more than one night . . . or even one night.

"It's only pain," he said, breathing quicker and heavier now, his hands hovering around her exposed waist, his biceps bulging in anticipation as blood raced through his body.

"Then share it with me," Mary said, dropping the cloth and stepping closer, moving her hands onto his shoulder muscles, squeezing them as she lifted her right leg slowly over his left, her eyes reaching into his, her moist lips hovering. "Share everything you feel with me . . . I want to feel it all . . . inside me . . ."

She slid her left hand behind his head, gently grabbing and pulling his hair back as she leaned forward, her lace covered breasts pressing against his chest. Her lips—full, wet and open—moved closer. She glided her tongue across his lips, up the side of his face to his right ear and whispered, "I know you want to . . ."

Dylan placed his hands on her bare sides, squeezed gently and lifted her easily onto his lap.

Mary wrapped her legs around his waist. Her lips touched softly on his, her tongue pushing between them, dancing with his tongue, lightly at first, then frantically. She grabbed his back, his shoulders, his arms. She pressed her breasts harder into his chest, sliding her half lace, half naked stomach over his, her pelvis rocking, searching.

He pulled her camisole off and then unfastened her strapless, black lace bra, letting it fall onto the faded pink carpet. Her breasts were more exquisite than he remembered—prominent but not large, firm but not hard. He caressed them softly, then cupped them, squeezing gently as he moved his tongue across and around her nipples, hardening with each moist caress.

Mary moaned with every touch of his tongue, gripping his hair tighter, her legs squeezing harder around his waist as she bounced rhythmically on his lap.

Dylan glided his hands up her legs, under her lace skirt, to her lace thong.

She screamed briefly and leaned back to look at him. She smiled excitedly and then lunged to kiss him again.

Dylan stood up with her legs still wrapped around his waist, turned and lifted her to stand on the window seat.

Mary grabbed his hair and pulled his head into her breasts, moving them slowly across his open mouth, his tongue catching her nipples with each pass. She smiled and moaned softly.

He unzipped her skirt and pulled it down. She stepped out of it, kicking her pumps off as she did. He kissed her smooth, taut stomach, moving his tongue down to her thong. He pulled it down slowly, kissing her lower with each pull, a short, excited screech accompanying each touch until he removed it.

Dylan leaned back and looked at her statuesque body, her beautiful face, her alluring eyes, suspended in the dull yellow light of a hundred dollar a night motel room, both of them wanting more, neither of them questioning if it could last.

Mary stepped down, her hands moving slowly across his shoulders, down his chest to his stomach. She slid them across his belt to his pants, stroking his groin, gently at first, then harder as he responded. She stepped closer, teasing her tongue on his lips, rubbing her nipples across his chest. Then she worked her tongue down his chin, to his chest, to his stomach, to the zipper on his pants, grasping it with her teeth and sliding it open. She took off his shoes and socks, then eased his pants down, kissing him firmly between his legs with every tug. She pulled down his stretch shorts, moving her tongue around, lingering with each reaction he showed.

When he was naked, she stood up, smiled invitingly, and sat down on the pink window seat. She leaned back and spread her legs slowly, panting softly, eagerly. "Give me everything you feel, Dylan . . . I want it all . . ."

Dylan opened the door slowly. A whiff of disinfectant and sweet perfume hit him as he stepped quickly into the room. He stretched his eyes wide to adjust to the darkness from the sunlight outside. The bed was empty, the bathroom door closed. He placed a bag of croissants and two coffees on the small table. It was 7:25 Friday morning at the Taylortown Inn.

The bathroom door opened, and Mary walked out, a towel hanging loosely on her right shoulder, droplets of water glistening on her smooth, bare body from the sun streaking through the blinds. Her damp hair hung loosely across her eyes. She stared at him, like he was unfamiliar, maybe unwelcomed. She let the towel slip off her shoulder, revealing her full naked body, as erotic and alluring as he remembered from last night.

A smile slowly crossed her face. She picked up the towel, wrapped it around herself, and said, "Sorry, no breakfast for you. I have to finish my story."

"But it's the most important meal of the day," he quipped.

Mary laughed lightly, picked up her clothes and went back into the bathroom. Ten minutes later, she came out looking as if she'd just bought a new outfit. She grabbed her coffee and a croissant, sat down in the pink lounge chair she had set up by the window seat, and started to review what she had already typed on her laptop.

She looked over her shoulder at Dylan and said, "I spoke with Rothstein. He wants to air the story in our three o'clock feature spot today. So, I have to be back by two."

"That's fast," Dylan said. "I thought he was skeptical of the story."

"I told him if I don't break the story today, he'll have to train a new reporter because I'll be lying dead in some swamp in New Jersey. He hates training new reporters."

"He sounds like a caring guy."

"Rothstein understands how big this is," Mary said. "It's going to dominate the elections and keep me and ICIN in the spotlight for a long time. This is a Pulitzer story. He knows that."

Dylan watched her—animated, striking and sexual, even in the dirty morning light of the decrepit room. The story was hers now. It was a vehicle, to take her where she had wanted to go ever since she decided to be a journalist. Except for the few hours last night when she thought she might die, the violent reality at the heart of this story had not affected her. She could cry for Caroline's death and feel Brad's pain, yet easily separate both of them from the opportunity the story offered. It was Mary Gannon he was watching. MG was gone.

He asked, "Was there anything about last night on the internet?"

"Only a report of a minor accident," she answered.

"How can that be?" he replied, shaking his head.

"I don't know, but there is some very interesting news on Blair Armstrong," she said, pulling up a story on ICIN's website.

Dylan walked over and looked at the screen. His mouth opened as he read the headline: "Jones Leaves Differential Capital To Launch Own Hedge Fund." The story reported that Rick Jones was taking half the team and half the assets amid rumors of massive client redemptions due to bad performance in Differential's two main funds. Dylan wondered what kind of kiss Blair Armstrong had given Jones when he told her he was leaving.

He walked over to the small dresser between the two beds and took out the gun that Brad had given him. It was a Glock 23. He checked it.

Mary heard the noise, turned and saw Dylan slip the gun under his shirt behind his back. She asked, "Where are you going?"

"Just outside to call Hank. I was planning to catch the bus into Manhattan whenever you're ready. I want him to meet us at the Port Authority."

"Okay," she said. "What about Brad?"

"I haven't been able to reach him. I've called twice."

"Do you think the police arrested him?"

"No, it would have been in the news. But something's definitely wrong . . . I still don't understand how he knew to be there last night."

Mary thought for a moment, then asked, "Is Granger going to try to kill me again?"

Dylan shook his head. "No. By now, he knows his men failed. He's too smart to risk another blatant attempt, unless he's working with the FBI."

Mary's eyes widened. "Then I need to get my story aired as soon as possible. It's the only thing that will protect us."

Dylan nodded and stepped outside to call Stewart. He walked around the side of the motel to where he had parked the rental car to keep it out of sight. Shattered glass covered the back seat. There were three splintered bullet holes in the front windshield and one in the driver's side. Both sides of the car were dented and scraped. As he dialed Stewart, he felt the cut on his head where the bullet had grazed him.

"Hank here . . ."

"Hank, it's Dylan."

"Dylan, are you and Mary okay?"

"Yeah, we're fine. Just a little roughed up." He then told Stewart everything that had happened last night, leaving out the very end. "Mary's finishing the story now. It should air later today. We're taking the bus back as soon as she sends it off."

"You want me to meet you at the Port Authority?"

"Yeah. I'll call you when I know what time. Bring your gun."

"Of course," Stewart replied.

Dylan asked, "Were you able to talk to anyone in the New York AG's office?"

"Yes," Stewart answered. "I just got off the phone with a woman I know there. She'll meet whenever you can. They're apparently very interested in Donald Granger."

"Good. Tell her we can probably meet around five today."

"I will," Stewart said, then added, "You know Granger's not going to let you expose him without doing everything possible to stop you."

"I know, but too many people know about the story now. The smart move is to deny everything and make us prove it."

"And if the FBI is in on everything?" Stewart asked.

Dylan thought for a moment, then he said, "If they are, I'll have to kill Granger myself."

CHAPTER 73
Friday, June 8, 2012

DRIVING A dented and scratched Buick with a blown out rear window and three bullet holes in the front windshield may not have attracted much attention in New Jersey, but he wasn't going to take any unnecessary risks. Dylan called Enterprise Car Rental and told them where to pick it up. Then he and Mary took a taxi to the Montville bus stop on Route 46 and caught the 11:25 a.m. Lakeland to Manhattan.

Hank Stewart met them at the Port Authority on 8th Avenue wearing the same gray, zippered Cornell sweatshirt he had on last night. Dylan assumed the slight bulge under Stewart's left arm was his gun. He noticed another similarly dressed man, younger and bigger, hanging back.

Stewart looked at Mary and asked, "You alright?"

She nodded, then turned her eyes to Dylan and smiled tenderly.

Stewart looked at Dylan and said, "The guy you're staring at is my backup. There's another one, but you won't see him."

"You mean the short, muscular guy in the gray suit looking up at the arrival instead of departure schedule?"

Stewart frowned.

They quickly went over the plan for the day. Stewart and his men would bring Mary to her apartment to change and then accompany her to ICIN to air the story. After she was done, they'd all meet at the New York Attorney General's office downtown on Broadway at five o'clock.

"You going to be okay by yourself?" Stewart asked Dylan.

"Don't worry about me. Granger doesn't think I can hurt him."

"Then he's not as smart as he thinks he is," Stewart replied. "Watch your back anyway. We still don't know what's happened to Brad." He looked over his shoulder and nodded to the two men, then turned back to Dylan. "We have a bullet proof SUV waiting out the back way."

Mary moved closer to Dylan and kissed him on his cheek, lingering an extra second. She stepped back, looked at Stewart and said, "I'm ready."

Dylan watched them leave, then went outside and flagged a taxi.

The city seemed subdued as he rode to his apartment, especially for a Friday. It would be a different city when he walked into FTS Monday morning, he knew. Stock markets around the world would be tumbling in response to Mary's story. And interest rates would be plummeting. He wasn't sure what would panic investors more—learning that the U.S. employment report was being manipulated, that the jobs data had been leaked, or that MQA would likely collapse, forcing the liquidation of a trillion dollars of investments. It was academic, he knew, just like Lehman. A tsunami was coming, and it wouldn't matter what started it.

Dylan suddenly felt nauseous, realizing that another financial crisis might be only hours away. He hadn't spent much time thinking about who the story would affect. Although he had planned in his mind how everything would play out, that was just strategy—chess pieces on a board. Not real people or real lives.

Undermining confidence in the fragile U.S. economy would hurt millions. But it was information everyone had a right to know—no advantages. Who was he to determine the truth by controlling what information people had? And he believed—as much as he believed anything right now—that the conspiracies Caroline had uncovered were tumors of a cancer that would eventually spread and threaten to destroy the U.S economy. That's what he told himself.

But revealing the story might destroy the economy regardless. Did he have that right? Was the cost of truth too great? He didn't know. All he knew was that people had a right to make their own decisions . . . and it was too late now to stop it.

Dylan stepped out of the shower in his apartment and heard his cell phone ringing. He got to it too late, but saw that Mary had called. Then he received a text message from her: "Story killed. Something happening. Be careful. Call when you are free. Mg"

He was stunned. He called Mary back immediately but got her voicemail. He left a message and then texted her. He tried to reach Stewart but got his voicemail too.

He tried to think. Granger didn't have enough influence with ICIN to stop Mary from breaking the story. It had to be someone bigger— the FBI. Mary had told him to be careful. Did she know something? His paranoia started to take over. His Blackberry rang, startling him.

"It's Dylan . . ."

"Mr. Regan, this is Ernie at the concierge. There's a man and a woman down here who say they're with the FBI and want to speak with you. They have real badges. Can I send them up to your apartment?"

"Uh . . . tell them I'll be right down," Dylan said and hung up. He figured it was Cole and Ricci. But they probably didn't have an arrest warrant since they would have come up without any warning. A wave of anxiety coursed through him. He had to make sure Mary was okay.

He threw on a T-shirt and jeans and then put on a long sleeved, white dress shirt without buttoning it or tucking it in. He grabbed the Glock, checked that it was loaded, and stuck it in the back of his jeans underneath the tail of his dress shirt. He slipped on his sneakers, grabbed his wallet and phone, and left his apartment.

Dylan ran to the stairwell. They'd expect him to go down, so he climbed two floors and then took the elevator up to the health club.

It stretched across the top of the complex. He reached the club and walked quickly to the elevator bank for the far tower because it had a separate lobby downstairs.

He took the elevator down and snuck out of Normandie Court without being noticed. He ran ten blocks to the 86th Street subway stop, avoiding the 96th Street stop in case the FBI was waiting there for him. He called Mary again but got her voicemail. Then he called Stewart—same thing. And finally Brad—voicemail again.

Sweat rolled down Dylan's face and neck as he boarded the 6 Local train downtown. His shirt clung to his back, and he worried that the bulge from the Glock might be conspicuous. He leaned against the door between the subway cars so no one could see.

At 59th Street, two police officers got on his car. Dylan caught them eying him and looked away, casually wiping the sweat from his forehead. Then two men in gray suits boarded at 51st Street—probably FBI. He checked the handle on the door he was leaning against—unlocked. At 42nd Street, he'd pull the door open, jump to the next car and make a run for it.

The train came to a stop. Dylan turned the door handle down quickly and stepped forward to yank it open. Then he saw the two police officers turn and face the train doors. They weren't after him. The doors opened, and they stepped off, along with the two men in gray suits and most of the other people on the car. Dylan breathed out and leaned back against the door.

At 33rd Street, Dylan got off, exited the subway and headed for Madison Avenue and 31st where ICIN occupied a pre-war high rise. At the corner of Madison and 32nd, his Blackberry rang. It was Brad. Dylan answered, "Brad, where are—"

"Dylan, listen, I can see you. Turn down 32nd and run—now! Run!"

"Brad, what are—"

"Get Down!"

CHAPTER 74
Friday, June 8, 2012

"THANK YOU for meeting with me on such short notice," John Wiley said as Mary walked into his office on the top floor of the ICIN building. "I know you're very busy."

Wiley gestured Mary to an old leather arm chair on one side of an antique Japanese coffee table in front of a Victorian styled couch. He sat down in a similar chair on the other side of the table. A wide picture window provided views looking uptown towards the MetLife and Chrysler buildings. His desk—modern and covered with several computer monitors—sat at the other end of the expansive, old office. Two large, flat screen televisions hung on the wall.

Mary sat down and said, "Well, your assistant and ICIN security were quite insistent."

"My apologies for the security folks, but it was urgent. And yes, my assistant can be aggressive. I plan to move her into a production position soon. I was going to ask you to spend a little time with her. Maybe give her some advice."

"You want me to give your secretary some advice? Is that what was so urgent?"

Wiley feigned a smile and said, "Mary, ICIN is a concept in media that has never been seriously or successfully pursued. Its full potential is far greater than what we've managed to achieve thus far. Yet, it has already grown bigger than either Gary or me. But it's still a basic business model that depends on talented people, like you. And talent attracts talent, which makes you that much more important to ICIN . . . and me."

Mary smiled politely but didn't say anything.

"Yes, I know," Wiley continued. "I need to explain myself. Let's see . . . The concept and environment we've created at ICIN to allow talent like yours to thrive has to be protected to ensure not only its survival, but its growth. In this global economy, businesses either grow or die. They don't just survive. Are you following me?"

"You haven't gone anywhere yet," Mary replied.

"Charming," Wiley remarked, then said, "Please don't take this the wrong way, Mary, but everyone is expendable when it comes to the survival and growth of ICIN, even Gary Rothstein. To ensure ICIN's future, I have to sometimes make decisions that may limit the very talent that is responsible for creating that future. I don't make such decisions lightly. Now, Gary knows that the day is approaching when he will need to relinquish some of his responsibilities to new blood to ensure that ICIN continues to evolve. And it's my job to manage that process."

Wiley stopped and looked at her. He smiled, confident that he had made his point.

Mary understood that Wiley was trying to bribe her. He was killing her story and offering her Rothstein's job in the not so distant future if she went along. She said, "John, if you want to tell me something, please do it quickly. I'm breaking a major story in ten minutes."

"I see. Your way then, just like Gary," Wiley said and paused to scrutinize her. "Are you going to continue to pretend that Gary hasn't told you your story is dead?"

"Actually, I would like *you* to stop pretending and tell me why you killed my story. Then tell me what you're really offering in return—today, not when Rothstein gets carried out of ICIN. Because we both know that's the only way he's ever leaving."

Wiley stared at her. After several seconds, he smiled and said, "My mistake for underestimating you. Alright, I killed your story because there are several acquisitions and expansions for my media interests, including ICIN, that will be blocked in Congress if I don't cooperate. This is coming from a number of influential players."

"Don't you have political leverage in Washington? Wasn't that the purpose of pumping up Governor Hayes as a Presidential candidate?"

"I'm impressed," Wiley said, "but this is even bigger than me. The reality is that very high people in Washington are determined to squash your story, regardless of whether I cooperate. And they're willing to punish my interests if I don't. It's going to be killed one way or another. I'm afraid you can't stop it. But if it's going to die anyway, then I want something in return. You should as well. As for Hayes, my strategy did achieve a number of goals, but unless he becomes President, which he won't, then I can't be perceived as taking sides. You never know who might win."

Mary asked, "Why are you so sure Hayes won't win?"

"Because Gary thinks he's a fraud," Wiley replied and smiled. "That's not the real reason, of course. Gary thought Obama was a fraud too. But I suppose I can tell you."

Mary glared at him, her displeasure obvious.

"This is confidential," Wiley started. "Governor Hayes is going to be charged with insider trading of SCT, that solar panel company that's been in the news. He got caught with his pants down, literally, sleeping with this woman who works for an expert network firm. She gave him inside information on SCT, and he traded on it. You shouldn't run for President if you don't know how to keep your financial and sex scandals separate."

Mary tried to suppress her surprise. The woman had to be Julie Watson. Hayes would have to drop out of the race. She asked, "How did this woman get inside information on SCT?"

"She's close to Donald Granger," Wiley answered. "His wife is connected to the Chinese company trying to acquire SCT. There are rumors he may be indicted too, but I'm sure he'll only get a slap on the wrist, if anything."

"A slap on the wrist?" Mary repeated in disbelief. "This story was supposed to protect me and my friends from Granger. He's already had three people murdered."

"I've been assured of your safety," Wiley said calmly. "I don't know about your friends, but I trust the people who told me nothing would happen to you."

"These people you trust—are they the same ones inflating economic data to manipulate the economy? I should just trust them?"

"I never said it was fair," Wiley replied. "And don't be so naïve. What government doesn't have its thumb on the scale? What matters is how hard it's pressing. I'll take this country and this government over any other by that measure. Your story is dead, Mary, and you're not. I've been assured that neither will change."

CHAPTER 75
Friday, June 8, 2012

"GET DOWN!" Brad screamed over the phone.

"Why are you yelling?" Dylan asked, glancing around to see where Brad was. He stopped breathing as his eyes fixated on Agent Ricci stepping out of a black SUV across the street, her right arm extended by her side, a gun in her hand . . .

Brad shouted, "Now—"

A loud, quick popping sound interrupted Brad's voice—a sound Dylan had heard before.

"Shit!" Dylan exclaimed, dropping his Blackberry as a bullet whizzed by his head.

Panicked screams erupted, and people scattered, frantic and terrified. Taxis blared their horns, slamming on their breaks to avoid hitting people fleeing across Madison Avenue.

Dylan dropped to one knee as people dove to the ground, his eyes darting around to see who was shooting. He heard Brad's muffled voice shout from his Blackberry, "Run!"

Dylan took off down 32rd Street. He glanced back and then ran into someone, sending him spinning and sprawling to the pavement, scraping his hands and knees. Scrambling to his feet, he sensed someone behind him and whipped his head around. A tall, thin black man wearing a dark blue windbreaker stopped abruptly, lifted his right arm and pointed a gun at him . . .

Dylan saw the man's finger move and rushed him. It was his only chance to survive. He dipped his shoulder to the left, faking like he was going for the man's gun, but then cut quickly to his right to avoid being shot. The gun turned towards him—a quick explosion sounded, followed by another, louder one . . .

A painful, hollow silence filled Dylan's left ear as he looked up and saw the man's right eye socket burst, blood and tissue splattering as his head snapped forward. The man's arm dropped just as Dylan hit him hard with his shoulder, knocking the gun to the ground. But the man's body had already gone limp. He fell sideways to the ground, heavy and dead.

Dylan's momentum sent him tumbling to the pavement. He grunted and started to get up quickly when he saw another gun out of the corner of his eye—Agent Ricci. The glare of the sun behind Ricci blinded him as he jumped to his feet. A loud ringing echoed in his ear.

Ricci lowered her gun next to her side. A black SUV roared around the corner and screeched to a stop next to them. Two large men wearing windbreakers with "FBI" on the back jumped out, holding their guns with two hands, pointing at Dylan.

His ear still ringing and his head swirling, Dylan stared at Ricci for a moment, then glanced down at the body on the ground next to him, a pool of blood forming around the dead man's head. It was the man from the coffee cave. He looked back at Ricci and started to reach for the Glock behind his back.

"No! Dylan, don't!" Brad's voice screamed from somewhere.

Dylan looked left and saw Brad sprinting towards him.

Brad shouted, "Don't, Dylan! They're here to help!"

Dylan stopped and stared at Brad, a large, white bandage just above his left eye. Dylan asked, confused, "Is Mary safe?"

"Yes, she's safe," Brad said and stopped a few feet away, breathing hard. "Trust me, Dylan. They're helping us. Please, give me the gun . . ." Brad reached out his hand and stepped closer.

Dylan looked at Ricci, then at the two men, then back at Brad. The ringing faded. He nodded, reached around and took the Glock slowly from his back. He handed it to Brad.

Brad took the gun and handed it to Ricci. She removed the clip, then looked at Brad and said, "We have to go."

Brad turned to Dylan and said, "You need to go with Agent Ricci to the FBI office downtown. I'll be there shortly. I'll explain everything, but you have to go now."

Dylan stared at Brad and then looked down at the dead man. His eyes turned up to Ricci. She had saved his life. He noticed the two men with FBI windbreakers holster their guns. A police siren screamed from a block away. Ricci walked to the SUV and opened the back door. He followed and climbed in.

CHAPTER 76
Friday, June 8, 2012

THE VIEW of the Hudson River from the conference room on the twenty-third floor of 26 Federal Plaza in downtown Manhattan was as nice as any Dylan had seen in New York City. And the coffee was decent. He could have been at a client meeting instead of a . . . he wasn't sure what it was—an interrogation, an execution, what?

The door at the other end of the room opened. Dylan stood up. Special Agent Cole and a tall, wiry woman with short dark hair walked in. She wore a navy blue suit and looked in her mid-forties, modestly attractive with angular features, glassy blue eyes, and a faded scar on her neck below her left ear. She had the look of a serious runner, Dylan thought.

Special Agent Cole and the woman walked over to Dylan. Cole said, "Mr. Regan, we meet again. This is Executive Assistant Director Foley."

Foley shook Dylan's hand firmly and gestured for him to sit down. She asked in a husky voice, "Would you like something else to drink or eat?"

"I'm fine," Dylan answered. "Is this where you normally interview people?"

Cole started to answer, but Foley interrupted. "This is our conference room for internal meetings. It's not an interrogation room, if that's what you're asking. And this is a discussion, Mr. Regan, not an interview. You're here at our request, but of your own volition."

Dylan realized it would be pointless to ask for a lawyer. He replied, "Do people die of their own volition here?"

Cole squirmed in his seat, looked at Foley and said, "Mr. Regan has a way with words."

Dylan said, "I want to know where—"

"May I talk first?" Foley interrupted. "I think I can answer most of your questions."

Dylan's jaw tightened. He said, "I'm listening."

"Thank you," Foley said. "So, your friend, Mr. Johnson, told us about all the events surrounding Caroline Brenner's death. We were already investigating it since she was an employee of a high profile government agency. As you know, her killer was recently identified, but because he was found dead in a car accident, we don't know why he did it. Fortunately, no national security issues were discovered. Now, do you have any other questions?"

"That's it?" Dylan asked, incredulous. "Yeah, I have a lot of questions, starting with where is Mary Gannon?"

"At her office, working, I assume," Foley answered.

"You assume?" Dylan replied. "And what about Brad Johnson?"

"He'll be here soon. Don't worry, they're both safe."

"They're not safe," Dylan snapped. "And neither am I. Someone just tried to shoot me in the middle of Manhattan . . . Listen, I know about everything—the data manipulation, Peter Zimmer, Donald Granger. I'm not going along with this charade." He knew he was taking a risk confronting Foley, but he figured he'd be dead now if that's what the FBI really wanted.

Foley smiled tolerantly, looked at Agent Cole and nodded. Cole stood up and left the room. She rolled her chair closer and said, "It's Dylan, right?"

"Yes."

"I'm Patricia," she said. "Okay, Dylan, I want you to listen because you'll never hear any of it again. You need to understand—you don't matter to the FBI. What you say, what you do, or what happens to you doesn't matter because no one is listening to you. I'm sorry if that's too blunt, but it's the truth. Yes, you could probably manage to make enough noise to be an irritation, but it wouldn't rise to the level that would get you attention from anyone we need to worry about. Do you understand?"

"That's why I'm here?" Dylan asked. "So you can tell me you don't care about me?"

Foley frowned and said, "Despite what you might think, we're the good guys. Our job is to look out for this country. There were things going on that needed to stop. We've taken care of them. You're in no danger from the FBI. In fact, we want to make sure all your concerns are addressed so you can move on . . . and stop being an irritation."

Dylan glared at her and said, "My concerns start and end with Donald Granger. He's had three people killed. Exactly how do you plan to address that concern?"

"I understand," Foley replied, "but Donald Granger has a lot more to worry about than you."

"What does that mean?"

"He's going to be indicted for insider trading of SCT. I assume you know the company."

Dylan's eyes widened, then he shook his head. "That's a long process, and anything can happen with lawyers. It won't stop him from coming after any of us."

"Again, Dylan, I understand your concern, but we've already met with Mr. Granger. He won't be a threat to you or Ms. Gannon or Mr. Johnson anymore."

"Then what was today—an accident?"

"A miscalculation, but it won't happen again. Trust me."

"Trust you?" Dylan replied. "Was Caroline Brenner a miscalculation too? Forgive my skepticism, but it seems like Donald Granger's miscalculations conveniently take care of whoever the FBI considers an irritation."

Foley took a deep breath. "You seem to be forgetting what we've already done to protect you. In any event, you'll just have to trust us. You have no other choice. But I'd like you to understand that sooner rather than later. So, there's someone I want you to speak with."

She stood up, walked to the door and opened it. Brad stepped in.

"Agent Johnson, he's all yours," Foley said and left.

Dylan stood up, shock quickly turning to anger as he watched Brad walk around the table and sit down across from him. He glared at Brad for several seconds, then sat down too.

After a long silence, Brad said, "I couldn't tell you this when we started."

"Exactly when did we start? How long have you been a fucking FBI agent?"

Brad took a deep breath and answered, "I joined out of Brown."

"Since Brown! Then what was the BIS?"

Brad leaned forward and said, "Didn't you ever wonder what the Bureau of Industry and Security was?"

Dylan shook his head in disgust and replied, "I assumed it was just another bullshit federal agency. Why get an MBA?"

"They needed someone new inside the Fed. I was interested in economics, and the Bureau was paying. I figured it would be good to have. You never know."

"You got that right," Dylan quipped.

Brad sighed and said, "Dylan, you have to understand. Growing up outside of Washington with my father in the defense industry, I was constantly exposed to all the federal security agencies, especially the FBI. I knew in high school this was what I wanted to do."

"Did Caroline know?"

Brad's eyes narrowed, then turned down. "No, not at first. When I finally told her, she felt betrayed. She thought I was using her to get information. I was, but only at the beginning. That's why she broke up with me. That's why she left the Fed and went to work at the BLS. She's dead because of me."

Dylan wanted to be angry, but he saw Brad's pain and guilt. They were friends, and Brad had saved his life. Mary's too. He wasn't going to punish him anymore. "Caroline wouldn't blame you," he said. "And she wouldn't let you blame yourself. Granger killed her, not you."

"Maybe, but it would have been my fault if you or Mary were killed. I had to do something. That's why I went to Cole. I needed the Bureau's help. It had gotten too big for us."

"So, you weren't feeding Cole information all along?"

"No. I didn't trust Cole either. But I had to tell him everything to get his help, so you and Mary were protected. Foley and Cole had no clue the jobs data was being leaked."

"How are we protected, Brad? I was just almost killed. Granger's still out there. And Foley didn't say a damn thing except to trust her. Trust doesn't stop bullets."

Brad said, "Okay. I'll tell you what I know, and what they want you to know. That's why I'm here—to get you to listen, and cooperate."

"I'm listening."

Brad took a deep breath and said, "So, the guy who tried to kill you today was Karl Robson. We don't know who he is yet, but he was probably working for Granger."

"I recognized him," Dylan said. "I saw him a couple of times when I was getting coffee. He must have been following me."

"Probably," Brad said. "The two men who died in the crash last night were Andre Leroy and Kevin Toner. Leroy was Ukrainian, an enforcer, do any job if you paid him well. He was the knife guy."

"And the other one?"

"Toner was a real professional. Worked for different outfits here in the city and in New Jersey. Both of them dropped off the grid three years ago, probably when Granger hired them."

Dylan shook his head slowly, then asked, "How did you find us last night?"

"I put a tracking bug on your rental car," Brad answered. "I had a good idea where you'd park when you were meeting with Zimmer. Unfortunately, it appears that Granger's men did as well. I'm guessing they also bugged your car."

"And how'd you know where I'd be today?"

"When I heard you gave Ricci the slip, I figured you were on your way to Mary's office to make sure she was okay. So, I called Ricci and told her to meet me there."

"But how'd you know about Robson?"

"I didn't," Brad answered. "I saw you across the street and started to call. Then I noticed Robson walking really fast behind you. He stood out—tall, black guy wearing a windbreaker in eighty degree weather. When I saw him reach behind his back, I knew he was going for a gun."

"Jesus," Dylan muttered. "So, I was just lucky you were there?"

"And Ricci," Brad said.

"I guess I should thank her. But I thought she was going to shoot me."

"She talks like she wants to. You really seem to piss her off."

"Yeah, her and Granger . . . but that's what doesn't make sense."

"What doesn't?" Brad asked.

"That Granger tried to kill me like that. It's not what I would expect from him."

"He was desperate," Brad said. "His other two guys failed."

"Granger was after Mary, not me," Dylan replied. "I was just a bonus. But once he failed, it was stupid to try again, especially in broad daylight. That's not how Granger manages risk."

Brad said, "Well, Foley wants you to know she met with Granger today. He supposedly got the message."

"And what message is that?" Dylan snapped. "How do you know the FBI, or whoever's behind the data manipulation, isn't encouraging Granger to take care of people who threaten them, like Caroline? And what if Foley and her bosses are more than willing to use people like Granger to do their dirty work?"

"The FBI saved your life," Brad shot back. "They don't kill good people. Trust me."

"You're sure about that?"

"Yes . . . but there's more, Dylan. I have to tell you how all of this is going down."

"What do you mean?"

"Granger's only going to be charged with insider trading for that solar panel company, SCT. And that probably won't stick. He's not going to be charged with murder or any of the attempts on you and Mary. Governor Hayes and Julie Watson are also being charged with insider trading. And Zimmer's retiring, effective immediately. He won't be testifying against anybody."

"That's bullshit!" Dylan yelled. "How can you go along with that? The whole point of all this was to get Caroline's killer. Are you just going to walk away?"

"I'm not walking away! But I need you to trust me."

"They know what Granger's done. Why aren't they going to charge him?"

Brad breathed out slowly, then said, "Granger knows the data's been manipulated. Bringing murder charges would risk him revealing everything. It wouldn't be like you telling everyone. Granger telling the world about the data would almost be the same as Mary telling the story. Everyone would listen. It would undermine confidence in the government and the economy . . . maybe trigger another financial crisis."

Dylan's jaw tightened. "So, the politicians want everyone to keep believing they can have it all. They get this country into a state where we can't afford the cost to get ourselves out of it, and then they just change the data and say everything's fine. And if that got Caroline killed, and if Mary had died, or me or you . . . well, that's just the cost someone else has to pay. Right?"

"You know it's more than that," Brad countered. "You said it yourself. It's about confidence and trust. If you destroy them, you'll destroy this economy and a lot of people's lives with it. I'm not saying we can go on forever like this, but I know something about destroying trust. I made that mistake with Caroline."

"But we're living a lie. Don't you see that? Who's going to fix it before the lie gets too big? The same politicians and business leaders who got us here? Maybe bringing down the economy is too high a price, but letting Granger get away with Caroline's murder is wrong. It all starts and ends there for me."

"I won't let Granger get away with anything," Brad sneered. He took a deep breath and said, "I'm asking you to trust me. Foley wants to know that you'll stay out of this from here."

Dylan shook his head. "But Granger's not going to give up. If Foley sent him a message and he still tried to kill me today, how can any of us be safe?"

"I don't know what happened today, but Granger won't try anything for a while now that the FBI is watching him so closely."

Dylan scoffed and said, "So, Granger lives to play—maybe kill— another day, just like a good risk manager. And he never pays for murdering Caroline."

"Never is a long time," Brad said. "But if that's the price to make sure you and Mary are safe, I'll live with it, for now."

"And what about Armstrong, and Sygowski? Does everyone just get to walk away?"

"They won't be indicted," Brad answered. "The risks are almost the same. But the SEC will figure something out. They'll pay somehow."

Dylan took a deep breath and blew out slowly. "And what happens to you now? Is it even legal for an FBI agent to be undercover in another government agency, especially the Fed?"

Brad said, "It's not about legal, it's about power. The FBI's had someone undercover in the Fed since Hoover figured out how powerful it was. Everyone with power is watching everyone else with power so no one gets too much of it. It's not a bad system, when it works."

"That's the FBI talking," Dylan replied. "It's a dangerous system. Once you're willing to manipulate the information you give to people, you open the door to greed and abuse. It's hard to control once it's in and even harder to get it out. That's how Granger got in, and Caroline's dead because of it. Fuck that system."

Brad lowered his eyes. "Anyway, I'll be leaving the Fed soon, but I'm not sure for what. Maybe a field assignment." He looked up at Dylan. "I still need to know if you're going to cooperate. I have to tell them."

Dylan laughed for a second, shaking his head. "You know, I'm probably going to be fired from FTS. It's ironic—Granger offered me it all if I would just go along, play along. Now, the FBI is telling me I have to go along, play along. And in return, I get nothing. Am I a good strategist or what?"

"Mary's alive, and you're alive," Brad said. "That's something, but you know there's always a cost."

Dylan nodded. He knew that Brad had already paid. And Mary was safe. It wasn't fair, but he'd take it. He sighed deeply and said, "Who's going to listen to me anyway? I'm at FTS, remember? I won't make any noise for a while. Tell them that."

"Thank you," Brad said. "One last thing—Mary doesn't know I work for the FBI . . ."

"Sure, what's another secret?" Dylan replied. He stared at Brad, a stranger to him now in many ways, but still the closest thing to a brother he had. "Granger's not going to stop, you know. We're still threats, no matter what Foley thinks. He can't be trusted. He cheats at chess."

"Then he needs to die," Brad said.

CHAPTER 77
Friday, June 15, 2012

DYLAN SAT at the bar at Sofia early Friday evening, drinking a Sam Adams and watching a repeat of Mary's most recent ICIN segment on the television above him. He'd been unemployed five days. The day after Granger tried to shoot him in midtown Manhattan, he was shot by Joe Brooks over the phone. Three months of severance pay, six months of health benefits, and a two-hundred thousand dollar good-bye bonus was what he was offered for three years of hard time at FTS—if he signed a non-disparage agreement. He never said goodbye to the Hispanic ninja cleaning lady.

"Isn't she amazing," the young, bleached blond bartender said to him as he watched Mary.

Dylan smiled and asked, "Why do you think so?"

"Look at her—she's smart, tough, beautiful, and a great reporter. All that and she's not afraid to be sexy. She has it all."

"You think she has it all?" Dylan replied, taking another drink of beer.

"She's working on it," a voice said.

Dylan turned and saw Mary standing behind him.

"But it's more important to know what you want," she added and kissed him on the cheek. Then she gently rubbed her lipstick off his face and sat down on the stool next to him.

Her perfume was rich and sweet, like lilacs, matching the color of her one shoulder, form fitting silk dress. Her long, shapely, tanned legs flowed to her lilac colored high heels, and her hair was pulled away from one ear by a lilac pin, matching her earrings.

Dylan said, "You look dressed to impress. Someone important, I assume."

"Thank you. I'm the keynote speaker at an awards dinner."

"Who's hosting?"

"My alma mater—Columbia Graduate School of Journalism. I'm receiving an award."

"Mr. Pulitzer, here you come," Dylan said. "Congratulations. That's great."

"Would you like something to drink?" the bartender asked, gawking at Mary.

"A glass of your Marco Martin Pinot Grigio, please?" Mary said, then turned back to Dylan. "You look good, rested. Everything okay?"

"Yeah, that's what unemployment will do for you. Everyone should try it. Wait, I think twenty million people are."

"You sure you're okay?" Mary asked.

"I'm fine, really. Just working on my new career as a comedian."

She frowned, then smiled and said, "I talked to Brad. He seems to be doing better."

Dylan nodded. "He seems to have found a place for Caroline that's letting him move on."

"I hope so," Mary said. "So, have you talked to Hank?"

"Yeah. I'm having dinner with him and his girlfriend tomorrow night."

The bartender returned with Mary's wine and asked, "Ms. Gannon, if it wouldn't bother you, could I get your autograph on this napkin?"

"Sure," Mary said, signed the napkin and handed it to the bartender. She turned back to Dylan, her expression now intense. "I'm not giving up on the story. With my new responsibilities, I think I'll eventually be able to tell it."

"New responsibilities?"

"Yes, that was the deal to get me to go along with killing the story."

"Good for you," Dylan said, trying to think what he had gotten out of all of it.

"Actually, it was Rothstein's doing," Mary replied. "His mistake, though. Now he has to listen to me. But this process has given me more respect for him."

"I thought you said he was an asshole?"

"He is, but he's sort of a genius, too. Kind of like you," she said and laughed.

Dylan laughed as well. "So, I'm a genius and an asshole. I need to get a BMW."

"You have other talents," Mary said, a coy smile appearing. "I'm serious. Which reminds me, have you thought about what you're going to do next?"

"A little."

"What about investment management?" she asked. "It seems perfect for your talents."

"MQA and Differential have changed my perspective. The buy-side may be better than Wall Street, but I'm not sure either adds a lot of value."

"But if you're good at it, why not take advantage of that?" she countered. "Then use the money you make to do what you really want."

"Hah, I can have it all if I just go along, play along," he replied. "I heard that from Granger, too. This country's just gone through three decades where everyone thought they could have it all, at no cost—just borrow from tomorrow. No one wants to admit it can't continue."

"What if I wanted it all?" Mary asked, trying to catch his eyes. "Would you deny me?"

"Probably," he answered, laughing and taking a drink of his beer.

"But why can't I have it all, too?" she asked, pretending to be hurt.

"Because you don't deserve it," he replied, laughing again. "No one does."

Mary rolled her eyes and said, "Since when has that stopped anyone? Look at all those executives who pay themselves millions for building bureaucracies. If they can have it all, why can't you and I? Or at least me?"

Dylan looked down at his beer. "The only way to have it all is to take what someone else has. That's what Granger did with Caroline . . . what he tried to do with you."

Mary reached over and lifted his chin to get him to look at her. "Dylan, I don't really want it all. But I know what I want, and I'm not afraid to go after it. You can have things, too . . . things you thought you couldn't. But do you want them?"

He feigned a smile and said, "I don't want what you want. We both know that. We could try to make it work. I'd be crazy not to. But that didn't work once already, for either of us."

"I'm what you wanted once," she said.

"You're not the same person now, and I'm not the same person who wanted you then."

"Has everything changed? Even calling me MG?" Her eyes were glistening.

"Yes, but it had to. I was holding you back when we were engaged. We both know that. I'm not going to do that again. Maybe it'd work for tomorrow and next week, even next month, because we have something special sometimes, and it's exciting. But it won't stay that way in six months or a year. You'll get tired of denying we don't want the same things. And then you'll get tired of me, of us. You're Mary Gannon now—a woman every man wants and every woman wants to be."

"Every man except you," Mary said, taking her hand away from his chin.

Dylan shook his head and said, "Even me. That night showed you. But that's not a good enough reason to wait around while I figure out what I want from the rest of my life. You know what you want, and you shouldn't wait for me or anyone to go and get it."

"So, that night was just sex . . ."

"No, it was more, but it wasn't the start of a life together. That's not what you want now either."

Mary looked tenderly at him. After a long silence, her expression turned somber. "I know Granger's still out there. Brad doesn't think he'll try anything again, but I think he will."

"I won't let anything happen to you," Dylan said.

"I know that. I was more worried about you." She smiled and looked in his eyes affectionately. "I have to get going. Did I tell you I think my new favorite color is dirty pink?"

Dylan gave her a warm smile.

Mary stood up and stepped closer to him. She put her arms around his neck and worked her legs up between his. She gazed into his blue eyes, then moved her lips closer to his as his left hand gently squeezed her leg. She smiled teasingly, as if she was going to pull away, then opened her lips and touched his, softly at first, then harder, her tongue moving in gently, then firmer . . . frantic. She eased her tongue out slowly, letting her moist lips cling a little longer to his before separating.

"That's what you want," she said, staring in his eyes. "Let me know when you figure it out." She stepped back, smiled seductively and strode away.

Dylan watched her leave, then turned back to the bar.

The bartender was standing, staring at him, her mouth open. She asked, "Are you someone?"

"Not yet, but can I have another beer anyway?"

CHAPTER 78
Saturday, June 16, 2012

PATRICIA FOLEY was standing on the far side of the round meeting table talking on her phone when Senator Murphy and Representative Boatman opened the door to the small conference room. She gestured for them to come in. Murphy closed the door, and they all sat down.

"Good, and make sure everything's ready for my briefing with the Director," Foley said and hung up. She put her phone on the table and looked at them, her glassy blue eyes intense.

Murphy gave her a disapproving look and said, "I thought Mitch was going to be here."

She replied, "He called and said he'd be a few minutes late."

Boatman fidgeted in his chair. "Is there someplace else we can meet in the future? This room makes me claustrophobic."

Foley squinted at Boatman as if she was trying to figure him out. "This room is protected. You'll have to live with it. Besides, these meetings will not be a regular occurrence."

"If you mean meeting on Saturday morning, I agree," Murphy said. "But we still need a regular meeting."

Foley said, "No, I mean we will not be meeting regularly, period. That's per the Director."

"We'll see about that," Murphy said indignantly. "Now, I'd like to discuss—"

"I called this meeting," Foley interrupted. "It's my agenda. We'll wait for the Speaker."

"Why do we have to—" Murphy started to say but stopped when the door opened.

A tall, muscular black man in a navy blue blazer stepped half-way into the room, looked around, and then opened the door wider. Mitchell Levy walked in, sporting a light blue blazer, a pink polo shirt and khakis, with tasseled loafers, but no socks. Levy nodded to his body guard, and the man closed the door, remaining outside.

"Good morning, Patricia," Levy greeted as he pulled back a chair to allow his long frame to stretch out. "Jim, Randy," he said and nodded to each of them.

"Mr. Speaker," Murphy replied, returning the nod. "I was just saying to Patricia—"

"Jim," Levy interrupted, "if it's alright with you, Patricia called this meeting. I think we should allow her to run it." Levy smiled perfunctorily, then turned his eyes to Foley.

"Thank you, Mr. Speaker," Foley said and leaned forward slightly. She placed her hands down on the table and stared at Levy. "Karl Robson, the freelancer we killed in New York last week. I need to be very confident that won't happen again."

The corners of Murphy's mouth turned up slightly. Boatman removed his glasses, rubbed his eyes and then put them back. Levy maintained his deferential smile.

Murphy spoke first. "Well, Patricia, I want to thank you for making sure that incident stayed out of the media, especially ICIN."

"Yes," Boatman added, "that was very good work."

Foley didn't acknowledge either of them, continuing to stare directly at Levy.

After a long silence, Levy looked at Murphy and Boatman and said, "Could you give us a few minutes alone, gentleman?"

Murphy frowned and stood up. Boatman followed, and they both left.

Levy returned Foley's intense stare for several seconds, then said, "Patricia, I think Jim already explained to you that it was a miscalculation. It won't happen again."

"Thank you, Mr. Speaker, for confirming that it was you who ordered that miscalculation. Do Murphy and Boatman know what's really going on?"

"They know what they need to know," Levy responded without changing his expression.

"Then they don't know Karl Robson was really Rodney Pearce, ex-Army Black Ops, kicked out for who knows what. We found the bug he planted in Regan's coffee maker. Very professional . . . too professional for the Army."

Levy didn't respond, continuing to stare at Foley with a deferential smile.

Foley continued: "It was a unilateral decision, wasn't it? You directed Robson to take out Regan. You figured we'd all assume Donald Granger had hired him. And you were counting on no one complaining about it."

Levy's smile vanished for a moment, then returned a second later as a wry grin. He sat up, his tall, wiry body looming in the small room. He said, "Okay, Patricia, cards up. I've been the head of the group barely two years, and you're even newer in your seat. We both have ambitions, we both have plans, and we both want what's best for this country. We can have a long, productive working relationship, if you want." He paused. "Now, this country—*this world*—has never seen anything like the financial crisis of the past four years. And it's not over, no matter what economists and politicians claim. As the head of the group, I need to make decisions that ensure the economic security of this country, and I need you to work with me on that. Those are my cards, Patricia. Show me yours."

Foley pressed her lips tightly together, the scar on the left side of her neck brightening. "I have no cards, Mr. Speaker, and I'm not playing games. You tried to have an innocent man killed in the middle of Manhattan for discovering our mistakes. Eighty years is a long time for this process to run smoothly and suddenly start to have these issues. It was set up for national security, not politics. But we opened the door to abuse, and now that's what we have."

"He's not innocent! He's a fucking Wall Street strategist," Levy snapped, the veins protruding from his temples. "He was going to keep pushing until he exposed something—him and that reporter from ICIN. You know that. That's why you tried to intimidate him. This country can't afford a scandal like that right now."

"It's not your responsibility to fix things," Foley sneered. "This miscalculation wasn't patriotism. It was politics. You were thinking about your Presidential ambitions in four years."

"Really, Patricia?" Levy replied. "And how is bumping up the jobs numbers the past three years good for me, or any Republican? I went along, even though I knew it would help Obama, because it was necessary for our national security."

"Always a politician," Foley said. "The truth is you don't want Romney or any other Republican in the running to have a chance. That's why you pushed for even more aggressive manipulation of the jobs data. But if Regan managed to expose everything, the fallout could have given Hayes the election. And you don't want to have to run against an incumbent in 2016. Another four years of Obama is just fine for you, especially if the employment data is revised down over that time to where it's supposed to be. With a sideways economy, it would ensure the Democrats go out looking bad. You probably figured you'd walk into the White House then."

Levy laughed, shook his head and relaxed in his chair. "Is this how you really want to play it, Patricia? There are no referees here, no judges. You don't call a foul on me and something happens. No one even acknowledges the process or the group. The President is intentionally excluded, and the Supreme Court is oblivious. But the

Director knows—your boss, Patricia. I can make things very difficult for you if this is the way you really want to play it."

Foley glared at Levy and said, "I told you, I'm not playing games. Until the Director directs otherwise, the group, especially its head, sticks to the protocol—recommendations only."

"Or what, Patricia?"

"Mr. Speaker, we know about your relationship with Donald Granger—his plan to set up Governor Hayes with that woman. Granger was going to make sure Hayes fell from grace, to clear the runway for you in 2016. It's a discreet and profitable alliance you have with Granger. I'm sure he expects to be well rewarded if you make it to the White House. And I'm sure he thinks he's protected, with the Speaker of the House in his pocket."

Levy snorted scornfully. "Again, you don't understand the game. Money is the easy part. I advise you to learn who really controls the cards."

Foley sat back from the table and said, calm but intense, "And I advise you to look more closely at Donald Granger's business associates, starting with his wife and her ties to the Chinese government. A public relationship with Granger and his wife might not be healthy for someone with Presidential aspirations. National security, you understand."

Levy stood up quickly and glared down at Foley. "And you said you weren't playing games. We're done here. Do what you need to with Granger. But be careful how hard you push with me, Patricia. That would be a real miscalculation."

CHAPTER 79
Friday, July 6, 2012

"255,000!"

Dylan sat inside at The Beer Bar Friday night and smiled at the one number text message from Atul. The employment report had been released this morning showing the U.S. economy had created 255,000 new jobs in June. He had bet Atul a steak dinner that the number would come in above 250,000. The message was to concede defeat.

May's data was revised modestly lower, and April's jobs number, which had started everything, was now a third of its original print. Dylan wondered where it would ultimately settle at in a few years when the real data had been fully reflected. No one would care by then, he knew. Whoever was behind the data manipulation knew that as well.

Dylan texted back: "Can taste my steak already! How is Ron Pahlavi doing?"

Atul responded: "Excellent! Great hire for us. I owe you again. Cheers!"

Dylan put his new IPhone on the bar, then sensed someone near him. He looked up.

Lina Sabatini was standing on the other side, smiling. "Chianti?"

"Yeah, thanks," he said. "You're working the bar now?" He already knew that she was. That's why he was there.

"Just a couple of nights a week. Better money, fewer drunk men grabbing me. You know, career advancement," Lina said and smiled.

Dylan watched her as she poured his wine. With her summer tan and wavy brown hair, streaked orange to match her lips, she was alluring and different. He didn't want it all. He wasn't sure what he wanted right now, except her.

An older man sat down at the bar three stools away and ordered a Sam Adams. As Lina reached in the cooler, she glanced over at Dylan and smiled—a warm, "I'm happy you're here" smile. He smiled back. Then she walked to the other end of the bar to wait on another customer.

Dylan took a sip of wine and closed his eyes. He was still unemployed, but he hadn't started looking for a job yet. Granger was still out there somewhere, watching and waiting.

It still bothered him that Granger had tried to have him killed in the middle of Manhattan in broad daylight. It was sloppy and undisciplined—not Granger. Dylan remembered what Petro had told him—a small group of senior politicians working with long-time data bureaucrats, with a gatekeeper to protect against abuse. Peter Zimmer and unknown others were the datacrats, the FBI was the gatekeeper, and the politicians had to be Congressmen, since the President wasn't involved, at least according to Zimmer. But they would have to be powerful politicians, the kind who might want to be President one day, the kind who might be aligned with a big money man like Granger . . .

Dylan's IPhone vibrated—a text from Mary: "News on Granger. Watch my report. Mg"

He looked up at the television. The ICIN banner streamed across the screen announcing breaking news. Mary appeared, and all the noises around him disappeared, except her voice.

"This is Mary Gannon with breaking news. Donald Granger, the founder and CEO of Macro-Quantitative Advisors, the trillion dollar investment management firm based in Stamford, Connecticut, has been found dead in his home in Greenwich of an apparent suicide."

Dylan stared at the screen, his mouth slightly open, the noises around him slowly growing louder. He waited for the replay, but Mary continued with her report. She said authorities believed that Granger had been distraught after learning that the SEC was going to indict him for insider trading and that the FBI was considering felony charges. She added that a story exposing an affair with a woman, Julie Watson, who was being indicted with him, may have contributed to his state of mind. Then she presented a summary of Granger's career and accomplishments, highlighting his pioneering work in quantitative investment management, before reviewing the recent insider trading scandal that had also ended former Governor Hayes' Presidential bid.

Mary concluded by saying, "Donald Granger was a man who seemed to have it all, but once again, we learn that you can never have it all—there is always a cost. Today, Donald Granger paid that cost. This is Mary Gannon, body and news, for ICIN."

"Bullshit," the older man at the bar with the Sam Adams muttered.

"Excuse me?" Dylan said, thinking the man was talking to him.

"It's bullshit," the man said louder, staring at Dylan now.

"Okay," Dylan replied, turning back to his wine and ignoring the man.

"Hey!" the man growled and leaned towards Dylan. "I know who you are . . ."

Dylan turned back and stared at the man for a moment, then said, "Yeah? Who am I?"

"You're a smart fucking guy, but stupid," the man slurred.

Dylan laughed. The man was probably right, but he didn't care. Granger was dead.

"You like her," the man said, nodding at the television showing another clip of Mary.

Dylan glared at the man for a long moment, then turned back to his wine.

"You know Granger didn't kill himself," the man grumbled.

Dylan looked at the man again. He wasn't a killer—too short, fat and old, unless the bad economy had forced him out of retirement. "What do you know about it?" he asked.

The man took a gulp of beer, then said, "Granger would never kill himself—no conscience. The fucking FBI did it. But he had to die. He was a bad guy." The man gulped some more beer, then added, "They set up Hayes, too. But he's a fucking fraud. No loss there."

Dylan's muscles tensed. "Why would the FBI kill Granger and set up Hayes?"

"You know why," the man slurred. "Protect a bunch of political asses and entrenched fucking bureaucrats. Control information— that's power." He squinted at Dylan. "You're worried, aren't you? Don't be. You're okay now."

"Who are you?" Dylan asked, facing the man and sitting up straighter to intimidate him.

The man finished his beer and said, "I'm the guy who tells people what they don't want to hear." He put seven ones on the bar. "I'm done," he said and shuffled out, weaving slightly.

Dylan shook his head slowly as he watched the man leave. Then he grabbed a menu. Granger was dead. He was hungry.

Lina walked over and said, "That guy comes in drunk every Friday night and never leaves a tip. And he's an asshole. Sorry, excuse my French, and Italian." She laughed, leaned on the bar and asked, "So, have you figured out what you want?"

Dylan fiddled with the menu. "Yes, but it doesn't seem to be on the menu . . ."

"If you know what you want, you need to ask." She stared in his eyes and said, "I'm waiting . . ."

He hesitated, then asked, "You free after work?"

Lina's face lit up. "Yes, my shift ends in ten minutes. Where do you want to go?"

"Well, you didn't seem to like the last place, so you choose."

"I did like it. It was just bad timing, or sushi, or maybe the wine. But let's try again. We can get some pizza and Chianti this time." She smiled playfully and left to close out her register.

He smiled to himself. *It was the white wine all the time.*

His IPhone vibrated—a text from Brad: "I told you I would . . ."

About The Author

William H. Cunningham

William Cunningham has been a top-ranked strategist for several Wall Street firms, the author of a weekly investment publication distributed to thousands of clients, and a successful money manager. He has been quoted and excerpted extensively in major news media, including *The Wall Street Journal*, *The New York Times*, and the *Financial Times*, as well as appearing on CNBC and Bloomberg Television in the U.S., Europe, and Asia. William is a graduate of Brown University and Columbia Business School.

CPSIA information can be obtained
at www.ICGtesting.com
Printed in the USA
LVOW11s0928060117
519967LV00001B/52/P